John Andrew Doyle, Susan Ferrier, John Ferrier

Memoir and Correspondence

in the possession of, and collected by, her grandnephew, John Ferrier - edited by

John A. Doyle

John Andrew Doyle, Susan Ferrier, John Ferrier

Memoir and Correspondence
in the possession of, and collected by, her grandnephew, John Ferrier - edited by John A. Doyle

ISBN/EAN: 9783337093938

Printed in Europe, USA, Canada, Australia, Japan

Cover: Foto ©Andreas Hilbeck / pixelio.de

More available books at **www.hansebooks.com**

MEMOIR AND CORRESPONDENCE

OF

SUSAN FERRIER

1782–1854

BASED ON HER PRIVATE CORRESPONDENCE IN THE
POSSESSION OF, AND COLLECTED BY, HER
GRAND-NEPHEW JOHN FERRIER

EDITED BY JOHN A. DOYLE

FELLOW OF ALL SOULS COLLEGE, OXFORD

WITH PORTRAITS

LONDON

JOHN MURRAY, ALBEMARLE STREET

1898

PREFACE

THE letters contained in this book have been collected and handed to me by Mr. John Ferrier, son of the late Professor Ferrier of St. Andrews, and, therefore, grand-nephew of the novelist. To him also is due, with hardly any exception, the biographical matter contained in the notes and elsewhere. My task has been confined to arrangement, in which I have been largely assisted by the advice of Mr. Ferrier, and to supplying the occasional comments which appear in the text. Mr. Ferrier has elsewhere expressed our sincere thanks to the Rev. H. M. Fletcher for the kindness with which he has placed at our disposal the letters written by Miss Ferrier to his mother. It is much to be regretted that many of Miss Ferrier's letters can no longer be found. Especially unfortunate is the disappearance of a number of very characteristic letters written to her intimate friend, Miss Anne Walker, of Dalry. These are known to have been in existence not many years ago, but have now disappeared.

J. A. D.

INTRODUCTION

MY great-aunt, Susan Ferrier, lived a life so quiet and uneventful as to afford little scope for a memoir. But an insight, however slight, into her simple stay-at-home life, derived from her correspondence, may perhaps be read with interest by those to whom the perusal of her clever and *still* popular novels has given pleasure. The very marked success that has attended the recent editions of these works gives a strong proof of their enduring excellence. Professor Saintsbury, a great admirer of Miss Ferrier, wrote (in the 'Sketch' Dec. 5, 1894), referring to the letters published in the Dent Edition, 'Indeed we can hardly have too many documents for determining the character of such a curious genius as Miss Ferrier's. "Genius" may seem a strong word, but I stick to it. Wherever there is the power of giving life there is genius varying in amount, constant in quality. And that she had this power, or the practically equivalent one of transferring life from living people to their copies in fiction, I do not think any one can reasonably deny.'

The larger portion of her correspondence Miss Ferrier desired to be destroyed ; but the letters to the friend of her youth and old age, Miss Clavering [1] (Mrs. Miles Fletcher—Mrs. Christison), are very lively and piquant in style, and touch upon the times when she and her friend were laying

---

[1] Charlotte Catherine, daughter of General and Lady Augusta Clavering, born 1790, died 1869. She was eight years younger than Miss Ferrier.

their hands and heads together in weaving the plot of
'Marriage.'   The letters to herself, which she seems to
have preserved, came to my father, the late Professor
Ferrier, at St. Andrews, after her death.   They consisted principally of critiques of her novels from her
different friends, chief among whom were Sir Walter Scott,
Sir James Mackintosh, Joanna Baillie, Mr. and Mrs. (afterwards Lady Theresa) Lister.   These and some others appeared in an article I wrote for 'Temple Bar' many years
ago, and are prefixed to Bentley's 'Edinburgh Edition,'
along with her touching 'Recollections of Visits to
Ashestiel and Abbotsford,' their only fault being brevity.
The picture drawn of Abbotsford is naturally in sombre
colours, as its master was then showing signs of the
decline of his great mental powers, and my aunt had quite
recently lost the father to whom she devoted her life.

To the Rev. Henry M. Fletcher my thanks are due for
the use of the Clavering letters.   His aunt, Lady Richardson, wrote to me, October 1873 : ' My friendship with your
aunt did not begin till about the year 1830, when I saw a
great deal of her when I spent most of two winters in
Edinburgh with the widow of my brother Miles Angus
Fletcher, who had been her friend from a very early period,
and I never knew a more constant and firm attachment[1]
than existed between them. . . . I have spent many delightful hours with her in company with James Wilson, the
intimate friend of both of us. . . . I was requested by my
sister-in-law to undertake what she had intended to do,
but was unable from her husband's illness to carry out—
to go over the revision of "Destiny" for the press.   This
led to our meeting daily for a long period and let me into
her inner mind more than I should otherwise been able to

---

[1] Their friendship commenced in 1797, and continued without interruption
till 1854.

appreciate from the shortness of our acquaintance. Her devotion to her father is well known, and strong family affections stand out in her, as in Miss Austen, in these comparatively unaffectionate days very strongly.'

Miss Ferrier in 1841 sold the copyright of her three novels to Mr. Bentley, who wrote to her, April 4, 1850:

'The works are now stereotyped, but even now I should be happy to make any verbal corrections in them if you would consent to give your name. I took the opportunity of enquiring whether you had by you any materials for another work of a similar kind, and was very sorry to hear you were so much of an invalid. . . . I need scarcely say how gratified I should feel if I could induce you to give the public another work of fiction. Although the honorarium which I should be happy to offer you might not be of importance to you personally, it might be gratifying to you inasmuch as it might enable you to exercise to a still greater extent your benevolent feelings towards others. But I should urge a still stronger motive to induce you to listen to my suggestion—the great value to society of such moral teaching as yours, for the influence of a writer so justly admired will not be doubted by any one. . . .'

Again he writes (1852): 'The times are now much altered from those when "Marriage" appeared, but if it were possible to meet your views in the event of your health permitting you to contemplate a literary work, I would certainly endeavour to do so ; for I should consider it a high honour to be connected with you in such an undertaking. . . . May 26, 1852.—Until the corrections are made in your three stories, "Marriage," "Inheritance," and "Destiny," I perfectly understood that your name was not to be announced. I sincerely trust that you may be able to contribute another work to those you have already given to the world and which have become classic.'

To Mr. Bentley Miss Ferrier wrote (Edinburgh, 1851) :

' I authorise the publication of my three novels, " Marriage," " Inheritance," and " Destiny," with my name prefixed to each, upon the following conditions :

' 1. The corrections and alterations made by me in the stereotyped edition shall be adopted.

' 2. The illustrations and vignettes shall be expelled.

' 3. That I shall have a certain number of copies for myself and friends, the boards to be lined with *plain* paper instead of the list of " Standard Novels." When these conditions are complied with I will then give up the penal bond I hold from Mr. Bentley.'

I desire in conclusion to express my sincere thanks to Mr. John A. Doyle for the care and labour he has bestowed on the arrangement and elucidation of Miss Ferrier's correspondence.

J. F.

April 12, 1897.

CONTENTS

LIST OF PORTRAITS

PRINCIPAL EVENTS CONNECTED WITH
MISS FERRIER'S LIFE

1744.   James Ferrier (father of S. E. F.) born.

1767.   James Ferrier married Helen Coutts.

1782.   Susan Edmonstone Ferrier born (September 7).

1796.   Janet Ferrier (sister of S. E. F.) married James Connell of
        Conheath, Esq.

1797.   Mrs. Ferrier died (February).

1800.   Archibald Ferrier (brother of S. E. F.) married Catherine
        Garden.

        Helen Ferrier (sister of S. E. F.) married James Kinloch,
        Esq., banker, London.

1801.   Lorn Ferrier (brother of S. E. F.) died in Demerara.

1804.   William Ferrier and James Ferrier (brothers of S. E. F.)
        died in India.

        Jane Ferrier (sister of S. E. F.) married Brigadier-General
        Graham.

        John Ferrier (eldest brother of S. E. F.) married Margaret
        Wilson.

1811.   Miss Ferrier and her father visited Walter Scott at Ashestiel.

1814.   Archibald Ferrier died.

1817.   Miss Clavering married Miles Fletcher, Esq.

1818.   Publication of ' Marriage.'

        Walter Ferrier (youngest brother of S. E. F.) married
        Henrietta Gordon.

1824.   Publication of ' The Inheritance.'

1826.   James Ferrier (father of S. E. F.) retired from office.

1829.   James Ferrier (father of S. E. F.) died.
        Miss Ferrier visited at Abbotsford.

1830.   Publication of ' Destiny.'

1831.   General Graham died.
        Miss Ferrier's second visit to Abbotsford.

1835.   Mrs. Fletcher married J. Christison, Esq.

1841.   Publication of the novels in Bentley's standard edition.

1846.   Mrs. Graham died.

1848.   Mrs. Connell died.

1852.   Fresh edition of the novels published by Bentley, with
        Miss Ferrier's name.
        The year she authorised her name to be given to her works.

1854.   Susan Edmonstone Ferrier died (November 5).

MEMOIR

OF

SUSAN FERRIER

CHAPTER I

PARENTAGE AND EARLY LIFE

IT may seem perhaps an ill-chosen way of commending
a book to the reader to begin with an apology for its
existence. Yet such may not be needless in a time when
biographies and the denunciations of biography seem to
multiply in equal proportions. Apparently the biographer
 in civitate nostra semper et vetabitur et retinebitur.' The
outcry against the writing of lives as excessive and superfluous is supplemented by two special pleas. It is said that
in many cases it traverses the express wishes of the dead ;
that even if there be not any explicit prohibition of a
biography, there may have been an aversion to publicity
which hardly falls short of prohibition. No doubt the
objector has a good case against many biographies as they
are written. But it does not argue any great arrogance on
the part of a writer to believe that he can avoid indecent
violations of confidence and gross sins against good feeling. Burns's death-bed petition ' Don't let the awkward
squad fire over my grave ' does not forbid all funeral
honours or require that every one who joins in the volley
should be a trained marksman. It would be easy to name
biographies raising large and bitter controversial issues, and
moving over the living embers of not extinct fires, which
yet have dexterously and not dishonestly avoided everything which would give pain to the living or in any way
deface or degrade the memory of the dead. And is it a

B

monstrous or unfeeling view to hold that in this matter the wishes of the dead need not be absolutely and for ever final, and that a somewhat morbid shrinking from publicity where there is no possibility of discredit need not wholly overbear a natural and legitimate desire to hear the praises of famous men and women?

Again we are sometimes told that, of all persons, authors are those whose biographies we should least wish to see. Almost always, so persons who are fastidious or cynical, or both, tell us, there are imperfections and weaknesses in the living writer which mar the pleasure with which we read the book. Let us take the poem or the novel, they say, as though it were a detached product of Nature. Enjoy the lines on Sporus without thinking of Pope's ignoble squabbles with Lady Mary. Do not mar your pleasure in 'Don Juan' by any recollections of Lady Byron. Others would say that there are few works which are not coloured by the individual experience of the author, and that those which are not, lose in human interest what they may perhaps gain in artistic completeness. The most attractive, if not intrinsically the best, products of the human mind can seldom be fully understood unless we know something of the soil and atmosphere in which they grew. And it certainly seems on the face of it somewhat strange and paradoxical to say that the completeness of our enjoyment will be marred by the completeness of our comprehension. To pry into novels for the recognition of individuals and the verification of incident, to speculate as to the indentity of Lord Steyne's parasites, or the historical truth of Diana Warwick's treachery, is not to show literary interest; it is to gratify tastes which would find more suitable pasture in the reports of the Law Courts or the paragraphs in a society paper. The desire to learn how the minds of Shakespeare and Scott were filled with all the personages of that vast and varied human pageant where king and beggar, men of action and men of thought, all move in unquestioned reality and due order, to know something of that strange seclusion which peopled Charlotte Brontë's imagination with figures, often so unreal in their outward seeming, ever living in their essential humanity, this surely is no unhealthy curiosity, but a feeling inherently connected with any true love for letters.

Here, I think, lies the main justification for this book. It would be an alarming display of biographical monomania if at the outset I placed Miss Ferrier on a level with the writers whom I have named. It is, perhaps, not claiming too much to say that her best work (and much of her work falls very far short of the standard of that best) does place her in that select band, whose writings have a distinct and unmistakable flavour of their own, and that its combination of merit and individuality invites us to a careful study of the conditions which gave it birth. To say that is not to deny that her letters have independent merit and interest. They are the writings, often spontaneous, in some cases more or less studied, of a vigorous, wholesome-minded, clear-sighted woman, with trained powers of observation and expression. Many of them describe a society interesting in itself, peopled with characters, noteworthy, well defined, and often singular. But the main interest lies in the fact that the persons sketched furnish the materials for her books, and that we see unmistakably the hand of the novelist at work. That is quite apart from any question as to the originals who served as models for the writer's various studies in the grotesque. In some cases recognition was so easy and obvious as to be a source of alarm to Miss Ferrier and her friends. In others there were rival claimants. The secret of Miss Pratt's indentity seems to have been effectually kept. Probably, if Lord Beaconsfield had lived in Edinburgh in the twenties he would have substituted her name for that of Junius in an often quoted epigram. But the letters are interesting, not because we meet with Miss Grizzy and Lady MacLaughlan, but because we are carried into a social atmosphere in which Miss Grizzy and Lady MacLaughlan were possible.

Nor is that all. The earlier letters reveal to us a good deal about Miss Ferrier's methods of workmanship. They show us how much she owed to the suggestions, and to the acute, and at times unsparing, criticisms of Miss Clavering.

The letters throw light, too, not only on the merits, but also on the deficiencies of Miss Ferrier's work. There, as in the novels, we see two distinct elements never able to assimilate. We see the comic Miss Ferrier, an observant, caustic satirist, just stopping short of cynicism, a boisterous humourist delighting in extravagant incident and mock heroics. We see the moral Miss Ferrier paying an honest but thoroughly conventional tribute to sentiment, treating it as her serious mission to exemplify obvious moral truths, and so buying the right to gratify an unregenerate and somewhat reprehensible love of mirth in her readers. And thus it would not be easy to name any writer with whom the published works and the life as set forth in correspondence so fully serve the purpose of mutual interpreters. Moreover, the literary judgments of an author are always of value, if not as criticism at least as revelations of his mind, and as throwing light on his views and methods. This certainly is so with Miss Ferrier. Her remarks on books tell us, indeed, more of her shortcomings than her powers, yet even in that lies instruction. It is not, let it be hoped, priggish or affected to say that her comments on books show an almost entire want of the literary faculty. She reads and likes 'Emma,' but describes it as 'having no story'; 'Emma,' which for compactness and effectiveness of plot has never been surpassed among English novels of genteel or romantic comedy, and would never, perhaps, have been equalled had 'Mansfield Park' and 'Persuasion' not been written! Miss Ferrier always judges books by direct obvious tests—in her younger days by their power of amusing, in her latter by their power of edifying. She shows no keen sense, one may almost say no sense, of construction and of style, of methods of character-drawing more finished and more balanced than her own.

This is not all loss. Miss Ferrier has the merits of her defects. She is always natural, and trusts with absolute confidence to powers which were, for the most part, guided by clear judgment and an acute sense of humour. She is at times conventional ; but she is so simply and naturally, not affectedly or artificially.

Miss Ferrier was born in Edinburgh on September 17, 1782. Readers of the late Mr. Hill Burton's 'Bookhunter' will not have forgotten his typical specimen of the conversation of a pedigree-loving old Scottish lady, ' And so ye see auld Pittoddles, when his third wife deed, he got married upon the Laird of Blaithershin's aughteenth daughter, that was sister to Jemima, that was married until Tam Flumexer, that was first and second cousin to the Pittoddleses.' In Miss Ferrier happily the genealogical instinct took a livelier and pleasanter form. She has left us a memoir of her father's early life marked by much of that discernment and definite unexaggerated emphasis which distinguish her best work. From that sketch, helped by a few slight but graphic references in the letters, and by one or two incidental touches in the correspondence and diary of his friend and colleague, Sir Walter Scott, it is not hard to see what manner of man James Ferrier was, what were those special features of his daughter's mind and character which came to her by right of inheritance, and how far his observed peculiarities formed a part of her literary stock-in-trade.[1]

TO J. F. F.

There is a natural desire in the human heart to connect the past with the future, and we are unwilling to consign to oblivion the memory of those we most loved and reverenced in life. I am now one of the few remaining links which connect the past generation of my family with that which is now succeeding, and I would fain transmit some slight record of my dear father's early life to those who may hereafter inherit his name, but to whom his character must be otherwise unknown. The particulars I had from himself, and I shall relate them as simply and faithfully as I can with few comments, though perhaps not without my own and others' inferences. His paternal grandfather, Mr. William Ferrier, possessed the small property of Kirklands, in Renfrewshire, subsequently sold to the Blantyre family, and which my father once pointed out to me as now forming part of their beautiful demesnes on the banks of the Clyde. As the smallest landed proprietor in those days had a 'man of business' in Edinburgh, Mr. Campbell, of Succoth, was the law agent of the small laird of Kirklands,[2] whose son John he also received into his office as clerk. There he remained till his marriage with

---

[1] Of this biographical notice Mr. John Ferrier writes thus : 'This short sketch from my aunt's pen of her father's early life shows the indomitable and persevering spirit that eventually led him to the top of an honourable, useful, though harassing profession. It was written for my father (Professor J. F. Ferrier), and endorsed by the writer " for his own private perusal," and I hope by laying it open to "public perusal" I have not acted unwisely.

'April 12, 1897. J. F.'

Some of the notes to this sketch are by Miss Ferrier, some by Mr. John Ferrier. They are distinguished by their respective initials.

[2] There was also, I believe, a distant relationship. (S. E. F.)

the daughter of Captain Walter Sandilands Hamilton of Westport (commonly styled Sir Walter),[1] when he removed to Linlithgow and took up his abode with his father-in-law in the family mansion at the west end of the town. This old gentleman had early in life been aide-de-camp to General Churchill, and on retiring from the army was appointed sheriff of the shire, for which duty, as may be supposed, he was quite incompetent, and soon had to relinquish. At the time of his daughter's marriage he was very gouty and infirm, a proof of which occurred within my father's recollection. Having been seized with a fit of the gout while in Edinburgh, and detained there longer than was convenient, he was anxious to return home, but, being unable to ride on horseback, he had no alternative but to be carried all the way in a sedan chair. There were no public carriages in those days, and the only private ones which ever performed the journey were those of the Dukes of Argyll and Montrose, which regularly *ploughed* their way (for roads were not) with six horses once a year to their respective family seats. My father was the third son of his parents; he was born in the beginning of 1744, and, according to the custom of those days, was sent out to be nursed. The following year the rebellion broke out and everything was thrown into such confusion (families not knowing when or where they might have to fly), that it was thought best to leave the nursling where he was, rather than add to other cares that of a teething and scarcely weaned infant. Towards the end of the '45, when the panic had somewhat subsided, he was brought home; but by this time his affections were

---

[1] His father, a cadet of the Torphichen family, had assumed the name of Hamilton on his marriage with the heiress of Westport. (S. E. F.) [Nisbet in his *Heraldry* says that this family is descended from Silvertonhill. The origin of the title of the family is from the mansion house having been built immediately within the walls of the town of Linlithgow, adjoining an elegant gateway towards the west, which was taken down about the year 1770.—From Anderson's *History of the House of Hamilton*.] The old house still stands (1897) overshadowed by a fine old tree said to have been planted by Mary Stuart. (J. F.)

so riveted to his nurse, that the separation seemed likely
to cost him his life.   The attempt was therefore given up
for the present, trusting that he would soon learn to prefer
the superior attractions of the paternal home to the poor
comfortless dwelling of his nurse.   But they had ill calculated on the strength and permanency of his affections,
which seemed literally to grow with his growth and
strengthened with his strength, as all endeavours to
counteract or overcome them proved unavailing.   It is
probable these had been injudicious, for a young heart
capable of such attachment might surely by love and tenderness have had its affections gently and gradually turned
into other channels, and how full and deep the stream of
his affection was, they can attest who were the objects of it.

Every method that was tried proved in vain.   When,
forcibly withheld from his nurse he neither ate nor slept,
but either wept or pined, or else contrived to make his
escape and find his way to the poor cottage where nothing awaited him but a scanty fare and a fond welcome.
This went on for a considerable time, till at last his parents
became so exasperated that when he did occasionally visit
home he found himself an object of dislike to them, and of
contempt and derision to his brothers and sisters.   This,
of course, only confirmed his preference for the humble
abode where he was fondled and caressed and consoled for
the humiliations he experienced at home.   His parents
now began to suspect that undue influence was used for
the sake of his board, which they therefore resolved to
discontinue as the most likely method of breaking the tie;
they accordingly warned the nurse and her husband that
if they continued to encourage him in his estrangement
from his own family it should be at their own charge, as
in future they should receive no remuneration whatever.
The poor people took them at their word, and declared he
should be welcome to share what they had to give with
their own children, and the only difference between them
was that they always spoke of and treated him (as far as

they possibly could) as the son of a gentleman and the grandson of 'Sir Walter.' Indeed, the nurse's affection was, if possible, increased, and its demonstrations redoubled, though the poverty of these warm-hearted people was such that my father assured me he never had seen a plentiful meal on their table during the thirteen years he dwelt with them, and had scarcely ever known what it was to have enough to eat even of the humblest fare. His parents kept their threat; they paid his clothes and schooling and nothing more, and every year increased the feelings of aversion and animosity between two parties placed in such unequal circumstances, where *power* was entirely in the hands of one had they known how to use it with love. At the Grammar School of Linlithgow he every day met his brothers, who never ceased to taunt him as the *son of Nurse Barr*; this *she* highly resented as an affront to him, whom she was most desirous to keep on a level with themselves in all outward appearances and appliances. In this it may be supposed she did not always succeed, as one little trait may suffice to show. Observing that his brothers' shoes were brighter than his (although the best in those days were probably not according to Warren), she procured some train oil with which she smeared his all over. The consequence was the smell was so insufferable he was hooted and driven out of the schoolroom. He used to mention this as one of the many mortifications he had to encounter, and which made childhood anything but a season of happiness to him. Added to these, he had the consciousness he was doing wrong in absenting himself from his father's house, and living on such unnatural terms with his own family. So after many struggles in his own mind, carried on for several years, he at last, of his own accord, went to his parents, acknowledged his fault, and asked to be forgiven and restored to his proper place in the family. The last request was immediately complied with, but it may be doubted whether the pardon was cordially granted, or at least till a later period, when his own good conduct must have gained their esteem if not their affection. At the time when this reconciliation took place he was about thirteen, his eldest brother (William)[1] had entered the navy, the second (Walter)[2] had gone, or was going, to India, and *his* destination would have been the army but for an accident which had befallen him some years previously. When at play with some other boys he fell with violence upon a piece of wood in which was a rusty nail that entered his eye, and after much suffering, and probably mismanagement, finally deprived him of sight in that member. Most likely skilful treatment might have preserved or restored it, and so have entirely changed his future career in life. Be that as it may, it rendered the choice of a profession for him a matter of doubt and deliberation, and the commission intended for him was transferred to his younger brother Islay.[3] Happily the other eye, so far from having been affected by the misfortune of its companion, seemed to have acquired a double portion of strength and clearness of vision, which, in spite of the very laborious duty it had to perform during the course of a long and busy life, continued unimpaired to the close of eighty-six years. He had been but a few months at home when his mother's only surviving brother, Major Hamilton, having obtained leave of absence from his regiment, then in Flanders, came to see his father, who was now quite superannuated, and, I believe, died soon after his son's return. He (Major H.) must have been a man of a superior mind, and of a penetrating and discriminating judgment. As so far from adopting the prejudice the other members of the family still harboured against the *alien*, he, on the contrary, had soon discovered the excellence of his nephew's character, and evinced a strong and marked predilection in his favour. Omitting several proofs of the confidence he had placed in him, the last was too remark-

---

[1] Succeeded to the Westport estate 1762 ; assumed the name of Hamilton. (J. F.)

[2] Married Miss Wallace of Cairnhill. (J. F.)

[3] Afterwards Major-General Islay Ferrier and Governor of Dumbarton Castle, where he died 1824. (J. F.)

able not to be mentioned.   Major H., having been suddenly recalled to his regiment (then about to be engaged, I forget on what occasion), before leaving Scotland he executed a trust deed empowering his nephew to act for him, and manage his affairs in his absence, overlooking the fact that his *appointed factor* wanted some months of being of an age when the law would have authorised him to act for himself. It was said his uncle's intentions in his favour went further than this, but that upon his death, which took place soon after,[1] his nephew cancelled every document which was in his own favour, and allowed the law to take its course. But of this he said nothing himself; it would have been most unlike him if he had.   I remember hearing my mother more than once repeat this trait, which she had from some member of his own family.   This appointment of his uncle's probably suggested the idea of placing him in a writer's office, and his father's former master, Mr. Campbell of Succoth, then at the head of the profession, received him into his when little more than fourteen. From that time his allowance from his father was ten pounds per annum, and with that and his own earnings he not only supported himself respectably, but as these increased he procured masters for such branches of education as he had not hitherto had opportunities of acquiring.   His good conduct, zeal, fidelity, integrity, and superior abilities, it may be inferred, gained for him the confidence and esteem of his master, by whom he had long been treated as one of his own family and with whose son, Islay (afterwards President of the Court of Session), he formed a friendship which lasted for life.   The second son had been destined to follow his father's profession, but disappointed these

---

[1] I am not sure whether he was not killed in battle. (S. F.) [He was not, as the following notices occur in the *Scots Magazine* :

August 13, 1762. At Portsmouth, on his return from Senegal, Captain Thomas Hamilton, youngest son of Sir Walter Hamilton, of Westport, Bart., deceased.

September 12, 1762.   At London, Sir James Hamilton, of Westport, Bart. (the uncle alluded to) ; he was wounded at Fontenoy.   (J. F.)]

expectations by falling into idle dissipated habits, and died abroad. As Mr. C. advanced in years, an able assistant became necessary for him to carry on the extensive and important business entrusted to him, and he gradually devolved upon his young *protégé* much of the confidence reposed in himself. He therefore prepared to follow out the course prescribed in order to qualify himself for taking his place in the highest grade of the profession. About this time, I believe it was when only three and twenty, he made what to many might have proved a ruinous step, but which, in spite of severe struggles and privations, proved a happy union. Helen Coutts was the daughter of a farmer near Montrose, and her sole endowments were virtue, beauty, and sweetness of disposition. She had come to Edinburgh to reside with an aunt, the Hon. Mrs. Maitland, the widow of a younger son of Lord Lauderdale. She had been left in poor circumstances, and lived in a small house in the Canongate, which she shared with the young couple, till their increasing family and my father's rising situation made it necessary he should have a house of his own. It was considered great elevation when he took possession of a flat in Lady Stairs Close, just vacated by Sir James Pulteney and his wife Lady Bath. I have often heard him mention this as a fact which would appear almost incredible to a future generation, as the situation is now one of the most beggarly description. At that time, such was the scarcity of accommodation, Mr. Campbell lived in a flat in James's Court, with a pretty large family of children, in which all his business was carried on. The small room, or rather closet, in which my father wrote had no fireplace, and when the Duke of Argyll or any of the principal clients dined with their agent (as happened occasionally), the only drawing-room was Mr. and Mrs. Campbell's bedroom. I am not certain at what period Mr. Campbell's death occurred, but when it did his assistant became his successor and to the greater part of his extensive and important business. That he managed to the entire satisfaction of his clients, with many of whom he lived in habits of great personal friendship, in particular with the benevolent and patriotic John, Duke of Argyll, to whom in his latter days he devoted a considerable portion of his time, and through whose interest (most strenuously exerted) he was finally appointed one of the principal Clerks of Session. The business of W.S. he then resigned to his sons. The duties of this office, while they afforded sufficient occupation for his able and active mind, enabled him to devote more time than he had hitherto done to the most important of all studies, that of the Holy Scriptures, which formed the greater part of his daily reading during his declining years, and opened up to him clearer views of the Divine character than had been conveyed to his young mind by those with whom his early days had been passed. In the conviction of the sinfulness of man in his unrenewed state, and in the humble hope in the atoning merits of Him whose blood 'cleanseth from all sin,' he departed this life January 18, 1829, aged eighty-six.[1]

---

[1] Mr. Ferrier's grandfather, old Captain Sandilands Hamilton, served in thirteen campaigns under Marlborough, and became in his old age quite doited, and had the chairs all drawn up in squadrons like the battle of Malplaquet, and old Aunty Moll (his sister-in-law), as she was denominated, was a lieutenant, and his nurse, an old woman who attended him, was a sentinel with a stick over her shoulder ! The circumstances under which Anne Ferrier (a sister of my great-grandfather) obtained a husband are strange and worth recording here. Dr. Glen, a rich old and miserly physician of Edinburgh, paid his addresses to her. She said she would marry him on one condition, that he gave her a carriage, to which he agreed. The marriage took place, and the carriage was presented, but when she asked for horses he said *they* were not included in the compact, and no horses would he give her. On which she instituted proceedings against him in the Court of Session, which ended in a judicial separation ! She then went to reside with her sister, Mrs. Burns, at Bo'ness, near Linlithgow. His fortune, which was considerable—30,000*l*.—he left to his niece, who married the eighth Earl of Dalhousie. Her father, I think, was Governor of South Carolina, and he built a magnificent drawing-room to his house, which stands quite near the entrance to the Palace of Linlithgow. There is an account of Dr. Glen in Kay's *Edinburgh Portraits*, a scarce and valuable work. My great-grandfather used to relate how he had as a boy walked all the way from Edinburgh to Linlithgow, sixteen miles, to see his grandmother, who set down before him as luncheon a pigeon pie, the aspect of which pleased him much, and he said as he stuck the knife into it he thought he would make his dinner upon it. ' Will ye so ? ' said his grandmother, and she immediately snatched it up and carried it off, leaving him to make his dinner upon the glance he had had of it ! He certainly could not have com-

Scott, James Ferrier's colleague in the Clerkship of the Session House, wrote thus of him : 'Honest old Mr. Ferrier is dead at extreme old age. I confess I should not wish to live so long. He was a man with strong passions and strong prejudices, but with generous and manly sentiments at the same time. We used to call him Uncle Adam, after that character in his gifted daughter's novel of the "Heiress." '[1] And three days later he writes, 'saw the last duty rendered to my old friend, whose age was

Like a lusty winter,
Frosty but kindly.

I mean in a moral as well as physical sense.'[2]

A characteristic story is told earlier :
'Uncle Adam (*vide* "Inheritance"), who retired last year from an official situation at the age of eighty-four, although subject to fits of giddiness, and although carefully watched by his accomplished daughter, is still in the habit of walking by himself if he can by possibility make an escape. The other day in one of these excursions he fell against a lamp-post, cut himself much, bled a good deal, and was carried home by two gentlemen. What said old Rugged and Tough? Why, that his fall against the post was the luckiest thing that could have befallen him, for the bleeding was exactly the remedy for his disorder!'[3]

A sketch of Mrs. Ferrier has already appeared in print. 'Mrs. Ferrier (*née Coutts*) was the daughter of a farmer at Gourdon, near Montrose. She was very amiable, and possessed of great personal beauty, as is attested by her portrait by Sir George Chalmers, Bart., in a fancy dress, and painted 1765. At the time of her marriage (1767) she resided at the Abbey of Holyrood Palace with an aunt, the Honourable Mrs. Maitland, widow of a younger son of Lord Lauderdale's, who had been left in poor circumstances, and had charge of the apartments there belonging to the Argyll family. After their marriage Mr. and Mrs. Ferrier occupied a flat in Lady Stair's Close (old town of Edin-

---

plained of being spoilt in his young days. (J. F.)

There may have been a dim recollection of this in the speech of Mrs. Macshake : 'Do ye mind how ye was affronted because I set ye doon to a cauld pigeon pie and a tanker o' tippenny, ae night to your foweroots, before some leddies ?'

[1] *Journal of Sir W. Scott*, vol. ii. p. 221.
[2] *Ibid.* vol. ii. p. 223.
[3] *Ibid.* vol. ii. p. 342.

burgh), and which had just been vacated by Sir James Pulteney and his wife Lady Bath.'[1]

The family of James Ferrier consisted of six sons and four daughters. Of the sons three pursued their father's profession. These were John, who died in 1851 and who was, by his marriage with Margaret Wilson, sister of Christopher North, the father of the metaphysician ; Archibald Campbell, who married Miss Garden, and died in 1814 ; and Walter, who married Miss Gordon, and died in 1856. Two other brothers, James and William Hamilton, went into the army and died in India, both in 1804. Between Susan and her brother James there was, as we shall see from this correspondence, a special intimacy and attachment. A sixth brother, Lorn, also in the army, died in 1801 in Demerara.[2] Susan was the youngest of the family and was the only one of the four daughters who did not marry. Jane married in 1804 Colonel (afterwards General) Graham, and died in 1846. Janet married in 1796 Mr. Connell of Conheath, and died in 1848, while Helen, who married in 1800 Mr. Kinloch, a London banker, survived till 1866.

Of Jane her great nephew writes this : 'Mrs. Graham was a very clever artist and copied the rich carvings that adorned the ceiling of the King's Room, Stirling Castle, a work published by Blackwood 1817 under the name of " Lacuna Strivelinense, or a Collection of Heads." It is now very scarce and seldom to be met with. In her youth she was a beauty, so much so that she fired the muse of Robert Burns when on her way home to her father's house in George Street. One verse is—

> Jove's tuneful dochters, three times three,
> Made Homer deep their debtor ;
> But gien the body half an e'e
> Nine Ferriers wad done better !

At the time the lady was twenty and was betrothed to one of the Campbells of Ardkinlass, who was subsequently killed in battle. Many years after she married General Graham. Her father would not give his consent to the marriage until he was a General, which rank he attained through the intervention of the beautiful Lady Charlotte

---

[1] Mr. John Ferrier's introduction to Bentley's edition of *Marriage*, p. 5.

[2] He was in the 42nd (the Black Watch).

Campbell with the Earl of Moira, who was then Commander of the Forces in Scotland. On her marriage Lady Charlotte (a friend from her early years) wrote to her :

'" For Mrs. Brigadier-General Graham. This comes to felicitate J. C."

Inside the cover :

'" Miss Ferrier *per ultima volta*,—Is it not strange that I should write for the last time to Jane Ferrier without sorrow? A thousand joys to Jane Graham. You have not time or power to read a long epistle. I merely trace these lines expressive of my best and kindest wishes, that since I cannot in person be present at the ceremony my heart may wing its way to you. My husband after his fashion manifests his sincere joy, and would have been very witty if I had allowed him. God bless you, my dear friend, not less so as a married than you ever were as a single woman, and in this pleasing belief I remain, with pleasure as well as with affection, Jane Graham's heartily affectionate

C. M. CAMPBELL.' "

(From *Memoir of General Graham*, by his son, Colonel J. J. Graham.)

The only surviving recollection, as it would seem, of Miss Ferrier's childhood is sufficiently characteristic. She had, it is said, great powers of mimicry. On one occasion her brothers and sisters, all, be it remembered, older than herself, had engaged in illicit pranks in the supposed absence of their elders. Suddenly they were alarmed by the sounds of their father's voice—sounds, however, which, as was afterwards discovered, really came from the youngest of the family.

The death of her mother and the marriages of her sisters left Susan Ferrier the mistress of her father's house. How she filled that post can be in a measure judged from her own correspondence. One of the few survivors of the generation who knew her in her days of youth and vivacity describes her as ' dark, tall and handsome, a most attractive personality, and a brilliant conversationalist ; the centre of a brilliant coterie in Edinburgh.'[1] Such is the recollection of Sir Douglas Maclagan, the son of the Dr. Maclagan more than once referred to in the following correspondence

[1] The tradition of her own family does not confirm this account of Miss Ferrier's good looks. The miniature shows a vigorous and expressive face, with fairly well-shaped but not very regular features.

as Miss Ferrier's family physician.[1] The same informant adds that his father found that the charm of Miss Ferrier's conversation invariably led him to spend three-quarters of an hour on his visits to her instead of the conventional quarter of an hour. To avoid this the duty of visiting was transferred to the son, with the result that a like waste of time followed in his case.

Few societies could have been found better fitted to give scope and pasture for Miss Ferrier's gifts than that of Edinburgh at the beginning of the century. It had the concentration which belongs to an intellectual oligarchy. The generation indeed was passing away with whom, as described by Lockhart, 'the style of visiting altogether was different from the ceremonious sort of fashion now in vogue. They did not deal in six weeks' invitations and formal dinners, but they formed at a few hours' notice snug little supper parties.'

Though that state of things was disappearing, much of the easy intimacy which it begot survived, while at the same time Edinburgh life became more and more leavened by widening literary influences. Such a society was just fitted to perfect the gifts which Miss Ferrier needed and to furnish her with the material on which to work. In the narrow limits of such a community satire does not require to be more than allusive, or to burden itself with cumbrous prefaces and explanations. It was, moreover, a self-describing and self-criticizing society. The reader of Lord Cockburn's 'Memoirs,' of Lockhart's 'Peter's Letters,' of the correspondence of Mrs. Grant of Laggan soon finds that he is moving in a limited society of recurrent persons and incidents. How vigorous the life of that society was is perhaps best shown by the diversified lights in which it presents itself according to the temper and prepossessions of the observer. In the pages of Cockburn [2] we read of a faction-ridden community full of bitterness and ill-feeling. In the early careers of Lockhart and Wilson we seem to see under the conventional amenities of biography a bear-

---

[1] Sir Douglas Maclagan, M.D., late Professor of Medicine in Edinburgh University, is the elder brother of the present Archbishop of York. The father was President of the Scotch College of Surgeons. His recollections of Miss Ferrier are communicated by one of the younger members of his family.

[2] This applies to the early Henry Cockburn, the vehement and often arrogant and embittered Radical partisan ; not to the mellower and more mature Cockburn, a Whig in politics, in all else the most strenuous of Tories.

garden of literary brawlers. Yet Mrs. Grant, something of an optimist, but no fool, could describe the world in which she lived as one where 'all the persons most distinguished and admired speak with a degree of respect and kindness of each other—no petty animosities or invidious diminutions, even though differing much on political or other subjects.' There were two other wholesome features in the Edinburgh life of the eighteenth century. It was neither prosaic nor provincial. Running through all the Scotch literature of that time we see that half-humorous, half-romantic personification which we have in Lady Nairn's 'Farewell to Edinburgh.' This was largely due to the fact that no inhabitant of Edinburgh was ever suffered to forget that the city was part of a wider community. In reading the letters and memoirs of that day we are reminded at every turn of the intimate connection between the life of Edinburgh and that of the aristocracy and landed gentry. This was largely kept alive by the fact that the townsman of Edinburgh never allowed himself to be divorced from rural pursuits and tastes. Lockhart tells us that 'It was looked upon as quite inconsistent with the proper character of an advocate, to say nothing of a judge, to want [1] some piece of land, the superintendence of the cultivation of which might afford an agreeable no less than profitable relaxation from the toils of the profession. It was understood that every lawyer spent the Saturday or Sunday of every week in the milder part of the year not in Edinburgh, but at his farm or villa.' Lockhart further illustrates this by describing Jeffrey at Craigcrook 'talking of Swedish turnips, and Frain grass, and red-blossomed potatoes.'

Thus no Edinburgh man of letters could look down on the country man as the London wit of the last century looked down on Squire Western and Tony Lumpkin. There was no danger of that sharp moral and intellectual severance between town and country from which France has suffered.

One feature of the world wherein Miss Ferrier lived was too noticeable and had too marked an influence on her writings to be overlooked, the existence of that 'singular race of excellent Scotch old ladies' whom Lord Cockburn has described in a well-known passage. They were, he tells us, 'merry even in solitude, very resolute, indifferent

---

[1] It is probably needless to say, 'to lack,' not to desire.

about the modes and habits of the modern world ; and adhering to their own ways so as to stand out like primitive rocks above ordinary society. Their prominent qualities of sense, human affection and spirit were embodied in curious outsides, for they all dressed and spoke and did exactly as they chose ; their language, like their habits, entirely Scotch, but without any other vulgarity than what perfect naturalness is sometimes mistaken for.' They meet us again and again in the pages of Scott, of Lockhart, and of Lady Anne Barnard, and we feel that with Miss Ferrier we are never far from them and their atmosphere.

It may not be out of place to see how one of the type could present herself to three observers of different temper and character, since in the cross lights thus given lies, I think, the key to a good deal of Miss Ferrier's humour. ' Miss Menie Trotter,' Lord Cockburn tells us, ' was of the agrestic order—ten miles at a stretch was nothing to her. Her attire accorded. But her understanding was fully as masculine. Though slenderly endowed, she did unnoticed acts of liberality for which most of the rich would expect to be advertised.' He then describes how every autumn ' an ox was sacrificed to hospitality ' and ' regularly eaten from nose to tail,' and how friends would be pressed to dine, with the warning ' we're terrible near the tail noo.' She figures with more dignity in Mrs. Grant's pages as a hostess of ' stately form, and firm, energetic, high-principled character,' entertaining a few visitors, ' always people of mind and intellect.'

We have a third description of her more sympathetic than Lord Cockburn's, and more observant than Mrs. Grant. ' Mystifications ' [1] is a rare enough work, and the character of Miss Trotter is germane enough to my subject, to justify a quotation in full :

' She was penurious in small things, but her generosity

---

[1] Miss Clementina Stirling Graham of Duntrune possessed a remarkable gift of impersonation, which she practised in the most intrepid manner on some of the leading members of Edinburgh society in the first quarter of the present century.

Assuming sometimes the character of some imaginary lady of an earlier generation—such as ' Lady Pitlyal ' or ' Lady Catherine Howard,' sometimes that of a beggar, or woman of the lower classes, she succeeded in completely ' mystifying ' or taking in such men as Lord Jeffrey, Sir William Fettes, Count Flahault, and others. In later years she was persuaded to print for private circulation some of her experiences ' in character.'

They were edited by Dr. John Brown and privately printed in 1859. A second edition was printed for publication in 1865. It is from this that the extract in the text is taken.

could rise to circumstances. Her dower was an annuity from the estate of Mortonhall. She had a contempt for securities, and would trust no bank with her money, but kept all her bills and banknotes in a green silk bag that hung on her toilet-glass. On each side of the table stood a large white bowl, one of which contained her silver, the other her copper money, the latter always full to the brim, accessible to Peggy, her hand-maid, or any other servant in the house, for the idea of any one stealing money never entered her brain. Indeed, she once sent a present to her niece, Mrs. Cuninghame, of a fifty-pound note wrapped up in a cabbage leaf, and entrusted it to the care of a woman who was going with a basket of butter to the Edinburgh market. My friend Mrs. Cuninghame related to me this and the following histories of her aunt:

'One day, in the course of conversation, she said to her niece, "Do ye ken, Margaret, that Mrs. Thomas R—— is dead? I was gaun by the door this morning, and thought I would just look in and speer for her. She was very near her end, but quite sensible, and expressed her gratitude to God for what He had done for her and her fatherless bairns. She said 'She was leaving a large, young family with very small means, but she had that trust in *Him* that they would not be forsaken, and that He would provide for them.' Now, Margaret, ye'll tell Peggy to bring down the green silk bag that hangs on the corner of my looking-glass, and ye'll tak' twa thousand pounds out o' it, and gi'e it to Walter Ferrier for behoof of thae orphan bairns; it will fit out the laddies, and be something to the lassies. I want to make good the words, 'that God wad provide for them,' for what else was I sent that way this morning, but as a humble instrument in His hands?"

'Miss Trotter had a friendship for a certain Mrs. B—— who had an only son, and he was looked on as a simpleton, but his relatives had interest to get him a situation as clerk in a bank, where he contrived to steal money to the extent of five hundred pounds. His peculations were discovered, and in those days he would have been hanged, but Miss Trotter, hearing the report, started instantly for Edinburgh, went to the bank, and ascertained the truth. She at once laid down five hundred pounds, telling them, "Ye' maun not only stop proceedings, but ye maun keep him in the bank in some capacity, however mean, till I find some other employment for him." Then she fitted the lad out, and sent him to London, where she had a friend, to whom she wrote, offering another five hundred pounds to any one who would procure him a situation abroad in which he might gain an honest living, and never be trusted with money.

'After all this was settled she went herself and communicated the facts to his mother.

'When she was confined to bed, and felt that her end was approaching, she bid Mrs. Cuninghame look at a little coarse engraving of a young man that hung on the wall of her room in a black frame.

'"Do ye ken, Margaret, whase picture that is? I would like to tell you about it. That's Jamie Pitcairn; he was but a young medical student in thae days, but he rose to distinction in his profession after that.

'"He was of a noble nature, and had a kindly heart, and he was the only one in the whole world that ever showed me any tenderness or affection; and weel did I love him; indeed, we were deeply attached to ane anither.

'"My mother and my sister Johanna were proud an' overbearing, and looked down upon Jamie, but my auldest sister, Mrs. Douglas, had a mair feeling heart, and often took me with her to visit at Dr. Cullen's, where I met Jamie, and mony happy hours we spent there. Whiles he wad come and drink tea with Mrs. Douglas; her house was at the head of the Links, and the windows looked out upon the country and up to Arthur's Seat and the Salisbury Craigs. One evening we three sat there building our airy castles; a happy party; the beautiful world before us, and the birds singing joyously, when the door opened, and four black eyes like a thunder-cloud darkened the room. They fell upon me like a spell that froze my very heart's blood. I can never forget the look of disdain they coost upon Jamie. He never spoke, but took up his hat, gave one kind look to me, opened the door and left the room, and I never saw him again.

'"They were cruel to me. I was ta'en hame to suffer, and he never married.

'"I had no friend left, for Mrs. Douglas went to France for the education of her only daughter, who in the course of time became Lady Dick of Prestonfield. So I wandered among the hills, and held communion with Him who is the father of the afflicted, and when I looked over the varied land and the restless sea, and down upon the broom and the flowers that were offering up their mute praise and incense to their Creator, I found the 'comfort that passes understanding.'

'"Mony ane thought when I gaed thae long walks among the mountains, that I was my lane; but I never was my lane, for the Maker of this beautiful world was my constant companion."

'She was a great reader, and had a highly-cultivated mind; but, continuing her remarks, said: "I never cared muckle for religious books; indeed, the only twa books that I thought worth reading were Massillon's Sermons and the New Testament. I didna gae often to the kirk, for I never profited by their lang prayers and their weary sermons; and I had nae pleasure in looking at the braw folk that cam' there on the Sundays."

'Pointing again to the engraving, she added, "Now, that's the picture of Jamie Pitcairn." A day or two after this conversation Mrs Cuninghame paid her another visit, and found her still in life, but very feeble. On asking how she felt she replied, " Very weel, but the candle is just done."

'She fell asleep the same evening, and her soul returned to Him who gave it.'

James Ferrier, be it remembered, was Miss Trotter's man of affairs, and the details of her life must have been familiar to Susan Ferrier. It may be fanciful to suppose that we can trace a direct reference to the incidents given above in the character of Uncle Adam. It is certainly not fanciful to see that this typical combination of eccentricity and shrewd judgment, of austerity and cynicism on the surface, with warm and tenacious affection beneath, is just that which inspires some of Miss Ferrier's best and most characteristic, though not most conspicuous, work.

I may seem to have dwelt at somewhat inordinate length on the features of that society in which Miss Ferrier was brought up and lived. But in her case, far more than in that of many writers, such external conditions were part of the history of her writings. No writer can make bricks without straw, and the work of every novelist will no doubt be largely influenced by those aspects of life with which he has been in contact. But it is obvious that this influence is not in all cases a fixed and equal quantity. A writer who deals with the travail of the human soul, with universal and elementary passions, a writer who prevails

by sense of proportion and artistic perfection of expression,
may be in a great measure independent of scenery and
circumstances. The solitude of the Yorkshire moors may
have been a needful element in the training of Charlotte
Brontë and her sister. The characters of 'Shirley' and
'Wuthering Heights' may be brought into fuller relief by
local conditions; they are not tramelled by them, nor
dependent on them. It is difficult to imagine a society so
barren and featureless, that a chronicle of its sayings and
doings by Jane Austen would not be a delight. But work
such as Miss Ferrier's, of which the main feature is
satire, qualified by kindliness, and restrained and guided
by good sense, but not marked by any artistic perfection
of style, needs appropriate material drawn from real life.
Edinburgh furnished her with exactly that which she
needed. The society in which she lived was compact and
homogeneous enough to be carefully studied, varied and
animated enough to be thoroughly interesting, grotesque
enough in some of its phases to give full scope to vigorous
and even extravagant humour.

That is a different thing from saying that Miss
Ferrier failed whenever she got beyond the bounds of that
life with which she was familiar. She is not a mere
realistic satirist of manners. She understood the absurdities and follies of humanity, not merely those of
Scotland. Her gallery of portraits could ill spare Lord
Rossville, who is only Scottish by accident, and Dr. Redgill,
who is not Scottish at all. Lady Juliana, too, must be rated
an able seawoman in that ship of fools which has Mr.
Collins for chaplain and Miss Bates for stewardess. But
even when the characters themselves are not Scotch, the
background against which their follies and absurdities are
thrown out is so. Miss Ferrier's comedy is so largely a
matter of action and incident that it depends almost as
much on circumstance as it does on individual character.
She may go abroad in search of individual characters;
she rarely does so for her scenery and atmosphere, and
when she does it is always with some loss of power.

One very notable and somewhat puzzling feature of
Miss Ferrier's character is explained by the traditions of
the society wherein she lived. 'Morbid' and 'affected'
are terms which plainly have no place in reference to her.
Yet her dread of publicity, her shrinking from the fame
and the responsibility of authorship, would on the surface

seem to deserve such a description. The reality and the strength of that dread cannot be doubted by any reader of these letters.[1] Partly, no doubt, it was due to a dread of the indignation, not wholly unnatural or unpardonable, which might be shown by the friends who had served as her models.

But the feeling was more than that. It was in truth a universal tradition, a superstition one might almost call it, which we find in full force among brilliant Scotswomen of that day, every whit as clear sighted and as fearless as Miss Ferrier. Lady Louisa Stuart is half beside herself with alarm and annoyance because a ballad with which Sir Walter had usually been credited, but which she had really composed, was being traced to its true author.[2] Lady Ann Lindsay makes a mystery of the authorship of 'Auld Robin Gray,' and Lady Nairn, in whom courage, frankness and strength of mind met as they have met in few women, or men, would fain pass herself off on her publishers as Mrs. Bogan of Bogan.

In all likelihood this was due to a feeling that there was about professional authorship a certain taint of Grub Street, a something of Bohemia and of uproarious and rather indecent publicity. That feeling was certainly not likely to be allayed by such an incident as the 'Chaldean' storm, or by the Boswell tragedy, nor indeed by the early careers and the many youthful indiscretions of Lockhart and Wilson.

The letters appended to this chapter throw light on Miss Ferrier's early relations to her family, and on what one may call her pre-literary life.

JAMES FERRIER, SEN. TO S. E. F.

Rosneath : October 12, 1798.

My dear Roe,[3]—You scared me from writing sooner by requiring a description of the illuminations in this quarter, as it exceeds the power of my pen to give any-

---

[1] Numerous instances will occur. One of Maginn's many literary indiscretions was a reference in a London paper to Miss Ferrier's authorship, before it was disclosed to the world. For this he received reproof from Blackwood. See Mrs. Oliphant's *History of a Publishing Firm*, vol. ii.

p. 27.

[2] See Scott's *Letters*, vol. i. p. 107. The ballad in question was called 'Ugly Meg.' One would like to know whether it had any relation, and if so what, to 'The Reiver's Wedding.' Lockhart throws no light on this.

[3] A pet name. (J. F.)

thing like an idea of them, but I shall attempt to outline
them, and leave the rest to your fertile imagination.[1] The
Duke first discovered that Mr. Vesy had lighted up the new
Inn at Ardencaple with great taste and lustre. On looking
at the other side of the house Greenock and Port Glasgow
were seen blazing through the trees, and on the opposite
shore the Town of Helensburgh was like one great lamp.
This roused his Grace, who desired his candle chest should
be opened, and that nothing might be spared of a com-
bustible nature, except the Castle itself, which he could
not well do without for that night, as he was not prepared
to move to Bellevue.[2] In a short time, the Castle, with the
assistance of potatoes and turnips in place of clay, was
highly illuminated, and people at a distance say it made a
very grand appearance. On the opposite point, Mr.
Buchanan's house of Ardenconnel was next lighted up,
and, last of all, Lady Augusta[3] took the hint and lighted
up Ardencaple. In the former part of the day, from
12 till dark, nothing was heard but the roaring of cannon
from the ships at Greenock and Port Glasgow, and volleys
from the volunteers on shore, so that it was on the whole
a very merry day. This victory has had a wonderful
effect upon the Duke's health and spirits. He has not
complained once since he consented to Lord John's joining
his regiment in Ireland, and for some days has taken to
his old trade of marking trees to be cut. Lady Augusta
and her whole family, including Miss Mure[4] and the

---

[1] For the naval victory of the Nile.
(J. F.)

[2] The castle was burnt down in
1803. Bellevue was a place the Duke
had opposite Rosneath. (J. F.)

[3] The duke's daughter, Lady
Augusta Clavering. She had a beautiful face, and it is said George IV.
wanted to marry her in her young
days. (J. F.)

[4] Miss Mure of Caldwell. She
was like one of the family, her father,
Baron Mure, having been guardian
to the duchess's son Douglas, eighth
Duke of Hamilton. She was a sister
of Colonel Mure, the well-known
writer on Greece. (J. F.)

Bessy Mure figures more than once
in Kirkpatrick Sharpe's correspondence. Writing in 1812 to Miss
Clavering he says : 'Then I have
discovered a new fault in her ; she
doth not understand a joke, which in
conversation and literary correspondence is certainly the sin against the
Holy Ghost.' *Letters to and from C.
Kirkpatrick Sharpe*, vol. i. p. 42.
I suspect from the tone of Sharpe's

Howdy,[1] are here at present to take leave before setting
out for Edinburgh. When she comes there, do all of you
take care to keep at a distance from that vile monkey she
carries about with her. Jacob, her manservant, who was
bit last year by her mad dog, is in danger of losing a
finger by a bite from that other favourite a few days ago.
Shawfield and Mrs. Campbell came here to dinner
yesterday, and are this morning gone to Woodhall?[2]
Adieu.

Yours most affectionately,

JA. FERRIER.

JAMES FERRIER, SEN. TO S. E. F.

Inveraray[3]: March 17, 1800.

At present I have no idea, my dear Susan, when I shall
get leave of absence from this place, and therefore I could
not make any appointment with you, even if there were no
other objections to my coming for you. But the truth, my
dear girl, is that, from a strain which I gave myself by over
fatigue in travelling near twenty years ago, I cannot take
such a journey without injuring my health, and therefore
must not think of it. I am in hope that your brother
William[4] is to be appointed a Captain at this time, and, as
he will probably be put on the recruiting service, that he
will choose Edinburgh for his station. In that case he will
escort you and the Tullochs[5] to Old Reeky, and the boy
belonging to them can be sent to Leith by sea. Having
sent Mr. Tulloch's letter to John after one reading I do
not remember perfectly what he said, but think the charge
is laid on me, and that amongst us we must execute

---

letters to Miss Mure that this was a
temporary outburst of spleen, not a
deliberate judgment.

[1] Monthly nurse. (J. F.)

[2] Mr. Campbell's place in Lanark-
shire. (J. F.)

[3] I have been told that my great-
grandfather was at Inveraray when

Dr. Johnson paid his memorable visit
there in 1773. (J. F.)

[4] His fifth son, a captain in the 13th
Foot. (J. F.)

[5] I don't know who the Tullochs
are. His daughter was in London, at
her sister Mrs. Kinloch's, when this
letter was written. (J. F.)

what is needful to be done.   We are now in frost and snow
here after an appearance of summer.   Adieu, my dearest.

Yours most affectionately,

J. F.

JAMES FERRIER, SEN. TO S. E. F.

Inveraray : October 11, 1800.

I rejoice, my dear Roe, to hear you are so able and so
willing to return to Old Reeky, where you may depend on
meeting with a hearty welcome if I happen to be there,
which is rather doubtful, for you must know that the Duke
appears resolved to winter here, although Lady Augusta,
Lady Charlotte, and even Mrs. Trot [1] are all to leave him and
to make their way to London, as is your friend Ashnish,[2] by-
the-bye, who is to carry up his daughter, and will be an
excellent hand to escort you down.   I do not mean, nor is
it expected, that I should pass the whole winter at this
place, but I suspect that about Christmas, or soon after, I
will be drawn towards it and be detained for some time.
Ashnish in these circumstances is quite the thing, because
if you miss me at Edinburgh and wish to join me here he
will . . .   [remainder of letter lost]

JAMES FERRIER, SEN. TO S. E. F.

Thursday : December 29.

My dear Roe,—I think you must have heard of a scheme
which some of my near neighbours had in view of providing
me with a housekeeper with one leg, if Jane [3] had not
fought her way through the snow, for you have only sent one
garter, which will not do for me, who have two limbs, such
as they are.   By-the-bye, they are very near well, so you
must make the other garter forthcoming and may begin
another pair as soon as you please, for I shall not spare my
legs now that I have got the use of them.   I have nothing

---

[1] I can't discover who Mrs. Trot was. (J. F.)

[2] Mr. Campbell of Ashnish. (J. F.)

[3] His eldest daughter. (J. F.)

to add but to wish you all a happy new year and to assure you of my warmest affection and esteem.

P.S.—The other garter is arrived, but I cannot be at the trouble of writing another letter.

JAMES FERRIER, SEN. TO S. E. F.

Tuesday evening.

My dear Susan,—I have just time to assure you that although I hurt myself very much by my excursion to the Islands I am geting [*sic*] every day better since I came home, and am already so well as to find no difficulty in discharging my official duty in the Court of Session in the morning, and frequently making visits to my female friends in the evening. For instance, this very night I am to meet Mrs. Hallyday [1] in a pitched battle at whist and the hour is arrived. Be not, therefore, my dearest, under any alarm about me, for I am become a perfect physician, and promise to take care of myself. I take the cold bath in the morning, which I think has done me much good. Adieu.

Your most affectionate

J. F.

The Duke of Argyll is in good health. I had a long letter from him yesterday.

JAMES FERRIER, SEN. TO S. E. F.

I am sorry, my dearest Susan, that I should have given you any alarm about my health, which I declare to you is as good as you ever knew it, but you must make allowance for tear and wear, and be satisfied with seeing me jog round Glenshira at the rate of five miles an hour in place of dashing

---

[1] She was an Edmonstone, and lived next door to Mr. Ferrier in George Street with her sisters, the originals of Grizzy, Jacky, and Nicky in *Marriage*. Their father, Campbell Edmonstone, was Governor of Dumbarton Castle and brother of Sir Archibald, first baronet, and their paternal grandmother was sister to the fourth Duke of Argyll. They are frequently alluded to in these letters. (J. F.)

up and down Glenaray with you at the rate of ten. Old
Slug and I are perfectly at one in this matter, for although she
is in the most perfect health, fat and sleeked as ever, she is
fully more averse to the quiet motion than I am, from which
I conclude that slow easy travelling is best for the aged,
and almost resolved, if ever I am obliged to go to London,
to transport myself in the waggon. I would prefer the sea
were it not for the sickness which would be the fruit of that
mode. Adieu, my dearest, do not think of leaving Helen
till she is better. Present my love to her and James, and
believe me,

¡Ever your most affectionate

J. F.

COLONEL JAMES FERRIER TO S. E. F.[1]

Paris : February 4, 1803.

I should have been perfectly charmed with this capital,
but as it is, I can but half enjoy the novelties of this abode
of luxury and pleasure ; it appears to me an age since I
heard *from* you, but if I could even hear *of* you I think I
should be contented. I, however, live in the hopes that
the first letters from England will say that my beloved
girl is perfectly recovered. Heaven grant it may be so.

I wrote Helen[2] last Monday ; since that time I have
been so much taken up that I have hardly had a moment
to myself. In the first place, I have to inform you that
to-morrow I am to be presented to the First Consul, along
with several others ; last Thursday I was introduced to
M. Tallyrand, the first Minster, by Lord W——, our
Ambassador ; this ceremony is absolutely necessary to be
gone through before the Consular levee. Lord Whit-
worth I am perfectly charmed with ; I think him the

---

[1] James Ferrier was at the siege of
Seringapatam in 1799, and came into
possession of some of Tippoo Sahib's
valuables brought home to England.
His sister, Mrs. Kinloch, states in a
letter that she remembers seeing in
Leicester Square a panorama of the
siege in which her brother figured.
He succeeded his uncle, Colonel Islay
Ferrier, in command of the 94th regiment. (J. F.)

[2] Mrs. Kinloch. (J. F.)

most affable man I ever met with.   I must delay a
description of this place until we meet, as it would fill a
volume.   I have been at four or five of the thirty opera and
play houses that are here.   Of all the houses I ever visited,
the French Opera is the most agreeable.   I shall never be
able to relish our own after it, the dancing being in such a
superior style to ours.

There is a politeness about the French that must
always make the stranger feel happy in their company;
you would think that their sole pleasure was to please and
entertain the company they may happen to be in; however, they certainly ought to have some good qualities. . . .
I shall write you a long letter either by the Monday's post
or Wednesday's, which are the days the post leaves this.
About the 20th or thereabouts I shall be thinking of
leaving this, so I hope still to see my dearest the first week
in March.   If it was summer I should like to return by the
low countries, and embark from thence direct for Scotland;
but this is not the season for travelling about.   Besides, a
long voyage in one of those small packet-boats must be one
of the most unpleasant things in the world.   I know I never
was so sick in my life as crossing from Dover to Boulogne,
although we were only four hours.   Adieu, my dear, dear
Hughie,[1] write your own Moor often, and say particularly
how you are.   God bless you, my love, and with remembrances to my father and all at home, I am ever
your own Moor,

J. F.

COLONEL JAMES FERRIER TO S. E. F.

Paris: February 15.

By letters from Helen of the 9th I was a little relieved
by hearing that my beloved Hughie was somewhat better,
but I am by no means satisfied yet that you are at all as
you ought to be.   I long much to hear from you, my
Hughie, and I trust you will be candid with me in telling

---

[1] There is nothing to show the origin or fitness of this name, nor of
Moor, which follows.

exactly how you are when I see you in Scotland. I shall be able to judge by your appearance, but I am already perfectly convinced that a change of air is absolutely necessary for your recovery, so I'm sure my father will see the necessity of your returning to England with me. I'm convinced he could not put you into the hands of a better *nurse*, for no one can love you better than your Moor.

I continue to like Paris very much. It is certainly the place of all others for a young man—plenty of amusement without dissipation, no drinking ; if a gentleman was seen drunk here he would be looked upon as a perfect *bête*. I think I wrote you I had been introduced to the chief Consul. I was on Sunday last presented to his lady, who I do not at all admire. The great man spoke to me then again, which is a very unusual thing, and I am told by the French I must be in his good graces ; however, I myself rather think it was my good fortune only ; at all events it has given me much pleasure, for it would have only been doing the thing half if he had not spoken to me.[1] I do not think any of the pictures like him much, although most of them have some resemblance ; they give him a frown in general, which he certainly has not—so far from it, that when he speaks he has one of the finest expressions possible.

JAMES FERRIER, SEN. TO S. E. F.

Inveraray : September 21, 1803.

My dear Susan,—I received your letter of the 22nd of last month, only about ten days ago, in the Island of Tiry, from whence I returned to this place two days ago, most exceedingly worn out, both in body and mind, by a very tedious and difficult expedition. I am already much resfreshed, and hope to be able in a few days to set out for Conheath,[2] to see Jess and her family before I enter on

---

[1] Napoleon questioned him much about the siege of Seringapatam, and about India. (J. F.)

[2] Near Dumfries, where his daughter Mrs. Connell lived. (J. F.)

business here, where I must afterwards spend the most of next month. You judged right in thinking that whatever was thought best for your health would be most agreeable to me. I hope Tunbridge will set you fairly up, and make you able to face the north early next summer. Adieu.

Yours affectionately,

JA. FERRIER.

FROM COLONEL JAMES FERRIER TO S. E. F.

(Endorsed by her ' Last letter from my dearest Brother James.')

Calcutta : December 17, 1803.

My dearest Susan,—I take the opportunity of an overland dispatch to write you a few lines, just to say that I am so far well, and am just on the point of setting out by Dawk or post to join the army under General Wellesley. If I should get up in time I may return home, sooner than you expect, a Nabob, as there is a famous rich fort to take, when we shall all make our fortunes. You must not be angry with me, my dearest sister, for sending so short a letter, as I have 150 things to do. I hope soon to be able to write you a very long letter, and meanwhile, Glod bless you, my love. Remember me to my father and all at home.

Ever yours,

J. FERRIER.

P.S.—I have written Helen a few lines by Colonel Nicholson, who carries home dispatches by sea. Possibly her letter will reach first, in which case Colonel N. will be able to give you all the news, as he has promised to call at B.[1] Square when he can possibly find time. Again adieu, my dearest. Heaven bless you.

JAMES FERRIER, SEN. TO S. E. F.

Inveraray : Sunday, August 4.

My dear Roe,—I am under serious apprehensions that some disappointment has made you take a rash step

---

[1] Brunswick. (J. F.)

either at Loch Coat [1] or amongst the coal pits at Hilderstoun, as I think nothing short of a broken arm could have prevented your falling upon some excuse for attempting to add a correspondent to your list. I shall not be easy, therefore, till I hear that you are in a sound skin, and desire in the most earnest manner to be informed of the worst by the return of the post.

We came here on Friday and found the cherries very plentiful and very good, but there is no enjoying every good thing at once. I have not yet seen your friend Mrs. Haswel; to make up for that loss, however, I had the pleasure of seeing Mrs. Campbell of Stonefield [2] this morning for a minute on her way to Lochgare. There is no pleasure without pain. I had the mortification to find that she had already got a Miss in her train, which prevented my applying to have you taken in tow; your sisters can shift for themselves, but one of your shy disposition would be much the better of such a friend. You must bear with your misfortune as well as you can, and look the sharper yourself. Adieu, my dearest Roe.

Yours most affectionately,

J. F.

FROM JAMES FERRIER, SEN. TO S. E. F.

Rosneath : Saturday morning.

My dear Roe,—If you have not employed my last epistle more to your mind, open it, and read it again, which will save me the trouble of describing what passed here last night, only adding to the view the arrival in the morning of our frigate Polyphemus, I think they call her, Captain Moore having in tow the French frigate which he had captured upon the coast of Ireland, with 500 armed Russians, who had left their own country to disturb and distress ours; and figuring to yourself the old Bailie sparkling through the trees at Clachan like the sun itself, with the Manses of

[1] In Linlithgowshire. (J. F.)
[2] Daughter of Sir Robert Anstruther, Bart., of Balcaskie, co. Fife. (J. F.)

Row and Rosneath, one on each hand, shining through the trees which surround them just sufficiently to add to his lustre. You must also take into the account that old Ann in good time lighted up Ardencaple house to great advantage, and that two large bonfires were lighted—one at Cairndow, the other at the Row. I am glad to add that no accident has happened so far as I can learn, and here am I left with the Duke and Mrs. C.[1] in the old Castle, all the rest having just set out, including Ashnish and James Menzies,[2] to visit the frigate, and then put Lord John on board Captain Beatson's cutter for Ireland. I suppose you have heard that John takes the opportunity of going to see Ireland, which was such a tempting one that I could not discourage his embracing it.[3] I think he grows more absent in conversation, and with the bulls which you may expect him to pick up, is likely to afford you some entertainment when he returns. Lord John going to join his regiment at this time is congenial to the Duke's feelings as an old soldier, and his health and spirits are at present luckily equal to the partings which have taken place. Adieu, my dear girl.

Yours most affectionately,

J. F.

S. E. F. TO HER SISTER MRS. CONNELL (MADRAS)

(Written from her sister Mrs. Kinloch's house in London.)

London : February 10 [year about 1801].

. . . As the India House dispatches are now closed, I am reduced to the necessity of making use of a private hand, a mode of conveyance I am in general by no means partial to, but as Mr. Spottiswoode is to have a letter of recommendation from James,[4] I think it as well to render him of some service, as I should be at a loss to get this

---

[1] Most probably the Duke's cousin, Mrs. Campbell of Carrick. (J. F.)

[2] Of the family of Menzies of Menzies, and related to the Argyll family at that time. (J. F.)

[3] His eldest son John Ferrier, W.S.

[4] Probably her brother-in-law, Mr. James Kinloch. (J. F.)

conveyed in any other way. We are in daily expectation of the arrival of the Triton, as I cannot help thinking it contains some live stock in which we have all an interest. The wind, however, is directly contrary, and as long as it continues so the poor Triton has little chance of getting into haven. The Bridgewater will have shipped her cargo before this time, which I dare say would meet with a hearty, or at all events a warm, reception from you and your gude man. I am afraid all the northern budgets will be too late to go by these ships, but I can assure you of their being all well and merry by the last accounts. Jane[1] seems to have made another début into the gay world ; her letters are filled with nothing but suppers, concerts, plays, &c., in all of which she seems to be bearing an active part. I have been nowhere yet except at *Court* (not of St James' but of Dyer's [2]), where I believe I was more in my element. George took Betsy[3] and I [*sic*] to the play, and on Thursday we sally forth under his wing to an assembly. You may believe with all this he stands very high in my good graces, and, indeed, I think report has much belied his *fair fame*. . . . Nabob Stewart is still at Edinburgh, where, if report says true, he has at last found a powerful attraction in Miss Davidson of Ravelrig. I would not give much belief to it, however, for I think he is one of fortune's most fickle favourites. He has got a sister and a female cousin to do the honours, but they are invisible to the prying eyes of man. I suppose they are in training, as they are but newly imported from the country ; their

---

[1] Her eldest sister, married in 1804 Brigadier-General Graham, afterwards Governor of Stirling Castle. (J. F.)

[2] Dyer's Court in the City, where Mr. George Kinloch lived with his sisters. He was a banker in Broad Street, and laird of Kair, co. Kincardine, and a bachelor. His brother, Mr. James Kinloch, also a banker, married Miss Ferrier's sister, and lived in Brunswick Square. Mr. G. Kinloch somewhat resembled Mr. Ribley in *Destiny*, and my aunt evidently had him in her mind when she drew that amusing character with his 'ain't it, Kitty, my dear?' On one occasion he was late for a dinner-party at Brunswick Square, and on arriving said to his sister-in-law, ' Very sorry, marm, very sorry ; couldn't come any sooner, cook in a fit, cook in a fit, stuffed burnt feathers under her nose,' repeating it several times in succession to each person as he went round the room. (J. F.)

[3] Miss Kinloch. (J. F.)

manners have not yet received the last finish. . . . Archy [1]
writes in high spirits about his little family. I should like
to view him taking his patrol with his wife, his lass, and
his wean. He says he expects to be in the print-shops
soon. I have written to request a copy whenever it makes
its appearance. When I tell you that I have got to
spangle a trimming for the great occasion of the ball, you
will certainly deem that a sufficient apology for concluding sooner than I would otherwise have done. I had
almost forgot to mention that we heard from William [2]
to-day, and that he is now perfectly recovered and was
just about to embark for Scotland, where he is expected to
land in the course of a few days. This is a sad scrawl, but
I am in great hurry and have only time to beg my love to
Mrs. C. and the little one, and to assure you I am,

Ever affectionately yours, my dear sister,

S. F.

S. E. F. TO MRS. CONNELL

Edinburgh : January 17, 1802.

My dear Jenny,—I had the pleasure of receiving your
billet by A. Kinloch a few days ago, for which I am very
grateful, as I am perfectly sensible of the exertion it must
cost you to continue a correspondence with so many of
your friends. You are very good to think of sending me
anything, as I'm sure I had little claim upon your remembrance. I am sorry you think it necessary to apologise to
me for the smallness of your present, as I am not so
mercenary as to judge of people's affection by the value of
their gifts. Whatever it is I shall make it very welcome,
and beg you will accept my sincere thanks in the meantime.

James has given us very agreeable accounts of you and
your little family, of which he seems very fond. I long
very much to see them, dear lambs ! and trust the time is

---

[1] Her brother Archibald ; he married in 1800 Miss Garden, daughter
of Mr. Francis Garden, a merchant
in Greenock. Her nephew was Dr.
Garden, late Dean of the Chapel
Royal, St. James's. (J. F.)

[2] Her brother ; he was captain in
the 13th Foot, and died in India, 1804.
(J. F.)

not very far distant when my wish will be gratified. My father is made very happy at the thoughts of returning and settling somewhere near him. I think he looks ten years younger upon it. Little Mary[1] is a great source of amusement to him now that she begins to run about and tries to make use of her tongue. She is a fine child, very lively and brisk, but I don't think her in the least pretty —farther than having a good skin and rosy cheeks. George[2] is my beauty, but that's, perhaps, partiality in me, who consider him almost as my own. Helen is very pressing with me to pay her a visit in spring, and I can only say it won't be my fault if I do not. I, however, have very little hope of obtaining my father's permission, as the family is now so small that one makes a great blank. I am much obliged to you for your invitation, and still more for the *inducement* you hold out to me, but I don't feel inclined to go quite so far in quest of a *husband*. I think you're very bold in promising to *insure* me one. I assure you it's more than most people would do, or even what I would do for myself. I was at a concert a few nights ago, where I was somewhat annoyed by widow Bell, who was there, heading *four and twenty maidens* ; she looked so queer and so vulgar, that I was fain to fight shy. She came bobbing along, sticking out at all points and places, keys and *coppers* jingling in her pockets, led in triumph by a frightful male creature with a large *bow window* bound in blue and buff, and a pair of pea-green *upper legs*. I thought I should have swooned with shame when she stopped and stared at me.

S. E. F. TO MRS. CONNELL (MADRAS)

(From her sister Mrs. Kinloch's house in London, 1803.)

June 19.

My dearest Jenny,—I congratulate you on the late increase of your family, and sincerely wish you joy of your

---

[1] His grandchild, daughter of his son Archibald. (J. F.)   [2] Her nephew, George Kinloch. (J. F.)

dear little girl, who I doubt not will live to be a comfort and a happiness to her parents. I long much to hear more particulars respecting her, as the last letters only announced her entrance into life, which she seemed to have made with great *éclat*, by her dad's account. I do not think I have written you since the arrival of the long-looked-for heir apparent. I presume it is unnecessary for me to say much on his personal or mental qualifications and endowments, as that is a subject which will be pretty well canvassed by other pens. I assure you, however (in case you should doubt the veracity of the papa or mamma), that he is a child of infinite merit, the chief of which consists in the largeness of his body, the strength of his lungs, and the greatness of his appetite. I am become quite an adept in the art of nursing, and whereas I used to hold by neck and heel I now support by top and bottom. I am also learning to talk nonsense, which you may think was not to do, but however easy I found it formerly, I assure you I think it a very difficult matter to sit down for the express purpose. I shall be quite ready for your little Helen, who I hope you will think seriously of sending home the first good opportunity; you won't miss her so much now that you have got another, and I am sure nothing would make my father so happy. He talks of paying us a visit here very soon, and of bringing Jane with him. Kiss your darlings for me, and believe me to be,

Affectionately yours,

S. F.

S. E. F. TO MRS. CONNELL.

(The water-mark on the paper is 1807.)

Saturday, 21st.

My dear Jenny,—As I understand our friend D——[1] is about to open another battery against you, I take the opportunity of coming under her cover, as I know it will give you pleasure to hear from myself that I continue to

---

[1] Probably Miss Dalmeny Edmonstone.

do well in spite of having the severest weather that ever was known to struggle against. As a proof of my convalescence, I need only tell you that my doctor, from visiting me daily, has now diminished his visits to twice a week, when he merely calls to tell me my pulse is perfectly good and 'just to go on as I have been doing.' I have still a little cough and pain in my side, neither of which he flatters me with getting rid of while this weather lasts, but as I sleep well, eat well, and am free from fever and sickness, I have great reason to be thankful to God for having restored me so far. I feel much flattered by your having given me a name daughter, but trust I shall not want such a selfish inducement to make me take an interest in her. I only wish for her sake it had been a prettier name, and that she had had a better and a richer godmother. As it is, none, I am sure, would feel more or wish her better than poor I. In a year or two I shall think I have some little title to put in a claim for her, so I hope you will always consider that and not allow her to become the pet of the house, as that would interfere with my plan of getting her for mine. I hear little of what is going on in this gay town at present, as I see very few people, and those not of the gayest. The Queen's Assembly was, as usual, brilliant on the whole, but nothing very striking in particular, except *Kate*,[1] who, I hear, was by far the most remarkable figure in the room, clad in a dark lead coloured satin (made at least six years ago, to the best of my remembrance), an immense black velvet beefeater's hat ornamented with large paste beads and high feathers, led by her brother Sandy in a pearl-coloured suit. Archie blabbed out that he heard the people declaring she was worth coming four and twenty miles to see, for which I dare say he would smart when they went home. I am ashamed to say anything about seeing you here when the ground is covered with snow, but I cannot give up the hope of having that happiness in the course of the season

---

[1] Her sister-in-law, Mrs. Archd. Ferrier. (J. F.

—it is a thing I cannot urge, because I feel it as a favour I never could repay. Remember me kindly to Mr. C., most truly do I rejoice at the brightening of his prospects. Pray tell him I have supped every night on *his porridge*, and reckon it my best meal. Adieu, my dearest sister; God bless you and your little darlings. Excuse blunders as I'm always too tired to look over my letters.

S. E. F. TO MRS. CONNELL

. . . He (her father) talks of paying us a visit here (London) very soon, and of bringing Jane with him. I return with him, and I believe she will remain with Helen,[1] but am not certain. I have proposed the Stag[2] as a third. She had begun her preparations for a second attack, I understand ; that there might be no delay on her part the night mutches were all in readiness, *starched and ironed*. She entertains fresh hopes, however, since matrimony has got amongst the female cousins, but I'm afraid it won't get her length. You will have heard of Miss K.'s[3] marriage to Colonel Cameron, a very pleasant, good-humoured *highlander*, which is quite recommendation enough to me, as I have a great predilection for the mountaineers you know. He has got a very pretty place near Tunbridge, where I have promised to spend a few days with them before quitting England. Betsy is keeping house in Dyer's Court, which she must feel very dull, now the family is so much decreased. She is very much with us, and will be still more, I hope, when I am gone, as H—— will then stand more in need of a companion. Jane desired me to send you a lace cap, but I have no means of getting it conveyed, so I must delay it till next time. There is nothing very new at present in the style of dress ; the fashionable sleeves have lace inserted in them

[1] Mrs. Kinloch. (J. F.)
[2] Miss Chalmer, so nicknamed. She was a cousin of the Kinlochs. (J. F.)
[3] Kinloch. (J. F.)

in this manner,[1] which has a pretty effect with a pretty
arm.   We were at the opera a few nights ago with Trot,
who had Lady Exeter's[2] box, so we were quite in style.   I
hope we shall hear from you soon.

S. E. F. TO WALTER FERRIER (1810)

Canaan : Friday.

. . . I am convinced nothing is so strengthening as
being much in the open air. I feel quite different those days
I don't get out from those that I spend in the fields, and I
believe, more or less, 'tis the case with everyone. A walk
is nothing, but *daadling* about from morning till night is life
to me, and I therefore prescribe it as the most sovereign
panacea for every disease under the sun.   I can't get you
to listen to my medical opinions in conversation, so to be
revenged of you I'm resolved to give you a dose every time
I write, so this is my first chapter.   I've not been in town
since I got your letter, but I shall go in to-morrow, and execute your orders to the best of mine and the blacksmith's
abilities.   I wrote to desire John to have the letter for Dr.
C. ready, so I hope to get the whole dispatched by Sunday's
mail.   I've been so engaged since you went away betwixt
business and pleasuring, that I've never had a minute I
could call my own.   You was hardly out of the door before
I felt sick and went to bed, but was obliged to rise to
receive the Laird of Makdougall and his daughter, a great
bumping miss in a blue riding-habit ; then in galloped Bessie
Mure, so that I was at my wits' end between a fine town
madam and a *rank Highland miss.*   On Friday we dined
at Dalry with a party of paper lords, and saw Mrs. Frank
for the first time, and think her the loveliest creature I ever
saw.[3]   Next day I was in the Elysian fields with my dear

---

[1] Here Miss Ferrier inserts an ex-
planatory sketch.

[2] Widow of Douglas, eighth Duke
of Hamilton, who was stepson to the
Duke of Argyll.   Married second the
Marquis of Exeter.   (J. F.)

[3] She was Miss Drummond, of
Hawthornden, and married Mr.
Francis Walker, son of Mr. Walker
of Dalry, created a baronet 1828.
(J. F.)

doctor, for such his grounds really are, and you may suppose his company did not lessen the delusion in my eyes.[1] Sunday we had our usual bill of fare from Q. Street, including Bob the Weaver, and that hedgehog Willie T. The rest of the week I was busy as any bee in divers and sundry ways. To-day we had the brothers Pringle, and Louis, and Lady.[2] To-morrow we dine at John's to meet Lord Frederick[3]; on Sunday we have them. On Monday, G. Thompson the poet; Wednesday, at Louis's; Thursday, the Pringles; and on Friday we set off. All this, I must say, is too much for me, and I'm so hurried that I've not time to mend my pen, as you may perceive. I've just snatched a few moments betwixt the departure of our guests and the commencement of Dumbie to scrawl thus far, and though it's almost pitch dark, by way of gaining time I'm trying to prove that it's broad daylight, a point by no means clear. That's a pun, if you please! maybe you'd not have found it out. You may imagine how delighted I was to hear of Helen's safe accouchement, and since then I've been gratified with daily bulletins, besides a long letter from Mrs. Conry giving a full and particular description of the late production, who, she says, surpasses the others for size and strength. . . . I have not heard from Cork for some time; there is a small parcel here for Mrs. G.[4] which I shall send, with the books, to your care. You left two pockethandkerchiefs, which I shall also send to relieve Marquis, who seems much disquieted about it.[5] I was obliged to bring

[1] 'My dear doctor' was Dr. Hamilton. He was one of the latest inhabitants of 'Auld Reeky' who still clung to the dress of a bygone age, the cocked hat, knee breeches, shoe buckles, &c., &c. He never wore gloves or carried an umbrella. Some one remarked these two peculiarities, to which Miss Ferrier replied, with her ready repartee, that he dispensed with gloves (she supposed) for fear of slipping the fees; and that an umbrella was unnecessary, as his three-cornered hat supplied the place of one! (J. F.)

[2] Her cousin, Louis Ferrier, of Belsyde. He married Miss Monro, daughter of Professor Monro (secundus) of Edinburgh University. (J. F.)

[3] Lord Frederick Campbell, Lord Clerk Register of Scotland. From him Professor Ferrier derived his second name. (J. F.)

[4] Mrs. Graham. (J. F.)

[5] Miss Charlotte Marquis, a dependant of the Argyll family. She was with Lady A. Clavering, and died in 1845. She had an annuity, paid by my grandfather. (J. F.)

my letter in with me to finish, and I've been trotting all
over the town, and am so tired, I can scarcely hold the pen
and must go to dress for the grandees. I long to hear
from you again, so pray write, and remember me to all
friends most kindly.

Queen Street [1] : Saturday.

S. E. F. TO WALTER FERRIER (1809 or 1810)

Friday.

My dear Wat,—. . . I am in convulsions at the history
of the 'Loves of the Pigmies,' and even my father (to whom
I read it) laughed most heartily at your description of the
gay Lothario. It is the best thing I have met with for a
great while, and really merits a place in my scrap-book,[2]
which is the greatest mark of honour I can give. Apropos
of books, there arrived for me a few days ago a huge packet
from Dublin Castle, which I doubted not came from my
Delight. You may therefore judge of my agitation when
opening it, and the disappointment that ensued when out
issued the effusions of Joey Atkinson's [3] fat brain in the
form of twenty-eight pages of a printed poem. There was
likewise a long letter filled with fine things, and complaints
of his beauteous rhymes having been so miscalled in Bobby's
paper. I suppose he lays it all to my bad spelling, but I
shall turn him over to the Printer's Devil for redress. There
were some songs for Margaret, which was the best part of
the bundle. I have to answer all this farrago, which is
rather alarming. He had parted with the darling at Lord
Grey's, pretty creature! I'm in hopes to make Joey my
cat's-paw, to help me to keep alive my flame,[4] for I don't

---

[1] Lady Augusta Clavering's house, No. 11. (J. F.)

[2] She had a most valuable scrap-book containing political caricatures by Gilray. She valued it, as she said, as 'the apple of her eye,' but it disappeared and never was seen again, stolen by some one who knew its value. (J. F.)

[3] Treasurer of the Ordnance, Ireland, and a great friend of Sydney Lady Morgan. (J. F.)

[4] This must allude to her admiration for John Philpott Curran, Master of the Rolls. (J F.)

wish it to die away, and yet I musn't burn my own fingers. I was yesterday regaled with the company of the charming *Christy* and her son. You know my opinion of *her*, and, to tell the truth, I don't think much better of him. I know no vice so detestable in youth as *narrowness* and *suspicion*, both of which ingredients seem to form his chief composition. Worldly prudence is very suitable at seventy, but at seventeen it is absolutely disgusting; in the one it is the result of experience, in the other it is the offspring of a little mind and base contracted heart. He goes off to the South on Saturday, where I hope he'll acquire more liberal notions, and get rid of some of his norland rust. I've seen little of Madam Worm since I wrote; she dined here one day with the Harry Davidsons, a most heavy handful. She was in one of her vicious moods; she's a sweet *crater*. We're to dine there to-morrow, it seems, which I'm sorry for; but she has a red-haired cousin staying with her, which saves the *misery* of a *tête-à-tête*. We had the Macdonalds dining with us the other day—rather a humdrum business, I dare say they thought it, for, as usual, we could get nobody, though not, as usual, for want of asking. However, just before dinner we met your friend Sir William, who accepted the invitation, and Janet Wilson was kind enough to come in Margaret's[1] place, who was confined with a slight cold. I'm a good deal disappointed in Colonel Mac; he's far from handsome, and, though he's frank and unaffected, there's nothing particularly pleasing in his manners, or captivating in his address. However, you'll be able to judge for yourself, as they don't leave this till November 1. The affair of the picture is very mysterious, to say the least of it; even Charity cannot avoid thinking evil in such a case. I don't wonder that Lord John has withdrawn from such a motley crew. . . .[2]

---

[1] Mrs. John Ferrier, her sister-in-law. (J. F.)

[2] I have not been able to find clues to any of the allusions in this letter or to the identity of Madam Worm or Christy, &c. (J. F.)

S. E. F. TO WALTER FERRIER

Canaan Grove : May 1, 1810.

My dear Walter,—If you think my silence requires any apology you will please observe the date, which says more for my despatch and agility as a correspondent then were I to write a hundred quarto volumes to prove it. I only received yours of the 27th this morning in town, and since then I have performed a journey that some years ago took Moses forty long years to make out, to say nothing of the various appendages and encumbrances I had along with me, and a pair of hackney horses, who, I'm sure, were worse to drive than all the stiff-necked children of Israel. So much for the improvement of modern times ! I like our little cot very much upon a closer inspection, and expect to pass my time very pleasantly in the retirement it affords. The only bar to my enjoyment is a vile east wind, which annoys me a good deal ; but as there's a bright sun along with it everybody says it's charming weather, and so I suppose it must be so. The doctor was very earnest with us about taking possession, in spite of wind and weather, and I dare say he was right, as I think it is impossible to gain health and strength in the streets. I'm sorry, however, that you should have experienced the fact, though it was no more than I expected, knowing what London is in the month of May. I trust you are now in a purer region, and that, in lieu of swallowing smoke and dust, you are now quaffing the limpid wave from the naiads of Cheltenham. You would be pleased to meet Andrew Millar there. I saw his mother [1] a few days ago, and she told me he was to be there at this time. I had a visit from D——[2] yesterday, but so brimful of charity that every other sentiment or emotion was quite sunk. She told me such stories of objects as you'd shudder at. She's just a walking Lazar House— however, I was really glad to see her, with all her imperfec-

---

[1] Mrs. Millar of Earnock. (J. F.)　　[2] Miss Dalmeny Edmonstone. (J. F.)

tions on her head. I was not quite so rejoiced at a visit
from the whole nest of Worms and the Oyster to-day just
when I was in the very midst of hurry and confusion. She
began to tell me all what she had had to do in her house,
upon which I cut her short, and told her it was quite
unnecessary for her to take the trouble of telling me what
she might easily see I knew. She never minded, but ran on
uttering nonsense and telling lies as fast as she could till I
could no longer be civil to her. She is an odious creature,
such a compound of forwardness and meanness as almost
exceeds credibility. To add to the other agreeables that
attended our stay in town for the last few days, we had
those two white blacks or black whites (which you please),
the T's for inmates till this morning, when they were
shipped off with a foul wind and my blessing. They are a
pair of the most hopeless creatures, I'll venture to say, ever
were sent into the world, not that I mean they've anything
bad in them. Paradoxical as it may seem to say, I should
have more hopes of them if they showed a tendency for
any one thing good *or bad*! But they do not seem to have
a single idea beyond *sitting*. I used to turn them out of
the drawing-room and my father, to find them each seated
in an armchair in the dining-room, with the blinds down,
doing nothing. He was obliged to hire chairmen to make
them walk or they never would have moved ; but they
seemed to be much admired at Conheath, and Jenny [1] wrote
the highest encomiums of them. For my part I don't know
a more deplorable sight than to see two young creatures
with souls and sound bodies such complete victims to
inveterate sloth and stupidity. I should envy you some of
your London sights if I were able for such things, but I
feel that quiet and retirement best accord with me now ;
indeed, at all times I believe there is more pleasure in the
retrospect than the reality. I am, therefore, glad you have
seen what will serve as a foundation for agreeable reflection
hereafter. I trust you will give the waters a fair trial, and

[1] Her sister, Mrs. Connell. (J. F.)

I think if you could manage to come down with A. Millar it would be pleasant for both parties. I am scribbling to you betwixt tea and cards, while my father is busy hoeing, so you must make due allowance for this being totally illegible, as it is all but dark. For the more heinous offence of extreme stupidity I must throw myself on your mercy, as I must honestly confess for some days I've not harboured a thought that did not relate either to painting or packing, but as these begin to yield to the influence of green fields and budding trees I hope I shall be able to acquit myself better. I had a letter from Cork about eight days ago, but have not yet found time to answer it. I have not a single word of news from any quarter to season this very insipid performance, but I know I need not apologise to you for the want of entertainment, as I'm sure you'll be better pleased to hear of my own health than were I to tell all the news and wonders of the town and country both.

CHAPTER II

'MARRIAGE'

IF the legal and literary circles of Edinburgh did not actually coincide, at all events they had so many points of meeting that they practically formed one society. Miss Ferrier was from the very outset brought into contact with Scott and enjoyed close intimacy with the family of Henry Mackenzie, 'The Man of Feeling.' There is tradition, too, of a friendship with Leyden, which he, at least, would fain have made more than friendship, and the total absence of any reference to him in the correspondence will probably be held rather to confirm that suspicion.

As we have seen, Mr. Ferrier's business brought him into close contact with the Argyll family, and there resulted a very hearty friendship between Susan Ferrier and the ladies of that house. The effect on Miss Ferrier's literary career was of no small importance. It introduced her to a phase of life which furnished a needful contrast to that with which she was familiar. Her fine gentlemen may be unreal in character, they are not stagey in demeanour ; yet less her fine ladies. We read of contemporaries wondering how Miss Ferrier, the daughter of an Edinburgh writer who had only had a few glimpses from without of the fashionable world, could reproduce the speech and the ways of that world so correctly, and the solution, we are told, was found in her intimacy with the household of her father's patron.[1]

The Argyll connection did even more than that for her ; it gave her the one literary friendship of her lifetime. As

[1] 'I visited Lady ———, who was engaged in reading Miss F.'s new novel (*The Inheritance*). I told her I heard she did not acknowledge being the authoress. Lady ——— observed it was surprising she should be so well acquainted with the living, talking &c., of fashionable people, as she had heard that Miss F. knew nobody belonging to that class of persons except the A. (Argyll) family.' Diary illustrative of the times of George IV. (J. F.)

we shall see, it is not easy to say whether the original design of 'Marriage' actually had its origin with Miss Ferrier or Miss Clavering. But it is pretty clear that it could never have been written if Miss Ferrier had not at her side a counsellor to whom she could open herself with full confidence and hearty enjoyment.

Miss Clavering, too, was much more than the mere recipient of Miss Ferrier's schemes. It was intended at the outset that the work was to be a joint one. Of Miss Clavering's actual share in the execution it is perhaps charitable to say little. It is indeed surprising that so acute a critic and so lively a letter-writer could have produced anything so commonplace and dull as the few pages which formed her contribution to 'Marriage.' Not even in the worst parts of 'Destiny' has Miss Ferrier produced anything so depressingly conventional as 'The History of Mrs. Douglas.' Miss Clavering's letters are not lacking in playful affectations of self-will and real evidence of self-confidence. All the more was it to her credit to have seen as she did at once the poverty of her own work, to have accepted dismissal without the slightest abatement of friendship or of hearty interest in Miss Ferrier's literary career.

Such slight injury as is inflicted on 'Marriage' by Miss Clavering's contribution is more than redeemed by her criticisms. If any reader takes the trouble to go through her letter of May 10, 1813, and to compare 'Marriage' as we actually have it, with 'Marriage' as she criticizes it, they will see how much Miss Ferrier owed to her friend's advice. One service alone would establish a strong claim for gratitude from all Miss Ferrier's admirers. Miss Clavering protests against the practice of making the fashionable characters interlard their conversation with scraps of French. No trace of the blemish remains, but it is terrible to think that the creator of Lady MacLaughlan and Miss Grizzy might have put on the form of Lady Fanny Flummery.

It is obvious, too, that over and above any direct advice or criticism that Miss Ferrier received, the continuous and intimate correspondence of the two friends had an important influence on her as a writer. The letters we have, we must remember, are but a fragment of the correspondence,[1] and over and above the correspondence there were those

---

[1] The correspondence itself shows plainly that many letters are missing.

'delicious splashy walks at noon and enchanting orgies at midnight,' over which Miss Ferrier laments. 'He was makin himsell' a' the time,' said Scott's friend, Shortrede, telling of the young advocate's days of sport and nights of feasting among the Liddesdale farmers. Miss Ferrier was 'makin hersell' while in her unstudied letters and more unstudied speech she was pouring forth boisterous fun and shrewd judgments on men and things.

S. E. F. TO MISS CLAVERING

Tuesday, 28th.

Your letter was quite a *cheering cup* to me, my dearest, and my heart was filled with gladness to see the joy with which yours overflowed. Long may it continue, in spite of all the *horrors* of London balls and London beaux, and may every wish and expectation it has ever formed be amply realised! But seriously I *was* delighted to hear you were going to leave your dogs, and cats, and owls, and mawkins, for though some of them may be very seemly appendages to elderly gentlewomen *comme moi*, I by no means approve of them as constant companions to beautiful young ladies like you. Ergo, I do rejoice with all my strength that you are going to explore the busy haunts of man. Now for myself, weary wight that I am, everybody says I am much better; in spite of a cough and a pain in my side, I'm obliged to believe them. I was sadly depressed during the dreadful cold weather, but begin to revive again since the change, which makes me hope much from a milder climate, as it is evident all my ails proceed from the excessive cold of this one. In the meantime I'm living like an *Arcadian shepherdess*, upon (asses) milk and grapes (which have really been my chief support for two months), and I only want a *certain hat* to make me complete the thing. The 'Siege of Rochelle' has been translated these six months and none of the book-sellers here ever publish such things, so your friend must betake him or herself to some other crafts. Apropos, no turning for me. I marvel not at you, for I perceive your

E

darling little pate has been completely *turned*; but pray, has Lord John's also run in the loom? But 'men were deceivers ever'! I meant to have written . . . no letter at all to you for daring to laugh at my claw, but shall remit your punishment to writing me 334 folio pages immediately upon your arrival, containing your life and conversation during your journey. Adieu, Pet of my heart, all good attend you. So prays the most affectionate of your friends,

S. E. F.

I'm glad you've dropped that odious freezing arm's length '*Miss Ferrier*'—in such cold weather it would certainly have chilled me to death. Should you see any comical catikitury, as a certain Burring dowager terms a caricature, will you get it franked and send me?

S. E. F. TO MISS CLAVERING

My dear Charlotte,—Do not think me the most ungrateful of living beings, for, indeed, I am only one of the most unfortunate. Your kindest of kind billets found me in an *unanswerable* state, in which I have remained ever since till within these last two days, when I have regained a small degree of strength, just sufficient to enable me to sit up and *hold* a pen, for, as you may perceive, I am not able to *guide* it. My complaint, as usual, is a violent cough; but what was not usual, it has been attended with a most excruciating pain in my side—both are abated, but far from gone. I never can thank Lord John and you for asking me to Ardencaple, so I won't even attempt it; but I hope you will both believe that I feel all possible love and gratitude for this kindness. At present I am too ill to go anywhere, but should I get better as the season advances I believe I am to be *transported* to England. It is a dismal prospect to think of travelling six or seven hundred miles in search of health, which, for my own part, I don't expect to find. Write to me if you really love me, for though I

can't write I can read, and that is my chief comfort. I
have nobody staying with me, for, since I can't have any
one I love, I prefer solitude to the society of those who are
indifferent to me ; you may therefore judge what joy it is
to me to hear from those who are so dear to me. As to La
Princesse, pray don't throw away a thought upon her ; at
present not all the princesses in the world could give me a
moment's pain or pleasure. When you give my love to
Lord John (which I desire you will do) tell him, in addition
to all his other favours, I must beg him to turn something
for me.[1]   I am quite childish and have taken a sick longing
for it, so I hope he won't deny me. I also wish for some
specimens of your handicraft. What a compliment to have
your fingers mistaken for a piece of ivory! Tell me what
it is you wish, and if I can't get it myself I'll cause others
to do it. This is the second time I have touched a pen
these four weeks, but I have taken my own time to this
elegant composition. Adieu, dearest, best of friends.

Ever, ever yours with affection,

S. E. F.

S. E. F. TO MISS CLAVERING

And you really have the pertness to tell me that I
ought to write you a letter every week without expecting
any answer ? Truly, child, you must have strangely forgot
yourself when you presume to talk in such a strain to a
person stricken in years as I am ! Methinks, on the contrary, you must have meant to say that (with my permission)
it would be no more than a piece of respect due to my
grey hairs and wrinkles were you to write me every hour
of your life, and render to me an account not only of the
deeds done in the body, but likewise reveal to me every
thought, wish, fancy, crotchet, and desire that enters into
and issues out of you in the course of the day ! From the
general incoherency that pervaded the whole of your

---

[1] Lord J. C. was very clever in a mechanical way; he used to turn
little ornaments in wood and ivory. (J. F.)

epistle, and extended even to the *direction* of it, I am willing to believe this was your meaning, and I shall accordingly expect a speedy and thorough reformation to be begun in the style and execution of your epistolary communications. And in the first step towards your amendments I must insist that you lay aside that odious practice of writing on *half-sheets* of paper. When I was your age *I* never presumed to lay a finger on anything less than foolscap, and had it not been by reason of my age and infirmities I should still have continued at it, so don't pretend to follow my example in that particular, for at my years I am well entitled to such indulgencies. The next thing that I have often tried to enforce upon you is to send me no *blank paper*, I can get as much for a half-penny as you sometimes make me pay a sixpence for. . . . I allow you all Sunday to meditate on my laws, Monday to put them in practice, and if Tuesday's sun does not show me your contrition I'll burn your letters, destroy my notes, and make a bonfire of your whole *remains* !

S. E. F. TO MISS CLAVERING

Edinburgh : February 21, 1808.

From your long silence, my sweet friend, I had begun to fear that your gentle spirit no longer sojourned on earth, and was therefore much relieved to find that it still lingered even amongst some of the ' thousand ills that flesh is heir to.' The effusions of your swelled face and sore eyes excited emotions of the deepest sorrow in my blistered breast, and was deplored by my broken voice in the most melting accents my cough could possibly assume. But seriously ill as I was myself when I received your letter, I was not so wholly engrossed by my own sufferings as not to feel truly sorry for yours, and would have written to inquire for you long ere now had I not heard of your convalescence from Miss Mure ; besides that, I have been, and still am, so great an invalid, that it's very seldom I have spirits to write even to those I most love. I am persecuted by a cough which will certainly be my death if I remain in this climate, and I have no chance of changing it for another. I have not been out to any party, in public or private, for the whole winter, and have seen about as much gaiety and fashion as you have done. From Miss M. you will have every information on those subjects, as I hear she shines forth the gayest of the gay throng. I hear the other rival queen, the Lamont,[1] is arrived, though if report is to be believed there is no longer much to be feared from that, for, as it is said she is at length going to bestow her fair hand on Maister Snodgrass. I heard of her a few nights ago at a ball in great beauty, arrayed in *crimson* gauze over sky-blue satin. Apropos of robes, have you got yours to fit? because if you have not, I must inquire for the cloth immediately, or it may be all gone, and of course your character will follow. We had Camillia[2] dining with us one day lately in very tolerable preservation. She went next day to take, as she thought, another family dinner at General Maxwell's, instead of which she found herself and her rusty fusty worsted robes in the midst of a brilliant assemblage of powdered beaux and perfumed belles. I visited Benbow[3] a few days ago and found her in the agonies of a ghost story. Shawfield[4] had just been amusing her with a story relating to an old lady, who is at present haunted in (and out of) every house she goes to. And now we are on the subject of ghosts, I have been reading 'The Fatal Revenge,' which I think quite delicious. I recommended to poor Benbow to take a dose every

[1] Miss Lamont of Lamont.

[2] This person is frequently mentioned, but I can obtain no clue to her identity; but Lord Frederick Campbell, Lady Charlotte, and Colonel Campbell came down from London to attend her funeral. Her ways seem to savour somewhat of 'Miss Pratt' in *The Inheritance*. I have also been told that the original of Miss Pratt was someone Miss Ferrier met at Inveraray, but she would never divulge who it was. (J. F.)

[3] Miss Ferrier used to nickname several of her acquaintances, thereby obscuring their identity. This old lady must have resembled old Lady Betty in *The Inheritance*, who was an insatiable reader of novels with marvellous names. (J. F.)

[4] Campbell of Shawfield. (J. F.)

night at going to bed, which I have no doubt will make her quite delirious, but should the worst come to the worst, there will be no difficulty in *providing her* with a *strait-waistcoat*. I see there is another novel published by the author of the above, which I am gasping for. Do write to me very soon and tell me whether you are to remain at Ardencaple or go to England this spring. If you do the latter, I wish you'd admit me and my child of your party. You promised me some poems, and I wish you'd send them now, when I'm sick and sad, and see nobody nor anything that in the least pleases or diverts me.

S. E. F. TO MISS CLAVERING

My Bower: Wednesday, 1808.

If you have a spark of gratitude in your nature, you will down on your marrow bones to me for having kept so long quiet, for you know that my silence has proceeded from naught but pure and genuine goodness on my part, for what could a poor homely maiden like me find to say that was worthy of engaging the time and attention of a fine dancing lady like you? Your account of your revels puts me in mind of those described in the 'Midsummer Night's Dream,' and methought I beheld you as Titania wooing the Blackburne as your beloved Bottom.

> Come, sit thee down upon this flowery bed,
>   While I thy amiable cheeks will coy,
> And stick musk-roses in thy sleek smooth head,
>   And kiss thy fair large ears, my gentle joy. . . .

You will say I am worse than John Brown of quoting memory, and so I am, for John quoted aptly, but I go by guess, for I know not whether the cap will fit your Bottom, never having had the felicity of beholding him. But to rise in my subject (for, you see, I'm an enemy to Bathos) and to go at once from the Bottom to the Top. How shall I express the shock I sustained on hearing of the foul murder that has been perpetrated on your hapless Pow? Did you never read St. Paul on the subject? Does he not say that 'long hair is the glory of women, and that it is their shame to be shorn'? And how dare you in defiance of Scripture commit this rape on your Locks? Indeed, I am mistaken if he does not also observe that the woman who is shaved is also to be stripped.

. . . The only consolation my affliction will admit of is for you to send me a ringlet as a relic of your past glories, so will it be both my bane and antidote. I would have sent your jewellery long ago, had I not, by your own authority, been waiting all this time in expectation of your lordly uncle's arrival [1]; they have been lying in George Street for more than six weeks, whereas you might have been blazing in them at the theatre, where I hear you shine forth a *fixed star*. I send you a little ring, as I think you liked the setting of one of mine, but I could not get a stone the same. You are surely in jest, my dear, when you talk of my *gifts*. God knows I have little to give, or I should be but too happy to give it to *you*, to whom I owe more than I hope I shall ever be able to repay, for, indeed, I would rather bear all the weight of your kindness to me, than you should ever be in a situation to require mine. I can only show the wish, and trust to your believing that 'a small gift may be the sign of a great love.'

I sent immediately on receiving your letter, and got a sixteenth of a lottery ticket for you; the numer [*sic*] is 16–820, and its fate still undecided. So set to work and build some castles, but don't make them too high.

. . . What novelties have you been reading lately? Have you been introduced to the McLarty family yet? I think they are the most exquisite family group imaginable.[2] Mrs. McC. is quite one of your darlings. . . . I shall get your trinkums franked to-morrow by the Postmaster. Pray write me a wee wordie immediately, as I shall be anxious to hear of their safe arrival. Remember me to Miss Mure.

---

[1] Lord John Campbell. (J. F.)
[2] In the *Cottagers of Glenburnie*, by Mrs. Hamilton.

Adieu, my Fairly Fair, believe me to be your most affectionate of friends.

Has Venus brought forth her Cupids yet ? I send this before, that you may make a row at the post-office if the packet is not forthcoming.

S. E. F. TO MISS CLAVERING (1808-9 ?)

Gasgow [*sic*].[1]

It is now ten days since I was torn from the root of my affection, eight of which I passed within fourteen miles of thy delightful presence ! Miserable thought that served but to poison those joyless days and sleepful nights. How different from our delicicus splashy walks at noon and our enchanting orgies at midnight ! But those times are past, and I live but to lament their loss ! I've neither time nor spirits to tell my miseries, for my heart aches as much as my head. Nothing now makes me sad but being doomed to the society of stupid, silly, disagreeable people ; sickness or solitude is paradise compared to it. We were some days at Ross[2] with Mr. and Mrs. M. Buchanan, who were very kind and pleasant, and we were at Garscube, where Sir Islay and his daughter were equally so, and at both of these places pure air I could breathe. But here, oh . . . what I've swallowed since I came to this region of smoke and vulgarity ! the nauseous *civilities*, the surfeiting hospitalities, the excruciating acts of politeness. Oh ! Miss Clavering, drop a tear to my woes ! I can liken myself to nothing but a hapless fly (mayhap a wasp) that has fallen into a pot of old thick stinking honey, where it wriggles and struggles in vain to get free. By the blessed influence of a pair of post-horses I hope to be emancipated to-morrow from this emporium of sweet civilities and tender assiduities, and on my arrival at Conheath I hope to be solaced by a letter from the light of mine eyes. I send you the ' Portuguese Nun ' which I amused myself

---

[1] Possibly because gas had just been introduced there. (J. F.)
[2] On Loch Lomond. (J. F.)

yesterday by hunting all through Glasgow, and could only
get her in that shabby state.[1]   She seems to be one of those
Furiosas for whom I have no pity, not but what I can
enter into her feelings, wild and ungovernable as they are,
for my own heart is a very whirlpool when once it is roused ;
but methinks, were I so unfortunate to love without being
loved, my heart should burst or break before it should ever
utter a single murmur or reproach. If I mistake not, yours
would do the same, would it not ?   Adieu, good night.

In 1809 Miss Ferrier found a spirit imbued with a
kindred sense of humour in Curran. More than one of her
letters, as we shall see, contains a profession of attachment
which may be compared with Miss Austen's expressed wish
to be ' the wife of the Rev. George Crabbe.'

*THE RIGHT HONOURABLE JOHN PHILPOT CURRAN
TO S. E. F.*

1809.

Dear Madam,—What I wished to say in verse I must
even say in prose. I thank you extremely for your kindness and courtesy ; it is simpler than song and full as true.   I
thought also to have wrote a line or two on the verses you
gave me, but my jade of a Muse was, it seems, engaged,
and disappointed me. She sent word, however, that on the
road she'd pop in and whisper something, but I scarcely
believe her. I have been courting her all my life, and she
has been uniformly coy and cruel. I don't, indeed, much
wonder that a poor Irishman should have so little chance
with her in Scotland. If, however, she should say anything
to me, I'll not keep her secret, but let you know it.[2]

I am, dear Madam, with great respect, your obliged
and grateful servant,

JOHN P. CURRAN.

My best respects to your father.

---

[1] The first English translation of this book appeared in 1808.

[2] Curran's Muse, however, did inspire him, and he wrote some verses in Miss Ferrier's album. This, containing many autographs of distin-guished persons, among them Scott, Burns, and Madame de Staël, is now in the possession of Susan Ferrier, great-granddaughter of Professor Ferrier the metaphysician. (J. F.)

S. E. F. TO MISS CLAVERING

1809?

My dear Charlotte,—Had you asked me to take Old Nick by the tail, or pull the man o' the moon by the horns, there's no saying what lengths my friendship might have carried me ; but really to expect me at this gay season I should forsake the flaunting town for your silent glens is a sacrifice too great for mere feminine affection ! 'Tis what the most presuming lover would hardly dare to demand from the most tender mistress, and were I to accord thus much to friendship what would I leave for love? You'll allow I could not carry my enthusiasm to a higher pitch in *this* world than to undertake such a journey upon your account, and the consequences would be that were he to ask me to accompany him on a jaunt to the *next* it would be thought monstrous disobliging to refuse ! This must, therefore, prove a deathblow to your hopes, as it must be evident to you that I would only undertake such a thing at the risk of my life, to say nothing of the little casualties of coughs, colds, &c. that would assail me in the course of my travels, and the whole formidable host of the materia medica who would be drawn up to oppose my progress. I've made no mention of the many delights I should leave behind, because I should be loath to mortify you by the comparison of my superior enjoyments ; but allow me just to hint to you that dirty streets are not to be exchanged for dry gravel walks, that black kennels are rather more pleasing to the eye than blue rivers, that the scrapings of a blind fiddler are full as melodious as the chirpings of a starved robin, that the flavour of stinking herrings is more satisfying (to the stomach) than the smell of seaweed, and that the sight of clothed men is as gladdening to the heart as the view of naked trees ! But to leave off fooling, and be serious on a subject on which, believe me, I only jest because I *can* say nothing to the purpose— how could you have the cruelty, not only to

tantalise me with the proposal, but also to insinuate that
it would be my own fault were it not accepted!

My dear Charlotte, I think you have known me long
enough to know that it is not my practice to make professions to any one, and I hope you will therefore believe I
say no more than I feel when I declare to you that had I my
choice at this moment of going to any quarter of the globe
or part of the kingdom I would without hesitation choose to
be with you.   I have no *bosom friend* out of my own family
save you alone (if such you'll allow me to reckon you),
and my sisters are now so engrossed with their respective
husbands and children that their society is no longer to me
what it was wont to be.   I have, therefore, no *great merit*,
you see, in preferring your company to that of any other
person, even setting aside the similarity of our tastes and
pursuits, which of itself would be a more and never failing source of pleasure and enjoyment.   But alas! such
pleasures must never be mine.

I'm doomed to doze away my days by the side of my
solitary fire and to spend my nights in the tender intercourse of all the old tabbies in the town.   In truth, your
solitude is not a whit greater than mine, unless you *reckon*
sound society—of that I own I have enough.   But somehow I don't feel my spirits a bit exhilarated, my ideas at
all enlivened, or my understanding enlightened by the
rattling of carriages or the clanking of chairs, and these be
the only mortal sounds that meet my ears.   As to conversation, that's quite out of the question at this season ; in the
dull summer months people may find time to sit down and
prose and talk sense a little, but at present they have something else to do with their time.   My father I never see, save
at meals, but then my company is just as indispensable
as the tablecloth or chairs, or, in short, any other luxury
which custom has converted into necessity.   That he
could live without me I make no doubt, so he could without a leg or an arm, but it would ill become me to deprive
him of either ; therefore, never even for a single day could

I reconcile it either to my duty or inclination to leave him. Therefore, my dear friend, believe what you are kind enough to ask is for me impossible to accord.

. . . Now as to the subject of your own personal sufferings, I need not say how warmly I enter into them and how much I feel for your being subjected to such severe trials; 'tis an evil for which there seems no cure, and which patience only can alleviate. Suspicion is a monster 'tis vain to contend with; it can swallow everything or it can live upon nothing; its patience is as inexhaustible as its ingenuity is wonderful, and it builds castles out of rubbish, and as often as they fall for want of a foundation it collects fresh materials and begins anew. The provoking thing is, it's always to be seen but never to be caught, so that there's no hopes of ever being able to overcome it. Sometimes, indeed, it dies for want of *air*, and I sincerely trust that may be the case in the present instance, for I know not a more irksome situation for an ingenuous mind than the one you describe in your own whimsical way. As to what you call your *perfect man*, I can only say our ideas on that subject differ very widely. I've lately discovered that I had the felicity of dancing with this prodigy about two years ago, and I remember I then thought him a *perfect child*, and could have patted his head and set him on my knee and fed him with sweetmeats for being a good boy and a pretty dancer. But as to his being a perfect man! Wait till he has attained the ripeness of my currant and had some fifty suns to warm him, and then I'll own it *possible* for him to be perfect. As to what I've heard, it was neither more nor less than that you loved and were beloved by a certain honourable cousin of your own at that time,[1] and this the perfect man declares, and also that he was a *perfect cat's-paw* to you on the occasion, so that I see he has some claims to perfection. . . . What do you say to this?

I sent you some paper by a Sylvan swain as having

[1] Lord Napier. (J. F.)

departed this world long before your letter reached it. I also used the freedom to introduce my favourite Julia upon you, but had not time to accompany her with a little anecdote of the author's family that occurred tother day; so here it is. You must know his eldest daughter has been begotten, born, and bred in such a delicate, elegant, chaste, modest, refined, sentimental manner as baffles the description of a poor, ignorant, homespun maiden like me.[1] Her father's Man of Feeling is a ruffian compared to her and Julia no better than she should be when placed alongside of this most sensitive virgin. It so happened that one day lately, as she was teaching her little sister to read, what should present itself in black and white but the word *bastard*! The lady, as all modest maids would or should do in a similar situation, trembled, turned pale, and would undoubtedly have swooned away but for the importunities of the child to be informed of the meaning of the word. After much hesitation she at length told her in a faltering tone that it signified a child without parents, 'just such as little Tommy,' naming a poor orphan she takes charge of. The child was satisfied. There was a very large party came to dinner shortly after, and one of the party happened to ask this little innocent girl what she was working. 'Oh,' quoth she, 'I am very busy indeed; I'm making a shirt for my sister's bastard.'

. . . Apropos of Sarks, did you ever see how to cut out a shift in a letter from a lady to a gentleman? I'll send it you before the noble lord leaves this[2]; that noble personage visited me yesterday, and I did not fail to ask permission to *suppose* him at Ardencaple, and though the favour was purely imaginary would you believe he had the churlishness to refuse it point blank! But, indeed, that was only of a piece with the rest of his behaviour, only, as

---

[1] This is probably the daughter of Henry Mackenzie whom Mrs. Grant describes as 'a lovely, meek creature, little known in the world, but very dear to her family! In her youth she had beauty of a particularly elegant kind, perfect good breeding, fine taste, and gentle manners.' *Letters*, vol. iii. pp. 188, 282.

[2] Lord John Campbell. (J F.)

Thady says, I don't choose to say what I think till I know whether you're staunch ; only let me know your sentiments, and whether you'd be pleased to abuse him by the hour or the yard, the year or the rood, name but your time and manner, and command my services. He told me of the scandalous and Satan-like device he had practised upon you, and he told it without the smallest symptom of contrition or remorse. I therefore deemed it incumbent upon me to manifest my disapprobation by one of the most awful frowns that I could possibly summon on such short notice, and it would be well if all honest people would follow my example and withdraw their countenance from such. . . I shan't say what ? Meantime, as he's to be here for some days, I desire you'll be pleased to send me a volume post haste under his cover. You need be under no apprehensions about it ; he dare not use any improper liberties with me, knowing I'm at the lug o' the law, as they say. Seriously I shall expect a letter from you on Sunday morning and shall have a Kiver [1] ready prepared to reply by return of post, as we must make the most of our time and *freedom.* You may perhaps expect that I should go off with a sneaking apology for the length, dulness, and illegibility &c. of this epistle, but be assured I shall do no such thing. All that I mean to do is to inform you, in case you don't know, that I am your more than any other person's most affectionate friend.

S. E. F. TO MISS CLAVERING

September 26, 1809.

I scorn your secrets, Shylock that thou art ! With your little haggling huxter-like ways methinks I see you seated in due state at a little stall retailing your penn'orth of apples and your farthing's worth of gingerbread, and trying to cheat poor children out of the coppers by imposing some of your trumpery upon them, even as you would beguile me of my sterling knowledge with palming some

[1] A frank. (J. F.)

of your pretended secrets upon me. You are worse than
Shylock or any of the tribe I ever heard of, for you insist
upon the money being paid down before the goods are
delivered, and without giving me any security that they
ever will be. Be sure you promise upon your honour, but
let me tell you, miss, a young lady's honour is too precarious
a substance to put much dependence upon ; for example,
what think you of the fate of Miss Latham, and if such
things come to pass in civilized countries, what are you to
expect in your barbarous regions ? For my part I think she
had better have pocketed the affront, seeing as how she
says it could not be helped.

   . . . I dare say all the old tabbies in town are sitting
on their sofas with *white sashes* on, ready to faint away at
the sight of a man ! By-the-bye, she must have been an
old-fashioned toad to have an handkerchief and a sash upon
her person, and there's the mischief of wearing clothes.
Had she been clad *al fresco* (as every modest woman ought)
the deed could not have been done for want of those
necessary implements of war ; but, to be sure, if people will
furnish arms against themselves they must stand the consequences ! And, to set you an example, I am going to tell
you that I'm deeply and desperately in love ! And what
makes my case particularly deplorable is that there's not
the least prospect of the dear man lending so much as a
little finger to pull me out of the mire into which he has
plunged me ! Were I possessed of the same mean spirit
of bartering as you, I'd have you to guess his degree ; but
you'd as [soon] bethink you of the great Cham of Tartary
as the Right Honourable John Philpot Curran, Master of
the Rolls, Ireland ! ! ! I wish I could give you any idea of
his charms but, alas ! my pen does not, like Rousseau's,
'*brûle sur le papier*' ; and none but a pen of fire could
trace his character or record the charms of his conversation.
Don't set me down for mad, for I assure you I'm only
bewitched, and perhaps time and absence may dissolve the
magic spells. He had the cruelty to tell me he liked me,

and then he left me. Had my eyes been worth a button they'd soon have settled the matter ; but there's the misery of being sent into the world with such mussel shells ! ! I (a modest maiden) said nothing, and it seems they were silent ; and so we parted, never to meet again ! ! ! But seriously, I have been very much delighted and gratified by a visit from this most extraordinary being, 'whose versatility of genius' (as Sir John Carr justly observes for once) 'is the astonishment and admiration of all who come within its range.' I'll certainly live seven years longer for having seen him. Lord Frederick[1] dined here with him, and was delighted. By-the-bye, I wonder how he can be plagued with that little fat *capon* (Mr. Cailly) always trotting at his heels ![2] . . . . My brothers go to Inveraray on Saturday morning, so if you want any duds, please to apprise me in proper time.

Adieu hastily, but affectionately,

S. E. F.

Please not to leave this in your ridicule, and write speedily.

S. E. F. TO MISS CLAVERING

Conheath : July 26, 1809.

I was so disconcerted at receiving your letter when I looked for nothing less than seeing your own dear self, that I have had no spirit to answer it sooner, but time (that seldom restores a blessing) has at length restored my wonted serenity. I was likewise somewhat consoled by a sight of Madlle, though certainly her appearance was not calculated to bestow much comfort, as she was in all the agonies of a sprained foot and eight children.[3] She told me how basely Lord John had behaved in giving her the slip and leading Lady Charlotte astray, for which (if there is truth in trans-

---

[1] Lord Frederick Campbell, brother of John, fifth Duke of Argyll ; he was Lord Registrar of Scotland, and died in London 1816. (J. F.)

[2] Mr. Cayley, a London lawyer, a kinsman to the Misses Berry. His name is misspelt in the text. (J. F.)

[3] The family of Lady Charlotte Campbell. (J. F.)

migration) his soul will certainly be transfused into the
body of a nursery-maid with the care of ten children, two
of them teething. I saw that noble personage as he passed
through Edinburgh, but during his stay there I suppose
he was, as usual, entirely engrossed by his beloved Bessy,[1]
and I hear he has nursed her to some purpose, as she is
quite recovered, contrary to my prognostics, as I took all
possible pains to convince her that she would never be
well until she had blistered her body all over; but she
vowed against all mortification of the flesh, so I presume
his Lordship's prescriptions have been of a more agreeable nature. Don't tell her this, or she'll be the death
of me, and I'm not the least in a dying strain at present,
being in high health and preservation, and *quite satisfied* with myself, which is more than many can say who
have rather better reason; but a sick bed is an excellent
school for future enjoyment. . . . I came to this *naughty*
place a few days ago, and am leading the life of an *absolute
beast*, for I do naught but wander about the fields, and eat
of the fruits of the earth and drink buttermilk, till I'm
become so fat I'm the admiration of all the cowfeeders in
the parish. By-the-bye, I expect to rival fat Lambert of
famous memory, or rather to fill his place in the world, and
to be wheeled about the country in my caravan with my
trumpeters and beefeaters; but even should I arrive at
that celebrity, I promise you I shall always make it a point
to pay you a visit gratis. I'm glad you like ' Cœlebs '—the
book I mean, for the *man* is insupportable. He's a good
well-meaning creature, to be sure, and is of great use in
making a pertinent remark or hitching in a hackneyed
observation whenever the conversation begins to flag, but
farther his merits I could not descry. There is a deal of
good sense and truth throughout the whole book, and the
Stanley family are delightful upon paper. Have you read
Edgworth's ' Fashionable Tales?' I like the two first, but
none of the others. It is high time all *good ladies* and

[1] Miss Mure. (J. F.)

grateful little girls should be returned to their gilt boards, and as for sentimental weavers and moralising glovers, I recommend them as penny ware for the pedlar. I lent 'Cœlebs' to Lord John, who has promised me some marginal notes upon it, which I think will prove a great addition to the next edition. I can't tell you what the world's about, for I'm quite out of it at present, and see nobody but innocent natives, and hear nothing but parish news. For myself, I'm just such another harmless innocent as Mrs. Commissary's monkey, for 'I joost play mysel' wi' a windle strae.' I hope your *sea Fowels* have taken flight; it must have been a tender squeeze from some of their amphibious fangs that broke my ring—deny it if you dare. I'm going to commit this to the care of your most puissant uncle— it is such another desperate expedient as putting a letter into a bottle and committing it to the mercy of the waves. I write at the risk of my life, for I'm dying of heat, but the only thing that will revive me will be to hear from you and that you are well and happy, not '*sick and melancholy.*'

S. E. F. TO MISS CLAVERING (1809)

I am overwhelmed with sin, in the shape of your letters, and like all agreeable sins I have paid dear for them, as all the world will agree when I declare that your first 'King Crispin' dispatch cost me a crown (and here it may be proper to apprise you that in the days of King Stephen a pair of handsome culottes cost that monarch no more than what I paid for your letter). Your next amiable packet amounted to the gross sum of four shillings, and your last cross composition completely exhausted the accumulated patience of twenty-seven years. To remedy those evils, and for the benefit of your correspondents in general, I shall sub- mit a small code of laws and regulations to which you will please to subscribe.

1st. All letters containing billets-doux or enclosures of

whatever description, whether relating to soul or body, to be either franked or post paid.

2nd. The contents of all franks, however light in their nature, to be duly weighed before being despatched, and not to exceed one ounce avoirdupois weight.

3rd. No commissions to be written across upon pain of their not being answered.

But seriously, are you not shocked to think of my having paid nine shillings for your two chits of letters? Such paltry suggestions are, to be sure, unheard of in the annals of novel writing, for never was the postman's demand known to interrupt the tender effusions of two sympathetic souls, even though their bodies should be starving in a garret or their last shift pawned for a sixpence. But I, alas! am a stranger to those exalted ideas. I am in use to eat a plentiful dinner, to wearing a flannel petticoat, so pray when you deign to write to a person of my low degree don't treat me as though I were one of your Signora Bianca della Manchas.

. . . And now I must congratulate you upon your return to this favoured land, where I pray you may long flourish and put forth branches and green leaves like a goodly tree. I was beginning to fear you were going to engraft your noble stock upon some of the little scions you wrote me about, particularly as I heard one of them was languishing for your love. Apropos of that passion so *miscalled*, did you hear that wee Wynne is going to clothe herself with a husband, and such a one! Apollo is truly a God compared to him. Were there ever such a pair of little infatuated foolies? I hope they're mad, poor things, as their best and only excuse. Your cousin Anne[1] is my authority, and I refer you to her for the melancholy particulars. She is, I think, grown quite handsome, and is vastly sensible and agreeable. As for your base attempts to depreciate the charms of my present mode of living, I

---

[1] Hon. Anne Napier, married, 1816, Sir T. Gibson Carmichael, Bart. (J. F.)

can only ascribe them to the blackest envy and grossest ignorance, else how could you compare the savage enjoyments to be found amongst your misty mountains to the elegant seclusion and refined pleasures to be met with in this queen of cities? *There* you behold nothing but decaying nature, such as dropping leaves, fading flowers, drooping trees. *Here* I contemplate the progress of the Arts in streets building, houses repairing, shops painting. *There* no sound salutes your ear save the monotonous din of some tinkling rill or tumbling cascade. *Here* I am regaled from morning till night with an enchanting variety, from the majestic rumble of a Hackney coach to the elegant trot of a post-chaise. While ever and anon intervenes the liquid notes of some sea nymph warbling ' Caller herrin'.' As to the olfactory delights, I need not expatiate upon them ; 'tis well known what a boundless store this town affords, rich and inexhaustible as nature herself.

As to my associating with *cats*, if I do let me tell you they are of a very different description from your wild Highland mousers, who would make no ceremony of tearing one's eyes out, while my tame domesticated creatures are quite content if you throw them some little bit of a tattered reputation to play with. Mine, thank my stars, is of a texture to defy both tooth and claw. . . .

But by this time you must be convinced of the vanity of supposing that I could forego all the dear delights of Edinburgh at this enchanting season for the purpose of vegetating at Inveraray. I was interrupted by a visit from Miss Lamont, wringing her hands and turning up the whites of her eyes in black despair at being doomed to sojourn in this wilderness of sweets. I tried to be very sorry for her, but I'm afraid I did not succeed according to her expectations. For my own part I'm quite contented so long as I have health, my books, work, a good fire, and my faithful blear-eyed dog. . . . I want but my child to complete my felicity. I wish you'd make haste and have one, and I'll engage to dry nurse it, and train it up in the paths of righteousness. At present I am obliged to devote my affections to petrified fish and preserved butterflies. Give my love to my love, and tell him I languish for some of his verses to sweeten my solitude. Do try and pick up some little morsel for me as an atonement for your sins, though you need never hope for my forgiveness till you've wet six pockethandkerchiefs with your tears, dried them with your sighs, and covered two pairs of sheets (of paper) with your apologies. You complain of your awkwardness at apologising. Let me see how handsomely you'll acquit yourself on this occasion, and as you hope for mercy, write instantly to your much aggrieved though still affectionate friend,

S. E. F.

S. E. F. TO MISS CLAVERING

. And then I believe we shall go by Taymouth and farther and farther and farther than I can tell, till at last we will come to a fine Castle,[1] and a beautiful Ladie,[2] called the Queen of the Dogs. Do you know her? Apropos of dogs, you had very near been the death of my darling, as you shall hear.

Air—MAID IN BEDLAM

One morning very lately, one morning in June,
I rose very early and went into the toon.
My doggie walked behind me, behind me walked he,
For I love my dog because I know my dog loves me !

Oh ! cruel was Miss Clavering to send me to the street ;
She sent me for to buy silk hosen for her feet.
And there my leetle dog a great big dog did spye,
And I love my dog because I know my dog loves I.

No sooner did my leetle dog the meikle dog behold
Than at him he did fly like any lion bold.
It was a sad and piteous sight for tender eyes to see ;
For I love my dog because I know my doggie loves me.

Oh ! sore did I screech and loudly did I pray
For some kind stick to drive the meikle dog away.
I never shall forget my fright until the day I dee,
For I love my dog because I know my dog loves me.

---

[1] Ardencaple. (J. F.)   [2] Miss Clavering. (J. F.)

And when I got my leetle dog his hind leg was bit thro',
And as he could not walk I knew not what to do.
At length I spied a coachman, beside a coach stood he,
And I love my dog because I know my dog loves me.

And I called to me the coachman, and unto him did say,
Lift my dog into your coach and then drive away.
The coachman looked full scornful till I showed a silver key,
And I love my dog because I k-no-w . . my d-og—g—y
     lo—ves m—e.—(*Da Capo.*)

This is a true and faithful account, and should be a warning to all ladies how they walk the streets with little doggies. Mine I assure you suffered severely in your service, and though his wound is now healed, I think his general health is considerably impaired by the shock his nerves must have experienced. The medical people are of opinion sea bathing might prove of benefit to him. I say nothing, but if you have a spoonful of marrow in your bones you'll sit down before you read another word and pen him a handsome invitation. As for the eighteen pence it cost me for coach hire, I shall let that pass, as I never expect to see it again. As for the airs you give yourself about wearing white silk stockings I like that mightily—you've a pair of good white satin ones of your own spinning, that will stand both wear and tear, and never lose their colour by washing, so you must e'en make them serve you through the summer, for none other will I send. I sent to Bessie Mure desiring her to surrender up her cheap glover, as I looked upon him as a much more desirable thing than a dear lover, so she made answer that she knew of no cheap men, but she directed me to where I could get *good gloves* at 1*s.* 4*d.* per pair. Well, away I trotted, resolved to become hand in glove with this pattern glover. So I went into the shop.

' Show me some good stout ladies' gloves,' quoth I ;
So he took down a parcel and gave me them to try ;
I picked out a dozen of pairs and said, ' Now, I'm willing
To take all these if you'll give me them at the shilling.'
Then the glover clasped his hands and said, ' Madame, I declare
I could not sell those gloves for less than *three* shillings a pair.'

Miss Clavering.

from a portrait by Kearsley in the possession
of her son The Rev. H. M. Fletcher.

So I said ' I was told you had very good gloves at sixteenpence,
And your asking three shillings for these must be all a pretence.'
Then he brought forth a huge bundle and opened it out ;
' There, ma'am, are the gloves made from the hide of a nuut,
But no more to compare with the skin of a kid or dog
Than the breast of a chicken to the back of a hog.'
So, having nothing to reply to a simile so sublime,
I was glad to sneak off and say I would come back when I had
    more time,
And I swear that's as true as I am now writing rime.

S. E. F. TO MISS CLAVERING

La pauvre Justine, 'tis very hard, as you observe, that
nobody will put her in the way of doing a good work.
I'm afraid, like the Dutch women, she'll be obliged to
engender a sooterkin herself, if so be it's for the love of a
child. What you relate to me of Madlle. gives me the
most serious concern ; as the improprieties of her life and
conversation cannot possibly be caused by the allurements
of the flesh, they must needs proceed from the assaults
of the devil. 'Tis a dreadful thought that he has got his
cloven foot inside your convent. The only remedy that I
can suggest is to summon the Rev. Paul to exhort you. I
meant to have written you such a letter as you never had
seen in your days before—it was to have been longer and
longer and longer than I can tell, but I must go and write
to a pure good honest woman, after having performed some
mental ablutions to purge away the iniquities I have
imbibed from so long communing with your evil spirit. I
must give you great praise for your last letter to encourage
you in well doing. Go on, my child, and prosper in the
path I have pointed out to thee, hold fast thy foolscap and
let it not depart from thee. But, without joke, your last
letter was without exception the wittiest I ever received,
which I impute to the great scope you had to indulge your
fancy in. While here am I forced to swallow and contain
such a quantity of the cleverest, wittiest, and most humorous
sayings as would fill a volume. But the foolscap fits not

my years nor dignity.   Write me instantly, I charge thee,
upon pain of my displeasure venting itself in the form of a
letter.   Farewell, pet of my heart.

S. E. F. TO MISS CLAVERING

20th.

In my journey as laziness has done in my letter I have
left you a gown, but not the one your wayward fancy had
fixed upon, for two reasons—the one is because it did not
look pretty in the piece, though you thought it so in the
pattern, and the other is because I do not think 'tis wholesome for young maidens of your disposition to get everything they desire, and, indeed, had I followed my own
inclinations, a full suit of sackcloth should have been thy
portion, for thou hast great cause, child, to fast, pray and
mortify the flesh in order to purge thy soul from the carnal
desires that seem to have taken possession of thee.   To
this end I do most earnestly recommend to thee to stripe
and physic thyself till thou art totally unable to stand, sit,
and, above all, speak.

20th.

. . . This is in revenge for your presumption in daring
to talk of *love* to a spinster of my years and discretion.
Know, Mistress, that I despise love and have no love for
anything in the world except wooden men and acting
magistrates.   How can you talk to me of balls and dances,
and drinking bouts—I, who lead the life of a saint upon
earth, and eschew all such evil and vain pursuits?   But
surely the town, *I'm told*, is very dull, for it is pretty much
the same to me at all seasons.   By-the-bye, was it in joke
or earnest that you said you were coming here in January?
I hope it was the latter, as I think you'd be the better of
six weeks of Reekie to *rub off the rusticity* you will doubtless have contracted in the country.   There are plenty of
houses to be had, so do pray make up your mind and get
your mamma to pack up.   You need not mind the expense,

because we're all to be dead before next summer. We're first to die of famine in the winter, and Bonaparte's to come and rob and murder us all in the spring. So says the Dss. of Gordon, and it must be so, because she says everything she has ever predicted has always come to pass.

S. E. F. TO MISS CLAVERING

Your letter, ma'am, with joy I read,
It seemed like tidings from the dead,
So full of fire and *fiddle*, too,
Of spectres green and spirits blue.

Give me credit for my prudence, which makes me withhold from your giddy pate the rest of my most adorable rhymes, but you may take my word for it that they are the cleverest, the wittiest, the sensiblest, the elegantest of possible verses, and that nothing the least like them has appeared since the day Eve first sported her green Dickie. As to your base rhymes, I had seen them before and deemed them far *beneath* your notice, for who, pray, when they purchase a fiddle ever thinks of looking to the case ? In my humble opinion you might, if you had pleased, have played a mighty pretty tune upon this same fiddle and danced to it also, not a *horn* pipe, but a good old-fashioned country dance to the tune of 'Money in both pockets,' which, let me tell you, Miss, is something better than your favourite air of ' Go to the devil and shake yourself.' Then to think of the happy consequences that would result to posterity from this union. For as the family of the R's are rather remarkable for the *saving graces*, how completely would that evil propensity be counteracted by having a few drops of the A——ll blood circulating in their veins ! As for Lord John, he need never hope to have rest in his bed if he don't make a marriage of it. The shade of Camilla will certainly haunt him, and her perturbed spirit hover over his couch upbraiding him with broken vows if he fails to accomplish this grand desire. Apropos, pray ask

him if he has a mind for another Bet upon that subject, as
I heard to-day that the physicians declare she is in no
immediate danger. I heard also (what, however, I don't
believe) that she says she has no fear of death as she has all
her life been kind to *animals*.

A most convenient creed I must own for some people,
and if our rewards hereafter are to be proportioned to our
merits in this particular, I know *one* little sinner who will
rank very high amongst the saints ; but woe to me for the
vengeance I used to take on the hides of your wretched
hounds ! What are your present pursuits and future plans ?
and is there any chance of your coming here in the course
of the winter ?

I am busied in the *Arts and Sciences* at present, japan-
ning old boxes, varnishing new ones, daubing velvet, and,
in short, as the old wives say, ' my hands never out of an
ill turn.' Then, by way of pastime, I play whist every
night to the very death with all the fusty dowagers and
musty mousers in the purlieus—and yet I'm alive ! Praise
be to oysters and porter. If you wish to be corpulent, eat
a score of the one and drink a bottle of the other every
day, and you'll soon be unwieldy, and, if you persevere, will
in time arrive at a *waddle*.

I send you a precious gift ! a piece of charmed cake,
which has undergone all the customary ceremonies, such as
being drawn thirteen times through the marriage ring, &c.,
&c. It is, alas ! not my own, but I trust that will follow ; it
is the daughter of my love, who was this day married to
my cousin, which makes a charming opening for me, as my
beloved is [now] left solitary, and solitude is the nurse of
love—but methinks eighty requires another sort of nurse,
and so I shall insinuate my services. Fail not to relate
your dreams unto me, and I will then expound. I hear
stocking working is (or was) the rage.

Make my obeisance to Lord John, and that no caricature has yet gladdened my sight. A Word to the Wise is
enough. Did you ever get my ' Princesse de Wolfenbuttle ' ?

As you never acknowledged her arrival, pray write to me speedily.

The first suggestion of 'Marriage' may be traced in the two following letters. In all likelihood the 'proposal' which 'enchanted' Miss Ferrier was a general scheme for a joint novel, amplified and defined by her in the subsequent letter.

S. E. F. TO MISS CLAVERING

Your proposals flatter and delight me, but how, in the name of postage, are we to transport our brains to and fro? I suppose we'd be pawning our flannel petticoats to bring about our heroine's marriage, and lying on straw to give her Christian burial. Part of your plot I like much, some not quite so well—for example, it wants a *moral*. Your principal characters are good and interesting, and they are tormented and persecuted, and punished from no fault of their own, and for no possible purpose. Now I don't think, like all penny-book manufacturers, that 'tis absolutely necessary that the good boys and girls should be rewarded, and the naughty ones punished. Yet, I think, where there is much tribulation, 'tis fitter it should be the *consequence*, rather than the *cause* of misconduct or frailty. You'll say that rule is absurd, inasmuch as it is not observed in human life; that I allow, but we know the inflictions of Providence are for wise purposes, therefore our reason willingly submits to them. But as the only good purpose of a book is to inculcate morality, and convey some lesson of instruction as well as delight, I do not see that what is called a *good moral* can be dispensed with in a work of fiction. Another fault is your making your hero attempt suicide, which is greatly too shocking, and destroys all the interest his misfortunes would otherwise excite—that, however, could be easily altered, and in other respects I think your plot has great merit. You'll perhaps be displeased at the freedom of my remarks; but in the first place freedom is absolutely necessary in the cause in which we are about to embark, and it must be understood to be one if not the chief article of our creed. In the second (though it should have been the first), know that I always say what I think, or say nothing. Now as to my own deeds—I shall make no apologies (since they must be banished from our code of laws) for sending you a hasty and imperfect sketch of what I think might be wrought up to a tolerable form. I do not recollect ever to have seen the sudden transition of a high-bred English beauty, who thinks she can sacrifice all for love, to an uncomfortable solitary Highland dwelling[1] among tall red-haired sisters and grim-faced aunts. Don't you think this would make a good opening of the piece? Suppose each of us try our hands on it ; the moral to be deduced from that is to warn all young ladies against runaway matches, and the character and fate of the two sisters would be *unexceptionable.* I expect it will be the first book every wise matron will put into the hand of her daughter, and even the reviewers will relax of their severity in favour of the morality of this little work. Enchanting sight! already do I behold myself arrayed in an old mouldy covering, thumbed and creased, and filled with dog's-ears. I hear the enchanting sound of some sentimental miss, the shrill pipe of some antiquated spinster, or the hoarse grumbling of some incensed dowager as they severally inquire for me at the circulating library, and are assured by the master that 'tis in such demand, that though he has thirteen copies, they are insufficient to answer the calls upon it, but that each of them may depend upon having the very first that comes in!!! Child, child, you had need be sensible of the value of my correspondence. At this moment I'm squandering mines of wealth upon you, when I might be drawing treasures from the bags of time! But I shall not repine if you'll only repay me in kind—speedy and long is all that

---

[1] Glenfern. Dunderawe Castle, on Loch Fyne, was in Miss Ferrier's mind when she drew this sketch of a 'solitary Highland dwelling.' (J. F.)

I require; for all things else I shall take my chance.
Though I have been so impertinent to your book, I nevertheless hope and expect you'll send it to me. Combie[1]
and his daughter (or Mare, as you call her) are coming to
town about this time, as I'm informed, and you may easily
contrive to catch them (wild as they are) and send it by
them, for there's no judging what a picture will be like
from a mere pen-and-ink outline; if that won't do, is there
not a coach or a carrier? One thing let me entreat of
you: if we engage in this undertaking let it be kept a
profound secret from every human being. If I was suspected of being accessory to such foul deeds my brothers
and sisters would murder me, and my father bury me
alive—and I have always observed that if a secret ever
goes beyond those immediately concerned in its concealment it very soon ceases to be a secret.

S. E. F. TO MISS CLAVERING

My dear Charlotte,—Had you known me you would
surely never have thought of apologising to me for writing
in a more serious (and shall I say confidential) strain than
usual, since so far from considering it as a 'piece of imper-
tinence,' I am much rather disposed to look on it as a sure
proof of your friendship. Every one that is not blind or
stupid must perceive without having it pointed out to them
that your present situation is one that to support must require
all the patience, good sense, sweetness of disposition you do
so eminently possess, and though I am far from approving
of weak regrets and unavailing complaints, yet as little
do I admire that sort of Spartan heroism that (like the
trite story of the boy and the fox) allows its very vitals to
be consumed in silence! I can easily enter into those
feelings you did not think proper to express, having myself
frequently experienced similar ones, and I do not hesitate
to declare that I think the thousand little gnawing mortal

---

[1] Campbell of Combie. (J. F.)

vexations of which the world takes no account are harder to be borne than even a severe dispensation of Providence, in *that* though the heart be bruised it is at the same time made better, and while the soul is elevated the passions are stilled ; but in the daily, hourly, petty, inquietudes inflicted by your fellow creatures we can discover no good purpose to be fulfilled, nor draw any consoling reflections from the excesses of ill-temper or the exercise of caprice. However, doubtless those bitter roots are destined one day to produce good fruits, though in the meantime the burden is hard to bear. Would I could bear yours for you, my dearest ! Many is the heavy load I have borne for myself in former days, and cheerfully would I now submit to carry one for your dear sake. But alas ! distance makes that impossible. I cannot in the smallest degree evince my friendship for you, though you have it in your power to prove the extent of yours towards me by showing that, though I cannot alleviate, you yet think me worthy of sharing your inquietudes. You apologise by telling me that ' out of the abundance of the heart,' and believe me I would not give a single word from your heart for the wittiest volume from your head. You will, perhaps, say I am as Job's comforters, but the truth is I think there can be nothing more irritating than the mistaken notion of one's friends trying to persuade them that their miseries are merely imaginary. I have always found that the heart too well knoweth its own bitterness and that sympathy is a more grateful balm than either remonstrance or advice. But enough of this you'll say. I am truly sorry to see the date of your letter, well knowing the change could not be for your advantage, though, as I hear you've got a road that has brought Inveraray to Ardencaple (or taken Ardencaple to Inveraray, I don't know which), I conclude you'll still pass most of your time there. How I wish some such blest scheme could be devised for bringing us some sixty miles nearer ! What great things might we not bring to pass by the junction of our heads, but alas !

what can we effect by the mere help of our hands? Your proposal enchants me, but how, in the name of impatience, is it ever to be carried into execution? Your brains are all bespoke, and had you the hands of Briareus I suppose they would be devoted to the service of the signoras; perhaps, indeed, as you're very ingenious, you may have trained up your toes to the business, but I should think them better adapted to *poetry*, as then you'd be sure your lines would never want metrical feet. You are kind enough to inquire after my health, life, and conversation. With regard to the first, I'm really excellently well; for the second, I eat, drink, and sleep it away to the best of my ability, and for the last I flatter myself few are the idle words or words spoken in vain that will rise up in judgment against me . . As to my pursuits (of which you are likewise pleased to express curiosity) learn that I'm at present in habits of the strictest intimacy with the Roman emperors. 'Tis well you did not ask me what the world's doing, for I know no more of its evolutions than if I were on the top of Mount Caucasus or on the plains of Bagdad! And I protest to you (but 'tis in confidence), that but for the rumbling of the carriages and the rattling of the chaise I should not know when Catalani sings or Apollo[1] is 'at home'! Apropos of the god, I heard of an entertainment he gave lately that eclipsed everything that has been seen since the days of Solomon, when gold and silver were accounted as nought, and his little lady, like the Queen of Sheba, arrayed in all manner of pleasant jewels, while his honest mother, cased in a salmon-coloured satin, went about whispering to the guests, ' Dear sirs, but Jeemie has a hantel a' quality amang his akquantans.' I am told the *G. Lamont* is going to be married to a Mr. Keith,[2] who's *deaf*, but, *entre nous*, I don't think her husband's a bit to

---

[1] Sobriquet for some well-known inhabitant of Edinburgh, but whom it is difficult to conjecture at this distance of time. (J. F.)

[2] She did marry Mr., afterwards Sir Alexander, Keith, of Ravelstone, Keeper of the Regalia of Scotland. (J. F.)

be pitied for that. 'Tis well for me I'm not within reach of a certain pair of Right Honourable Claws when I expressed such a sentiment! Apropos of the owner, pray what is become of him?[1] Is he gone on an Embassy to the moon, or is he still an inhabitant of air? I've, to oblige you, been making particular inquiries after the amphibious animal described in your last, and find he has by some extraordinary chance been thrown within a few doors of me.

S. E. F. TO MISS CLAVERING

My dear Chatty,—It seems I am not to go to the devil with a dish-clout at this time, for from a sorry kitchen wench I'm now transformed into a gay ladye, and instead of staying at home to dress dinners I do nothing but go about devouring them. In plain terms I have got a cook, a very bad one, but better than none, and I've invested her with all the regalia of the kitchen, and given her absolute dominion over the fish of the sea, and the fowls of the air, and the cattle of the earth, and over every creeping thing that creepeth on the face of the earth. I have not a minute to speak to you, for really I do nothing but go out to my dinner, and I'd a thousand times rather eat a raw turnip at home as go to a feast abroad and play at ladies and gentlemen all in a row ; but our career ends this week and then we're to go into our graves and bury ourselves alive for the rest of the winter! And then I may sit and hatch plots and compose poems as long as to-day and to-morrow if I choose! The very pen is like to jump out of my fingers for joy, though it has small chance of partici-pating in these glorious achievements, as its race is very nearly run—and a weary life it has had under me it must be owned. Apropos, what would you think of writing the life and adventures of a pen? It has this instant flashed upon me that something might be made of such a subject.

---

[1] Lord J. Campbell. (J. F.)

Think well of it, Miss, and you shall have the honour of beginning the story and continuing it, and if that won't satisfy you shall conclude it too. As to your poem I'm sorry I can't serve you, but you might just as well have *seriously* asked me to compose you a Latin oration better than any of Cicero's as have asked me to write verses after Lady Charlotte! If you call those pitiful doggerels (I sent you in an access of folly) poetry [1] I'm sorry for you, Miss Clavering, but I can't help it. I could not write *poetry* if my life depended upon it, and I never even wrote a *single* jingle of a rhyme but those I have sent you as aforesaid. To be sure there is one encouraging circumstance, that the writer of them is supposed to be no genius, and I'm sure anything I can send will afford ample confirmation, if any is required. I enclose you, therefore, the beginning of a thing that I shall finish if you think it will do, but I hope you won't stand upon the least ceremony as to rejecting or receiving it as you think fit. At any rate, I *entreat* you won't tell *Miss Adair that it is mine*, *because* God forbid I should set up for a writer of poetry! I would give anything to see your novel ; do send me a morsel of it, I'm sure I shall like it ; and you really could not do me such a favour as to initiate me into the mysteries of your imaginations. When will you be ready to join hands with me ? I've just seen Lord John about half a minute since he came here ; Bessie Mure keeps him in her ridicule and never lets anybody get a peep at him ; they dined here on Monday, but they got such a beastly repast, and were so scurvily treated, that I've been sick ever since with pure shame and vexation of stomach.

S. E. F. TO MISS CLAVERING

In vain dost thou hope to overwhelm me with torrents of ink, to strike terror into my soul with the point of thy

---

[1] Possibly the verses on p. 70, or they may be some rather conventional and humourless verses in Popian metre, addressed by Miss Ferrier to Miss Clavering, and preserved among the letters.

pen, or to smother me in a sheet of foolscap. Even in thy
hands these enemies of destruction have no terrors for me !
For know I am descended from a race of Scribes ; I was
born amidst briefs and deeds ; I was nurtured upon ink ;
my pap-spoon was the stump of an old pen, my christening suit was a reclaiming petition, and my cradle a
paper poke ! . . . 'Tis doubtless, therefore, from these
first rudiments of education I imbibed that surprising
elevation of soul which enables me (like certain savage
tribes) not only to support the malice of my foes, but even
to triumph and rejoice in the torture they inflict. It can
only be this ennobling principle which not only sustains me
under the weight of thy vengeance, but even causes me to
laugh and exult with true savage delight in the punishment inflicted by thy most merciless hand ! Of this therefore be assured, that to whatever lengths your fury may
transport you, even though you were to scourge me with
pure white serpents, or set me to scour out the stains of
blood as they trickled from the stuccoed ceilings of the
Signora Bianca !—nay, even should your vengeance think
proper to visit me in those unquestionable shapes, I shall
not shrink from the visitation, dreadful as it may be. I
am ready to receive it, so do thy worst. I defy thee, Satan,
and all thy devices and dead works. But, really and truly,
you have inspired me with the most ardent longing to
behold this production of yours, and as I begin to suspect
I'm with Book myself, there's no saying what the consequences may be if my inclinations are baulked.[1]

On my bare bended knees do I therefore beseech you
to gratify me with a sight of your babe before he makes
his appearance in the world. Only consider how many
casualties he will experience before he attains maturity,
and then he will be so changed that I shall never be able
to recognise him as your child. He will be maimed by the
publishers, mutilated by the press, corrupted by the printer's

[1] The obstetrical metaphor is, as we shall see, rather a favourite one
with Miss Ferrier.

devil, and even should he escape these dangers, who can
tell whether he may not be cut in pieces by those foul friends
the critics, who, like death, spare neither sex, nor youth,
nor beauty, nor talents, but sweep all that comes in their
way with the besom of destruction? Moreover, consider
how precarious is human life! I may make my exit without having had the benefit of the delightful lessons of thy
wisdom! I shall never know how the tail of a serpent came
to be transformed into the head of a young man, and the
dreadful secret will, alas! ever remain a dead secret to me!
Then think with what *éclat* I shall enter Pluto's dark
domains with the spirit of an unpublished novel by a lady
of distinction! It will be the best possible letter of introduction to me, and I shall immediately be received into the
first circles there. Not an old dowager who will not be at
my beck, nor an authoress but will hasten to embrace
me. To yourself the advantages will be incalculable. Your
fame by my means will be spread abroad throughout the
whole kingdom ; your arrival will be most anxiously looked
for ; the banks of the Styx will be covered with crowds
waiting to hail your approach, and, in a word, you will
be received with every mark of honour it is in the power of
ghosts to pay. But seriously, will you not contrive some
means of indulging me with a sight of your book? Miss
Mure will be coming to town soon ; send it by her, or any
other trusty and well beloved, and I'll sit up all night to
read it, and get it franked and returned to you safe and
sound next day. What do you say? I think the verses
you sent me quite beautiful ; there is in them, as in all
Lady Charlotte's poetry, so much delicacy and feeling as
show them to be the effusions of a tender heart and culti-
vated mind. A few more such favours will be highly
esteemed and carefully concealed. Mortal eye shall never
behold nor ear hear aught from me. I have the terror of
Midas' barber ever before me, and I shall not whisper it even
to the walls for fear the stones should sing forth the secret.
Mark the sympathy that subsists between us. At the self-

same time you were gracefully smiling over the witticisms
of the incomparable Fidget was I likewise indulging my
mirth at her expense—a striking proof of the similarity of
our pursuits in the paths of literature, and a strong argument that while you are revising the first volume of a book
I ought to be reviewing the second.

S. E. F. TO MISS CLAVERING

Feb. 1810.

What a glorious vision burst upon my sight as I
behold our heroine, even the beauteous Herminsilde,
sailing over the salt seas in an old beer barrel!!!
My dearest of dear creatures, you must excuse me for
having skipped over all the dry land and plumped in,
heels over head, into the water, since really the barrel is as
buoyant in my imagination as erst it was in the Archi-
pelago. Methinks I behold the count and the squire
ramming her in like so much raw sugar, and treading her
down as the negroes do the figs, to make them pack
close! 'Tis no wonder you pride yourself upon your
invention; that is truly an incident for which you'll find no
parallel in the annals of novel writing! A mere matter-of-
fact writer now, had they really wanted to drown a body,
would most likely have tied a good thumping stone about
its neck, and there would have been an end of it; but your
count knows a trick worth two of that—he either goes to
a cooper and bespeaks a good, stout, watertight cask (tho'
he seems such a scurvy old knave, I doubt if he'd have
been at the expense), or he picks up an old rum puncheon
belonging to the ship's crew, into which he *crams* his
victim, and then (tho' by what means the story does not
inform) this said enormous pipe or puncheon is in a trice
whisked out of a little cabin window!!! Now if this is not
something new I should be very glad to know what is?
Solomon, to be sure, some time ago gave it as his firm
opinion that there was nothing new under the sun; but I
should like to know what he would have said to this!

And here I must observe what a cruel thing it was of that wise monarch to lay down the law so positively in that particular. How many a bright genius has been stifled by this smoky saying! For my part I'm discouraged from all attempts at novelty, when I think if there was nothing new in those days what must it be now, when every bit of ground from Parnassus Top to the Mummy Pits of Egypt has been so poached! However, I rejoice to see your spirit soars superior to the shackles King Solomon thought to impose; and while I lament that my grovelling nature cannot accompany you in your aerial flights I shall yet do my best to speed your success in this nether sphere. You say there are just two styles for which you have any taste, viz. the horrible and the astonishing! Now I'll groan for you till the very blood shall curdle in my veins, or I'll shriek and stare till my own eyes start out of their sockets with surprise—but as to writing with you, in truth it would be as easy to compound a new element out of fire and water, as that we two should jointly write a book! Not but in some things we perfectly agree—for example, bating the barrel. I give the most unqualified praise to the rest of your plot, which I think rich in fancy and novelty and perfect throughout, until we come to the end, where it again offends my nicety. It is a vile catastrophe, a man sticking himself and dying like a calf, and a woman throwing herself from the top of a high wall as one would toss a dead cat! You don't say how much of it is your own and how much borrowed, so that I may speak freely under favour of these little incidents being the work of some bloody minded Frenchman's horrible imagination.

. . . In all things else, as I said before, I do highly admire and applaud the story, and am of opinion that it might form a most interesting romance if properly worked up; but there's the rub! For my part I feel it would be a work far beyond me. You, who are learned, and witty and wise, and know all about the world, may pick and choose

your country, and be as much at home in one as in
another, but for a poor, unlettered, illiterate, unskilful
wight like ¦me, what a figure should I make in foreign
parts! . . . You may laugh at the idea of its being at all
necessary for the writer of a romance to be versed in the
history, natural and political, the modes, manners, customs,
&c. of the country where its wild and wanton freaks are to
be played, but I consider it as most essentially so, as nothing
disgusts an ordinary reader more than a discovery of the
ignorance of the author, who is pretending to instruct and
amuse him. If you'll wait a year perhaps I may have picked
up a little lair in that time, for, as you observe, I'm on the
right road to it at present; but alas! I have but just entered
upon it, and many a long day's journey lies before me!
As to your other plans, I reject and spurn them all without
hesitation. A Hottentot heroine and a wild man of the
woods would be in truth a pair most ' justly formed to
meet by nature,' but I should despair of doing justice to
their wild paces and delicate endearments, though, by-the-
bye, I do think something might be made of such a couple.
Then as to your men of the moon, I shall have nothing
to say to them; this globe contains men enough for me.
Better have one earthly man as a score of moonshine ones
methinks; and as for their lives and conversation :

> What, I prithee, ist to us,
> If men o' the moon do thus or thus ;
> How they eat their porridge, cut their corns,
> Or whether they have tails or horns.

In short, I don't think we'll come to any understanding
upon paper, so we had best give up thoughts of the thing
till we meet, which we'll surely do some day or another—
at any rate, I'm determined not to engage with you till
this of Lady Charlotte is at an end. And you likewise
mention one with Miss Adair![1] Cæsar piqued himself, as

[1] Daughter of Sir Robert Adair, K.C.B., brother of Viscountess Barrington and Mrs. Charles Clavering. She married the Hon. Edward Grey, Bishop of Hereford, and died in 1829. (J. F.)

I have been told, upon dictating three letters at a time. How must his great shade be racked with spite and envy if he sees a young lady composing three novels all in a breath!!! No, no ; as the old saying says, always finish one thing before you begin another. I've the highest respect and admiration of your talents and genius, but I don't think there's a head in the world capable of containing and clearly arranging materials for three books, be they what they may ; besides that, you can do nothing but write, and though I approve of it as an amusement I by no means commend it as the business of life—too much application is bad for the health and will spoil your eyes and complexion, and, to tell you a bit of my mind, I don't think you will ever write half so well as nature has written upon you . . . I've said nothing of my own obstacles, because I consider those on your side as sufficiently powerful ; but I assure you I could no more accomplish such a letter as you propose every week than a poor wretch could promise to be witty and agreeable when writhing in the cholic. In the first place, I really have not much time I can absolutely command, for in a town, however privately or retired one may live, they're still liable to a thousand interruptions ; in the next place, I have enough to do with my time in writing to my sisters three, sewing my seam, improving my mind, making tea, playing whist, with numberless other duties too tedious to mention ; and, in the third and last place, there's sometimes for a week together that I can't bear the sight of a pen, and could no more invent a letter than I could have discovered the longitude. So for the present let us put our child to sleep and hope for better times to wake him. Only, once for all, let me promise to you that I *will not* enter into any of your raw head and bloody bone schemes. I would not even *read* a Book that had a spectre in it, and as for committing a mysterious and most foul murder, I declare I'd rather take a dose of asafœtida ; so don't flatter yourself with the hope of associating me in your crimes and iniquities, for

I'll be partner in none of your bloody purposes, Miss. . . .
But enough of this. Why won't you tell me that you're
coming here with Lady Charlotte? Thou cruel Lady of
the Mountains, thou dost nothing to cheer me. If you could
come with her I might prevail on *mon père* to go back
with you, would not that be foine? Say instantly what
you think possible. As to my sending my letters to you
under Lord John's cover, that's morally impossible for two
reasons: the first is that he positively forbid me, but said
if I chose to send them via London I might (which, by-the-
bye, I've a great mind to do, as they're never in a hurry);
the second is, that the post-office here has his address and
orders to send his letters to London; and to my making
love to Members for such base purposes I'd have you to
know, Miss, I scorn such things, that I do, and, more than
that, there's not a Member in all this town at present nor yet
in all the country, I'm told. . . . And so you have the
assurance to compare that little ignoble paw to my own
graceful pothooks and hangers, which have no parallel
save in the hieroglyphics of Egypt! But I scorn to waste
time upon one so ignorant of their value, and shall only
add my desire that you write directly and tell me whether
you're in a storm or a dead calm against me. Oh! that
barrel, it will always be uppermost, do what I will. Farewell,
my nutmeg of delight! that's one of the titles of the Grand
Signior, but I ween you're more worthy of it—if so, look
upon me as your most attached Grater. I would have
written sooner, but have had a fit of the *ophthalmia* ever
since reading your last letter. You advise me to have
a reservoir of *red ink* always in the house. Horrible hint,
a human one I wot you mean! I suppose the Goloch is
yours and that you dab a bare bodkin in her every time the
spirit of composing comes upon you; 'tis no wonder your
writings have imbibed such a bloody character.

S. E. F. TO MISS CLAVERING

Feb. 13.

Miss Clavering,—Madam, I have so many crows to pick with you, I am quite at a loss which first to try my hand upon. They're all much about one age and all alike black, and the only way to choose is to begin with the biggest. But belike you'd relish them better in a *pie*, and though I can't promise to season mine so much to your taste as the gusty ones you had at the minister's once upon a time, and yet such as it is, hot or cold, you must stomach it, so fall to. Pray what do you mean by writing to me in the most vindictive, revengeful, unchristian, bloodthirsty manner of the conduct of a noble personage, thereby inflaming my choler, increasing my bile, agitating my chile, and causing my gall to overflow, even to my finger-points, and then when, like a doughty champion, I draw my dirk and step forth to espouse your quarrel and redress your wrongs you turn upon me with a stare of astonishment and a ' What d'ye mean ? I declare I don't know what you'd be at. I never was the least angry with anybody, nor ever said a word against any human being ; you must have dreamt it,' and then you steal away and leave me fighting and thrusting at my own shadow.

Allow me to help you to another crow, Miss. I've suffered you to daub me all over many and many a time with an odious composition of honey and butter, such as they were wont to anoint criminals with for the cruel purpose of aggravating the torments by attracting wasps and flies. To this most inhuman operation I have submitted in silence nor ever breathed a murmur of complaint ; but when in pure kindness I attempt to offer you a morsel of fresh butter or a teaspoonful of virgin honey, just by way of a little nourishment to you, you fly upon me like a very fury and accuse me of a design to butter you all over, and, in short, seem to suspect me of the same evil designs you practise upon me.

. . . Do you really think me capable of flattering, i.e. of saying what I don't think ? Attend to what Julie says on this subject—the sentiment is the same, whether applied to love or friendship—'L'amant qui loue en nous des perfections que nous n'avons pas les voit en effet telles qu'il les représente. Il ne ment point en disant des mensonges,' &c. Now, I never did pretend to say you were bona fide —and—and—all that I maintain is, that I think you so, which proves nothing, because an ancient philosopher has proved, or tried to prove (which is all the same in the Greek), that there's no such thing as reality ; that life's a dream, pain a fancy, and that we've no further certainty of our existence than what our own imaginations give us. For aught I can tell, you may therefore be as ugly as an ape, as stupid as an owl, as venomous as a toad, as cruel as a hyena ; you may destroy your offspring before they're born, like the silly ostrich ; or you may carry them about with you in your pouch, like the tender kangaroo. All these things you may be or do, and yet to my fancy you may be fairer than an Houri, wise as a Genii, benevolent as a *Brownie*. For my part, were you to cry me up to the skies and tell me I had the grace and innocence of Eve, with the beauty and amorous inclinations of Cleopatra, the virtue and delicacy of Lucretia, &c., &c., I never could have the incivility to tell you it was all a lie, or that you were speaking nonsense. . . . Neither should I perhaps be able to persuade myself it was so, tho' I should give you credit for thinking so—flatter me, then, as much as you've a mind for, and the worst that can be said is that I've 'cast glamour in your e'en.'

Now comes crow the third. Pray where did one of your illustrious pedigree learn that pitiful trick of saying 'how much do I owe you for this yard of ribbon, and how much for that half of half a quarter of catgut and '—(oh ! that I should soil my paper with such shop sneaking sentiments)— ' I'll send you the four and tenpence ha'penny by the first opportunity, &c., &c.'? Are you not ashamed of yourself ?

I'm sure you are.   Only see how these pretty sayings look upon paper and say whether they don't smell stronger of the shop than the castle.   However, I'll let you off for this time upon condition that you make a handsome apology, beg my pardon, and promise never to do the like again.

I condole with you upon having fallen into the hands of the Philistines, i.e.—— ; like smoke to the eyes, and vinegar to the teeth, so is their tongue to the reputation—only, greedy as the world is for lies and nonsense, its maw is not quite so rapacious as to swallow all that their evil imaginations engender and their slanderous mouths bring forth.   I am not surprised that B.'s purity should take the alarm at your *dead works*, since she held me up to the scorn of the virtuous and the detestation of the pure in heart for having written a letter to her poor brother, who is now gone, on the subject of *corn cutting*.   You will allow I must have had some ingenuity if I could extract either immorality or indecency from a corn !   But so it was.   I was reprobated by all the members of that *Holy* family as one of the abandoned of my sex.   I dare say B., if she were in your situation, would think it a far more innocent way of passing her time to fall into the vapours, or yield herself up an unresisting victim to sullenness and spleen, than exert her faculties, call in the aid of imagination (a thing, by-the-bye, I suppose she thinks no modest maid should have), support her spirits, and, while amusing herself, at the same time take the chance of amusing others—rather than do all this, I ween she would think herself better employed sitting with her ' hands folded eating her own flesh.'   You'll say I'm very illnatured ; so I am I own in the present instance when she seeks to deprive you of the only enjoyments you have in the resources of your own talents ; take them away and she certainly leaves you little to make merry with at present.   I understand she remains here.

You've never told me what's to be the fate of the book since they have seen it ?   I hope it is not to spoil the sale of it. And now having bubbled over like a great boiling cauldron, and got rid of my froth and scum, you shall come to the good things at last ; but they deserve a page to themselves, so please turn over.

When will you write me such a letter as this with your wide lines, long tails, and blank paper ? I mean this as a pattern for you, and as soon as you've taken it off, I beg you will throw it into the fire, as you'd do with the shape of a cap or tucker. When you write, please put ' single ' upon your letters, as the post-office people, rightly guessing that they are worth two of any other person's, choose to charge me accordingly.

S. E. F. TO MISS CLAVERING

Sunday evening : 20th.

Did I not promise you a literary letter ? Alas ! my hand turns pale and my pen is ready to swoon at the bare mention of such an undertaking ! How shall these inexperienced innocents who have never strayed beyond the precincts of folly, save to peep into the flowery field of fiction—how shall they ever find their way through the mazes of literature and criticism ? Will they not be plunged into the bogs of ignorance, driven against the rocks of pedantry, or bewildered in the mazes of error ? Will they not have to combat prejudice, to conquer partiality, to beware presumption ? Too surely all those dangers beset those monsters that besiege the paths of science, and unless vanquished at the very entrance seldom fail to make the unwary passenger their prey ! Unlike the fabled dragons of old, we cannot bribe them to let us pass unmolested, but rather, like the fascinating syrens, they charm us to our ruin !!! There's an exordium for you, that even out-Montagues Montague ! The cause of this extraordinary burst of eloquent moralising proceeds solely from that source of the true sublime in letter-writing. I chanced to take up a volume of hers to keep me awake

after dinner, and the fancy took me to try whether, without
a grain of her talent, I could not write something about
nothing as flowery and pedantic as she had done. I
admired her letters at first reading, and still think some
of them the wittiest that ever were written—but that everlasting eternal preaching and prosing is execrable in every-
day letters, don't you think so?

But to bring my criticism and remarks nearer home.
. . . I yesterday sent off your production to your own
care sealed up and directed by one bookseller to another,
so all you have to do is to commit it to a penny post.
Whether it will be received or rejected the fates who preside
over the Minerva press alone can tell, and they're such
tongue-tied jades that they never speak but by signs. As
I told you before, its extreme shortness is its chief crime
and its excessive *personality* another; it was in vain I pro-
tested there was not a word of truth in the whole volume,
but that it was a compilation of lies from beginning to end.
The man of learning shook his head, said it might be so,
but that it *looked so like* truth, few would care to publish it
for fear of being called to account (for you must know,
Ma'am, that according to law truth's a libel). I confess I
don't in the least wonder that a poor innocent bookseller
should doubt the fact of its being a falsehood when I, in
the sober certainty of its being a fiction, read it as Gospel!
Most people complain of having their facts taken as false-
hoods, but I should suppose it was quite a new species of
distress in the annals of authorship to have lies mistaken
for truths. However, as the taste of the times is undoubtedly for private memoirs and personal satire I can't
believe that will be any serious objection to a London
publisher; therefore, if it is returned you may ascribe its
failure entirely to its brevity and act accordingly. With
regard to the others I am very desirous that you should get
some person who is up to the art of bookmaking and book-
mending to revise and correct it before you give it to the
world, because you may be well assured the authors will

be no secret.   Robert Campbell [1] speaks of your writing not as a thing *suspected*, but quite ascertained.   I affected to disbelieve it, but he said anybody that had ever seen it could not for a moment doubt its being the work of two people, &c., &c.[2]   This being the case, you certainly ought to take all possible pains to have it unexceptionable as possible, and the only way to accomplish that is to show it to some friend on whose taste and judgment you can rely and to whose correction you will submit.   Lady Charlotte has so many literary friends she can be at no loss. Lewis [3] I should conceive might be of use, and is not Mrs. Damer *un bas-bleu*?   It seems mighty impertinent in me to interfere, but you cannot for a moment mistake the motive.   I sent what I had copied by the Duchess.[4]   There are several blanks and, I fear, many blunders ; one in parti- cular I observed when too late to remedy.   I hope it won't be too ridiculous.   After the two friends leave Leoni and Philiberto together what followed was so blurred and blotted that I mistook and made them fall to their prayers, but as I presume they are *Papists* the error is not so great as if they had been pure Protestants or stiff-necked Presby- terians.   I've kept the originals, so if you want a clue to any of the blanks I'll send them ; if not I'll burn them. You may send me as much as you please—if you really approve of my copying, but not otherwise, as I promise I shan't be affronted should you dismiss me.   I try to imitate your hand as closely as I can, but there's a stiffness in it defys all human pens.   I've a mind to enclose you a wee morsel of Lady MacLaughlan, though I think the dinner scene is carried too far, but I write down everything that folly suggests at first and leave it to reason to abridge it afterwards.   Would Mamie [5] deign to read it ?   If so

---

[1] Robert Campbell of Skipness, co. Argyll. (J. F.)

[2] One would infer from this that the book under discussion was one in which Miss Clavering was engaged with her aunt, Lady Charlotte. Pro- bably it was *Self-Indulgence.* (J. F.)

[3] The author of *The Monk*. He was frequently at Inveraray Castle, where Miss Ferrier met him. He wrote several poems in her album. (J. F.)

[4] The Duchess of Argyll. (J. F.)

[5] Mademoiselle de la Chaux, gover- ness in the family of Lady Charlotte Campbell. (J. F.)

I'll send the beginning if she'll give me the benefit of her critiques.

. . . Your love speech is quite beautiful and eloquent and must have come from the heart—the head never could produce anything so warm and tender, and I love you all the better for it. My only fault to you is that you've never been in love, but I trust your time is coming, and that you'll live to swell the streams with your tears and shake the trees with your sighs! How I should doat on you as a love-sick maid! I long to see the beauteous Rawdon;[1] it seems but as yesterday since these aged arms used to hold the crowing babe! Give my motherly love to him. I suppose he's too big to be kissed now? When do you go to Inveraray? When does the Duke come to it? Who's to be there? How long are you to stay? Is it to be very gay? Have you got in your hay? Answer me quickly by 'Yea,' or by 'Nay'? And don't let it be in the old way—for I declare I never grudge to pay. No more will I say, for this is Sunday.

S. E. F. TO MISS CLAVERING

And so you vile little spendthrift that you are you have the effrontery to declare that you only wish to be married that you may have the opportunity of squandering your husband's substance among your friends and needy acquaintances? A most laudable motive, indeed, for entering into the holy bonds of matrimony. Are you not ashamed to be already plotting the ruin of some honest unsuspecting man, instead of bethinking you of accomplishing the ends for which matrimony was ordained? Go, attentively peruse your Prayer-book, ponder well upon its contents, and that you may soon have it in your power to obey its precepts and fulfil the Scriptures is, and shall ever be, my most fervent prayer. None but a saint would sit down to

---

[1] Rawdon Clavering, her brother. He married Miss Dunbar, of North- field, and was father of Sir Henry Clavering, Bart. (J. F.)

scribble to you in the state I'm in at present, with a head like a mill-stone, eyes like fountains, fingers like horns, and my brain in my pocket-handkerchief—in fact, my head feels exactly (as I should suppose) as though it were in labour. I hope you'll therefore prove a skilful *accoucheur* and be the means of delivering me, and whatever I produce, even though it should be a second Minerva, I promise you shall have it. Apropos of such things, I rejoice to hear your Bantling thrives so well, and is so much improved since I saw it. I always thought there was promise in it, but it wanted a little pruning ; by-the-bye, I hope you've restored the serpent to the third chapter of Genesis. It was unaccountable to me how a person of your wisdom could ever think of ever appropriating such a notorious fact to yourself; you might just as well have stolen the Regalia and thought to walk the streets unmolested with the Crown of Great Britain on your head. I must be allowed to give my opinion and advice also, because on the success of your works I build all *my* hopes of fame and fortune. But that you may not impute to me the paltry design of treading on your foot-steps, know that I mean to choose a nobler path, and intend to immortalise myself by giving to the world a work which shall be read when reading is no more ! A work whose fame shall extend from the Taboozamanoo Islands to the last stone of the Mull of Kantyre [*sic*] ! A work which shall penetrate to the remotest unknown regions ! A work which, to sum up all, is to contain your life, character, conversation, and correspondence ! ! ! I only wait till your book shall have gone through seventy-five editions ; you will then either expire with joy or fall a victim to envy ; the world will call loudly for your Life (or *remains*, as it is now called) ; I shall be prevailed upon to undertake the painful task at the solicitation of your friends, the request of your acquaintance, the commands of your sovereign, and the prayers of all the world. I shall begin with a biographical sketch of your life, followed

by some account of your writings, interspersed with notes
and observations critical and original. To these succeed
the editor's preface, and to every edition shall be a new
note by the editor. Then begins the correspondence
from the age of five years to the day of your death, the
whole to conclude with a grand elegiac ode to your
memory. I shall have three copies three feet and a half
long by two and a quarter broad ; they shall be printed on
white velvet (white satin having become so common), and,
to suit the solemnity of the subject, every page shall be
trimmed with a deep black flounce ! I designed one for
the Emperor of China, another for the great Cham of
Tartary, and the third I shall allow you to suggest the disposal of, in case there is any crowned head in particular you
may wish to confer it upon. They shall be bound in the
hides of your hounds, and surmounted with a plume from
the rumps of your peas.[1] Remember me to Lady Augusta
and her Foot, which I hope is no longer carried in state.
Commend me to Miss E—— unto whom breathe none of
my murmurs as you value my life, because she is the
bosom friend of the *Pot of Honey*. I've got nothing done
nor even imagined since we parted, and I know not when
I shall, ill-fated woman that I be ! I find I unintentionally
carried off the first chapter, but you shall have it again
whenever you please.

> I shall write no more,
> For my eyes are sore,
> And my heart is tore,
> With rage I could roar ;
> But I must only snore.
> So good night, as I said before.

S. E. F. TO MISS CLAVERING

Edinburgh : May 26, 1810.

I hope you won't set me down as stark staring mad,
for I assure you, in spite of appearances, I'm only a *wee
daft* and just wanted to divert myself, and I know I'd be

[1] Pea-fowl.

H

safe with you, for you're a good dear and won't make a fool of me—for a good reason, you'll say, because it's done to your hand.' But seriously and truly I think you have just as much malice in you as would make you think it fine fun to show what an old goose-cap I am ; but I give you warning, if ever you show a single line of mine to any man, woman, or child, I'm done with you for ever and ever ; so if you want to get rid of me there's a genteel opening for you. I've been languishing to write to you this age, but I've had such a fulness of blood about my head and chest that I thought I was going to break a blood-vessel, and so dared not put pen to paper—and that's the true cause of this long cessation.

S. E. F. TO MISS CLAVERING

. . . I send you your gown, which I hope you'll approve of. It came to 1*l.* 3*s.*, and gave the account to my brother and have got my monies. I sent a yard more, as it wasn't for a lady ; by-the-bye, you should have told me what kind of a person it was for, as there's some sizes between fat Fanny and Miss Wynne. I see Mrs. Robert has got a third son.[1] I saw her walking with her lord, and she just came up to his knee, and so I thought he had got a monstrous swelled leg, till I drew near and discovered that it was his rib ! I met Betsy,[2] too, one day—a fine thing in a salmon-coloured suit came galloping up and made an awkward kind of a speak, and so I made a cold reply, and we parted, never to speak again, I suppose. The Misses Mure came and dined with me one day in my cot, and we talked of you, and we all three agreed that you are the most——[3] in the world[4] ; so take that,

---

[1] Mrs. Campbell, of Skipness, co. Argyll (née Wynne). She was called 'the Pocket Venus.' (J. F.)

[2] Elizabeth Campbell, of Shawfield (Mrs. Thriepland). (J. F.)

[3] A blank. (J. F.)

[4] Perhaps it was after this that Miss Mure wrote to Miss Clavering : 'I dined with Susan Ferrier two days ago. I believe she was somewhat piqued at a letter you wrote her some time ago, but has always talked of

Miss. I like them vastly, and am very sorry I don't see them oftener. Bessie told me Lady A.[1] was going into the Lions' Den at Hamilton.[2] Is that so? And are you, sweet Doo, to be left bird alane? Oh! that I could make unto myself wings and fly! Pray write to me post haste and tell me everything, for 'tis an age since I heard from you and Elfin! . . .

When am I to be blest with the book? You might easily send it by the coach, and I'll ensure its safety for the price you put upon it, if a price it has. How did you like the family? My head aches and I'm sure so may yours by this time, so farewell, my pretty. Pray write to your faithful and affectionate friend,

S. E. F.

S. E. F. TO MISS CLAVERING

Wednesday evening.

I am at the greatest possible pains to furnish you with an abridgment of my brain in order to save you double postage when, just as I had finished by letter, my brother sent me a frank big enough to carry a folio. 'Tis well for you that I did not know of it sooner, for, as I'm in a scribbling mood, there's no saying where I might have stopped had not the form of sevenpence held my hand. However, I am overflowing with spite, and you need not wonder should my gall show itself soon on a new sheet of paper. Meantime, I charge you on your allegiance herewith to assume the form of a letter and transport yourself into my presence. 'Tis very hard, methinks, that serpents and skeletons should have more of your company than what I have, but, I suppose, were I a snake or a spectre I'd be prettily courted; but let me tell you flesh and blood

replying. Perhaps she waits till her choler cools; she tells me she is very cholerick and proud; perhaps she is like all the family, who are always busy supporting their dignity . . . She is very civil to me and I like her very well.' (J. F.)

[1] Lady Augusta Clavering. (J. F.)
[2] Hamilton palace. The Lions' Den alludes to the celebrated Rubens there, ' Daniel in the Lions' Den.' (J. F.)

won't bear this, as I'm cast off by Lady Charlotte, abandoned by Mamselle. La Chaux and treated with contumely by Miss Clavering, but I'll be revenged of you. I shall write a book to which yours shall bear the same proportion as Joe Miller to Mrs. Radcliffe. *You* have but one serpent ; *I* shall have nine. *Yours* can only speak (which they could do in the days of Adam); *mine* shall sing and play on the harp, and waltz. You measure out blood (like laudanum) in drops, but I shall dispense it like the shower-bath! I—but I shall say no more lest you burst with envy at my superior genius, and thereby deprive me of the satisfaction of seeing you pine a slow death at my unrivalled success.

S. E. F. TO MISS CLAVERING

Thursday.

Deign, Madam, to withdraw your lofty eyes for a while from the flowered chintz of Lady MacLaughlan, and fix them upon the enclosed patterns of silk, with the prices (oh! vulgar sound) thereto affixed, while I (oh! degradation unparalleled in the annals of novel writing) must descend from the sublime region of fiction to—the back of a counter! How shall I ever be able to clothe this vulgar translation in elegant language, or where find terms to commune (as one author ought to commune with another) upon the price of sarcenet, and the width of lutestring ? Let me try. That whose hue doth emulate the rose, and on its surface smooth doth bear the stars of heaven impressed by heaven's skill, doth on the top shelf of a little shop languish amidst dusty duffells, in which the village dame arrayed to church or market hies, and fustian strong, in which for thrift clad by wise parents is the wanton schoolboy, and hard and obdurate, rattling in form of petticoat against the bare legs of country girl, and broad cloth, drab and blue, of which the careful farmer, after much conning and prudent confab with his dame and neighbours all, doth chuse his

Sunday's coat.   And flannels, Welsh of smell most potent, in which the rheumy Granam seeks to shroud her shrivelled limbs.   All these and many more my muse could sing do with that starry robe abide.   Six times the length of thy finger is its breadth, by some three-quarters called ; silver seven times told, by vulgar called seven shillings, the price of each fair yard.   Turn we now to where the various hues, such as of painted rainbow, doth delight the roving eye of fickle youth.   There's pink, denoting pride and vanity ; and straw-colour, mocking the hue of pining maid ; and purple, by some styled the light of love ; and buff, symbolic of our happy state of nature ; and white, emblem of virgin inno-cence.   All these may then be thine for slips or linings, stout and warm, for twelve times four of pence, formed of base brass, and stamped with Britain's power triumphant and monarch's head with laurel bound.   And now to paint the lilac I essay.   Pride of the spring, welcome thy blossoms fair and odoriferous !   But fairer still to sight of youthful fair when by the Indian artist's cunning hand thy beauties are with green and gold inwove and stripes of silvery white. This in the coffers of a dame doth dwell, whose niggard hand doth only draw it forth for love of sordid lucre ; its extent doth much surpass thy utmost wishes, but she swears no shears shall e'er sever it in twain so long as she doth own it.   Seven yards, eke an' half, it owns, and for each yard this flinty female doth demand ten shillings good and bright. . . .   But enough of bathos.   I wish there was not quite so much pathos in the price of that lilac silk, for I think it would suit you vastly, it belongs to a member of my brother-in-law's family, and I've been straining every nerve to get her to part with it for love or lucre, instead of which the vile copper-hearted creature has the conscience to ask ten shillings a yard for seven yards and a half, which would be a useless quantity, as it is too much for one dress and not enough for two.   I said I would send you the pattern, but I didn't suppose you would care to give so much, upon which the Jew said it didn't signify.   I don't know what's doing about the plain one, as Mrs. Kinloch is at Brighton at present, but in the last letter I had from her she said she had some hope of being able to procure a figured one, but was not certain, so I don't advise you to have anything to do with this, as I think it shamefully dear. My sister, Mrs. Graham, got some of the same from a good woman of the family, rest her bones! and I believe she gave hers to Lady Charlotte, but this hunks has no idea of giving.

I approve highly of christening each chapter, but I think we'd as well motto them afterwards. Which of the heroines is to be Constance? The good girl or the bad? Call them what you will. Apropos, don't you think Monteith would be a better family name than Douglas? The second chapter should open with some history of the family, as one is brought quite slapdash into it without knowing anything about them; not but what I think people should always *speak for themselves* in books, but it may be proper to tell that the mother died when they were all young, and that the laird had got his sisters to superintend his family &c. What think you? . . . I waste my whole time and substance in scribbling to you, but I'm determined to turn over a new leaf, mistress, and not put pen to paper to you for a month to come, or at least not till I've heard three times from you, and until you've told me something to make amends for your secrecy. You go and gossip with Bessie Mure, and tell her everything that opens and shuts, and I suppose your whole kin may be dead or married before you'd think proper to let me hear a word of the matter. Go, go, you bad girl, you deserve to be put in a dark closet; but if you'll *promise* to be good I'll forgive you, so kiss and be friends, and there's a pockethandkerchief for you to wipe your eyes with, and hem it neatly, and put a loop to it and wear it at your side, and every time you blow your nose you'll become better and better; by the time it's dirty you'll be quite perfect. Adieu, my dearest.

MISS CLAVERING TO S. E. F.

Postmark 1810.   Ardencaple Castle [1] : Sunday morning.

I am so charmed with you in every possible way, that I should have written you so every day, had I not thought on what you were to pay, which, though a mean idea, you'll say is one very proper to be considered in this world of straits and difficulties.   The moment Lord John comes letters shall pour upon you in bushels.   First of all, I must tell you that I approve in the most signal manner of 'Lady McLaughlan.'   The sort of character was totally unexpected by me, and I was really quite transported with her. Do I know the person who is the original?   The dress was vastly like Mrs. Damer,[2] and the manners like Lady Frederick,[3] tell me if you did not mean a touch at her.   I love poor Sir Samson vastly, though it is impossible in the presence of his lady to have eyes or ears for anyone else. Her kissing Lady Juliana and holding her at arm's length is capital.   Now you must not think of altering her, and it must all go forth in the world ; neither must the Missies *upon any account* be changed.   I have a way now of *at least* offering it to publication by which you never can be discovered.   I will tell the person that I wrote it. (' Indeed, quoth a',' cries Miss Ferrier, 'and no great favour now ; see how she loves to plume herself with borrowed fame.')   Well, however, my way is quite sure, and the person would never think of speaking of it again ; so never let the idea of detection come across your brain while you are writing to damp your ardour.   Positively neither Sir Samson's lady nor the 'foolish virgins' must be displaced.   I don't propose to compose anything just

---

[1] Near Helensburgh, where Miss Clavering lived with her mother, Lady Augusta Clavering. (J. F.)

[2] Her cousin, the celebrated sculptor, and friend and also cousin of Horace Walpole, to whom he left Strawberry Hill. (J. F.) It is like meeting a familiar friend unexpectedly in a strange country to remember that the supposed original or part-original of Lady MacLaughlan was the child who was a petted visitor of Horace Walpole, the daughter of the Eton friend to whom he clung through life with such loyal affection.

[3] Wife of Lord Frederick Campbell, and widow of the ill-fated Lord Ferrers. (J. F.)

now till you send me some more of Lady MacLaughlan, and when you do I must repeat that you are to let me know exactly when and where you want me to add a little of my babbles, though I don't expect to shine till you come to the killing of the people. Now I think on't, I am quite ashamed of what I sent you, but there is no helping it, and you can always leave it out, that's my only comfort. Constance I intended should be the name of the good girl, and let Matilda remain as she was. Monteith is a very good name, but I'm not sure that I like it better than Douglas; however, it signifies not a great deal. I was thinking that I had seen the name of Alvanley[1] in some beggarly book, so we must have another. I had a nice one in my head yesterday, and I've forgot it to-day. You would make a delightful auctioneer. Christie would be a joke to you. Never did I see goods set off in such a brilliant manner. What a pity you have such a stupid correspondent as I—I have often thought it very odd that a person of your wit should take up with such a dull person as Miss Clavering. It certainly says a great deal for your heart that you should like a person through thick and thin —through all the thickness of their brains, and thinness of their understanding. Well, to fly from the lining of the skull to the covering of the body. You will do me the favour if you please, Ma'am, to buy me seventeen yards of the crimson *starry mantle.* I suppose you think I am going to make a sack with five and fifty flounces and six yards in circumference. No, Madam, I want eleven yards for my- self, out of which I am making two gowns—one for myself and one for a compliment—and the remaining six yards are for Miss Annie Mure, who wishes to purchase the same. All this, provided there be seventeen yards of it, which I don't at all consider a certainty. If there is not such a quantity I must just have the eleven yards, and I will send you the money as soon as ever I can get a

---

[1] It may be presumed that this was to be the title of the stupid Duke. It seems strange that Miss Claver- ing should not have remembered that the name of Alvanley is to be found in that 'beggarly book' the *Peerage.* Altamont, with all its stage associa- tions, was hardly a happy choice.

frank, which will be in a few days, as Lord John is to be at Glasgow to-day, if his skull does not prevent him. The lilac is transcendent, but my purse says nay, and I am such a discreet *crater* that I'm never carried away with the vanity of the eye. I recognised it to be the same Lady Charlotte had. I am doatingly fond of the price of the lutestrings, and think I must have a sixteen-shilling go of the white one if it is ¾ wide. If it is narrower I mun hae mair, and if it is wider less, but I don't think 'twill be wider—that will be 4*l.* 13*s.* I shall owe you besides two guineas for Miss Mure's red silk, if you can get the quantity always *bien entendu.* It is really shocking to be *bodering* you about such troublesome concerns, but really such good-humoured people as you are always taken advantage of in this wicked world. I assure you you wrong me by saying I gossip things with Bessie Mure that I withhold from you. I had heard of the Duke's marriage some time ago, and was desired not to speak of it ; and it was not till, by the currency of the report, Bessy wrote it to me that I ever let on that I knew anything of it. My other reasons for not talking of it you know already. However, one must hope the best, and whenever I find a number of fine qualities in my ' Lady Duchess ' I shall write about it to you. I think for the present I have nothing more to add than that I am always, with many thanks for the pretty painted muckinger,[1]

Your most affectionate friend,

C. C.

Let me have the continuation of Lady MacLaughlan directly. How am I to get those beautiful delicious silks when you have bought them ?

MISS CLAVERING TO S. E. F.

Sundridge,[2] Inveraray : December 10, 1810.

And now, dear Susannah, I must tell you of the success

---

[1] A handkerchief, spelt Muckender in Bailey's *Dictionary.* (J. F.)

[2] The Duke of Argyll sits in the House of Lords as Baron Sundridge. The letter was franked ' Sundridge ' on the cover. (J. F.)

of your first born. I read it to Lady Charlotte in the carriage when she and I came together from Ardencaple, Bessie having gone with Mamma. If you believe I never yet in my existence saw Lady C. laugh so much as she did at that from beginning to end; seriously I was two or three times alarmed that she would fall into a fit. Her very words were, 'I assure you I think it without the least exception the cleverest thing of the kind that ever was written, far surpassing Fielding'; then she said, that as to our other books, that they would all sink to nothingness before yours; that they were not fit to mention in the same day, and that she felt quite discouraged from writing when she thought of yours. The whole conversation of the Aunties made her screech with laughing, and, in short, I can neither record nor describe all that she said; far from exaggerating it, I don't say half enough; but I only wish you had seen the effect it produced. I am sure you will be the first author of the age. The Duke bids me to tell you to say to your father that he has received his letter and will answer it in a few days, and, in the meantime, he will be very happy to see him and you at Inveraray. If Lady Charlotte puts her plan in execution of taking me to London I am afraid I shall miss seeing you, which will be a very great disappointment to me. However, Mamma has not been asked yet, and I look forward with dread to the feuds it will occasion. We never see the Duchess[1] except in the evening, for these two are philandering all morning together—far from taking upon her to do the honours of the house, she labours to appear to have no more to do with it than I. She is vastly sweet and gentle, but desperate shy. I dare say I shall like her vastly well when we are better acquainted. Her two children are very nice

---

[1] Caroline, daughter of the Earl of Jersey, married first Lord Paget, which marriage was dissolved 1810. She married in the same year the Duke of Argyll. (J. F.) That scurrilous writer, Eaton Stannard Barrett, in *Six Weeks at Long's*, attacks the Duchess, but can find nothing worse to say than to quote a description of her by her sister-in-law, which tallies with Miss Clavering's. 'Elle est jolie comme une fleur, aimante comme une tourterelle, et paisible comme le sommeil.'

creatures—the eldest pretty and like herself.[1]   I never saw anybody appear so fond of another as she does of him ; she sits for hours gazing on him with fixed eyes. I do not think Lady Charlotte is strong ; her cold, however, is better.   I wish she could stay here a little longer to recruit her health, but she will not hear of it. Tell me if you want to have the whole of your novel together, and I will send it ?   Do go on with it as fast as you can.   I am sitting for my picture, and, though you may not believe it, Bessie and I have been squabbling about it ; she says she is to keep it herself, but has made me a promise to copy it for you.   I don't suppose she will have time, however, to do it here, as she intends painting a head of Lady Charlotte. I should like to see her do one of her Grace, for I do think she is beautiful.

Well no more at present from your humble servant and affectionate friend,

CHARLOTTE.

How fares the Savage ?   Give him my tenderest love.

MISS CLAVERING TO S. E. F.

J. D. Campbell,[2] London.
April 2, 1811.   Cadogan Place : Sunday.

For these two days I have been more particularly thinking of writing to you, my dear friend, and have been racking my brains to compose a well turned and new excuse. At least I think of one which must, unless you are the most unreasonable person in the world, entirely satisfy you.   Not writing to one's dear friend is generally reckoned a proof of not thinking of her, but you will, I am sure, acknowledge it to be a venial trespass when I declare that you are then more constantly in my thoughts, and your merits more present to my fancy, than at any other

---

[1] Lady Caroline Paget, afterwards Duchess of Richmond. (J. F.)

[2] Lord John Douglas Campbell He franked this letter. (J. F.)

time. I am then continually haunted with the idea of your wrongs. Everything you have done for me rises up in judgment before my contrite spirit. I long for your letters, and yet cannot hope or expect them. I will say no more on this subject except the assurance that my heart is perfectly unchanged, if that can give you the least satisfaction, and upon the strength of that you ought to make allowance for me, and putting yourself in the same situation as me, and taking upon yourself the same infirmities of character, I think you will not find me so much to blame. I have not, and am afraid never shall acquire, that energy of character to make me snatch stray moments of time, and dragging my mind from its foolish pursuits set it down at a chance time in quite a different mood. This incapability has been very much increased by always living in the country, where the happiness of having much longer portions of time at my own disposal, without any jarring pursuits coming across me, has given me a lazy habit of mind, which incapacitates me from abstracting my mind at a minute's warning. This is an infirmity of my nature for which I am more to be pitied than blamed ; which, when added to my having very little time and (from my poverty) a great deal to do with my ten fingers, makes, I hope, my transgression less. I candidly confess that I have not a correspondent that I have not treated in the same way ; moreover, I've scarce opened a book since I came, and, above all, I enjoy life very little. I am very thin and very ugly, which mortifies me, I confess, a good deal.[1] I therefore study to make myself fat by all sorts of laziness and indulgence, such as lying in bed like a *very*

---

[1] Kirkpatrick Sharpe, fastidious and fault-finding in female beauty as in other things, writes : 'Miss Clavering strikes me as being pretty, but nothing more, for she hath got tender eyes and no flesh to cover her nakedness. She is a sort of ghost of Lady Charlotte, dead of a consumption, and much compressed by whipping through the key-hole.' Nevertheless he banters his friend, Henry Adams, about his devotion to 'his charming Pastora,' as he calls Miss Clavering. (*Letters*, vol. i. p. 559 ; vol. ii. p. 13.) Her beauty is vouched for not only by her portrait, but by what may be considered most unimpeachable authority, that of a mother-in-law much attached to her son. Mrs. Fletcher, in her *Autobiography* (Ed. 1875, p. 132),

London lady, sleeping after dinner. We have no carriage, so depend upon our toes for a walk, which takes up a good deal of time, as we are so dreadfully out of the way. This is acted every day of our lives as the weather is so exquisite. Another thing which swallows up a good deal of time is our visits to Lord Abercorn in the country.[1] We have been three times there, and as there is always a great deal of company one's days are necessarily devoted to idleness. I went there yesterday week and did not return till Thursday last. There was a great christening of Lord Abercorn's grandson,[2] at which there was a gathering of all the old women in the kingdom. Lady Hamilton, mother of the child, is a very beautiful young creature, only eighteen; her husband is a poor sick looking bird, but seems to adore her. My favourite in the family is Lady Maria Hamilton, Lord A.'s daughter. She is a most charming amiable woman, very uncommon and odd. She is reckoned the most completely amiable and moral character that can exist. Certainly the Priory must have been very much wronged in its time as being filled with dissolute company, for both Lady Maria and Lady Aberdeen were brought up there, and I don't believe there are two such rigidly proper and strictly virtuous women to be found in the three kingdoms. I once wrote to Bessie Mure some account of Miss Owenson,[3] who has been living there these three months. Did she ever tell you anything about her? I've had rather a surfeit of her, so I don't feel as if you cared to know anything about her. However, I cannot in honour pass her over entirely. First, to speak of her merits, she is perfectly different from what I had fancied her from her works. She hardly ever talks sentiment, and her *forte* is the *folâtre grâce*. Though vain

---

speaks of Miles Fletcher bringing home 'his very lovely bride.' She also gives (p. 203) a very touching description of her daughter-in-law's composed courage at the time of Miles Fletcher's death, when she thought that her own mind was in danger. 'I never,' she says, 'saw any living thing so deadly, so pale, emaciated, and unearthly.'

[1] At Bentley Priory, Stanmore. (J. F.)

[2] The late Duke of Abercorn, (J. F.)

[3] Lady Morgan afterwards. (J. F.)

of her works and fond of talking of herself, I don't think her affected. She is extremely good-humoured, likes to talk nonsense, loves to have men quiz her, and is never affronted at being laughed at. Indeed I think her *sensibly* good-humoured, for I take fools upon an average to be cross and touchy. She does anything to make society agreeable, always ready to dance, play, or sing, none of which she does well. She is, I believe, a very good-hearted, amiable person, very kind to her relations, and I expected she would speak nothing but Greek and Latin; instead she never obtrudes pedantry upon one and never speaks of wise things, which is quite proper, as I take it she does not understand them the least. She has not a better head than thousands of people who never thought of writing a novel. As for her person, I thought her pretty at first, and now I think her frightful. She has a great general look of Mrs. Robert Campbell, and I don't believe is above an inch taller—a great deal fairer, and her eyes would be very pretty if they did not squint *à faire dresser les cheveux.* Her figure is not the better of being obtrusively crooked, and her head is ornamented with a frightfully ill-cut crop; and now I will dismiss the subject. I'll tell you who I have fallen desperately in love with—Lady Harriet Leveson. She was a daughter of the Duke of Devonshire, and was lately married to Lord Granville Leveson-Gower.[1] This passion of mine is amazingly strong, though I have only met with her three times. The first night I was introduced to her I was in such a state of distraction of mind that I did not know whether I was standing on my head or my heels. I was to have gone to a ball at the Duchess of Gordon's, but as we went first to a party at the Princess's,[2] Lady Charlotte could not go, and so she insisted upon sending me from Kensington. . . . Lord John intends to depart for Hampshire in a fortnight, and takes me to

[1] Miss Clavering's opinion agrees with a universal social tradition, fully borne out by the recent publication of Lady Granville's letters.

[2] The Princess of Wales. Lady Charlotte Campbell was in her household. (J. F.)

Southampton.   After staying there some time we go straight to Scotland, so I think I shall see you in less than a month from this time, which idea, believe me, gives me more pleasure than my engagement in London.   I have never been able to call on Mrs. Kinloch; first, because Lady Charlotte has no carriage, so that when we go out to walk it is for the good of our health, and we don't go into town at all, but walk for air and exercise in the park. I have only been twice in Lady Clavering's [1] house since I came.   Mrs. Kinloch came to see us yesterday morning, and I was really happy to see her; she looked very well and put me very much in mind of you.   She told me you were rather angry at my not writing, but I hope this letter will, not that it deserves it from its own merits, but hopes it from your clemency, and in this trust believe me most truly

Your sincerely affectionate friend,

CHARLOTTE.

FROM LORD JOHN CAMPBELL TO JAMES FERRIER, ESQ.

Ardencaple : October 16, 1812.

My dear Sir,—Although I would by no means have given you the trouble of coming so far as Inveraray upon account of my election, yet if you would come for the sake of the ball, and bring Miss Ferrier with you, it would give us all much pleasure.   If you consent to this, send me a line directed to Inveraray, where I go on Sunday, and I will prepare rooms for you in the Castle.

I am, yours very sincerely,

J. D. CAMPBELL.

MISS CLAVERING TO S. E. F.

Bywell Hall [2] : December 20 [1812?]

My dear Friend,—I was sorry for the anxiety that stopped your lucubrations so suddenly that I hope by this

---

[1] Daughter of John de Gallais Count de la Sable of Anjou, married, 1791, Sir Thomas Clavering, Bart. (J. F.)

[2] Where her uncle, Mr. Charles Clavering, lived in Northumberland.

time your father has recovered ; you know that, painful as the gout is, it secures from all other disorders, and is hardly ever a dangerous thing. I should like to get a word from you to say that you are relieved from your anxieties ; if you write immediately I should get your letter, as I don't expect to leave this till the end of the week. The last time I heard from Lord John he told me that his business would be concluded as yesterday, but that, as Lord Frederick [1] had invited him to Coombank,[2] he did not think it proper to offend the old gentleman by a refusal, therefore he will delay his departure for three or five days ; but he is to write again to tell me the day. Do you not remember you said he would not be back till July !! I had an immense packet from Lady C. the other day, which I confess rather disappointed me, for I expected volumes of new compositions, and on opening it what should it prove but your book returned, so I shall keep it safe till I see you. She was profuse in its praises, and so was Mamie,[3] who said she was particularly taken with Lady Juliana's brother, he was so like the Duke.[4] Lady C. said she had read it all deliberately and critically, and pronounced it *capital*, with a dash under it. Lady C. begs that in your enumerations of Lady Olivia's peccadilloes you will omit waltzes. I back the request, and agree with her in thinking that people will immediately say she wrote it, and was Quixotising her own character. You may say she danced quadrilles in London if you choose. There were quadrilles, otherwise called cotillons formed entirely of married women of quality, in London when I was there. A few days after, I got another parcel, five times as big, and was all on the alert to open it, when, to my infinite mortification, what should present itself but 'Self-Indulgence !!'[5] She wrote me that Mrs. Damer had

---

Another letter, p. 251, shows that Miss Clavering was there in December 1812. (J. F.)

[1] His uncle. (J. F.)

[2] In Kent. (J. F.)

[3] Mlle. de la Chaux, Governess to Lady Charlotte's children. (J. F.)

[4] George, sixth Duke of Argyll. (J. F.)

[5] A novel by Lady C. Campbell. It is of this book that Kirkpatrick Sharpe, writing to Miss Mure says

charged her with the fact of being its mother, had begged
and entreated that she would correct its inaccuracies to
make it fit for a second edition, which she declared would
soon be called for, and made her sit down and read it out
in a slow audible voice, marking with a pencil where it
should be corrected and amended. Well, then, this copy
Lady C. sends me to make the alterations . . . but I
don't mind so much, as I am not obliged to look out for
faults but those that are marked with a pencil . . . Who
do you think we expect to-day? No less a personage than
Rawdon.[1] I am going away to meet him as soon as I am
done scribbling. I have not written a syllable of composition since I came here. At first I used to work, and Miss
Adair read to me ; so now we have no reading, as we have
a visitor in the house, with whom I sit from morning till
night, and never leave her for an instant. I don't mean
that I sit with my hands before me, but yet she makes me
dawdle a little, and I have not a moment to read or write.
During the time I did read I am sorry to say it was
nothing but nonsense. I have been purifying my mind
with Beaumont and Fletcher's plays. They are not so
harmonious in versification as Massinger, less absurd and
inconsistent in plan and character, though enough so, and
pretty near as improper. The play of 'Philaster' is very
beautiful, and there's many other pretty things, and some
funny ones. I am improved a little in seal manufacturings,
but I have not been able to procure more than five or six
impressions. I am charming well again, as the man says
in the caricature. I have not been in such glorious health
and spirits since I was a little girl. I hope I shall not lose
the latter, but they are very slippery untenable goods . . .
I am going to trouble you with a very impertinent concern,
but necessity forces me. Will you ask Mr. John Ferrier
to send me ten of Lady Augusta Clavering's good pounds

(vol. ii. p. 45): 'I have read your
novel, or Miss Clavering's, or Lady
Charlotte's, for to all these ladies it

hath been attributed.' (J. F.)
  [1] Her brother, Rawdon Clavering.
(J. F.)

I

sterling? She told me I might draw on her, and I could not bear writing to him; it looks so impertinent to say to anybody give me some money, and I have nothing more to say to you. Good-bye. Will you send them me directly, that I may get them before I leave this place? You can ask Bessie to get me a frank from Mr. Drummond. Adieu, my dear Susan,

Believe me your most affectionate

CHARLOTTE.

MISS CLAVERING TO S. E. F.

May 10, 1813.

My dear Susan,—I received the box only yesterday, yet, strange as it may appear, and contrary to my natural ferocity, I did not feel one emotion of the rage which you seem to lay your account of. Indeed I never suspected that the fault or the misfortune lay with you, but attributed it to delays of the carriers. I, at least, sent word to the innkeeperess at Dumbarton to deliver up my property if she had it, and the box forthwith made its appearance. I like the bonnet very much, and am exceedingly obliged to you for the seals. They were perfect, except two that were cracked through and through, and those luckily I had before—the Dumbarton Castle one and the warrior. You quiz me monstrously about my party-coloured garments, but I am not quite so bad as you imagine, as the article which was to be allied to the lustre you sent is of the same colour, only with stripes of pink intermixed. I am distressed to the utmost degree, and my feelings deeply wounded by the immensity of trouble you have had trotting after that bonnet for me, and I know not what remuneration to make unto you for your expenditure of time and patience in that cause, not to mention the wearing out of your boots, and feel all I can do is to assure you in the name of my head, feet, and hands that they are ever your humble servants to command. We were to have gone to Sir M. Stewart's yesterday, but they were engaged from home and could not receive us. What put it into your head that I was going to meet my sailor friend there ?[1] He is Lord Keith's flag-lieutenant, and has been this long time at Plymouth. The ferocity of my nature you have also overrated, when you supposed that I should behold with such fury the mutilation of my MS ; certainly if you had discarded it altogether I had no right or reason to complain, as the story was constructed by you, and I know very well you only suffer my little interpolations out of good nature not wholly to discard my labours from the concern, having been intended to be a joint one. You need not be afraid but what I shall think your alterations always improvements, and I had a thousand times rather copy out your works than my own.[2] As to the part in which you wish to have Lady Ju set up against the duchess, I think there is no need of much of that, because it can bring about no event and will not further display Lady Ju's character, that the vol. will be enormous at any rate, and that the succeeding ones will treat of the daughters. I don't like those high life conversations ; they are a sort of thing by consent handed down from generation to generation in novels, but have little or no groundwork in truth ; and the first part of the book will please because the scenes are original in a book and taken from nature. These you now wish to add could at best but amuse by putting one in mind of other novels not by recalling to anybody what they ever saw or heard in real life. What you have written I like very well except the speech of the Duchess of M., which is the style of conversation of duchesses only in novels. Far from giving occasion to describe character, I know nothing more insipid or uniform than fashionable manners and conversation, and to attribute designs to them from their

---

[1] Her cousin, Lord Napier.

[2] Miss Clavering's share in the work as it stands is 'The History of Mrs. Douglas' in Chapter XIV. The retention of a separate heading rather suggests that Miss Ferrier wished to see it distinctly ear-marked.

conduct is ninety-nine times out of a hundred quite a mistake. These polished individuals, smoothed down by continual jostling and *propinquity*, have not the characteristic traits that fit them to be drawn, and a true picture of the fashionable society of London would be very dull. Miss Edgeworth fails in this, even the personages too plainly move *à ressorts* worked by the author. They go through their evolutions like puppets, and their affectation sits awkwardly on them, and one sees it is done half by guess, half by memory, and greatly by imagination. Will you have patience to hear my other remark, which is that I disapprove very decidedly of Frenchifying Lady Ju's conversation ? It puts me in mind of plays and novels innumerable, though I cannot exactly designate them, and does not the least paint real life to me. It is not, nor has been, I'll answer for it, the least the mode this century (I cannot answer for the last), and it looks more like an affectation in the author than the personage he draws ; then they are always ill spelt, and readers are so ill-natured they would prefer quizzing the author to laying the blame on the printer. Now I have a doubt to propose. Is it allowable to write of events which must happen at a time yet to come ? Because you lay the mother's history, as I conjecture, in about this last seven or eight years, then the daughter's history to the end of the book will reach at least nineteen years beyond. This does not shock me in the least, but I don't know what other people might say to it, as it has no parallel, and I merely mention it in case it did not strike you. Your conclusion is without the least shadow of doubt immeasurably superior to mine. I don't, however, much like General Cameron being so vulgar, as I had figured him a contrast to Henry's natural relations, a man of the world, and a remarkably well-bred stern officer. He, however, appears so little on the stage that it is no great matter. I agree with you that the *page* may have a fine effect in the second volume, and will do much better where one enlarges more. I like the idea of the twin daughter being worse than her mother—she ought to be full of whimsies, and have engrafted on her mother's character more *firmness* and *stamina*, which in that style of education will not fail of completing the badness of her disposition, as she will then be deceitful as well as frivolous, passionate as well as humorsome, tyrannical as well as forward, proud and designing as well as vain and affected. I don't see any other way of the amiable cousins escaping the infection, except by making them totally neglected by Lady Ju, and having a capital governess who shall also be by ways of guiding Lady Ju's daughter, who will always have her own ways, and merely pick up a smattering of learning (she may be excessively quick) by fits and starts, for the pleasure of surpassing and eclipsing her cousin. Tell me if you wish me to wait till the first volume is copied out ; or whether you will begin it soon, and whether I am to do any of it ? This is the most diabolical paper to write on, it puts me in a fury ; it is so rough it blunts all the pens, and so greasy that I cannot get my words made intelligible, hang it. I should like amazingly to see that same ' Pride and Prejudice ' which everybody dins my ears with. Hannah [1] likes it excessively, only she says the heroine's a little vulgar. I should like to have seen Douglas enacted. I dare say Margaret Fletcher [2] would be a famous actress ; indeed, her mother looks as if she was cut out for it. There is nothing in the world I should so much like to do as to act a play, though I am morally convinced I should do it detestably. I don't believe a word about Miss B—— starving her brother and sister. Do tell me if you are to have a country house near Edinburgh or not ; you will be wishing by-and-bye to bask in the shade, though at present there's no basking desirable but upon the hearthrug. The east winds have of late attacked us with greater fury than I ever experienced

[1] Miss Mackenzie, daughter of the ' Man of Feeling.' (J. F.)
[2] Married afterwards Dr. Davy, brother to Sir Humphry ; Miss Clavering married her brother, Mr. Miles Fletcher. (J. F.

since I have lived here [1]; it is as cold as winter; we had one warm day and all the rest hurricanes. I am sorry to hear the Duchess's child has vaded away, as they say in Old English. My health has never mended much, only I'm tired swilling camomile tea and sipping antimonial wine, which will not make me sick though I were to go down on my knees to it. I never have an appetite, and I have no other variety but from headaches to squeamishness and back again. I wish you could send me some drugs when Lord John comes down. One of my symptoms is having the blue devils, than which nothing appears to me more proper and reasonable, notwithstanding that I often repeat to myself the words of my beloved poet:

> The moments past, if thou art wise, retrieve
> With pleasant memory of the bliss they gave.
> The present hours in present mirth employ,
> And bribe the future with the hopes of joy.

You may lay them up in your understanding box for your own use. And now adieu. I hope you will write speedily, and believe me, ever yours entirely,

C. C.

Do you wish that I should send payment for the things?

S. E. F. TO MRS. CONNELL

George Street : Saturday, December 5, 1812.

My dear Janet,—I should have written before now to acknowledge the safe arrival of the box of apples, but having nothing but my poor thanks to express I was rather averse to making you pay postage for them, so gladly avail myself of this opportunity of doing it. The apples arrived in the best possible condition, and I have almost lived upon them for the last eight days without seeming to make any diminution in the quantity, which is indeed enormous. I think you must have sent me the whole produce of the garden. There was not above half a dozen

[1] At Ardencaple. (J. F.)

of them spoilt, and the rest were in perfect preservation, and most excellent of their several kinds. I had a visit yesterday from Miss Farquharson to consult me about a cloak, that it seems you have been corresponding about, and whose fate depends on my fiat. She has sent it to me to look at, and I certainly think it so cheap, and she seems so anxious about your taking it, that I have given my assent, so I hope you will not disapprove. I understand there is also a bonnet, but that I have not seen. I was glad to hear, by Miss Morrison's letter, that you are in good health, as I was afraid this dreadful weather would have quite overset you.

. . . I never remember anything half so bad in all the variety of wretchedness which this climate is given to. It is a fortnight to-day since I have been watching a *fair* opening to get to the old town, but in vain. In that time I have only been able to get out twice, and the streets were in such a pickle that I was splashed up to the shoulders, even on the pavements. The only change we have is from mist to rain and from rain to mist; our only comfort is that any change *must* be for the better. I pity those who are obliged to be exposed to such noxious elements. For my part I should think it sinful to repine, having a good comfortable fireside to sit by, and though I feel considerably stupefied for want of air and exercise, yet I have every reason to be thankful for the good health I enjoy. . There is a great deal of sickness here at present. I scarce know a family some part of which is not laid up. Archy's children have been very ill of an influenza, but are now well again. She had it, too, she said, but Archy himself escaped and is wonderfully well, walking about as usual, though he still looks thin and pale. Walter has been complaining of rheumatism for some days, but otherwise is better than usual, which is surprising, considering the sedentary and laborious life he leads at the desk from 9 in the morning till 10 at night, with only the intermission of an hour for dinner. I have said everything that was possible to him on the *wickedness* of sacrificing himself in that manner, but in vain ; and he is of such an anxious temper, that if he was not busy he would be fretting or pining, which would be still worse. I do not hear a word of news as I see nobody, and am as much out of the world as if I was a hundred miles from a town, instead of living in the heart of one. The only thing in the matrimonial way that has caused any sensation lately was the marriage of a daughter of Dewar's to a son of the *Earl of Winterton's*.[1] She is remarkably pretty and was greatly admired here. . . . Miss Clavering was here for a few days lately with Lord John, on her way to visit her uncle in Northumberland.[2] Lord J. was very ill while here, and she has been dangerously ill since she left this, having carried away with her an Edinburgh cold as a travelling companion, but happily she has got the better of it. I heard from Lady Charlotte t'other day *from bed*, where she was laid up with a severe cold she had caught in her gardening operations, for she is grown a perfect *hedger and ditcher*, and works an hour every day in her garden with her own hands, which she thought did her a great deal of good, and in dry weather I dare say it did, but the season is now too far advanced for outdoor work— at least for ladies. I hear the fashionable cure for nervous disorders now is *Rosemary Tea*. Several people here have been recommended to take it ; amongst others, Mr. Jeffrey, the reviewer, who is afflicted with the most violent palpitations, and has hitherto tried everything in vain. Annie Mure was smitten with a sort of blindness last summer . . . was blistered, bathed and bled to no purpose ; but the medical people, thinking it must be nervous, ordered her Rosemary tea, and she is now perfectly cured. It should be drunk in place of other tea to breakfast and in the afternoon ; and as the experiment is neither troublesome nor expensive, it is surely worth trying.

[1] Mr. James Dewar, S. Edinburgh. (J. F.)

[2] Mr. Charles Clavering ; he married Miss Adair, sister of Lady Barrington and aunt of the Miss Adair so often alluded to. (J. F.)

S. E. F. TO MISS CLAVERING

'Twas when the seas were roaring
  With hollow blasts of wind,
A damsel sat by the fireside poring
  Till she was almost blind.

Such is the situation—poetical, geographical, atmospherical, intellectual, and optical of the damsel who now addresses you ; and these lines, descriptive of her unhappy circumstances, may prove no less instructive to posterity than they are interesting to present times. As I find my correspondence is carefully preserved by you, I flatter myself it is with the view of being one day presented to the public in twelve handsome octavo volumes, embellished with a portrait of the authoress, and enriched with a facsimile of her handwriting. Having this hope before my eyes, I carefully abstain from the vulgar practice of dating my letter, aware how greatly uncertainty adds to interest.

With regard to this letter, my future biographer will say (for my Life must go along with my head and hand): ' It has been found impossible to fix any precise date ; all we can ascertain is that it must have been written somewhere in the vicinity of the sea during very tempestuous weather, and we also learn that the author was much addicted to reading by the fireside (probably with her toes on the fender), and that her sight was materially affected by this unremitting attention to her studies. Of the nature of these studies it would be presumptuous to hazard a guess. We certainly cannot deny what has been alleged, that " Jack the Giant Killer " at this time formed a part of her course of reading, but it is not probable a mind such as our author's could take much delight in such scenes of rapine and bloodshed ! ' O me, how wearied I am of walking upon stilts, and how glad I am to get down to my very stocking soles ! I only mounted to try and please you, as you are not satisfied with me, it seems, in my ordinary dimensions. Forgetting how much Time has bent me with his iron hand, you want me to be as tall and as straight as in the days of my prime; alas! my dear Chatty, my mind as well as my body has long been past playing antics, so don't quarrel with me because 'sprightly folly no longer wantons in my lines, and dull serenity becalms my page.' Nobody ever had less to make them gay that had nothing to make them wretched than I have; if I was thoroughly good I suppose I ought to be excessively happy; but as Waverley says of your country :—

> There's nought in the Highlands but syboes [1] and leeks,
> And lang-legged callants wanting the breeks, &c.[2]
>
> There's nought to be seen here but mountains and heath,
> And lang-backed lassies wanting the teeth, &c.

N.B.—This is quite matter of fact, except that there is no heath in sight; and the girls have got bran new buck teeth, which they are always showing, like me; and as I hate to be imitated, I'm going to have all mine pulled out and a handsome transparency of Mount Vesuvius put in their place. I'm infinitely obliged by your invitation; this place is quite *handy* for a trip to Greenock, as there are vessels sailing every day for Liverpool, and from thence I could be at no loss to get myself a berth; but as I have just half-a-crown in the world, I suppose I would have to work my passage; seriously, I can only say I would rather be with you than anywhere I know at present. You may well say we have no comfort in each other in town, but from the nature of things it cannot be otherwise, as you have your ways and I have mine; but in the country we could *blend our beings* together, and go on vastly well. As to the 'Chiefs of Glenfern' I shall say nothing till you have read it, and then I shall expect a candid opinion from you. I cannot offer to send it to you, as I have no copy

---

[1] Scotch for onions. (J. F.)
[2] *Waverley*, it will be remembered, was published in 1814. This helps to date this letter.

for myself, but I hope you will contrive to satisfy your curiosity some way or other. I was delighted with your account of Lord John [Campbell]. I had had a bad dream about him, which made me very apprehensive. I wish he would go and winter in Italy, however, and take you with him to nurse him. If Lady Charlotte comes, how enchanting that will be; but I fear nothing but an earthquake will roll her hitherward. I stood the Quake very well; what did you do? Some ladies, I saw in the papers, were papering their hair at the time. I rather think my curls must have been compleated, but I never could say positively whether I must have been tying my night-cap or buttoning the collar of my night-gown. My brother Walter is away to Holland; I'm afraid he'll never come back. When we who dwell on mountain tops can hardly keep our heads above water, what must it be in such Puddock Land? Not but what I would go to the Antipodes to shift the scene a little and see something strange and new, for truly this side of the world is become prodigiously *flat*, and I'm very weary, Miss Clavering, and do nothing but send forth clandestine groans. I'm reading heaps of books, but they tell nothing but the truth, and I know it already; but if you could send me a batch of lies I should take it very well of you, and they would do me a deal of good; they would be like foxglove to the dropsy, and arsenic to the ague. I would try my hand myself, but that I know you are very incredulous and wouldn't believe me, though I were to swear that my father wore a pink silk coat and bagwig, and that I rouged and danced waltzes with my brother-in-law's black servant. Ah prop oh! [*sic*] did you ever receive my communications on that subject, i.e. waltzing, and was it not as plain as print where they came from? I desire you will write instantly and tell me how you like the latitude and longitude of my lucubrations. I mean to cover this page down to the very ground, that you may have no white paper to cast in my teeth. I don't know what to put upon it, but as I began in poetry I scorn to end in prose, so I bid you adieu, as I am going to blow my nose.

S. E. F. TO MRS. CONNELL

Montpelier[1] : Friday, 7th.

My dear Janet,—Before I left town I was so poorly I had no spirit to write to anybody, but as usual the change has had a good effect, and though I don't reckon myself quite well, I am certainly much better than I was. We had not much advantage in weather at the time of our moving, for I scarcely recollect such storms of wind as were at that time ; but *country wind* is but a slight annoyance, it is only *town airs* that are to be accounted amongst the miseries of life. I walked in yesterday to try to arrange my effects, which I had left very much to the mercy of Betty Horn.[2] After that I made some sick visits, inquired for your friend Betty, who is better, but still confined to her chamber. Saw Miss Combie,[3] who is also convalescent, but looks much more like death than matrimony. Indeed, I think everybody looks sick and dying at present. Miss Clavering is come to town very *spectreish*, and living upon camphor julep, and tonic drops for her nerves. For my part I have entirely lost faith in physic and *almost* in physicians, but that is the result of sad experience. Except of diseases I have no knowledge of anything that has been going on in Edinburgh, as we have passed this winter even in a quieter manner than usual, though that seems quite unnecessary ; but I cannot say I have any wish that it should be otherwise, as I could not submit to lead a *gay life* unless I was very *strong* and very *rich*. Having no prospect of ever being either, I am satisfied with such enjoyments as my own fireside offers in winter and my *elegant* flower-garden in summer. I am now very busy labouring in that department, having the whole work of it

---

[1] An old house near Morningside, Edinburgh, which Mr. Ferrier had for the summer. (J. F.)

[2] A servant. (J. F.)

[3] Miss Campbell, of Combie ; she married, in 1815, Mr. Campbell, of Sonachan. (J. F.)

to perform with my own hands, unless some of my friends come to my assistance. I have told Helen that I must have a day's work out of her, and Miss Clavering has promised me another, so I hope I shall get it accomplished without the aid of man. All my sedentary employments are completely at a stand. I never *sew* (except in my garden), scarcely ever put pen to paper, and have not read anything fit to be named since 'Guy Mannering.' I dare say you will be much delighted with that performance, as it seems to have given unbounded pleasure to everybody but me ; but I do not like it half so well as 'Waverley,' though I dare say it is a work of greater power. I am happy you like 'Discipline,'[1] but you have mistaken me in thinking I meant it to be returned, as it was intended as a small addition to your library, being one of the very few novels I think fit for family use. I must leave it to Mrs. F.[2] to give you any news that are going. For my part I hear nothing but the cackling of hens and the routing of the cow, who, by-the-bye, is to be *confined* in a few days, an event which will excite no slight sensation in the family, I assure you. I have not heard from London or Stirling for a great while, but, like you, I have become a very lazy correspondent, and have therefore no right to find fault. Remember me affectionately to Mr. C. and the youngsters, and believe me to be

Ever affectionately yours,

S. E. F.

S. E. F. TO MRS. CONNELL

Montpelier : October 12, 1815.

My dear Janet,—You would hear from Walter [her brother] of our safe arrival at home atfer all our weary wanderings, and since my return I have been as busy as I can be, which, I believe, is being about a hundredth

---

[1] By Mrs. Brunton. It appeared in 1814. (J. F.)

[2] Mrs. John Ferrier, sister of Professor Wilson and remarkable for her beauty. She was mother of the late Professor Ferrier, of St. Andrews, N.B. She died at 12 York Place, Edinburgh in January 1833. (J. F.)

part as active as other people. Had I prolonged our absence, I don't suppose we should have got into our own house [1] this winter, as it is not yet ready for us. I've done nothing but run after masons, painters, and upholsterers ever since I came home. This carries a great sound with it, and you'll naturally conclude that I'm not only painting and new furnishing the house from top to toe, but that I've been pulling it down and building it up again. The upholstery is merely making up the drawing-room curtains anew, but, trifling as these matters are, the workpeople here are so slow and so stupid there is no coming either to an understanding or a finishing with them. I believe my father would not be sorry for an excuse to remain here till the meeting of the Session, but I wish to be in earlier on account of the Festival and the preachings, not that I'm at all clear of attending the former, as it is expected that even the morning performances will be extremely crowded, and in that case I certainly shall not run the risk of being laid up for the winter ; but if they are moderately attended I'm in hopes I shall get to one, which would probably satisfy me. Everybody agrees that it will be the grandest thing that ever was seen or heard throughout the kingdom. I'm certain it would do *me* more good to hear fine sacred music than to listen to fifty sermons. I therefore consider it a *religious duty*, and as you are not much in the way of the Church, I think you are bound to be forthcoming at the Festival. . . . I hope you will write and tell me that you are coming, and what day. It begins on the 31st, and you ought to arrive some days before, that your thoughts may be composed for the occasion. Of course Anne will accompany you, leaving Helen [2] at the head of the government. I hear she is now fairly *come out.* James Walker [3] told me he had danced with her at a circuit ball, and I hear she has since been figuring off

---

[1] No. 25 George Street, Edinburgh, where Mr. Ferrier lived from 1784 till his death, 1829. (J. F.)

[2] Mrs. Connell's daughters. (J. F.)
[3] Of Dalry. (J. F.)

with that indefatigable old cow. Will nobody put that creature to death? I see a flaming account of your Dumfries doings in the papers. Helen will be exulting in the splendours of her darling city; many a dispute we used to have on that subject, but she would have the best of the argument at present. I heard from Helen [1] yesterday, after a very long silence. Her health, she says, is now very good. I expect Jane will be in to the Festival, as it won't be like her to absent herself from so remarkable a spectacle. I was very much delighted with my visit to the Castle [2]; it is really a most agreeable residence, and the children quite delightful. . . . Miss Clavering writes me that the Duchess of Argyll is again in the way of providing an heir. I trust she will be more successful than on former occasions. Tell Jane I saw Miss Connell two days ago in good health. My father was much amused at the idea of your wanting my assistance to expel G. C.,[3] and indeed I had enough of business of the same sort upon hand at *Spitcaithley*.[4] Remember me affectionately to Mr. C. and the girls, and believe me to be affectionately yours.

Friday evening.—I had no opportunity of sending this to town to-day, and upon Walter's coming out to dinner he told me he had this morning a letter from Mr. C. mentioning that you and Anne would come to pay us a visit, which makes me very happy indeed. We shall be in town by the 27th I expect, but if you can come sooner, let me know, as a day or two is of no consequence to us. Everything I find will be ready for us in the course of next week.

S. E. F. TO MISS CLAVERING (1816)

What a cruel Christian you are thus to heap coals of fire upon my poor head, already hot enough, God knows. . . .

---

[1] Mrs. Kinloch. (J. F.)

[2] Stirling. (J. F.)

[3] G. C. stands for George Chalmer, brother of the 'Stag.' (J. F.)

[4] Miss Ferrier's jocular name for Pitkaithly, a place in Perthshire with mineral waters. (J. F.)

Your letter cut me to the heart. As for your drawing, it is really exquisite, and I should have admired it had it been the work of my bitterest foe ; but as the freewill offering of a friend, I value it beyond its weight in gold, or its size in fine gold. Truly and seriously, I have received many an expensive present that did not afford me half the gratification of your little etching. You know I don't flatter, so you may believe me when I assure you you have conferred a very great pleasure upon me. I showed it to the Mackenzies,[1] and they all fell into convulsions the moment they clapt their eyes upon it, and Hannah's visage became dimmed with 'pale ire, envy, and despair'; so for the sake of her health and complexion I left it with her for a day and a night, which was a great sacrifice on my part, as I have not half explored its wonders yet. I have not climbed up to the Castle above fifty times, nor sat under the trees for more than half an hour, morning and evening. It looks like one of the impossible tasks the cruel Grognon would have imposed upon the beautiful Princess Graciosa, and I'm in hopes you have a Prince Percinet, who did it all for you with a stroke of his wand. I never beheld such human touches, so almost invisibly fine and yet so firm and expressive. Bessie Mure will be filling herself with treasures ; but she's a scrub, and won't give me any, for which I mean to hate her some day. I dare say Mr. Jenkinson[2] and she draw very well together. I should like to see a joint production of theirs.

 . . . . . I have been reading ' Emma,'[3] which is excellent ; there is no story whatever, and the heroine is no better than other people ; but the characters are all so true to life, and the style so piquant, that it does not require the adventitious aids of mystery and adventure. I have also read M. Simeon's ' Tour Through Britain,' a compilation

---

[1] Family of H. Mackenzie, ' The Man of Feeling.' (J. F.)

[2] Afterwards Sir C. Jenkinson ; he married a Miss Campbell, of Shawfield. (J. F.)

[3] Published in 1816.

of old newspapers, travellers' guides, Joe Miller jests
impertinent gossip, and vulgar scurrility, all tacked together
in the most grating, disjointed style that sets one's teeth on
edge, and makes them feel as if they were trotting on the
back of a donkey.   His account of Inveraray is that it contains some very ugly old-fashioned tapestry and coloured
prints in the very worst taste, and that the trees are
pyramids stuck upon *pivots*.   Glencoe he describes as
having fine steps with a *green carpet* spread upon them,
that it is well *swept*, and free from litters.   Even a chamber-
maid would have scorned such figures of speech upon such
an occasion.   The nightingale, he says, sings in a vulgar
manner ; he quizzes Shakespeare, condemns Raphael, and
abuses Milton—but you must read the book and the copy,
if you can get it, enriched with my marginal notes.
Modest ! . . .

I have not heard from Lady Charlotte since she came
home, and I can't write to her for want of a frank, so
continue to tell me all you know of her.   I can tell you
nothing of what's going on in this dull town, as I seldom
stray beyond Prince's Street, where I sometimes go to sun
myself.   Yes, I went to the Catholic chapel one Sunday
with my spectacles on, that I might see all their *marches*
and whirligigs, and strange sights I saw as ever sour-faced
Presbyterian looked upon ; but the strangest part of the
whole was the lecture or discourse, which was a red-hot
exhortation to matrimony, and that from a Catholic priest
I was not prepared for.   He began by showing from
Scripture how highly marriage was approved of by Heaven,
and then proceeded in all the richness and energy of a
first-rate brogue to describe the joys of holy wedlock ; he
then changed his tune :

' An what's the raason ye are all such meeserable craaters
in the maareed staate ?   What's the raason of the scandalous
tumults, the dirty *squibbles* you're for ever engaged in ?
It's *becaaze* ye don't maary in the spirit, but for the graatifica-
tion of your *owne* vile bodees ; it's the Deevil himsaalf

that presides at your maarages. Now as for the dewtees of husbands and wives, I'll *taall* ye plainly what they are ———But for the dignity of this *chyer*, and for sake of deacency an modesty, I shall go no farder. An' as for you of both *saaxes* who are still single, an' of coorse *laading* vicious an' profligate lives, I advise you as a friend to alter your behaviour unless ye all wish to go to Hell.' But I beg pardon for the familiarity I have fallen into—allow me to turn over a new leaf.

S. E. F. TO MISS CLAVERING [1816?]

I relent; here is a letter for you, so dry your eyes, wipe your nose, and promise to be a good child, and I shall forgive you for this time. I'm sure you must be very sorry for having displeased me, for I know my friendship is the only thing in the world you care about; everything else compared to it is as cold porridge to turtle soup. Tell me how you have sped in the long night of my silence. Did not the sun appear to you like an old coal basket, and the heavens as a wet blanket? Was not the moon invisible to your weeping eyes? Were not the fields to your distempered fancy without verdure, and the boughs without blossoms? And did not the birds refuse to sing, and the lambs to dance? Did not the wind sometimes seem to sigh and the dogs to howl? All these and a thousand such prodigies I know have appeared to you in the long interval of my silence; but now the spell is broken, and all these fearful visions will vanish; you will see the sun break out as yellow as your hair, and the moon shine as white as your hand; the fields will grow as green as grass in December, and the birds will dance waltzes all the way before you from the post-office; you will taste of five more dishes at dinner to testify your joy, and you will toss off an additional glass of ale in honour of every sentence I shall indite. You would hear how Lady Charlotte[1] had

---

[1] Lady Charlotte Campbell. (J. F.)

tarried in this place ten days,[1] but I got very little good of
her. She was so *cherché* and *recherché*. She dined with
me one day, however, and had John Wilson to show off
with, and there arose a question whether a woman of a
right way of thinking would not rather be stabbed as
kicked by her husband (observe this burn hole, Miss, it is
a sure sign that either you or I are going to be married;
but keep that to yourself, and excuse this parenthesis,
which, indeed, is rather too long, but I hope you have not
such an antipathy to them as Dean Swift had; he, honest
man! could not abide the sight of them, which was
certainly a prejudice on his part; for mine, I think there
are worse things in the world than parentheses). But to
return to where I was (which, indeed, is not such an easy
matter, as I must turn the page to see where I left off; it
was at the burnt hole, and here I am just coming upon
another, which looks as if we were *both* going to be wed; I
wonder who it will be to!), I am for a stabber, but I
dare say you will be for putting up with a kicker. It was
talking of Lord Byron brought on the question. I maintain
there is but one crime a woman could never forgive in her
husband, and that is a *kicking*. Did you ever read anything so exquisite as the new canto of 'Childe Harold'?
It is enough to make a woman fly into the arms of a
tiger; nothing but a kick could ever have hardened her
heart against such genius.

. . . I thought Lady Charlotte looking more like herself, for she would dance and sing and go about and *talk
blue*, and that is hard work in this town. I think Miss
Campbell critically beautiful, and *nothing more*.[2] She has
all the Argyll elegance, but she wants their look of *esprit*;
and, in short, she is a person I don't think I could ever
feel much interest in. With Lady Cumming it is quite
otherwise. She may not be so handsome, but she is a
vast deal more attractive. She carries her heart in her

---

[1] Edinburgh. (J. F.)
[2] Afterwards Countess of Uxbridge; died 1828. (J. F.)

countenance, and it is so good a one that it makes one happy to look at it.[1] Mr. Wilson [2] remains faithful to your charms; he does not allow your cousin to be at all comparable to you, but he became so improper in the comparison that he really made it odious. Lady Charlotte seems more eat up with sentiment than ever; all *her* sayings and doings are delightful, to be sure, in her, but how odd they would seem in the ugly part of the creation! I hear your brother Douglas is in town, but he does not come near me, and I have not a genius for running after the men, *à la* Bessie, so I suppose I shall never cast sawt [salt] upon him. If you come to town this winter I hope you will come and visit me at the Tolbooth; I expect to be there very soon, having lost my purse containing near four pounds. I've some thoughts of trying a penny piece subscription, like Lord Cochrane, but I doubt if I could raise more than a shilling by it. What is your opinion of the extent of friendship in brass? I've read 'My Landlord's Tales,' and can't abide them; but that's my shame, not their fault, for they are excessively admired by all persons of taste, Bessie Mure amongst others. I thought my back would have broke at 'Old Mortality,' such bumping up and down behind dragoons, and such scolding, and such fighting, and such preaching. O, how my bones did ache! I trust it is unnecessary for me to say a syllable on the subject of a speedy answer, as I am sure your own feelings will point out to you the propriety of an instantaneous reply to your much injured and forgiving friend,

S. E. F.

The Grand Duke Nick o lass is arrived.

---

[1] Eldest daughter of Lady C. Campbell; married Sir Wm. Gordon Cumming, Bart., died 1842. The reference to her as Lady Cumming shows that the letter is later than September 11, 1815. (J. F.)

[2] 'Christopher North.' (J. F.)

MISS CLAVERING TO S. E. F.

Postmark : May 2, 1817, Wednesday.

My dear Susan,—I sincerely congratulate you upon your good luck in the sale of your brains, and most disinterestedly I do so, as you cannot suppose me mean enough ever to think for a moment of sharing the profit where I have not aided the labour.   What I have written is the only few pages that will be skipped,[1] and as for the time I have lost in writing what was fit only for the fire when it was done, it is ten to one I should have been wasting my time in something else that might have been equally profitless, so that it is not worth mentioning.   You are really in luck, and I should think you would not long hesitate in closing with such terms.[2]   As for myself, I could not positively engage never to look at you when the book was mentioned, but as there is no likelihood of my being near you at all that need not deter you.   Make haste and print it then, lest one of the Miss Edmonstones should die, as then I should think you would scarce venture for fear of being haunted.   I was glad to hear that you had got out to the country.   I think I know the house, but thought it was a school, which certainly would not suit you.   Is it rather an old-fashioned looking house with two stairs to go up to the door?   This unprecedented fine weather will make a new creature of you and will render your garden quite a paradise to you.[3]   Take care the boys on the links don't break your legs with their balls.   I think there has been only two showery days the whole month of April.   Did you ever get a message I sent you about money, by Bessie?   Upon looking over that letter just now, I think I can descry

---

[1] Note by Miss Ferrier. *History of Mrs. Douglas,* vol. i. subsequently altered and abridged.   (J. F.)

[2] The terms were not magnificent for *Marriage.*   She received 150*l.* from Mr. Blackwood.   (J. F.)

[3] Old Morningside House was the house old Mr. Ferrier and his daughter removed to every spring from Edinburgh; it still stands. (J. F.)

a sort of vague meaning as if you had got the money ; if so,
well and good. I owe you six shillings, which you shall
surely get somehow or other. I have never thanked you
for the 'Moral Waltzing,' which is very diverting. I suppose long ere this you have solaced yourself with 'Six
Weeks at Long's.' I have never seen it, and Sir William
told me it was not fit for a young lady to read ; however,
as I am an old one, I should certainly have ventured had it
come in my way.[1] I am convinced Miss Adair no more wrote
the 'White Cottage' than you did.[2] It is so absurd people
fancying that anybody would write the same kind of story
twice over. I think it very pretty indeed ; it is like a man's
writing. I do think I shall hasten to burn your last letter
as you mention something of looking out for a father for
your *bantling*, so I don't think it would be decent to let
anybody get a sight of such a letter! I am sorry to
hear Hannah Mackenzie is not looking well. . . . Poor
Bessie is very melancholy about her sister. This world
does, indeed, teem with woes of every description. Have
you seen the picture she has done of Rawdon ? He wrote
me he had had his last sitting, but carefully omitted saying
a single word upon the subject of the picture. Douglas
and he[3] are coming here the end of this month, for I believe
this is the 1st of May. I had rather they stayed where
they are, this will be terribly dull to them ; duller than
this letter, which I ought to make many apologies for. I
am really sorry to make you pay for it, but you desired

[1] Any one who has read *Six Weeks at Long's* will probably agree with 'Sir William's' opinion. It is written by Eaton Stannard Barrett, best known as the author of *The Heroine*. It is a mixture of extravagant and rather dull melodrama, with personal satire, sometimes amusing, always scurrilous. In the opening scene Lord Byron and Beau Brummel are introduced under the transparent pseudonyms of Lord Leander and Mr. Bellairs. The friends of the former ' hope that he will discard his cynicism and misanthropy, as he has already discarded his neckcloth.' That Lord Byron was the subject of revolting personal charges at the very outset of his career, is shown by the fact that he is here represented as drinking iced claret !

[2] After writing ' I,' she puts ' you ' over it, and says, 'After putting *I*, I thought you would imagine that was a get off, and meant that we had both written it, so I hereby testify I don't know who is the author.' The author was a Dr. Mower. (J. F.)

[3] Her brothers. (J. F.)

me to write, and I should certainly make myself gay and happy if I could, both for my own sake and yours.

Believe me, however,

Always your sincerely affectionate

CHARLOTTE.[1]

The following note was written after Miss Clavering became Mrs. Fletcher (1817), and endorsed by Miss Ferrier ' To be kept.'

Many thanks for the China, my dear Susan, which is very pretty and useful. As for the novel, I read it all before Mr. Fletcher came home yesterday, and I admire it more than I can express. You are improved even beyond my expectation, and Lady Emily is dazzling with her wit. Altogether it is perfectly amusing, and much of the old lady is excessively affecting, and absolutely made me blow my nose. Indeed, her character is particularly well drawn. Lord Lindores (I don't like his name) is well done, too, but I wish there was more of him and of the details of their wooing. Pray have you written any more, and is that the end of the second volume ? I am pining for the rest and to have the whole *dénouement*. I thought you, lazy woman, would have been still at your breakfast. As for me, I have been at mine these two days at half-past eight! I am afraid it will not be in my power to see you to-day ; I have so many places to go to, you cannot imagine ; however, if not to-day, certainly to-morrow, and probably early. Your messenger is horribly impatient. Farewell.

Ever your affectionate,

CHARLOTTE.

From one of the eminent guests whom Miss Ferrier met in the Campbell society came a word of warning against a career of letters. It is in the fitness of things that one of the most dismal and affected of literary masqueraders should have sought to silence the voice of a

---

[1] It was in this year that Miss Clavering became the wife of Mr. Miles Fletcher.

satirist, from whom dulness and pretence ever looked in vain for quarter. 'Monk' Lewis wrote thus :

I hear it rumoured that Miss F——r doth write novels, or is about writing one. I wish she would let such idle nonsense alone, for however great a respect I may entertain for her talents (which I do), I tremble lest she should fail in this bookmaking, and as a rule I have an aversion, a pity, and contempt for all female scribblers. The needle, not the pen, is the instrument they should handle, and the only one they ever use dexterously. I must except, however, their love-letters, which are sometimes full of pleasing conceit : but this is the only subject they should ever attempt to write about. The fact is, I am full of the subject, being at the present moment much enraged at Lady —— for having come out in the shape of a novel, and now hearing that Miss F——r is about to follow her bad example, I write in great perturbation of mind, and cannot think or speak of anything else.[1]

FROM GEORGE, DUKE OF ARGYLL TO S. E. F.

Inveraray Castle : December 19, 1817.

A thousand pardons, dear Miss Ferrier, for not answering your mermaid letter sooner. I leave it entirely to your taste whether my mermaid disports herself in the waves or combs her hair out on a rock, though I rather think her tail may oppose some difficulties to the sitting posture, but I particularly wish she may not have so *armorial* an appearance as the pattern seal has, nor do I like the *triple* end of her dorsal fin. If there is room, I should like the word *Georgy* on the seal. Forgive my giving you so much trouble.

Yours very truly,

ARGYLL.

Caroline desires her kindest love to you.

---

[1] From *Diary, illustrative of the Times of George IV.* M. G. Lewis was well known to both Miss Ferrier and Lady C. Campbell ; he used to visit at Inveraray, where Miss Ferrier was in the habit of meeting him in her young days. His doubts as to her novel writing were never determined, as he died in 1818, the year in which *Marriage* was published. (J. F.)

Wednesday evening.

Dear Miss Ferrier,—I regret missing you this morning, but perhaps I may find you in George Street to-morrow or Friday, before two o'clock, when I go to Lord Rosebery's. I brought some parcels for you, but I cannot take yours for Charlotte, as I am not going to Ardencaple for ages. I am going to Altyre [1] and many other places *a visiting*, so you had better send your Bonny *Dys* [2] by the coach. I can assure you I did not either touch the Bible or the flute, but I made all square and then came away.

Yours sincerely,

J. D. CAMPBELL.

The correspondence with Miss Clavering serves to let us into some of the secrets of Miss Ferrier's workshop An extract from a letter by a common friend carries our knowledge a little further. It shows how Miss Ferrier cast about for suitable material, and how deftly and appropriately she incorporated it when found. It serves, too, to throw some light on the embarrassments and fears which the secrecy of her authorship involved her in.

Before ' Marriage ' was published we find Miss Mure writing to Miss Clavering :

' Since I began this I have been out at Susan Ferrier's with Mary Campbell. Susan does not go to Gilsland till the twelfth. You remember the thing I had of my aunt's writing on the change of manners. Mr. Mackenzie once asked my leave to copy it, which I permitted, and it was a few days ago printed in a New Edinburgh Magazine, published by Constable. I don't think it was the thing to do it without my consent. I told Susan ; she was like to go into a fit, as all Mrs. Garshake's character and conversa-

---

[1] Where his niece, Lady Gordon Cumming, lived. (J. F.)

[2] Lord J., in a footnote, asks, ' Is that the way to spell Bessie Mure's language?' ' Bonny Dyes' is Scotch for ' Fine Things.' (J. F.)

tion turns on that theme. She advised me to prosecute him for damages and hire Mr. Jeffry for my lawyer' [1817].[1]

It remained for Miss Ferrier to find a publisher. The historian of the house of Blackwood, loyally anxious to do honour to the founder of it, has, I think, a little exaggerated his services to letters in this matter. She pictures Mr. Blackwood as a munificent patron taking by the hand a timid and distrustful young writer.[2]

No doubt Miss Ferrier's strenuous determination to remain unknown made it specially difficult for her to make terms.[3] But I think we may take it as certain that when Blackwood gave a hundred and fifty pounds for the copyright of 'Marriage' he was running no very hazardous venture. Miss Ferrier, too, had active friends in close contact with the literary world with whom her secret would have been safe, and some of whom indeed already knew it. It can hardly be said that Blackwood showed any exceptional insight in perceiving that if he failed to secure Miss Ferrier's work, a Scottish rival to Miss Burney might make the fortune of another publisher, or any peculiar enterprise or liberality in the measure which he took to prevent that calamity.

W. BLACKWOOD TO S. E. F.

Edinburgh : May 6, 1817.

Mr. Blackwood now returns the author the enclosed, which he has perused oftener than once with the highest delight. He feels not a little proud that such a writer should express a wish to receive any suggestions from him. The whole construction and execution of the work appear

---

[1] In 'Marriage' as published Mrs. Garshake becomes Mrs. Macshake.

[2] I shall have occasion again to dissent from Mrs. Oliphant's estimate of the relations between Miss Ferrier and Mr. Blackwood. I should be, indeed, sorry if my criticisms seemed to imply any disparagement of the book. It is enough praise of it, I think, to say that it does not need the favour to which it is fully entitled as the last work of its author. The Victorian age has produced better writers than Mrs. Oliphant, though none too many. It has, I venture to think, produced hardly any who succeed in the same way in establishing a claim on the goodwill, one might almost say on the personal friendship, of the reader.

[3] Some years later Miss Ferrier wrote thus : 'Secrecy at that time was all that I was anxious about, and so I paid the penalty of trusting entirely to the good faith of the publishers.'

to him so admirable, that it would almost be presumption in any one to offer corrections to such a writer. Mr. B. begs to assure the author that unmeaning compliment is the farthest from his thoughts, and he flatters himself that at no distant period he will have the high delight of assuring the author in person of the heartfelt sincerity of the opinions he has ventured to offer.

Mr. B. will not allow himself to think for one moment that there can be any *uncertainty* as to the work being completed. Not to mention his own deep disappointment, Mr. B. would almost consider it a crime if a work possessing so much interest and useful instruction were not given to the world.

The author is the only critic of whom Mr. B. is afraid, and after what he has said he anxiously hopes that this censor of the press will very speedily affix the *imprimatur.*

W. BLACKWOOD TO S. E. F.

Edinburgh : May 30, 1817.

Mr. Blackwood embraces this opportunity of returning the MS. to offer his warmest thanks to the author for the high enjoyment he has received from it. It is unnecessary for him to repeat how much he is flattered by his observations being considered as at all worthy of notice by one who is so far above his feeble praise, and who stands so little in need of criticism.

Mr. B. cannot forbear remarking how admirably the cold selfish character of Lady Juliana continues to be sustained, as well as the fine contrast afforded by the sensitive and feeling heart of her deserted daughter. Every one has felt in youth the glow of enthusiasm so well pourtrayed in Mary, and any one who has ever associated with the English of a certain class will at once recognise in Dr. Redgill the living portrait of hundreds, though never before hit off so well. The first paragraph of the second chapter is alike remarkable for its truth, beauty, and neatness.

Mr. B. hopes he will be excused for making these observations, which he has been tempted to make from the portion he now has before [him] being so small. If he had attempted to say what he felt on perusing the former part of the work, he fears he would have said too much for the author's patience, and at the same would not have been able to have done justice to his own feelings. He anxiously hopes the author will not lag, but finish the work with all convenient speed. When it suits the author's conveniency Mr. B. need but add how happy he will be to receive either a large or small portion of the MS.

W. BLACKWOOD TO S. E. F.

Edinburgh : August 7, 1817.

Madam,—I return you the enclosed with a thousand thanks for the very high delight I have had in perusing it. Mrs. Lennox's character is most interesting, and our old friends support their parts most admirably. You are quite in the true spirit at present, and I anxiously hope you will go on without doubt, let or hindrance. I am quite impatient that I should have it in my power to let others enjoy what I have enjoyed so much myself.

I am, madam,

Yours very respectfully,

W. BLACKWOOD.

W. BLACKWOOD TO S. E. F.

Edinburgh : December 10, 1817.

Madam,—I now 'return the two portions of MS. you lately favoured me with. As you proceed, I think you are still happier in your delineations. I have never read anything that gave me such strong impressions of real life. Your picture of the blind mother and her son is

most striking, but if I were to praise any part more than
another it would be the admirable way in which you have
hit off Lady Matilda &c., &c.   I anxiously hope you are
proceeding without let or hindrance, and that I shall very
soon have the pleasure of seeing the work fairly at press.

I am, madam

Your most obedient servant,

W. BLACKWOOD.

W. BLACKWOOD TO S. E. F.

Prince's Street : Tuesday, five o'clock.

Madam,—Mr. Mackenzie is in the highest degree
pleased with the second volume, so far as he has read, and
is anxious to see the remainder.   I now send you the last
portion I got, and I hope you will be able to give the
whole to Mr. M. to-night or to-morrow morning.

I am, madam,

Your most obedient servant,

W. BLACKWOOD.

W. BLACKWOOD TO S. E. F.

Prince's Street : Saturday.

Madam,—I am very sorry it will not be in my power,
as I intended, to call on you this evening, and I am likewise unfortunately engaged on Monday ; but if it would
answer you I would call on you on Monday betwixt ten
and eleven.   If I do not hear from you to the contrary I
shall therefore call at that time.

In the meantime I send you the whole of the first
volume fairly copied.   The printer tells me it would make
about 440 such pages as 'Tales of my Landlord,' 'Rob
Roy,' &c.   This, you will see, is nearly a hundred pages too
much.   I expect to have the remaining portion of the
MS. copied in a few days, when I will send you an exact
calculation of the extent of the whole.

The two chapters you last finished are, I think, excellent
and I wonder at you not being satisfied yourself. Continue

(as there is no doubt you will) with the same spirit, and success is certain.

> I am, madam,
> Your most obedient servant,
> W. BLACKWOOD.

I have addressed the packet to Mrs. Graham. Besides, there is none of my people who will suppose anything whatever.

I hope you will be able to give me on Monday a part of the MS. for the printers.

W. BLACKWOOD TO JOHN FERRIER, JUNIOR

Dear Sir,—Since we can now give a name to the work which we have so long had in hands, I beg to mention to you, on behalf of the author, the terms which I originally proposed to Mrs. General Graham.

I hereby offer for the copyright of 'Marriage,' a novel, one hundred and fifty pounds sterling. Booksellers commonly expect twelve months' credit, but I shall pay the money shortly after publication if you wish it.

Your answer in behalf of the author will close the transaction, and oblige,

> Dear sir,
> Yours truly,
> W. BLACKWOOD.

S. E. F. TO MISS WALKER

Newington House : 29th.

My dear Anne,—I was beginning to feel rather queer at you for your long silence, when yours arrived and put all my feelings into their right places. I could not answer it instantly because I was in the heat of my preparations to take possession of this chateau, which we did yesterday, and instead of unpacking my trunk I sit down to unpack myself to you. In the first place I must plead innocent to the lily white robes which seem to have given such offence. I was merely used as a tool in the matter ; my taste was not consulted, though my name has been used as a sanction. . . . At the same time I consider it not only as an act of charity but a positive duty in you to array yourself occasionally in costly raiment ; you not only encourage the industrious manufacturer by it, but you inflict upon yourself a severe penance and practise that highest of virtues, self-denial. Possibly, some people might object to view the wearing of white satin as any penance, but these must be voluptuous Catholics, who would shudder at a suit of sackcloth ; besides, penances, like other things, must depend on taste, and I've no doubt but that you would greatly prefer a good stout black hair cloth smock to being clothed *à la* lily. As to the watch, you, who can patronise painters, what is your objection to befriending watchmakers? Probably the making of your watch saved a family from starving, perhaps a man from hanging himself, or poisoning his wife, or braining his small family. In short, I defy any one to say that the purchase of your watch is not the best action you ever committed. I was very glad to leave town on any terms, as I found myself very poorly ; the warm weather had no other effect than that of weakening me, but I think I feel revived by the change already. My malady, however, is no better, and I see plainly there is but one remedy, and I must try to make up my mind to it, and trust when the time comes God will give me strength, both of mind and body, to bear His dispensation. I expect Mrs. Graham next for a few days, but I long very much for your return. However, the 10th is now so near that I shall try to wait patiently till then. This is a huge house, something quite out of our humble sphere, but at this season a large house is pleasant, and we have plenty of room for our friends ; the only drawback is the great distance and the disagreeable access from your quarter of the town. I am reading Mrs. Hamilton's 'Memoirs,'[1] which I think just readable and no more, but I have not read

---

[1] Authoress of the *Cottagers of Glenburnie.* (J. F.)

much of them. I saw H. Mackenzie[1] yesterday, and she says her sister writes from London that 'Marriage' is much admired and generally attributed to Walter Scott, but Hannah said her father had good reason to believe it was Miss Campbell of Monzie.[2] *Whose ever it is I have met with nothing that has interested me since!* I long for your allegory, I dare say it will be fine. I saw Helen yesterday in great preservation. Adieu, my dear Anne. Write to me and tell me when I shall see you. I'm very dull at present, so excuse me. My father is well and desires his remembrances.

Ever yours affectionately,
S. E. F.

S. E. F. TO MISS ANNE WALKER

Wednesday, 14th.

My dear Anne,—It is reversing the order of nature in me to write to you first, but as you are one of those eccentric bodies who observe no order yourself you will not be surprised at my deviation. I heard of your safe arrival yesterday from Helen, and that you were storming for letters, which is the cause of this one. She walked out in the rain and Julia[3] came for her in the carriage, seemingly quite well, so you must find some other legitimate object to trouble your head about, for she is no longer the least interesting, and I hear all is smooth at home, so you have nothing to do but to eat, drink, and be merry abroad. That is not so easy in this weather, and if you are living like me, in the midst of wet leaves, I dare say you'll feel it dull enough sometimes in spite of your teeth. I don't mean this in a Redgill sense, as I know your teeth are not the chief instruments of your pleasure. I've got nothing done

---

[1] Hannah Mackenzie, daughter of the 'Man of Feeling.' (J. F.)

[2] The cousin of Kirkpatrick Sharpe to whom he addressed unwontedly amiable letters, and whom he describes (vol. i. p. 196) as 'a staunch friend and the best monitor in the world.' His drawing of her represents a face and figure of great beauty. (J. F.)

[3] Afterwards Lady Hall, of Dunglass. (J. F.)

since I saw you, but I shall try to sketch a little some day soon, and I hope your pencil is not idle ; the merest scratches of yours have always some merit, so be doing. There has only been one good day since I saw you, and this place [1] swarmed like a bee-hive. Amongst others was Miss Moneypenny, who is fain to take up with Hannah Mackenzie in your absence. I wonder what I am to cover this white sheet with ; I don't think I have a blot yet, and you'll despise me if you get a clean letter, so I shall leave room for one ; it will both raise me in your estimation and give you something for your money, for I know nothing so grudging as to pay postage for white paper——that is an imposition I must say you scorn to practise on your friends. I am thinking of building a brig, not a bridge, but a vessel to cruise about my grounds in. Have you named your boat yet?

> The rain is pouring, the wind is roaring,
> I wish I was snoring, and so do you ;
> But perhaps you are sailing, while I am wailing,
> And my time is failing, so I shall bid you Adieu.

There is poetry as well as painting for you ! But as I know you are not blessed with such a genius, I shall only expect in return a good mess of plain prose telling me that you are well and tolerably happy, and don't think of returning before September. God bless you, my dearest Anne,

I am yours truly affectionately,

S. E. F.

We have seen from these letters how 'Marriage' was received in the immediate circle of Miss Ferrier's kinsfolk and friends. There is a family tradition of its reception by old Mr. Ferrier which, it must be confessed, bears a somewhat suspicious likeness to the well-known story of Miss Burney.

'Old Mr. Ferrier had a great contempt for female authors, according to the fashion of his day ; and on one

[1] Morningside House. (J. F.)

occasion, when confined to his bed through illness, he asked his daughter to bring a book from the library and read it to him, bidding her be careful not to choose one written by a woman. “ Marriage ” being then completed, she was desirous to have his opinion of her maiden effort, and read it, seating herself behind the curtains that her father might not see the MS. So delighted was he with the story that he hardly gave her time to take her meals, and on its conclusion she was told to get another by the same author. There was no other, his daughter told him. “ I am sorry to hear that,” he said, “ for it is the best book you have ever brought me.” “ Then what will you say when I tell you it was written by a woman ? ” “ Nonsense,” was the rejoinder, “ no woman could ever write a book like that.” My aunt placed the MS. in his hands avowing the authorship, and the old man burst into tears.’

This story is on the authority of Mrs. Richardson, who was a frequent visitor at Abbotsford, having been first the wife of Sir Walter’s friend, Daniel Terry the comedian.[1]

Of opinion beyond the immediate circle of those who might be prejudiced in Miss Ferrier’s favour two instances are worth quoting. Mrs. Piozzi, writing at the end of 1818, says : ‘ Meanwhile ladies leave cards and starving females write romances. The novel called “ Marriage ” is the newest and merriest. How marriage should be a new thing, that is at least as old as Adam, the author may tell : but ’tis a very comical thing, and would make Lady Fellowes laugh on a long evening.’[2]

In less than a year from the publication of ‘ Marriage ’ we find it receiving what to the author—what, indeed, to any Scottish writer of that day—was the supreme and crowning honour for fiction, a word of praise from the author of ‘ Waverley,’ ignorant, it may be, that he was befriending the daughter of an old friend and colleague.[3] In the epilogue, as one may call it, to the ‘ Tales of My Landlord,’ which ends the legend of Montrose, Scott says :

‘ I retire from the field [of Scottish fiction] conscious that there remains behind not only a large harvest, but

---

[1] This incident is told in the words of Mr. John Ferrier.

[2] Mrs. Piozzi to Sir James Fellowes, December 1, 1818. (*Life and Writings*, vol. ii. p 456.)

[3] More than ten years later Miss Ferrier, as we shall see, speaks of mentioning her authorship to Sir Walter for the first time. Her language suggests that she believed the authorship to be a secret from him. It does not follow that it was so.

labourers capable of gathering it in.   More than one writer has of late displayed talents of this description, and if the present writer, himself a phantom, may be permitted to distinguish a brother or perhaps a sister shadow, he would mention in particular the author of the very lively work entitled " Marriage." '

CHAPTER III

'INHERITANCE' AND 'DESTINY'

AFTER what one may fairly call Miss Ferrier's triumphant entry into the field of letters she did not long remain resting on her oars. Of the formative process which gave birth to 'Inheritance' we hear nothing. The letters to Miss Clavering, now Mrs. Fletcher, came to an end, and there is no correspondent to whom Miss Ferrier discloses her literary schemes or reveals her best self. One need not suppose that the old frank and affectionate intercourse ceased.[1] No doubt the circle into which Mrs. Fletcher's marriage brought her, one of earnest Whig politics, had no very great sympathy with Miss Ferrier's literary ambitions, and less perhaps with her habitual modes of thought and expression.[2] And no one can study Miss Ferrier's character, as disclosed in her books and letters, and not see that she was a person with whom intimate confidence did not flow very easily, and that the stream which fed it might be easily dammed up or turned aside. And even if there was nothing in the nature of alienation, there was not the same motive for confidence. Miss Ferrier had learnt her methods and tested her strength, and had no longer the same need of a counsellor and a critic. She was shrewd and clear-sighted enough to discount the extravagant praises of friends. She could profit by general criticism all the better because her own interest in the matter was a secret shared with few.

There are other reasons, too, why the letters should be no longer the same joyous and reckless self-revelation. The whole cast of Miss Ferrier's humour is observant

---

[1] Many letters from Miss Ferrier to Mrs. Christison were destroyed by the writer's request. One can easily understand why Mrs. Christison should have been specially anxious to preserve what one may call 'The *Marriage* correspondence.'

[2] This did not prevent, as we shall see, a very warm friendship springing up between Miss Ferrier and members of the Fletcher family.

rather than reflective, and that is not the kind of humour which defies the encroachments of time.

Moreover, there was now the impending prospect of separation from that father of whose vigorous, self-repressed nature and outer shell of cynicism Miss Ferrier had inherited so large a share. How real and absorbing was her devotion to him is clearly shown by more than one incidental reference made by her friends. If henceforth a sense of the *lacrymae rerum* becomes increasingly more and more manifest, alike in Miss Ferrier's published writings and in her letters, we must remember that there was now almost immediately before her the severance of the chief tie of human affection which bound her to the world, the cessation of the main interest and purpose to which her life had been for years devoted.

S. E. F. TO MRS. CONNELL

You must think me the most thankless of beings in never having acknowledged the magnificent salmon you have been sending us, and which might have graced a Lord Mayor's feast ; but by some mistake I was told the sumptuous *jowl*, which came via York Place, was from Stirling, and I paid my thanks there accordingly, when I found out my mistake. I would have written to you, but John [1] had just sent off a frank and could not get another at that time, so I have been waiting till I could get my acknowledgments covered, as they have not the face to go forth in their own nakedness. Both fish were very fine, but I beg you won't take the trouble to send any more, as my father seldom, or rather *never*, eats salmon now, and I ought not to taste it. Henry,[2] to be sure, does it all justice, but he leaves us in a few days for Kair,[3] and from thence to London with the Laird and Charles.[4] They were in Edinburgh nearly three days, but we only saw Charles one day at dinner. He seems a nice smart boy

[1] Her eldest brother, John Ferrier ; he held various lucrative appointments, among others, Deputy Keeper of the Seal of Scotland, under the Duke of Argyll. (J F.)

[2] Her nephew, Henry Kinloch. (J. F.)

[3] The residence of his uncle, George Kinloch, in Kincardineshire. (J. F.

[4] Another Kinloch nephew. (J. F.

with a very pleasant voice and manners. Mrs. K. wrote me that you had half *trysted* to meet at Harrogate, but she seems to think they must be stationary all summer, which I am sure must be bad for both. . . . The Walkers found Harrogate dreadfully dull—not a kent face to be seen, but perhaps it is gayer now. Anne[1] has been the better of the water, but with regard to your Helen I should think the Airthrie water would be of service to her, so perhaps you will take a trip to Stirling, and we shall have a peep of you as you pass. I have taken a small course of it and my head feels much better. . . . My father is quite well, but feels his eyes weak ; fortunately the weather has been delicious, and he is very much out, and when he is in I read to him. This, with my attention to my flowers, picking currants, pulling peas, eating gooseberries, &c., fills up the measure of my days completely. Peggy[2] is, however, to be back to us to-day, which will be a great relief to me, although poor Beenie has done wonders. The Johns are gone to Dalmeny,[3] for two days. James[4] is off to Windermere[5]. . . . I see nobody but the Mackenzies[6] and Wilsons, who never have any news. The town is a perfect desert, as I am told, for I see little of it. The time for our sale is not fixed, but I shall bid for the books you mention. The Madame Genlis will be in great request, as everybody is delighted with her ; it certainly is about the most amusing book that ever was written. I always find writing occasions a slight return of headache. In spite of my specs I must stoop a little, and I never feel right but when I carry my head high, so excuse a letter with nothing in it. . . .

Monday.—James[7] dined with us yesterday, and I wanted

---

[1] Miss Walker. (J. F.)

[2] Their cook, who was (like the servants long ago) with them for years. (J. F.)

[3] The Ferriers had acted as agents for the Rosebery family for several generations. (J. F.)

[4] The late Professor Ferrier, of St. Andrews. (J. F.)

[5] To his uncle's, 'Christopher North,' at Elleray. (J. F.)

[6] The family of the 'Man of Feeling.' (J. F.)

[7] Her nephew, James Connell. (J. F.)

him to put something into the frank, but he said he had
nothing to say to any of you. Margaret F. joined the
party unexpectedly ; she has come to town to take home
a carriage, and Mrs. Riddell is to accompany her to Cairnhill. The Hamiltons have taken a house in Ayr for two
months for bathing, so she says they will have plenty of
room for their friends, and are in hopes Mr. C. and you
and some of the Misses will pay them a visit.

Helen [1] is grown a good deal, and I think all the better
for her travels. She is really a fine creature, clever,
natural and ladylike, with an inexhaustible flow of good
humour and good spirits. I hardly think you will see
them at Conheath at present, though there is no saying,
as when people have acquired the habit of moving they
cannot settle all at once. We are once more *settled* here [2]
for seven months to come, I suppose, and glad I am to
find myself out of the smoke and dirt of the town, which
always disagrees with me at this season. Jane is shocked
at my leanness, and I have not felt very well of late, but
the air of this place suits me so particularly well that I
dare say I shall soon pick up a little beef to cover my great
bare bones. You may believe I am still somewhat hurried
and confused, so will excuse this illegible scrawl, and with
kind love to the girls, believe me,

Your ever affectionate,

S. E. F.

S. E. F. TO MRS. CONNELL

Monday, January 8.

My dear Janet,—Your magnificent donation arrived
safe and sound on Saturday night, and I hasten to make our
acknowledgments to Mr. C. and you for so substantial
a mark of your remembrance. Nothing could be more
apropos than the arrival of the ham, as we had not a
morsel in the house, and the turkey is more seasonable
now than it would have been at Christmas, as we had one

---

[1] Miss Ferrier's niece, Helen Graham. (J. F.)
[2] Morningside House, where *Inheritance* was written. (J. F.)

from the Dean [1] and another from Mrs. Wallace.[2] I was beginning to long for some tidings of you, and was relieved to find by Mr. Connell's letter to Walter that you had neither been buried in the snow nor blown into the Solway, but were all living on the surface of the earth. I never remember to have suffered so much from cold as I did during the late storm ; in a colder house I think I must have died outright. I suppose it is my extreme old age that makes me require so much heat to warm my icy veins ; you know I reckon myself ninety-nine in constitution. . . .

Walter made a flying excursion to Stirling at Christmas, and was much pleased with his visit, though he found the cold excessive, . . . and now that the military are gone the general must be badly off for society. To be sure they could hardly have less of it than we have had for these six weeks, as, except the Dean and the Walkers, we have not had a soul within the doors. It is really no compliment to ask people to family dinners and *porridge and potato* suppers at this season, and with books, bagatelle, and *two-handed* whist our evenings glide away very easily. . . . I was in the old town lately for the second time since you left us, and made out a visit to Mrs. Riddell. Her husband had been confined for a fortnight with a sore throat, and she does not look well herself.[3] She expects her mother about the end of the month. . . . I return Mrs. Duncan's book, which I have read again, but I like the first edition the best. I think the last too much spun out and too *prosing.* Not that I think religion ever can be made of

---

[1] Mr. Ross, Dean of the Faculty of Advocate. (J. F.)

[2] The widow of Miss Ferrier's uncle, Walter Ferrier, of Somerford. She resumed her maiden name on inheriting the estate of Cairnhill, co. Ayr, after the death of four brothers, and was known as Mrs. Ferrier Wallace. After her death her daughter called herself Miss Wallace Ferrier, to distinguish herself from Miss Ferrier and others of the name. (J. F.)

[3] Daughter of Mrs. Ferrier Wallace. Thomas Riddell, of Camiston, co. Roxburgh, her husband, was a friend of Scott's, who much lamented his death, and notes in his diary, April 20, 1826 : 'Another death. Thomas Riddell, younger, of Camiston, Sergeant-Major of the Edinburgh Troop in the sunny days of our yeomanry, and a very good fellow.'

too much consequence to oneself, but I think people may err in saying too much about it to others. However, it is an excellent work, and we may all learn a great deal of good from it. . . . I hear of no new books at present, and therefore content myself with Henry's 'History' and Eustace's 'Tour Through Italy,' both very excellent in their way ; then with working and walking when the weather will permit fill up the measure of my days. Helen's[1] life, I fancy, is a great contrast at present with her five sons on her hands. She cannot have many quiet moments.

I met Miss Chalmers on the street one day, and it was so long since I had seen her that I really felt something like pleasure at sight of her, poor hunted stag ! but then I felt remorse when I thought of my impudence to her, and upon that I pressed her to come and dine with me, but she was cruel and would not. . . .

S. E. F. TO MRS. CONNELL

Morningside : Monday.

Although I am not quiet so bad as I must appear to you, yet I am bad enough to make me feel rather at a loss for a good thumping excuse for my silence. I have sundry small ones which, if strung together and properly arranged, might make a very creditable appearance, but you know I have no knack at doing up anything neatly, and besides I hate either to make or to take long-winded excuses, so will rather trust to your taking my word for it that I am not *inexcusable*. I don't pretend to make my health upon this occasion, as it has been better than it has been for upwards of a year, and, though I never shall be well, I am now very thankful when not positively ill. My father has been in great health and good spirits—better than I have seen him for a long while, but he had a slight attack last week in consequence of a merry-making he had with

[1] Mrs. Kinloch. (J. F.)

Lord Eldin, Mr. Charles Ross, and James Walker—the
latter, I believe, was merely an accessory not a principal,
but the other two are very jovial, and only fit for entertaining once in a lifetime. Miss Monypenny, A. Walker,[1] and
I were left to our own devices till ten o'clock, by which
time we were getting rather tired of one another, and were
beginning to fight about *dress*, but luckily the party broke
up before we had begun to pull caps. . . . I was sorry to
hear by a letter from Helen that Mr. K. was so poorly in
his health, but I trust change of air will set him up again,
as he has always benefited by it, and Tunbridge seems to
agree particularly with him. As you have had a sufficient visitation of Henry,[2] and the schools are now
opening their jaws again, he must be returning some of
these days. There is nothing fixed as to our movements,
so I can't say whether we shall be in just before the Festival,
or in the very midst of it, or immediately after it, but as
it must be one or other I hope you will make up your mind
and your plans to come in *bodily*, and you and some of the
girls to remain, as you could be at no loss for a day or two,
supposing we were not there to receive you, which, however,
I think we probably shall, and that, too, in a fine new
painted dining-room ! Wonders have not ceased, you see,
or at least you will see when you see that. New window
curtains, too ! In short I shall not be able to eat my dinner
for pride. We have given up our airings long ago, the
journey to Newland Burn was the finish.[3] I blessed my
stars we had not set out there in the chaise, as I'm sure I
must have died by the way. I was dreadfully tired, for
four and twenty miles is a prodigious journey to me now.
The town is still a desert, and the weather is so broken and
the days so short, we have very few visitors, so I have no
news of any kind. I have been reading the 'Tales of a
Traveller,' which are elegantly written, but the greatest

----

[1] Sister of Lord Pitmillie, one of
the Lords of Session. (J. F.)
[2] Kinloch. (J. F.)

[3] A country retreat of the Misses
Edmonstone near Edinburgh. (J. F.)

trash in themselves that ever were put forth. . . . Mrs. John and I agree that the stone teapots are not so good as the silver ones ; however, I have sent for one for a trial, as they are not costly, but I could not get one to hold more than three breakfast cups, and I thought I might as well send a thimble to your table.   Tell H. the gardener says the stocks lift better in the Spring.[1]

S. E. F. TO MRS. CONNELL

My dear Janet,—Having thanked your daughters for the beautiful specimens of their work, I must now take to a vulgarer theme and acknowledge the safe arrival of the jolly leg of veal you were kind enough to order for us.   It was excellent, and my father enjoyed it very much, so we shall be glad to receive another when it comes.   I wish you would let me know the price, that I may pay it to James, and also the cost of the collar, which is almost *distressingly* beautiful.   It makes me wae to think of human eyes straining themselves to such a pitch for their daily bread !   Pray pay the *full amount* without any prigging, as I shall not grudge it whatever it is, and tell me what it is, as I don't like long accounts.   My father continues well in his general health, but was annoyed for some days with an attack of rheumatism in his elbow, which made him rather helpless, but it is now gone, and the only symptom remaining is its being an excuse for wearing his old ragged duffle great coat and not shaving

[1] John Clerk Lord Eldin, mentioned in the foregoing letter, was a well-known resident of Edinburgh in his day ; he was a very talented artist, and had a very good collection of pictures in his house in Picardy Place, and used to say ' If any one wants gude picters, let him gang to Tours, for Sir John Dalrymple has been there and picket oot a' the bad yuns.'   He was very eccentric, and had several cats, two of them named Aminadab and Rebecca, and had a regular class for them with a Dux and Booby ; and once a terrific cats' concert took place behind his house, on which he threw up the window and read the Riot Act.   He had also a collection of teapots and said (feeling tired of life, it must be inferred), ' I weary of mysel', I weary of a' things, I weary of my Sister, I weary of my cats, but I *never weary* of my ten teapots.'   (J. F.)

his beard, so you may imagine he is rather a *picturesque* figure, not that I should like many to draw his picture in his present state.

In the two letters which follow we find reference to Lady Charlotte Campbell's novel, ' Conduct is Fate,' published by Blackwood in 1820. If any one pushes his spirit of literary inquiry so far as to read it, he will probably think that both Blackwood and Miss Ferrier were very lenient critics.

W. BLACKWOOD TO S. E. F.

Edinburgh : January 18, 1820.

Madam,—I have to apologise for not writing you sooner with regard to the novel.

I have already mentioned to you the high opinion I have of the talent displayed in it. I need not say that, commercially speaking, I would be happy to publish the work. At the same time I hope the author will pardon me for the liberty I take in hinting that I feel confident that she could very greatly improve the first volume so as, in my humble opinion, to make it more acceptable to British readers, who are not accustomed to a husband knocking down his wife, nor yet to some other traits of Continental manners. Of all this, however, an author, and not a bookseller, is the best judge. If she is determined to publish I shall be happy to take charge of the book, and when I see the conclusion of the work I will let you know what sum I could afford to offer for it. I have no doubt I shall be able to arrange all this entirely to your satisfaction.

I am, madam, your respectful servant,

W. BLACKWOOD.

S. E. F. TO MRS. CONNELL (1820)

Saturday.

Your letter came very apropos for receiving an answer, as I was going to have written you a line at any rate to beg your acceptance of a copy of 'Conduct.' I believe it is scarcely published yet, so I have no idea how it is to take or what is to be said of it in the world ; but for my own part I think there is a great deal of talent in it, though not very well directed. Some of the descriptions are beautiful, but there is too much of them to please the generality of readers. Altogether I am not sanguine about it, but I shall be very happy if it succeeds. My father did not go to the election and seems to have no thought of moving farther than Morningside, where he is always wishing himself. . .

Jane had an attack of the bleeding of her nose while in London, and the General had also been ailing, but they had both recovered and set off for Norfolk [1] on a visit to Lady Suffield, where I was glad to learn by a line from Jane they had arrived safe and sound. It required some spirit to pay a visit and renew an old acquaintance under such circumstances, but they are both largely endowed with locomotive powers. . . . The storm seems to be *awsome* and appears to be endless ; last night was almost as bad as any we have had—nine trees blown down at Morningside, the stack of chimneys of this house was discovered to be hanging by a *thread*, and when it was repairing one of the men was blown down, and would have been precipitated to the street if he had not caught at the skylight and smashed it to save himself, poor creature ! In short, after having stood this winter, I shall never speak of my nerves again. . . . I really never lived in such *profound retirement*. Except the Walkers and James on Sundays we scarcely ever see a soul. . . . I have not read 'Sir Andrew Wyllie' as I can't endure that man's writings, and I'm told the vulgarity of this *beats print*. 'Adam Blair' is powerfully written, but painful and disagreeable to the greatest degree, and in other respects not fit to be mentioned.

[1] Blickling Hall, a very fine old Tudor mansion, left to Lady Suffield by her father, the Earl of Buckinghamshire. (J. F.)

The following letter from Mr. Blackwood no doubt refers to the same offspring of Lady Charlotte's prolific and rubbish-producing brain.

W. BLACKWOOD TO S. E. F.

Edinburgh : June 27, 1821.

Madam,—The friend to whom I sent Lady Charlotte's MS. has only just finished it, and I now send you the third volume.   I have been so much hurried since I saw you that it has not been in my power to write at length as I intended, but I will do either to-night or to-morrow morning.

Your friend here will be wearying to hear about her MS.   I enclose you a note I had the other day from the amanuensis.

I am, madam,

Your most obedient servant,

W. BLACKWOOD

S. E. F. TO MRS. CONNELL

Morningside : July 12, 1821.

My dear Janet,—You must certainly think I am going to figure at the Coronation from the sumptuous garment you have sent me.   I know not what has possessed you all to take to the decking of my bare bones at such a rate. I spend a great deal too much upon them myself, and it is really grievous to see other people wasting their substance upon them, especially those who have fair young bodies of their own to clothe.   I would say I was *almost* vexed to think that Mr. Connell should have been throwing away his money on finery for me, but I dare say you would not believe me if I were to swear it.   It seems so very improbable that one should be sorry to receive a very handsome present from a person they like, but I really must say for myself I am not a greedy creature, and I have already had so many proofs of his and your generosity that any additional ones are really more than superfluous.   So much for my *gratitude*.　As to my admiration, that is not so easily expressed, as I think it is the handsomest silk I ever saw, really beautiful, but too much so for me ; and as for the quantity, there seems enough to make my father a coat and waistcoat, *let a be* a gown for me.　In short, it is quite a thing I would have chosen if I had been a *rich, handsome lady*, but I think you might have made less serve me.　I was very happy to hear you had all enjoyed your jaunt so much, and with such right feelings of being happy while away and happier still to return ; it is not always that people are happy and contented both ways.　It must have been a delightful tour, and you seem to have quite *creamed* England.　It must also have been a happy meeting with Helen ; she writes in raptures of all of you, and only laments having had so little of you, but I hope next summer she will return your visit and pay us one. Although it is so long since I have written you I don't remember anything at all remarkable that has occurred in the interim, indeed one day is so like another with me that when I look back upon a few weeks or months I can scarcely believe I have really *lived* them.　I don't know whether everybody seems to dream and idle away existence as I do, but I certainly never have anything either to tell or to show, so I fear I shall have a very bad account to give at the last.　Last Saturday, indeed, was a remarkable day in my life, as I had a jaunt to Hawthornden and dined there—the first time for nearly three years I have been so far from home ; but the Clerks of Session had a dinner [1] and I took the opportunity of being gay too, and so went with the Walkers to the woods and wilds of Roslin and Hawthornden, and then dined at the Drummonds, and so spent a delightful day.　That is like to be

---

[1] The Clerks were Scott, Hector Macdonald Buchanan, Colin Mackenzie, James Ferrier, and James Walker (Dalry).　A coach, called the Clerks' coach, used to call for them at their respective family residence to take them to the Parliament House.　Mr. Walker used to do a good deal of Scott's work in the Court while he was penning his romances, and for which kind service Scott presented him with a complete set of the *Waverley* Novels.　(J. F.)

the extent of my travels this summer as my father seems
to have no intention of leaving home, and, indeed, I could
hardly expect it, as it would seem downright *wastery* to be
leaving our cow and our sheep and our *berries* and our
flowers to be wasting themselves upon the *desert air*. I
think the best time for him to visit now would be the
spring, when the Session rises, before coming out here, for
after he is fairly settled there is no getting him to move—
so you must not look for us this season. As to my
promising a visit, you surely have very erroneous ideas of
my power if you think I could take upon me to promise
anything of the kind—perhaps if I were to tease him very
much he might be wrought upon to consent—but that I
never do and never will do for any purpose whatever, as I
think it much more fitting and reasonable that he should
have his way than I should have mine. We have had
many kind and pressing invitations to all the points of the
compass, I believe, but all were rejected with the same
answer, that he would go nowhere. Walter and his family
go off to Moffat to-morrow, and I hope the change will
prove of service to them all ; he seems very well himself at
present, but Mrs. F. and the children have been ill of
a sort of influenza, which has reduced them a little ; they
are very nice creatures, and my father will miss them
much, as they are just at his favourite age, and Agnes is
very amusing. We don't see so much of your youngsters as
we could wish, as they are busy all the week, and 'tis only
on a Saturday or Sunday they can come to us ; they seem
quite happy now and much more sociable and frank from
mixing with other girls. They seem very fine amiable
creatures, and I admire the strong attachment they have for
each other and the warmth they feel towards home, though
Mary certainly did carry her feelings (or rather allowed her
feelings to carry her) to a great excess ; but in youth I
would rather see too much than too little feeling. But the
one character certainly requires much more management
than the other, and if you are to keep them at home I

hope you will be fortunate in a governess, as I think
Mary would require one superior to the common run of
mere *two handed* animals that pretend to govern those who
are fitter to govern them.   James [1] seems to give great satisfaction in every way.   His aunts quite dote upon him, and
Mr. Rae [2] speaks highly of his good behaviour and attention.
He is grown quite a man in his exterior, so you may be
prepared for a full sized gentleman.   John takes up his
son James to Greenwich early next month, which I think
a good plan, as he really requires brushing up.   I wish he
could hear of a good school in the North of England for
the other James F. [3] as he would also be the better of a
little polishing.   Do you happen to know of any about
Carlisle or Penrith that are well spoken of?   Helen has
signified to her grandfather that it is her mother's intention
to take her home the twenty-fifth of this month.   I would
fain have had her remain another year with Mrs. Seton, as
she seems very fond of her.

S. E. F. TO MRS. CONNELL

Monday.

. . . I was much struck with the notice I got of the
death of Miss Clerk [4] of Eldin, whom I saw but a few
weeks ago in her own house apparently in perfect health
and surrounded with all the eye could desire to look upon
of fine pictures, costly furniture, and all that was rich and
rare.   But all in vain!   This is a very sombre strain of
writing, you will think, but it is a solemn subject, and one
I fear I do not think upon half so often as I ought to do,
and certainly it is not the prevailing topic of conversation
in this town at present, where Yeomanry balls and such
things are far more engrossing subjects.   My father continues quite well and ready to resume his station at the
Clerk's table . . .

---

[1] J. Connell.   (J. F.)
[2] His tutor.   (J. F.)
[3] The son of Archibald Ferrier.
(J. F.)

[4] Sister of Lord Eldin, the Edinburgh judge, and one of the Penicuik
family.   (J. F.)

M

S. E. F. TO MRS. CONNELL (1822)

. . . The entry[1] was a finer and more gratifying sight than the procession; there was more pageantry, to be sure, at the last, but the badness of the day and the dirtiness of the streets very much spoiled the effect; it was really grievous to see the rain pouring upon white satin cloaks, and pages wading through the mire in satin shoes. I hear the King's equipage was by no means so splendid, and he himself invisible to mortal eye; there were no other carriages in the procession, so neither judges nor clerks nor anybody else had any part to play. Walter had excellent windows provided, and the Connells enjoyed it very much, as did also Cousin Mag,[2] though she was in despair at not having seen the King, and I fear she is not likely to be gratified now; neither could she procure a ticket to the Peers' Ball, which was the finest thing ever was seen, only the peeresses *mobbed* his Majesty—at least, crowded him so much that he could not stand it. Mrs. Graham went with me to see the Duchess of A.[3] dressed for the Drawing-room. She was very splendid in French white satin and tulle, embroidered with silver and diamonds and all the rest of it, but I thought I had seen her more beautiful when less gorgeous. She had an *At Home* the other night, and pressed me to go; but keep me from such things! She says never was anything seen like the awkwardness and uncouthness of the *novices* at the Drawing-room, which I can well believe, though I dare say they all thought (Miss R. M. amongst others)[4] that they had acquitted themselves to admiration. I was interrupted by Cousin Mag, who came to spend the day, and is just gone brimful of delight, having been at the Hunt Ball, patronised

[1] Entry of George IV. into Edinburgh, 1822. (J. F.)
[2] Miss Wallace Ferrier. (J. F.)
[3] Argyll. (J. F.)
[4] Miss Robina Millar (Earnock), married H. W. Williams, the artist, known as 'Grecian Williams'; he was much thought of in his time. Many of his water-colours are in the Edinburgh Royal Academy. (J. F.)

by Lady Rollo and squired by my Lord, and standing
within two of the King. Her brother[1] goes off to Cathlaw
to-morrow, but she remains a day or two longer to be
present at Miss Greig's[2] marriage to Macleod, a ten years'
engagement ; he has some property in the Highlands and
a good situation in India, but it must be a great struggle
to leave her frail father and mother. . . . We had Sir
Archibald Edmonstone and sister dining here on Saturday,
and D.[3] on Sunday overflowing with loyalty. . . .

S. E. F. TO MRS. CONNELL

. . . Mrs. John has been out, but is still far from well.
I saw her yesterday in the drawing-room, but she said she
was still *rheumy* and her pulse at 120. General Graham
has been confined to bed for a fortnight from the same
cause, and Mrs. Riddell's fever was a rheumatic one, but
last time I heard of her she was recovering. To add to
their misfortunes their house has been broken into and all
their bits of plate and linen taken away ; so much for the
miseries of human life, which seem to be all that I hear of
at present, though happily exempt from experiencing them,
as my father is in his usual robust health and I feel
stronger than I have done for some months. Our greatest
distress is how to dispose of our apples, but that seems also
an *epidemic*, and one which I dare say you have felt very
severely. The town is in a state of deathlike repose after
its late excitement, but as most of my friends happen to
be in it I find it particularly agreeable. I went with the
Fletchers one day to see Holyrood, and we thought black,
burning shame of ourselves for having been such gowks as
to go and look at a bare room and an old empty throne. The
presence chamber is just decent and no more, so you lost

---

[1] Colonel Ferrier Hamilton, of
Westport ; he had a small and very
pretty property near Linlithgow,
Cathlaw by name. His wife was
a daughter of the first Viscount
Gort. (J. F.)

[2] Her sister was Lady Rollo ; her
husband became Sir John Macleod.
(J. F.)

[3] Dalmeny Edmonstone. (J. F.)

nothing there. . . . The weather is very broken and the trees getting a very wintry aspect, but I have still a fine show of flowers, and I feel no inclination to leave them, so am not sorry to look forward to another month at Morningside.

We still keep our two little guests, who are a great amusement to their grandfather at present, though in another year they will have reached the snubbing age, and then Thomas Henry will be in request.

S. E. F. TO MRS. CONNELL

I have been suffering so much from headaches for some time that I have almost resolved to give up writing entirely ; however, I must write you a line in the meantime to tell you so. I put on eight leeches lately in hopes they would have relieved me, but they did me no good ; and now the doctor wishes me to try some mineral water, so I have written to Jane to send me some of the Airthrie spring, which I would fain hope will clear away some of the monstrous mass of *hot rubbish* which seems to fill my head and makes me at times feel as if it were a burden on the face of the earth. I find stooping very bad for me, so I do nothing but read and hold up my head, and walk about when the weather permits . . . so don't wonder if I am long of writing even short letters . . . as for me, I forget everything I hear and have neither incidents nor ideas to record. . .

S. E. F. TO MRS. CONNELL

January 14, 1823.

This is the first letter I have attempted this year, and I believe I may add to that some weeks of the last one, so I feel somewhat awkward at setting about it, as I think I *ought* to have a great deal to say, and yet I fear I have very little. . . . I have been wholly taken up with my father, who has had a slight inflammation in his eyes, which threw him out of all occupation ; but I am happy to say it is quite gone, and he is now at the Court in his usual health and good looks. When he heard you were ailing he said the best thing you could do would be to come and keep him company at the fireside, and I do hope we are to see you (though not for that purpose) in the course of next month. James [1] dined with us on Sunday, seemingly in perfect health and, we all agreed, quite fat enough, though it seems you and Aunt Bess are quite alarmed at his thinness ; but everything is by comparison. I don't suppose he looks very pretty alongside his father and you . . . but he is a stout, fat man beside me. The Johns are all well and very gay, I suppose, with Elizabeth's [2] marriage, which took place on New Year's day ; the pair are to be here for some weeks, so there will be a deal of revelry, I dare say ; he is really an uncommon, handsome, genteel man, and has the character of being very clever and amiable, so that *emigration* to Persia is the only draw-back, and she seems to think nothing of it at present. Julia Walker [3] is going to be married to Sir James Hall's eldest son—a match which seems to give great satisfaction to both parties. I don't know him, but she is a very un-spoilt creature to have been an only child, and reckoned a beauty, though I never could discover her claims. I see less of my friends Anne and Helen since they have em-barked in the cares of housekeeping and visiting, which is really a business of its own in this town, and no avoiding it without offence. . . . I am reading ' Peveril,' and like it, as I do all that author's works for the imagination, wit, and humour that pervade them. 'Osmond' is very finely written, though painful. To descend to birds of another feather, your turkey was most excellent, and much

---

[1] Connell. (J. F.)

[2] Elizabeth Wilson, Mrs. John Ferrier's youngest sister, married Dr. McNeill, afterwards Sir John McNeill, envoy to the Court of Persia ; he died at a very advanced age, 1888. He married for his third wife Lady Emma Campbell, sister to the Duke of Argyll. (J. F.)

[3] Half-sister to her great friends, the Misses Walker. (J. F.)

applauded by all who partook. Many years may you rear turkeys, and we eat them! This is a modest way of returning thanks, you'll say!

S. E. F. TO MRS. CONNELL

I have much to answer for to you, but I trust you will give me credit for having had more to do than I have time to tell. Our dear father's illness occupied me entirely both in mind and body for some time, and I assure you I often wished for your assistance ; he was low and apprehensive for some days, but happily I was not alarmed, as it never appeared to me that his illness was anything else than the epidemic cold which has been so prevalent here, and so it has proved. He is somewhat thinner than when you saw him, but otherwise looking well ; he both eats and sleeps well, and you may judge of his strength when I tell you that a few days ago we drove as far as Dalmeny Park and all through the grounds, went over the house, did not get home till five, when I was quite worn out, and he was so little fatigued that he played two long *tough* rubbers with Mrs. H. and D., and carved a still *tougher* fowl for their supper with great glee. Yesterday he walked about Morningside for upwards of an hour, and James will tell you he seemed nothing the worse for it at dinner. He is now very impatient to be settled there, so we are to move to-morrow, and I don't think even a fall of snow will stop him.

S. E. F. TO MRS. CONNELL

My dear Janet,—I blushed at the sight of the bag of meal, which I ought to have withstood when you proposed sending it ; but I stupidly forgot to say anything about it, and so my silence was mistaken for consent. I am really sorry Mr. C. should have deprived himself of any of his small store, and beg he will never do so again, as I assure

you we are very well supplied by our *Commissary General*
Buckstone.

In the meantime we eat yours with great zest, and I
doubt if the shearer who cut, or the miller who ground it,
makes a heartier breakfast than my father does upon it
every morning; he is indeed *perfectly* well, and very impatient to be at his rural avocations at Morningside, though
the weather is by no means inviting; however, we are to
march next Tuesday if the wind and rain permit. We
were both disappointed at not seeing you here this winter,
but you must have felt thankful you were safe at home,
and not exposed to the same jeopardy as the Carlisle
travellers. I was glad to hear from James they had not
been the worse of their adventure. We are all going on
here much as usual, Mrs. Walter making little progress, I
am sorry to say; but when the weather settles and she
can get out, I would fain hope she may gain some strength.
Walter has been colded and *bileish*, but upon the whole I
think better than usual, and the children all quite well.
The Johns are in perfect preservation except Eleanor, who
looks thin and yellow, but I dare say will rally when the
summer comes round. She will be very handsome if she
gets fat and blooming.[1]

. . . James won't allow there is such a thing as beauty
to be seen in all Edinburgh. Anne Walker told me she
had got him an heiress for a partner at her brother's dance,
but she had found no favour in his sight, it seems. She
has been very poorly of late, and as for Helen, she has
half killed herself working for the charity sales. I went to
them, but the mob was so great I could see little or
nothing, and bought nothing but monstrosities of screens.
I send you a slight cap which was made from one of Mrs.
Fletcher's, which I thought looked well; but perhaps you
may not like it, as there is nothing so *ticklish* as choosing
caps for others. Lady John[2] has been in the very jaws of

[1] Eleanor Ferrier, married, 1843,   Leith, Bart. (J. F.)
George Leith, Esq., son of Sir George   [2] Lady John Campbell. (J. F.)

death, but has got out of them, and is now very well. I forget whether I sent you Lady Charlotte's book of prayers, which I think far superior to her novels, and highly creditable both as compositions and as showing so much Biblical research. Our good neighbours are in their usual glee, and dine with us regularly once a week *forbye* occasional evening visits, so we shall miss them much at Morningside.

S. E. F. TO MRS. CONNELL

(Endorsed 'per favour of Mr. J. F. Ferrier's[1] Fish-basket.')

Morningside.

I think it very doubtful if this ever reaches you, as it is to go in a fisherman's *creel*, which I don't take to be the safest of conveyances. However, as it won't be worth 8*d.*, it is as well to let it take its chance, and if it should land with the trout, I wish them much good of it. My father has got so well since we came here that he is not like the same person he was in winter; except being a little deaf, and not quite so active as he used to be some years ago, I should say he was as well as ever he was. The weather has been charming ever since we came here, and we both almost live out of doors. We have got a gardener not so old as the hills, but as old as this place, for he talks of what he did five-and-fifty years ago as if it were an affair of yester-day. He does very well notwithstanding, but as he is somewhat stiff at the *sowing*, I have to take that in hand myself, and have done nothing but make round patches and stick sticks in them for a month past, and still am not near done. Tell Helen of all things to sow large beds and long rows of dwarf rocket larkspur; there is nothing makes a garden look so brilliant. The Grahams went off this day week, and the General returned to town on Friday— Jane says to get a *warm*, he says upon divers bits of

---

[1] Miss Ferrier's nephew, the late Professor Ferrier, when young, used to be often at Conheath. (J. F.)

business.   One of them he is gone upon to-day is to bury his old friend, Sir H. Macdougal,[1] who will be a great loss to him. . . . We have returned to our old courses in seeing *nobody* and having *somebody* at dinner almost every day; but who they are I cannot tell, as I never see the face of a stranger or hear a syllable of news.   Anne Walker has just been here straight from her brother Frank's,[2] where she has been spending some days with a bride and bridegroom [3]—Miss Connell and Mr. Knatchbull; she says he is very handsome, and has 500*l.* a year, so for a poor *plainish* miss it is no bad match. . . . Have you read 'Common Events?'[4]   I think it very clever and amusing as well as profitable, and it seems to be better liked than 'Rich and Poor.'   I am become a member of a book club, so I buy no new books now; but I don't think our association will last long, as nobody seems pleased.   My complaint is that there are more books bought than I can find time to read, and very few that are worth reading. . .

S. E. F. TO MRS. CONNELL

Wednesday.

Mr. C. has charged me to write to you, otherwise I would rather have delayed it, as I feel myself particularly stupid at present—the effects, I flatter myself, of a cold which, however, is now on the decline.   You will be happy to hear that our dear father is now quite recovered from a pretty severe cold he had had for some weeks, but, thank God, he is now perfectly well.   He was at the Court yesterday, and the doctor, who has just been here taking leave, says he may now do what he likes, for that he is done with him; in short, he is now quite himself again and

---

[1] Sir Henry Macdougal, of Mackerston, co. Roxburgh.   He came into the world twenty years after his sister, who was long considered the heiress of the property, thereby cutting her out of it.   She married Scott, of Gala, to whose family it has now returned.   (J. F.)

[2] Sir Francis Walker Drummond; he married the heiress of Hawthornden.   (J. F.)

[3] Daughter of Sir John Connell, judge of the Admiralty at Edinburgh. (J. F.)

[4] By Anne Walker.   *Rich and Poor* was also by her.   (J. F.)

looking as fresh and well as ever. . . . I every day feel a greater repugnance to forming new acquaintances, as I'm long past forming new friendships, and I feel it a tax to visit people whom I don't care for, having so many dear intimates to associate with. The Walkers are at present in Fife, but are to be home soon to a house of their own, a measure which has been long in contemplation and will be much more comfortable for them. . . .

We have seen already how, prompted by the success of 'Marriage,' Blackwood stirred up Miss Ferrier to further efforts by quoting the appeal made to her by the writer of 'Waverley.' Miss Ferrier was nowise backward in answering to the call, and by 1823 'Inheritance' was sufficiently advanced for her to open negotiations with a publisher. After an abortive negotiation with Mr. Murray, the copyright of 'Inheritance,' like that of its predecessor, was made over to Mr. Blackwood, but not until he raised his offer for it from five hundred pounds to double that sum.

JOHN FERRIER TO S. E. F.

London : April 18, 1823.

I called for Mr. Murray to-day and was received very graciously when he understood the business I had come to him upon. He talks of 'Marriage' in the most flattering terms, and says he will be proud to be the publisher of another work by the same author, and in so far as any one can judge on so slight an acquaintance it appears to me that he is open and candid and much of a gentleman in his manner and appearance. He says if he got a perusal of the MS. or such parts of it as may be written, that he will at once give his proposal of terms. In short, he appears to me to be *the man*, as he dwelt upon the great talent of the author of 'Marriage' in such a manner as would make me think he will give liberally for its successor. It would be desirable if you could send up a volume while I am here so as Mr. M—— might peruse it and send it back by me.

JOHN FERRIER TO S. E. F.

London : May 7, 1823.

My dear Susan,—I have only time to inclose a note from Mr. Murray along with your MS. which I shall take special care of.   If you wish me to do anything more here you will need to write me *in course* of post, or I shall certainly be off early on the next morning, Friday next, if not sooner.

There does not seem to be any occasion for haste, and therefore it may be best to do nothing more until we meet. In the meanwhile the formal communication, so far as I can judge, is of an agreeable nature.

Yours ever affectionately,

J. F.

Indorsement.—The negotiation with Mr. Murray was broken off at Mr. Blackwood's *earnest intreaty* and upon his assuring me it would be a serious injury to him as a publisher if I gave the work to another.   It would have been well for me if my feelings had not prevailed over my self interest.

S. E. F.

W. BLACKWOOD TO JOHN FERRIER

Edinburgh : September 19, 1823.

Dear Sir,—I hereby agree to give the sum you mention as the price of Miss Ferrier's work, viz. one thousand pounds sterling [1] to be settled for by a bill at twelve months from date of publication.

The work to be in three volumes, and the second and third it is understood will extend to about 360 MS. pages each, similar to the first volume in my possession.

I am, dear sir, yours truly,

W. BLACKWOOD.

---

[1] Five hundred was the sum originally offered by Mr. B. and refused. (S. E. F.)

P.S.—I now return the first volume of the MS., the portion of the second volume I have at home, and it will be sent to-morrow.

W. BLACKWOOD TO S. E. F.

P. S. : Saturday.

Madam,—I cannot go home without telling you how much I have been delighted with all the packet you have just sent me.

I intreat of you to go on, and to have no advisers but your own heart and feelings.

Yours respectfully,

W. Blackwood.

W. BLACKWOOD TO S. E. F.

Friday evening.

Madam,—Before I gave the MS. to the copier I read the whole of it, and I cannot help telling you how much I have been delighted with it. You have only to go on trusting wholly to yourself, and you will very soon be at the end of your labours.

I am, madam, yours very respectfully,

W. Blackwood.

W. BLACKWOOD TO S. E. F.

Princes Street : Friday night, ten o'clock.

Madam,—The sheet which I now send you I have read with even more pleasure than when I first perused this portion in MS. I am sure you will not have a letter to obliterate here.

W. B.

W. BLACKWOOD TO S. E. F.

One o'clock.

Madam,—This sheet is excellent. You will see that there are two pages wanted to complete it. The printers have delayed it too long. Be so good as to give my son whatever MS. you have ready and he will instantly return with it to the printers. You need not keep him to correct

this sheet, as he will ride out again with the sheet completed if you give him the MS. Do not mind my sending
out again as I can perfectly spare him.

Yours,
W. B.

All the sheets that are printed off are to be sent off by
the steamboat to-morrow morning, and the others I shall
send by mail coach, so as to publish in London in the
beginning of next week.

W. BLACKWOOD TO S. E. F.

Monday morning.

Madam,—I am almost sorry when I ought to be glad now
that I send you the *end*. I have had more enjoyment and
pleasure in the progress of your work for the last twelve
months than I have ever had in any that have passed
through my hands.

I am now as impatient to have it fairly afloat as I was
to have it concluded, being confident that there will only
be one opinion of its merits.

I am, madam, yours respectfully,
W. Blackwood.

W. BLACKWOOD TO S. E. F.

Madam,—You have introduced Uncle Adam most
happily, and I lost not a moment in sending it to the
printers when I had read it. There is a hurried and
breathless kind of interest in these last chapters which
keeps the mind of the reader in almost as feverish a state
as that of your heroine. She is indeed a heroine, and in
my humble opinion the only one I recollect of in modern
works that one could care much about.

You are in such a vein for it just now that I hope you
have been able to shut yourself up to-day and not be dis-
turbed by the Saturday's young folks.

Yours respectfully,
W. B.

W. BLACKWOOD TO S. E. F.

Princes Street : Monday.

Madam,—On Saturday I lent in confidence to a very clever person, upon whose discretion I can rely, the two volumes of ' The Inheritance.' This morning I got them back with the following note :

' My dear Sir,—I am truly delighted with " The Inheritance." I do not find as yet any one character quite equal to " Dr. Redgill "—except perhaps the good-natured old tumbled [1] maiden—but as a novel it is a hundred miles above " Marriage." It reminds me of Miss Austen's very best things in every page, and if the third volume be like these, no fear of success triumphant. Yours &c.'

I could not resist sending you this, and I hope you will be pleased with it, and drive on to your conclusion with full confidence in your own powers.

I send you another sheet. I sent one on Saturday night to George Street, but I have not got it back.

I am, madam, yours respectfully,

W. BLACKWOOD.

W. BLACKWOOD TO S. E. F.

Salisbury Road : Tuesday evening.

Madam,—I sent to George Street before three the conclusion of the second volume, and I expect my son will be able to send to the post-office to-night the first sheet of volume III.

I had not time till now to read the two new chapters, and I wanted merely to tell you how much I have been delighted with them—particularly the last one. Lyndsay is admirably brought out, and you have only to go on as you are going to sustain the character which Sir Walter gave me of ' Marriage,' that you had the rare talent of making your conclusion even better than your commencement, ' for,' said this worthy and veracious person, ' Mr.

---

[1] *Altera lectio*, ' troubled.' The writing is indistinct.

Blackwood, if ever I were to write a novel, I would like to write the two first volumes and leave anybody to write the third that liked.'

I am, madam, yours, respectfully,

W. BLACKWOOD.

W. BLACKWOOD TO S. E. F.

Princes Street : Saturday, three o'clock.

Madam,—Nothing can be better than the way in which you have managed with Gertrude and Lyndsay, and with Lyndsay and Lewiston particularly. Lyndsay's character rises in every new scene, and Gertrude's feelings are admirably brought out, and her whole character is supported in the most interesting way possible. I have not the least doubt of your managing the Colonel with the same tact, and winding the whole story up in a way that will, I am quite confident, place your work along side of those of the author of ' Waverley.'

Do not, I beg of you, think for one moment that I am saying anything but what I most sincerely feel. I merely wish to have the pleasure of first telling you what I am certain will be said by those whose opinion will be of more consequence than,

Madam, your very respectful servant,

W. BLACKWOOD.

Edinburgh : June 11, 1824.

Madam,—You must by this time have heard that all I said of ' The Inheritance ' from the first has been confirmed by the opinions of those whose opinion is of some value. On Wednesday I dined in company with Sir Walter Scott, and he spoke of the work in the very highest terms. I do not always set the highest value on the Baronet's favourable opinion of a book, because he has so much kindness of feeling towards everyone, but in this case he spoke so much *con amore*, and entered so completely, and at such a length to me, into the spirit of the book and of the characters, that showed me at once the impression it had made on him.   Everyone I have seen who have read the book gives the same praise to it.

Two or three days ago I had a note from a friend, which I copy:

'I have nearly finished a volume of "The Inheritance." It is unquestionably the best novel of the class of the present day in so far as I can yet judge.   Lord Rossville, Adam Ramsay, Bell Black and the Major, Miss Pratt and Anthony Whyte are capital, and a fine contrast to each other. It is, I think, a more elaborate work than "Marriage," better told, with greater variety, and displaying improved powers.   I congratulate you, and have no doubt the book will make a prodigious *sough*.'

I do not know a better judge, nor a more frank and honest one, than the writer of this note.

I am, madam, yours respectfully,
W. BLACKWOOD.

We have, unhappily, no record of the process of observation and construction by which 'Inheritance' was built up such as we have in the case of 'Marriage.'   We do know, indeed, that one scene, the happiest perhaps of all the author's ventures in the comedy of incident, was taken from an actual episode in the history of the Ferrier family.   Shortly after the appearance of 'Inheritance' a niece of Miss Ferrier's wrote thus:

We are all delighted with 'The Inheritance,' which is read aloud in the evening, although most of us have read it before.   We are come to Miss Pratt's extraordinary arrival in a hearse.   I mentioned some people objected to that as being overdrawn.   Uncle Walter (Mr. Walter Ferrier) said he had heard so too, but he mentioned a circumstance something of the same nature that had happened to himself. During the severe winter, several years ago, he was returning in the mail from Dumfries to Edinburgh during one of the dreadful storms, and was one of the few who insisted on the mail going on, which it did, till it came to one of the Moffat hills, where it was totally unable to proceed.   In this dilemma his ear was caught by piercing cries, and on looking behind was a hearse drawn by six or eight horses stopped in the same manner, and the screams came from it.   The desolation around, where nothing but snow was to be seen, and a lowering winter sky, the sombre appearance of this vehicle of death, and the cries altogether filled him with awe and horror.   Upon inquiring what it was he found out it was some poor soldiers' wives and children, who were thankful to get this conveyance, which was a hearse sent from Edinburgh with somebody who was to be buried in that part of the country and was now returning, but upon finding themselves in this state the poor creatures had begun to scream and cry.   They provided for them and the other passengers in the mail as well as they could, and those who were anxious to go on got the horses taken out and rode on them.

Uncle Walter got one of the hearse horses to ride.

S. E.|F. TO MRS. KINLOCH

Morningside : Saturday, 1823.

My dear Helen,—Although I certainly was hurt at the idea of your having divulged the secret of my authorship, yet I cannot bear that another work of mine should be announced to you by any but myself.   John has now completed a bargain for me with Mr. Blackwood by which I am to have one thousand pounds for a novel[1] now in hand, but which is not nearly finished, and possibly never may be.   Nevertheless, he is desirous of announcing it in his magazine, and therefore I wish to prepare you for the *shock*.   I can say nothing more than I have already said on the subject of *silence*, if not of secrecy.   All that I

---

[1] *The Inheritance.*   (J. F.)

N

require of my friends is to answer impertinent interroga-
tories by saying that as *I* don't acknowledge it, nobody
else has a right to say it's mine, that is surely no untruth ;
but as to giving it to any other person, that I neither
require or desire. I never will avow myself, and nothing
can hurt or offend me so much as any of my friends doing
it for me ; this is not *façon de parler*, but my real and un-
alterable feeling. I could not bear the *fuss* of authorism !
You may judge how well my secret has been kept in some
quarters when I tell you that neither Helen Graham nor
Margaret F. (York Place) have the least suspicion of it. I
fear that brat Eleanor may do me some mischief ; she is so
inquisitive to know what I am writing, and this house is so
small, it is very ill-calculated for concealment. As for the
money, I'm surprised how little I care about it, but I have
no desire to die a rich old aunt and leave a *posi* behind me
like poor Moll. The account of her *remains* was really
tempting. Such [*piece of letter cut here*] and Goupins
of gold ! No wonder that he [Mr. Alexr. Connell is here
meant] was 'neither to haud nor to bind' at getting
nothing, and I understand he was quite in a passion at the
reading of the will. I wish she had left his sisters something more. I had Mdlle. Le Chaux spending a day with
me on her return to Switzerland. She is to send me a
French copy of 'Marriage' to your care, which you will
forward to me.[1] I had a long visit of the Man of Feeling
t'other day—very infirm in body, but as gay and *spirituel*
as ever. We had also a grand dinner-party, as the 'Globe'
calls it—the Forbeses,[2] Monros, and Miss Mackenzie, who is
an enchanting creature ; but, nevertheless, I hate 'grand
dinners.' Mrs. John and Babe are *bravely* ; it is a nice fat
little thing, the picture of its grandfather. They are at a
loss what to call it. I propose William, but she seems to
like Henry better. . . . Don't be uneasy though it should

---

[1] *The Inheritance* was also translated into French by the same person
who translated Scott' novels. (J. F.)

[2] Lord Medwyn and Mrs. Forbes,
Professor and Mrs. Monro of Craig-
lockhart. (J. F.)

be weeks before you hear from me again ; this is to serve as
an answer to your next letter.

The following letters show that Miss Ferrier did not
pay for the popularity of 'Marriage' by any reaction
against its successor.

MRS. CONNELL TO S. E. F.

Conheath House : June 21, 1824.

My dear Susan,—I congratulate you most sincerely on
the happy termination of your labours. 'The Inheritance'
is delightful and certainly does great credit to both the head
and heart of the author.   I cannot presume to analyse it,
but upon the whole I never felt more interested in any book
than I have been by this.   James[1] lived upon it as long as
it lasted, and the girls are charmed.   Mary and Sue think
there ought to have been five volumes, and my only disappointment is the third is so many pages shorter than the
others.   However, I shall just begin and read it over again,
as a first reading is always hurried.   The Misses have
dubbed me Mrs. Black, but unfortunately we have no
Major Waddell, otherwise I think I should come best off.
Helen and Anne dined at Cowhill, on Friday[2] when one
lady at the other end of the table from them spoke of it
as superior to 'Marriage,' and said it was either by Miss
Campbell of Monzie or Miss Ferrier. . . .

S. E. F. TO MRS. CONNELL

Wednesday.

Your letter, my dear Janet, was extremely gratifying,
and I take shame to myself for not having acknowledged
it sooner.   I am very glad you all liked 'The Inheritance'
so much.   It seems to have been wonderfully successful,
but both Sir Walter and Mr. Mackenzie took it by the
hand at the very first, which of course gave it a lift.
Nevertheless the author will not confess nor allow any of

---

[1] Her son. (J. F.)
[2] Residence of Admiral Johnstone, near Dumfries. (J. F.)

her friends to do it for her. *Everybody* knows who the characters are, but no two people can agree about them. I have heard of five or six Lord Rossvilles and as many Miss Pratts, and Lady John Camp[1] signs herself Mrs. Major Waddell on account of her care of her husband, which she says is her to the very life. In short, whenever characters are at all *natural* they are immediately set down for being *personal*, which is a grievance. I think 'Red Gauntlet' extremely interesting, and the ghost story *delicious*, to say nothing of my bonnie Willie and Peter Peebles, who are inimitable. It will be particularly popular, I should think, in Dumfriesshire on account of its locality. I am happy to say my father continues in great health and good spirits, and I feel better than I did ; but as to our going from home, at my father's time of life, and with his habits, travelling would no longer be a recreation or amusement.

MRS. KINLOCH TO S. E. F.

Brunswick Square : June 23.

. . . I am enchanted with 'Inheritance,' and you must be sensible that it turns the 'Red Gauntlet' *quite pale* ; there's no comparison, and it's neither partiality nor flattery that makes me say so. It sells much better, the booksellers say, and is altogether a very superior work.[2] Mr. K. says he prefers it infinitely to 'Marriage,' and there he is at it till two o'clock in the morning weighing every word and sentence. He was impatient to get home from Mrs. Edmonstone's grand ball last night to finish a volume, while I was so weary I could hardly pull my things off. I felt a little nervous till I read a few chapters, so seldom do things answer our expectations, and so many failures are daily occurring in the literary way, witness 'Trials' by the

---

[1] Lady John Campbell (*née* Miss Glassel), mother of the present Duke of Argyll. She was a favourite pupil of Mrs. Grant, of Laggan, and is described in her letters.

[2] It is not altogether surprising that Miss Ferrier did not exchange many literary confidences with her sisters.

'Favorite of Nature,'[1] such trials to be sure to read such
stuff! And yet what a beautiful thing the 'Favorite' is.
But you have outdone yourself and come off with flying
colours, and I hope your health will improve now it is off
your mind. . . . .

MRS. GRAHAM TO S. E. F.

Stirling Castle : June 19.

Well, my dear Susan, I have finish'd it, and I am
delighted and so glad I did not read it piecemeal; it came
with such freshness. I truly enjoyed it. The faults, if
there are any, are lost amidst so much talent, and I have
read nothing like it for many a day. The interest is great
and rises with every volume, and though one is sorry when
the curtain drops, yet one retires quite satisfied from the
banquet. The strain of religion and morality through it is
refreshing, not wearisome like some of the late novels; in
short, we are all charmed with it. Miss Rutherfurd[2] dreams
of nothing but Edward. Helen's[3] favourite chapter is Miss
Pratt issuing from the hearse. The general was in fits at
Uncle Adam, who is truly rich, and there are so many
beauties, and so much fine writing I can scarcely select any
one, but I was greatly struck with the first interview between
the sisters, and the scene at the cottage is capital. I hear
there are extracts from it and a most flattering, or rather
favourable, critique in the 'Courant' . . . . We had a dinner
party yesterday, Lord and Lady Abercromby and their
daughter, who, by-the-bye, is a beautiful and sweet girl,
and the Tytlers. Colonel T. asked me if I had seen 'The
Inheritance,' as there was such a favourable account of it.
I said I had. How did I like it? Very much indeed.
Did I know who was the author? No, I do not. Lady
A., who was at the other end of the table, look'd up and
gave me such a stare, but said nothing. There was a sort

---

[1] By Mary Anne Kelty. (J. F.)

[2] Sister of Lord Rutherfurd, a judge of the Court of Session, Edinburgh.
(J. F.)　　　　　　　　　　　　[3] Her daughter. (J. F.)

of titter went round, and as none of them had read it, the conversation launched into other channels ; but Miss Johnstone,[1] who dined here two days since, told Helen it was in every house in Edinburgh, and the author as well known as if the name were prefixed to it. I was aware of what you say about lending and had determined not to do it. It is unfair to all parties—to the author and the publisher, and there is a little man here who gets the new books in whose way I should be sorry to stand. Mrs. Cameron,[2] who was very impatient for it, was to get it from him. . . . What a disgusting mind and imagination the author of 'Mathew Wald'[3] must possess. He is only fit to write in the 'Terrific Register'. . . .

FROM THE HON. LORD MURRAY[4] TO MISS WALKER

122 George Street : Wednesday evening.

Dear Miss Walker,—I received a message this evening about the admission of some person into the West Church poor house. I am unable to give you any aid in that, as I am not a member of the session and never attend its meetings. I was about to write to you on another subject. Indeed I have been prevented by absence from town from doing so long ago. I received a copy of 'Inheritance' in the name of the author, and as I do not know who the *author is*, and I suspect that you know more than I do, I trust that you will find some channel through which you will convey my thanks. I read 'Inheritance' with very great pleasure, the characters are very well conceived and delineated with great success. I may add that I have heard it highly commended by much better judges. Jeffrey speaks very favourably ; he is particularly pleased with the Nabob (Major) and Spouse, the letter from the lakes, and the P.S. to it. Lord Gwydyr, who lives entirely

---

[1] Miss Johnstone, of Alva, afterwards Mrs. Hamilton Grey. (J. F.)
[2] Lord Abercromby's sister. (J. F.)
[3] By J. G. Lockhart (1824).
[4] A judge of the Court of Session. (J. F.)

in fashionable circles, said to me much in its praise, in which I concurred.

From many other symptoms I have no doubt of its complete success. With best compliments to Miss Helen,

Believe me, ever yours truly,

JOHN A. MURRAY.

THE DUCHESS OF ARGYLL TO S. E. F.

Waterloo Hotel : Saturday evening.

My dear Miss Ferrier,—You have been so kind in taking so much trouble for me, *my books*, and *my baskets*, that I hardly know how to thank you for it. I only hope you will not hate me as much as people generally do those who give them commissions, though I was not *quite* as unreasonable as the Lady in 'Inheritance.' Did *you* ever read that book ?

You make a very good selection for us, and they are all new to us. I am very willing to accept you as a *middle man*, but you forgot to tell me what I am in your debt for these very perfect baskets, and I am not going to rob you of them. The Duke is very happy you admire his handwriting, and has sent you two *beautiful* specimens. I hope you were none the worse for your cold walk to-day or for *my minced collops*.[1] We set off, I hope, *early* to-morrow, as we propose sleeping at Belford. The Duke is so well, I am happy, and desires his kind remembrances to you, and believe me ever,

My dear Miss Ferrier,

Yours affectionately,

CAROLINE ARGYLL.

---

[1] A favourite dish of Miss Ferrier's. (J. F.) I fear there is no convincing evidence to identify her with the old lady who, when a cook was recommended to her as a very decent body, replied, ' Damn her decency ; can she cook collops ? '

MADEMOISELLE DE LA CHAUX[1] *TO S. E. F.*

Yverdun : August 20, 1825.

At last, dear Miss Ferrier, I have obtained possession of the long wished for book !   I cannot say how delighted I have been on reading it.   For this year past I was led by the nose by the vain promises of Paris and Geneva booksellers, and finally applied to the fountain head of all good things, *London*, by means of a friend, and I got a copy of the *second edition*.   I observed the proof of success with exultation, though I already had read in several periodical works the most favourable account and extracts of it announcing a translation 'to be speedily published,' but of this I am not sure after having been deceived about that of ' Marriage.'   I read ' The Inheritance ' during a short stay on the Jura, two or three leagues above Yverdun.   The situation was not unworthy, I thought, of this pursuit.   I was with my friend, Madame Huber, who has known English from her childhood, her mother being an Englishwoman, and she enjoyed your work *con amore*, I assure you.   We were both deeply in love with Uncle Adam, thought Miss Pratt abundantly provoking, Gertrude one of the most interesting heroines produced since the time of Evelina, because she was only sufficiently handsome, accomplished, and amiable not to be above mortal, and quite unfortunate enough to have had Mrs. St. Clair for her supposed mother. I found Lord Rossville very like a friend of mine, and several English people told me it must be a portrait from nature.   But I fear you will think all these observations very commonplace and beneath your notice since you have had those of the great wits and geniuses laid humbly at

---

[1] This lady, a native of Switzerland, had been governess in the family of Lady A. Clavering, and when Lord John Campbell was there in the year 1803 with his travelling companion, Dr. Argyll Robertson, she disguised him in her clothes, &c., to enable him to get back to his native land ; otherwise he might have been detained a prisoner by Napoleon. But for her presence of mind, he would certainly have been among the *détenus*, as Marshal Ney had sent an officer to seize him. (J. F.)

your feet! Of course Mr. Ferrier has been one of the
first to testify his approbation, and with a due share of
pride very enviable for a father. I suppose you understand what I mean, though my English is a little doubtful
now and then. Perhaps Miss E. M. has told you it was
my intention to go to England in autumn to pay a con-
doling visit to my friend at Waddon, who has lost a most
amiable sister, and one whom I loved and esteemed very
particularly. It will be a great privation to me to be in
the house where her presence was so essential. I hope
your venerable father continues to wear well and allows
years to pass over his head as though they were zephyrs.
Pray remember me to him as one who never forgets his
constant friendliness and wishes much to see him again. I
have fixed October as the time of my setting out for
England, as Mr. Baillie, my former travelling companion,
offers to take me again under his protection. If I don't
hear from you before, I trust I shall when at *Waddon, near
Croydon, Surrey.* I am particularly anxious to know how
you are in health. The long absence of my friend, Miss
E. M., from Edinburgh has deprived me of the advantage
of hearing *of you* through her letters. I owe an answer to
Mrs. Fletcher, and when you see her I wish you to tell
her she knows the effects of procrastination, and that I
regret being under that fatal spell towards her, but that I
don't forget her for all that, and should be very happy to
see her and hers. I trust Lady Augusta's scheme of going
to join Rawdon has been laid aside and that his wife is
recovering, but gives him no more *heirs* to inherit his want
of fortune and *good guidance* into the bargain. How is
Mrs. Graham and her family? I once heard of her by
Miss Bruce of Stenhouse. What does she do with her
sons? Remember me to your brother John and his
family. I could ask you fifty questions about all sorts of
people and things, but I fancy you might think it rather a
bore to answer half that number. I will wait to hear how
far you are generously disposed towards a sort of exile, as

I reckon myself when far away from dear Scotland ! . . . .
By-the-bye, the 'Tales of the Crusaders,' with some happy
accidents de lumière are not fit to keep up the *Great Unknown's* fame, I think, except that he shows an acquaintance
with Saladin's talent for quackery, which historians were
ignorant of, fortunately for his dignity. 'Richard Cœur
de Lion' is good, but not equal to his 'Louis the Eleventh.'
Adieu, dear Miss Ferrier !

Ever your sincerely attached

C. D.

MISS HANNAH MACKENZIE TO S. E. F.

I hardly know what to say for myself—I am so entirely
ashamed of not having before now answered your kind
note, and sent you my hearty congratulations on the birth
of your second daughter ; had I been able I should certainly
have come to rejoice over it with you, and to get cake and
caudle. Papa is very much pleased with much that he
has read (to the end of the second volume), and mama,[1] as
is no common case with novels, likes the third greatly
the best, thereon I agree with her. Walter Scott dined
here one day, and both he and papa joined heartily in their
admiration of Uncle Adam and their wish to know who
he is. Sir W. also admires Miss Becky Duguid, and said
he thought her quite a new character. I should like much
to see you and talk all over at length, but fear to invite
you to my own bower for fear of suspicion, but I trust
you will soon come and boldly face my whole family. I
do not think you need fear them much—of course, like
other people, they have their 'thoughts,' but by no means
speak with certainty. Margaret has this minute assured
us that she 'does not think it Miss Ferrier's.' I wish you
had told me how you are—I fear, suffering from the nasty
east wind ; I have not gained much under its influences.

---

[1] Henry Mackenzie married, in 1776, Penuel, daughter of Sir Ludovic
Grant of Grant, Bart. (J. F.)

Hope has got a cold which will not leave her. But I am thankful to say papa has got quite well in spite of it, and of having had a very long fit of illness ; mama, too, is very well. Chatty is very good in coming to see me, and I think her looking well and in good spirits, and very agreeable. Can you read this ? Pardon it, and believe me

Ever yours affectionately,

H. M.

Monday night.—The woman of the needle lives still in her old quarters.

CAPTAIN BASIL HALL[1] TO S. E. F.

81 High Street, Portsmouth : August 15, 1824.

Captain Hall presents his respectful compliments to the author of 'Inheritance,' and begs she will do him the honour to accept a copy of his work on South America, in humble but sincere testimony of his gratitude for the pleasure and, he hopes, improvement which he has derived from the perusal of her very admirable work. Captain Hall, without the slightest affectation of humility, is fully sensible of the superiority of interest, and very often of instruction, in works of fiction over those of mere matter of fact, and as an author willingly offers his homage accordingly. In order that either shall prove useful or interesting it must be written with perfect honesty. One has the privilege of dealing as it pleases with events, but it must be true to nature in all that relates to sentiment and character. The other must be true to actual occurrences, while the imagination may be called upon to assign the motives. In the hands of one author the fancy is an engine to be used at will and with confidence ; to the other its use is utterly denied in description, and must be very carefully handled in judging of the causes of events.

[1] Author of a charming book entitled *Schloss Heinfeldt*, an account of a six months' visit he and his family paid Countess Purgstall (*née* Miss Cranstoun) at her residence in Styria. He was a son of Sir James Hall, Bart., of Dunglas, and an officer in the Royal Navy. (J. F.)

The vast field of human society is open to the novelist ; the traveller is circumscribed by narrow boundaries, and yet in the course of natural events circumstances will sometimes arise which the imagination could scarcely have created. To describe these with effect probably does not require much less labour than it does to do justice to the creations of fancy, though certainly far higher praise is due to the author who not only describes but conceives, than to him who merely opens his eyes and writes down what he sees.

In both cases there is enough always left to the taste and skill of the author to establish a sort of analogy between two things at first sight so very dissimilar as a novel and a book of travel. The author of the travels would assuredly be very well pleased, at all events in this case, could he hope that his dry details would in any degree afford a similar gratification to the author of the novel that its pages have bestowed upon him.

MRS. GORE TO S. E. F.

47 Connaught Square, London.

Madam,—I have to apologise for intruding upon you having very little hope that the production of a few ephemeral novels will induce the authoress of ' Marriage ' to admit me to the high honour of sistership in her craft, An explanation of the motive of my letter may perhaps afford its best apology. Two years ago I was so fortunate as to produce a successful comedy, which necessarily introduced me to the chief comic actors of the day, all of whom without one exception successively made it their request that I would dramatise the novel of ' The Inheritance,' allotting them such and such parts. Having other engagements to perform, I gave the subject little attention, more particularly as the work, although the most original and various in point of character, did not strike me as peculiarly adapted to the stage. Since the management of Covent Garden Theatre fell into the hands of Laporte he has favoured me with a commission to write a comedy for him, and the subject proposed by him is again the French novel of 'L'Héritière,' which turns out to be a literal translation of 'The Inheritance'; he is quite bent, he says, upon having Miss Pratt on the stage. I have not chosen to give Monsieur Laporte any positive answer on the subject without previously applying to yourself to know whether you have any intention or inclination to apply to the stage those admirable powers which are so justly appreciated in London, and whether 'The Inheritance' suggests itself to you as the subject of a drama. If not, I shall probably lend my aid to his projects; but, believe me, it would afford me sincere gratification to announce to him that the task was committed to so much abler hands.

I forward this letter to Mr. Tait, the bookseller, hoping that it will reach your hands, and that you will pardon the liberty I have taken in addressing you.

I have the honour to be, madam,

Your obedient, humble servant,

CATHERINE FRANCES GORE.

S. E. F. TO MRS. CONNELL (1832)

My dear Janet,—I have been all day expecting the arrival of the Grahams with great anxiety. They were to embark in the 'Adelaide' on Saturday evening, and the weather has been most unfavourable ever since; Sunday night must have been fearful at sea—the wind blew so strong from the north-east. Oh that they were safely landed! I am told it is a very slow sailing vessel, and is commonly a day longer on the voyage than the others, and upon going to the office before dinner the agents said they never looked for its arrival before to-morrow morning; but this has been a long day, and seems a lonely evening as I sit here listening to the vile roaring east wind, and think of what *they* may be suffering! Yet, to use Samuel's expression, 'there is a Providence at sea as well as on land,' for He in whom we live and move and have our being is present everywhere. Oh, if we could but *believe* that we are each and all of us the objects of His peculiar love and care, how much easier we should feel under every circumstance of life! Even now my heart condemns me for the misery I feel at every blast of wind; but I must try to write of something else, though I cannot change to a much more cheerful theme on turning to poor Mrs. F.,[1] who is certainly not gaining ground. Yesterday she felt so uneasy and became so languid they were obliged to administer the foxglove; to-day she has not been worse, but that was all the doctor could say; happily she is still able to take food, and the morphia agrees with her, so her nights are better than they were, and we must still hope that it may be God's will to restore her in His good time. It was well that Walter was persuaded to give up his journey to Dumfries, as he was ill able for such an expedition; he has much need to save, not to squander, the little health and strength he has. I heard to-day, which gave me much pleasure, that the King has ordered a pension of 200*l.* to Miss Scott, and that will give her about 300*l.* per annum, and with that any one may be quite independent. Mrs. Gore, the author of 'Pin Money,' &c., has been applied to by the managers of Covent Garden to dramatise 'Inheritance,' so Miss Pratt will be figuring there by-and-bye. I have not yet got servants, though I have seen and spoken with multitudes; it is frightful to think how few characters will stand the scrutiny even of their own sinful fellow creatures! I was shocked to hear of the delay of the box, and that you were eating fish exactly a week old, as they had been sent *off* on the Thursday before. I should have sent more, but they have been scarce, and it will probably be next week before I can send any. The linen was sent by me in lieu

---

[1] Her sister-in-law, long an invalid. (J. F.)

of the flannel, and if there is any balance in my favour you may give some more flannel to the Millers and Hunters.

Thursday.—Thank God our dear Jane is arrived safe after a very stormy and perilous voyage; she looks ill, and is much fatigued, but a day or two's rest will set her all to rights. Helen is quite brisk, and both seem very happy and thankful to find themselves on dry land, and happy I was to see them! Jane will write soon and give you all her adventures. Mrs. John is decidedly better to-day. I end in a blither key than I began. I called at the repository to look for some new work, and there is a very simple affair which I think you will like; it is called a *fanchette*, and is used to put over the head, and clasps under the chin to keep the head and ears warm, or else round the throat; the day was so bad, and I was so hurried, I could not get worsted or netting needles, but if you want them I will send them next week with the pattern—it's a net boa from London. The *fanchettes* are all colours, but silk is better than cotton where it is used. I dare say this is illegible, for I write in the dark—my eyes are so painful. I am just going to have eight leeches applied.

MRS. GORE TO S. E. F. (about 1831)

5 Ulster Terrace, Regent's Park.

I have to thank you for writing to me again respecting 'The Inheritance,' for nothing but my apprehension that you might write me down a Miss Pratt has prevented my addressing you on the subject. Very shortly after I had the pleasure of communicating with you last I was informed that a dramatic version of the novel had been laid before the reader to Covent Garden Theatre, which (unless I wished to establish a previous claim) would be accepted. Not having written a line of my play, and having no clue to the merits of the one in question, I judged it unfair to a brother dramatist to interfere with his labours, and withdrew from the field. I have since learned with regret that the play is the production of a certain Mr. Fitzball,[1] the distinguished author of the 'Flying Dutchman,' and sixty other successful melodramas, represented with great applause at the Surrey, Coburg, City, and Pavilion Theatres, &c. &c.—in short, a writer of a very low class. . . . I greatly fear that neither comedies nor other works of fiction dependent for their interest on the successful delineation of *character* will for many years to come fix the attention of the public. Nothing but books or plays administrant to unnatural excitement, or of a nature to gratify the outcry for useful knowledge, have now any vogue in London. I venture to say outcry, because I perceive that the greater number of Miss Martineau's readers care nothing for her stories, which are certainly as good and interesting as if they conveyed no instruction. . . . I have presumed to trespass very long on your time, and yet I would willingly detain you a moment longer, to beg that, if you have not already read it, you will look at the third volume of the 'Recollections of a Chaperon,' containing 'Ellen Wareham.' I would willingly find you of my own opinion, that it is the most forcible tale produced since those of Mrs. Inchbald.

Though Mrs. Gore's scheme fell through, Miss Pratt was allowed dramatic existence of a sort over and above that provided by Mr. Fitzball as we see from the following letter:

MISS MARY CAMPBELL[2] TO S. E. F.

Kennet[3] : January 8, 1826.   Alloa.

My dear Susan,—I must first wish you a good New Year in the common way, and I may just add my best

---

[1] Readers of *Bon Gaultier* will remember the 'terrible Fitzball,' Wordsworth's opponent in the tournament which decided the Laureateship. Miss Ferrier would have had an almost unique experience among modern novelists if he had not dramatized her. His list of victims, as set forth in the British Museum Catalogue, includes Sir Walter Scott, Michael Scott (the author of *Tom Cringle*), Cooper, Marryat, and Victor Hugo. Miss Ferrier does not appear, and there are probably other omissions. The Catalogue also discloses the fact that his real name was Ball.

[2] One of Miss Ferrier's very oldest friends, daughter of John Campbell, of the Citadel, a cadet branch of the Breadalbane family. Her mother was a Callander, of Craigforth, and her brother, Mr. John Archibald Camp-

wishes for your health and comfort and that of all those
near and dear to you during this and all the long years
that I hope and trust it may be the will of Providence to
permit you to enjoy in this life.   How are you ?   I hope in
your *frail ordiner*—no, something better than that.   I have
enjoyed a part of the Xmas gambols here exceedingly.
Dressing up in character and *guizarding* (I don't know
how to spell the word) was the order of the day, or rather
of the evening ; and at last, the actors waxing bold, it was
proposed to get up a scene from 'The Inheritance.'
Unluckily there was no copy in the house, but after all I
don't think it signified, for we were all so perfect in the
speeches of Bell Black, Major Waddell, Uncle Adam, and
Miss Pratt, that there was *small* occasion for any kind of
prompting. Sir Gilbert Stirling did your Uncle Adam to the
life ; his face was excellently painted, a red silk handkerchief,
old great coat, hose drawn over his breeches knees—in
short, the costume I do think very much as you would have
wished ; it was, we thought, in the hilarity of the moment,
quite perfect. My sister Georgina was Bell Black, and
clacked the Major in great style, who was Mr. Bruce.
She is a funny, quick girl, and entered into the spirit of the
character, both before and after marriage, astonishingly.
Miss Pratt deserved a better fate, for she fell to Willy
Bruce, who did her no justice. Cumming Bruce[1] took
Colonel Delmour, and Amelia Lamont Miss St. Clair.
The scenes they chose were the first introduction to Uncle
Adam and his visit to Gertrude. I have no doubt, my
dear Susan, you would have spit fire at the exertions of
the party and pronounced them a complete failure ; but we,

bell, a well-known inhabitant of
Edinburgh. In her youth she was
very beautiful and somewhat resembling Marie Antoinette, 'Santa Maria,'
as she was called by her friends, from
the depth of her human sympathy and
divine love. She died in 1872 at
Albyn Place, Edinburgh, aged ninety.
(J. F.)

[2] The residence of Robert Bruce,
Esq., and now the property of his
son, Lord Balfour of Burleigh.
(J. F.)

[1] Brother of Sir W. Gordon Cumming ; took the name of Bruce on his
marriage to Miss Bruce, of Kinnaird
(J. F.)

poor creatures, we roared and laughed, and shouted excellent! bravo! encore! Now don't you perceive the mixed feeling of mind by which I am at this moment actuated, evidently telling you this expecting you are to receive the intimation as a compliment, and at the same time not without fear that you will highly disapprove the temerity of the attempt. There has been a large party here, but except a Mrs. Bruce of Grangemuir I once told you about, I think the bulk of the people were genteel, but dull, gentlemanlike, and melancholy. Amelia goes to Edinburgh next week, and I shall desire her to call and tell you her news, as I have been so busy all day at the Kirk. I have no time to add the nothings I intended to follow this detail. Adieu, my dear friend.

Believe me always affectionately yours,

M. H. C.

There was, as we have seen, a connection by marriage between the Wilsons and the Ferriers. Of the Wilson family, the one with whom Miss Ferrier seems to have been most intimate was James, a brother several years younger than Christopher North.[1] He was a learned naturalist and figures in the Chaldee MS. as 'the stork which buildeth upon the housetop and devoureth all manner of unclean things, and all beetles and much worms.' For once two critics differing as widely in cast of mind as Lockhart and Mrs. Grant are agreed. In Peter's letters James Wilson is described as 'very young, many years junior to his celebrated brother, and no casual observer would suspect them to be of the same family. James is a thin, pale, slender, contemplative looking person, with hair of a rather dark colour, and extremely short-sighted. In his manners, also, he is as different as possible from his brother. His voice is low and his whole demeanour as still as can be imagined. In conversation he attempts no kind of display, but seems to possess a very peculiar vein of dry humour which renders him

---

[1] James Wilson was born in 1795, and died in 1857. His marriage to Isabella Keith, sister of Sir Alexander Keith, took place in 1824, and is referred to in the following letter. A life of him, by the Rev. James Hamilton, D.D., was published in 1859.

extremely diverting. . . . Professor Jameson informed me that his young friend is in truth no less a poet than a naturalist, that he possesses a fine genius for versification, and has already published several pieces of exquisite beauty, though he has not yet ventured to give his name along with them.'

Mrs. Grant describes him as 'a younger and graver brother of the "Isle of Palms." When I speak of gravity I mean the grave countenance with which he says things irresistibly ludicrous. He is, in fact, the author of some of the best, at least the most refined, wit in "Blackwood's Magazine."' His biographer, Dr. Hamilton, says of him 'Charles Lamb and James Wilson would have understood each other.'

JAMES WILSON TO S. E. F.

53 Queen Street : October 11, Tuesday morning, 1824.

Dear Susan,—You will have heard of the scrape I have got into ; you will probably never hear that I have got out of it again, but let us hope the best ; it is not Dalmeny Edmonstone, neither is it Marianne Millar. My mind must have sunk under the sparkling sylph-like intelligence of the one and my body been soon overcome by the robust indefatigable pedestrianism of the other. But it is one, who, though less accomplished in the English tongue than the Sylph and more ignorant of strong shoes than the Satyr, is about as much to my mind as either, and much more so than both. As I am just on the eve of giving myself an airing with the view to inspect an estate in the neighbourhood of Morningside, I think it right to write these few lines lest you should think that I have taken any undue advantage in planting myself so near you without timeous warning.[1] Should the house prove cold and damp, and the summer unfavourable, you will enjoy the satisfaction of hearing an additional widow's gun fired off before the fall of the leaf.[2] If I am allowed to walk

---

[1] A small place, Woodville, where he lived and died, and which he bought from his brother-in-law, Mr. John Ferrier, W.S., for 1,000*l.* Miss Ferrier and her father lived at Morningside House in summer. (J. F.)

[2] Neither of the editors can offer any suggestion as to the nature of a 'widow's gun.'

up to Morningside to-day I shall do so, and hope to find you deriving some benefit from the change of air. I myself shall have nothing else but air now, so hope it will be frequently changed. Do they bring fish round regularly? Is there a baker and butcher at hand? How are you are off for soap? Spirits, I am told, are down (mine are so), but then, from the increased price of tallow, I fear candle is looking up. Do you wash and dress in the house? I hope so, for I always thought it very improper for any lady to be seen either washing or dressing by the roadside. The thing itself may not be wrong, but then idle people talk, and wicked people doubt one's motive, and you know, Miss Ferrier, one must sacrifice something to the opinion of the world, however anti-ablutionary it may at present be. However, I would fain hope that both yellow sand for the kitchen floor and camstane [1] for the lobby may be had either at Burrow Muir head or the toll. On these and several other points of deep importance, I shall hope the same friendly and unreserved confidence which has hitherto subsisted between us will induce a free and impartial communication. What is upon the whole your opinion of Sunday salt compared with salt of the week-day kind? Do you buy your potatoes by the peck or the boll? Do you look upon small bread as not more objectionable on the score of cheatery than the standard quartern loaf? Do you fatten and then kill your own poultry? Do you harden your heart by so doing? Do you train up a pet lamb in the way it should play itself and murder it when it comes to years of dishcretion? Do you boil your lobsters alive? Do you poison your neighbour's pigeons to preserve your own peas? Is it justifiable homicide to shoot other people's cats when you have none of your own? But I am anticipating what I hope we shall have ample opportunity of discussing in the course of the ensuing summer. For the present I shall conclude by observing

---

[1] A substance used for floor cleaning.

in regard to *the creature* that had I been as blooming as
Mr. Spencer, as upright as Anny Walker, as rich as Prince
Esterhazy, as innocent as Alexander Millar, as lively as
his sister aforesaid, as healthy as Mr. Rollo, and as fat
as Professor Leslie, I could neither have hoped for nor
expected anything better than I have obtained. I trust
you will also be of the same opinion.

Believe me, your very sincere friend,

JAMES WILSON.

P.S.—Feeling a little tired from want of sleep, and I
have changed my mind as to going with my mother and
Jane [1] to-day *out yonder*, but I hope to see you soon either
here or there.

J. W.

JAMES WILSON TO S. E. F. [2]

Woodville : July 4.

Dear Susan,—Isabella [3] agrees with me on the propriety
of *not* dining with you at this time, as you are just on the
wing for a foreign country. In fact, on her own account, as
well as yours, I think she is better for a while at home ; from
having been so long without paying any visits she would
perhaps be expected to go *through with it* if she once
began. However, she will not be in town during your
stay without paying you a visit, and I need scarcely say
how gratified and how grateful she will be whenever you
afford her an opportunity now or hereafter of seeing you
here. . . . I am a good deal engaged at present with
Uncle Sym [4] who, though not suffering from any definable

---

[1] His sister, Miss Wilson. Old
Mrs. Wilson was a very fine-looking
old lady, and sister to Mr. Robert
Sym, W.S. Jane Wilson had her
miniature painted for her sister, Lady
McNeill, who was in Persia, her
husband being Envoy at that Court.
James Wilson, hearing that it was going
to Persia, said to her, 'I'll tell you
what will happen, Jane. The Shah
will see it, and he'll send for you for
one of his wives, and when you
arrive he'll cut your head off, for you
are not the least like it !' The portrait is supposed to have slightly
flattered her. (J. F.)

[2] As I can find no clue to the date
of this letter, I have placed it with the
only other one from the writer.

[3] Mrs. James Wilson.

[4] Robert Sym, W.S. ; he was
'Timothy Tickler,' in the *Noctes
Ambrosianæ*, and was remarkable for
his stature and good looks ; died 1845,

complaint, is languid both in mind and body and more dependent than usual on the attentions of the few with whom he finds himself at ease. He has several times quoted, with high approbation of its beauty and propriety, a sentiment from a certain recent novel [1] that the affectionate ministrations of the young to the old ought rather to be regarded in the light of delightful privileges than as mere duties which they are bound to pay, and although the allusion was made without any reference to himself I have great pleasure in endeavouring to imitate the example of those by whom the sentiment has not only been finely expressed but long practised. [2] If you won't grudge a postage I shall be glad to let you know occasionally what is doing among the birds, bairns, and other beasts of this corner of the world.

Sincerely yours,
JAMES WILSON.

S. E. F. TO MRS. CONNELL.

Wednesday, March 3, 1825.

My dear Janet,—I really would have written to you before now, but for my father's indisposition, which was of a nature that puzzled me what to say about it. One day he was pretty well, the next complained of being very ill. Even on the same day he varied several times, but in general his appetite remained perfectly good, and he acknowledged that he commonly slept seven or nine hours at a stretch with these symptoms. I could not believe there was anything materially wrong, and therefore I was not alarmed, though I was uneasy and restless; but I thought it would be cruel to communicate my feelings to you, especially as I could not have asked you to come to

---

in George Square, Edinburgh, aged 95. His portrait, by Sir H. Raeburn, is one of that great painter's finest works, and is now in my possession. (J. F.)

[1] Either *The Inheritance* or *Destiny*. (J. F.)
[2] In allusion to Miss Ferrier's well-known filial devotion. (J. F.)

us, for at that time he would have been quite angry had I
hinted at such a thing. He is now, I am happy to say,
much better. He still complains occasionally of a sort of
confusion in his head (which, however, never appears in
anything he says or does) and a degree of deafness which
at his age is certainly not a *prodigy*, but he continues to
eat and sleep well and looks well, and takes a drive to
Morningside two or three times a week, or walks in the
garden when the weather admits. At the same time that
I rejoice in these good symptoms I am sensible that his
strength is not what it was, and that he walks slower and
more feebly than he did some months ago, but I would fain
flatter myself that when he gets to Morningside he may in
some degree recruit even at his advanced age. . . . He
has been obliged to withdraw from the business of the
Court, even before his successor was appointed, but he has
had it in view for many months, and is now in daily
expectation of seeing everything settled, which will be a
relief to his mind as well as body. With regard to your
kind offer of coming to us as usual in time of need I read
it to him, and he seemed sensible of the kindness and
affection which had dictated it ; but the season is now so
far advanced, he seemed to think it would not be worth
while, as our stay in town will depend so much upon the
weather ; at present it is very bad, but should it set in
fine we shall probably move very soon. My cold is almost
gone, but for some days it was very severe, and I was so
hoarse I could not speak, or at least my father could not
hear me; but now, mercifully, we are come to an understanding. Jane will tell you of her sufferings, but everybody has been ill of something or another: Mrs. John,
toothache and rheumatism ; Mrs. Walter, a bad cough,
which is now better; Mrs. James Wilson you would see
has produced a daughter, a real human creature, and
neither fish nor fowl, as was apprehended, but a very fine
child, and its papa the happiest of men. They are to be at
Woodville this summer. Mrs. Wallace came to town about

a fortnight ago, chiefly, she said, to see my father, but he was so much of an invalid when she came, that he would not see her for some days, although you know what a favourite she is. Since then she has dined twice, but except that, and having the lads[1] as usual on Sundays, we never have a soul. I think one or two intimate friends now and then would be an agreeable variety, but it won't do. Even Anne Walker in her fur cap would be taken for a *company*, and I'm almost afraid of having asked Mrs. G.[2] to meet Mrs. Wallace to-day, it will be such a brilliant party! Mrs. K.[3] is certainly very fortunate in having both a rich and an indulgent husband, as there are few Scotch wives at least who can travel about for their health as she does. I had a letter from her t'other day with a history of her boys having shot a fine painting all through with their bows and arrows, the *blame* of which she seems to land on Mrs. Conry,[4] the *pity* upon herself for not having heeded them better. Mrs. Conry must be much better than I am to be blamed for other people's boys! You must have done a great deal the short time you were in Carlisle, and, I hear, made many conquests, which is very *impolitic*. Remember me to Mr. C. and believe me, dear Janet,

Your most affectionate

S. E. F.

S. E. F. TO MRS. CONNELL

Monday, 10th.

This is the first free opportunity I have had of thanking you for your letter and its accompaniments, which I can scarcely add were most acceptable, although my father grumbles a little at the degeneracy of modern partridges, and always discovers after having picked one to the bone that there is nothing upon it. From this you may infer

---

[1] Her Nephews. (J. F.)
[2] Graham. (J. F.)
[3] Kinloch. (J. F.)
[4] Mr. Kinloch's sister. (J. F.)

his appetite is not failing, and, indeed, I never saw him better in every respect than he is at present; he has recovered his hearing by having had his ears syringed, and altogether is in such good health and spirits that I am impatient for you to see him. We shall be moving to town about the end of this month, when we must, I fear, bid a last farewell to Morningside. I *could* be very sorry to think of it, and time was when I *would* have been, but I have lived long enough to have discovered that all such unavailing regrets and repinings are at best but weakness and selfishness, mere disturbers of our own peace and the peace of others. As for my *bodily* feelings, they are much the same, if anything better; my head became so very bad after drinking the Airthrie waters that I was obliged to have recourse to my good old doctor, and his prescriptions, together with sponging my pate &c., have relieved me in some degree of the intolerable weight, though it still continues stupid and confused, and I suppose will do all the days of its life. I have been reading a book upon the stomach, which has convinced me that we are all *gourmands* and eat and drink a great deal too much and of too many good things, and that almost all diseases are occasioned by our *intemperance*; this is no new doctrine, and I don't pretend to pass it for such, but 'tis a great point gained when one is brought to believe it, and a still greater when one can bring themselves to act upon it. I dare say that is not easy at your good table, but at our meagre board the temptations are seldom powerful. . . . . I hear James Walker is going to be married to a Miss Mackenzie of Scotsburn, but I have heard no particulars of the lady, except that she has no fortune, so I trust she has better things and will be an acquisition to the family. Anne and Helen are still in Isla, but I hope they will be home soon, as they make a dreadful blank to me. Mrs. Fletcher, too, is away, so I have nobody but the Mackenzies and James Wilsons to befriend me. I send you hieroglyphic newspapers, which are said to be the best things of the kind

since the days of Hogarth. Whatever Sir A. F. or anybody else may say, you know what you have to say.[1]

S. E. F. TO MRS. CONNELL
December, 1826.

As I think it too much to make one's friends pay for
bare thanks I delayed sending mine till they could travel
free. The partridges were excellent, and your offer of a
credit upon your poultry-yard most generous and kind ;
however, I hope I shall never be so ravenous as to play
Tod Lowrie and carry off your hens and chickens—it is
quite enough that we are liberally supplied with the birds
of the air. . . . My father continues in perfect health, eats
well and sleeps well, and is in good spirits, but he is feeble
in his walking, which is the natural consequence of ad-
vancing years—except in that particular he really shows no
symptom of old age . . . but I hope you will judge for
yourself by-and-bye.

The Grahams are to be with us on Saturday ; they say
for a week, but I trust for a month, after which they go to
Mrs. Hay, and when they leave us we hope Mr. C. and
you, and one of the girls, will come for a few weeks, as the
G.s, being in Edinburgh, will be an additional inducement, and if you don't come then there is no saying when
we may meet, as we shall be off to Morningside, as usual,
in March.

I don't think I have written you since the death of poor
Beenie, who slipped away very suddenly one morning without any warning. She had gone to a niece's wedding the
evening before and wanted to get up to put on the fires
about an hour before she died. She was a quiet, inoffensive
creature, and so little had been given her in the way of
understanding that doubtless little would be required of
her in attainments. I can't be so hypocritical as to
lament her loss, as she had long been worse than nobody

---

[1] Adam Fergusson. (This last sentence evidently alludes to the secrecy of
her authorship.) (J. F.)

to me, and I have now got a nice, stout, neat-handed young woman in her place. . . . We have a regular weekly dinner of our neighbours and their cousin, Miss E., who is a very pleasant, sensible creature.[1] . . . Walter looks fagged and ill; at present both John and he are so very busy I see very little of either—indeed, everybody is busy in their own way at this season, for the days are so short and dark there is no getting anything done. We don't breakfast till about ten, and at one I commonly take a drive to Morningside with my father and walk about there, which, with seeing my friends, putting on and off my things, and managing my domestic affairs, leaves me scarcely a moment to myself.

S. E. F. TO MRS. KINLOCH (1826)

Saturday.

You judged truly, my dear Helen, that I would be much occupied upon coming to town, though not so much but that a letter from you would have been very acceptable. As for my old letters, the only purpose for which I wanted them was to burn them, and I am very glad you have saved me that trouble. It seems you thought I was going to publish them!!! I begin to think you don't know me or you never could have imagined such a thing. I wish I could destroy every letter I ever wrote, for I am sensible my mind has undergone many and great changes in the course of my life, and that my sentiments and opinions in many respects are totally changed from what they were; indeed, I find them *still changing*, for though I trust and believe I am not *insincere*, I am conscious I am somewhat *fluctuating*, at least in *some* things and people; in others I am uniformly steady. 'Judge before friendship, then confide till death,' is good advice, but alas! my judgment has often followed my liking in many things; but this is a long digression from the subject of my old scrawl, and all I have now to say is that I beg all my new ones

---

[1] Mrs. Halliday and her sisters, the Misses Edmonstone. (J. F.)

may share the same fate. My father continues quite well and bears his retirement from business better than I could have expected.[1] The great blank in his life is the want of an old friend, for it is very sad not to have one remaining ; but we all need to be weaned from this world, for, with all its pains and privations, we are all too fond of it. I'm sure I am, in spite of my many warnings.

ALARIC WATTS TO S. E. F.

8 North Bank, Regent's Park : July 12, 1826.

Madam,—I fear you will pronounce me guilty of an unpardonable liberty in venturing, without the pleasure of any personal acquaintance with you, to introduce myself to your notice by requesting a favour from you ; but the great delight I have received from your writings (kindly presented to me by Mr. Blackwood), an admiration which I have more than once had opportunities of publicly avowing, makes me anxious to include some brief production of your pen in the forthcoming volume of the little work of which I have now the pleasure to request your acceptance. This volume will be found to contain original contributions in prose and verse by a large proportion of our most popular writers, and the illustrations I think you will find have seldom, and in two or three instances never, been surpassed as book illustrations.

A northern friend had kindly undertaken to endeavour to interest you in behalf of the 'Literary Souvenir' some time ago, but as I am of opinion that a direct application to you would be forgiven, even although you should be indisposed to comply with my request, and that 'a faint heart never won a fair lady,' I have, at the risk of being set down for an intruder, ventured upon this address.

Any sketch resembling the numbers of faithful delineations of society in your published writings, or any little legend or essay of a light character, will confer great

---

[1] He retired on June 5, 1826, on a pension of 860*l.* per annum. (J. F.)

interest upon, as anything from the author of 'Marriage' would aid in conferring popularity upon, my little volume.

Having suffered grievously by the failure of my late booksellers (from ten to eleven thousand of the work having been printed), I am particularly anxious to concentrate as much talent as possible in my next number. In addition to most of the friends who contributed to the last, I am promised and have received papers from various other quarters.

As the book must make its appearance on the first of November, the favour of an early line mentioning whether I may hope for something from your pen will greatly oblige.

I am, madam, with great respect,
Your obedient servant,
ALARIC WATTS.

DUCHESS OF ARGYLL TO S. E. F.

Upper Brook Street :[1] Friday, January 12, 1827.

My dear Miss Ferrier,—I assure you I was much pleased to receive your letter, for I feared by your silence you were ill or had not received the book, not that it deserved the thanks you so kindly bestowed on me for sending it. I was anxious for your opinion of it, and now I really wish you were here to have a discussion with the Duke, who thinks you very *unjust*, but he says *poor Truth* has always suffered from misrepresentation. However, so determined is he to endeavour to convince you that *his* opinion is right, that I should not be surprised if he writes you a letter on the subject the first leisure moment he has. The Duke begs me also to tell you that he shall have great pleasure in appointing your friend his chaplain if his number is not full, or if that number is not limited, neither of which facts he knows how to ascertain. Perhaps your friend will take that trouble. You will probably have

---

[1] The site now occupied by Lord Tweedmouth's house, Brook House, at the corner of Park Lane. The number was 29. (J. F.)

heard how very ill poor Eleanor has been,[1] indeed dangerously so, but I am happy to tell you she is now *better*, but in a very weak state. I hope, if she continues improving, she will be able to be moved to town in about a week. . . . I hear we have another *dairymaid* added to our family ; we must hope that in due time she will do honour to the profession. I conclude Lady Augusta is in Edinburgh by this time ; if so, pray give my kind love and tell her I shall send the box by to-morrow's mail. Excuse my giving you this trouble. We beg our kindest regards to your father, and thanks innumerable to you both for your good wishes for the New Year, and we return them most sincerely to you. I thank you very much for your promise of writing to me. Your *new hand* is very ingenious, and I shall like a specimen of it, otherwise I do not like my friends to make *any change*, and I shall hardly fancy it is your letter. I will administer any book you recommend to the Duke with pleasure, but I will not answer for the effect. Adieu, my dear Miss Ferrier,

> Believe me always,
>> Yours very affectionately,
>>> CAROLINE ARGYLL.

Georgy[2] is not with me at present, but I shall *forward* to her the few lines you wrote in her favour.

DUCHESS OF ARGYLL TO S. E. F. (1827)

The Duke will have *great pleasure* in signing the paper in favour of your friend whenever he receives it. I assure you *I* am delighted at having it in my power to send you a favourable answer to anything you wish. I am always, you know, interested in your *sayings* and *doings*, and hope *very soon* to benefit by the first production. I do not think the Duke has had time to study sufficiently your good book ; his business bothers him too much just at present, but he

---

[1] Her daughter-in-law, Lady Uxbridge. (J. F.)

[2] Her daughter, Lady Georgina Paget. (J. F.)

begs to be most kindly remembered to you and your father.

We have seen how those immediately about Miss Ferrier received 'Inheritance.' Mrs. Grant may be taken as a good exponent of the average educated opinion of her time. Writing in June 1824, she says:

'There is a lady here whom I think you must know—Miss Ferrier; her father is a very old man, and she, who is not very young, and has indifferent health, secludes herself almost entirely with him. The fruits of this seclusion appeared three or four years since in the form of a novel called 'Marriage'; it was evidently the production of a clever caustic mind, with much good painting of character in it, that could not be produced without talent and considerable knowledge of men and books. I have just finished a hasty persual of a new work by the same author, called 'The Inheritance,' and join the general voice in pronouncing it clever, though there is, perhaps, too much of caricature throughout. Pray read it ; there is strong sense in it, and it keeps attention awake even when it does not entirely please. There are some here who praise this book beyond measure, and even hold it up as excelling the invisible charmer.'[1]

And a little later we find her writing, 'A month hence, Theodore Hook's sayings will not be less clever nor less abrupt. Miss Ferrier will not be less observing nor sagacious.'

When Miss Ferrier actually began upon 'Destiny' does not appear. But it evidently had not got far in January 1829, when her father died. None of the letters preserved belong to that period or refer to that incident. But no one who has read the correspondence can doubt that the sombre tone which overlays so much of 'Destiny,' the lack of that joyous and boisterous humour which marks Miss Ferrier's earlier work, tells of the shadow of a great loss.

<hr>

[1] Vol. iii. p. 57.

There were other troubles and hindrances. The infirmity of eyesight, which had so long given trouble, became so acute, that in 1830 Miss Ferrier found it necessary to visit an oculist in London, without, as it would seem, much profit.

The view has lately been set forth that 'Inheritance' was commercially a failure, and that in consequence Mr. Blackwood was content to let 'Destiny' fall into other hands.[1] The former part of the statement may be well founded, though the general reception of the book would certainly seem to make against it. There is nothing in the dealings about 'Destiny' to confirm the second part of Mrs. Oliphant's view. That it fell into other hands was due mainly to the intervention of Scott. In the autumn of 1829 Miss Ferrier was paying a visit at Abbotsford, which will come before our notice again, and she then for the first time took Scott into full confidence about her novels. He at once told her that 'Inheritance' had been sold below its value, and entering into negotiations with Cadell, received seventeen hundred pounds for the copyright.

DUCHESS OF ARGYLL TO S. E. F.

Upper Brook Street : May 12, 1827, Monday evening.

What am I to say sufficiently to express my thanks either to *you*, my dear Miss Ferrier, *or* to the author of 'Inheritance,' whoever she may be, for the most perfect edition of that *most perfect* book that ever was written ? Now that I may be allowed to have my suspicions I shall read it again with double pleasure. It was so kind of you to remember your promise ! When I received your kind letter and books this morning I was quite delighted with my beautiful present, and to find I was not forgotten by one of my best friends. I wish I had anything to tell you from this place to make my letter amusing, but indeed we are all more dull and stupid than you can imagine, and the abominable weather contributes to make one feel so. I am sure an east wind and fog are bad for the mind as well as the body. The dear Duke, though

---

[1] By Mrs. Oliphant. *Annals of a Publishing Firm*, vol. i. p. 45.

recovered from the gout, is by no means as strong in walking as he ought to be, nor do I expect it till we have some
warm weather. I am very sorry to hear your father has
been suffering. Pray give our kindest regards to him.
You are quite right not to venture much out, and I hope
you continue as well as when I saw you in Edinburgh. . . .
Give my kindest love to Mr. and Mrs. Fletcher when you
see them.   The Duke begs I will not forget to mention
him to you most kindly.

I sent your letters to your sister immediately and shall
be always happy to do so.

W. BLACKWOOD TO S. E. F.

Edinburgh : August 8, 1827.

Madam,—I have read your MS. with the most intense
interest and delight. While the story is natural and easy
in its progress, the characters have all your originality and
force. If I might venture a hint, however, I rather think,
with all his excellent and original points, the laird of Inch
Oran is perhaps not sufficiently brought out before you
kill him off. The *Moderate*[1] minister is capital ; he is,
one would say, the concentration of the excellencies of the
class. The breed of these beasts is happily getting scarcer,
and let us hope that it will soon be extinct. I might fill
several sheets if I were to value at all the characters and
incidents which have struck me. All I shall venture to
say is that I anxiously hope your health and spirits will
soon enable you to finish this work, which I feel confident
will be a most instructive as well as amusing production.

Mr. Pollock, the author of 'The Course of Time,' is, I
am sorry to say, in a very bad state of health. As he is
threatened with consumption, he is going to the Continent
by the recommendation of his medical advisers. To enable
him to do this some of his friends have begun a private
subscription, and with what I have been able to give him
on account of his poem we hope to be able to send him

[1] Mr. McDow.

away quite comfortable as to his pecuniary matters. Mr. Henry Mackenzie has taken a most lively interest in the matter, and, besides giving five pounds himself, he is applying to his friends here and in London. I would be much gratified if you would give any little aid to this matter, and if you could privately mention it to Miss Walker or any of your friends. I hope you will excuse me for applying to you.

> I am, madam, yours very respectfully,
>
> W. BLACKWOOD.

Miss Ferrier writes in answer :

Sir,—I am much gratified with your remarks on the MS., and send you the remainder, but at present there is no prospect of my carrying it on.

Miss Walker has been taking a great interest in the subscription for Mr. P., and I had already given him my mite towards it, otherwise I should have been happy to have contributed through your means.

> I am, sir, your most obedient servant,
>
> S. E. FERRIER.

S. E. F. TO HER NIECE, ANNE CONNELL

Cairnhill[1] : Friday, September 3, 1829.[2]

My dear Anne,—. . . I have had so few letters since I came here that I am rather in the dark as to what is doing beyond the shire of Ayr, and indeed I have been so busy traversing this corner of it that I have had little time for anything else.

Mrs. Wallace had not been in the way of visiting for many months, but since I came she discovered it was necessary she should return the civilities of her neighbours,

---

[1] Cairnhill was the residence of Mrs. Ferrier Wallace, near Kilmarnock. She outlived her four brothers, and became heir to the estate. On the old tower at Cairnhill is a curious stone with inscription and a coat of arms, Wallace and Mure of Rowallon. A niece of Elizabeth Mure, wife of King Robert II., married Sir Hugh Wallace, of Cairnhill. (J. F.)

[2] Miss Ferrier lost her father in the January of this year. (J. F.)

though I believe it was only a pretence to show me the
beauties of the country ; and she was so set upon doing it
that I was obliged to acquiesce in her kind intentions.
Our first destination was Netherplace,[1] and the first person
we there encountered was Mr. —— all alone in the
drawing-room, as nauseous as ever, and only to be endured
from a sense of duty which *ought* to make all things
endurable !   I suppose you will soon be put to the test, as
I understand he goes to Conheath after the Ayr gaities ;
I think he won't stay long. . . . Miss Connell and Mr. A.[2]
are expected at said Netherplace about this time, and I
hope we shall have Miss C. here for a day before I leave
this, which I intend to do on Tuesday if Hamilton can get
away then ; but there is talk of some parish business that
may detain him a day or two longer.   I mean to pay but
a short visit to Cathlaw, and to be in Edinburgh either the
end of next week or the very beginning of the one following.   But to return to my past travels.   We were also at
Barskimming and Sorn Castle—the former I knew, and
the latter I was charmed with ; it is quite a Paradise of its
kind, but I pity the poor solitary Eve who possesses it ;
she looks so melancholy amidst all her wealth and beauty,
without a single creature (not even a parrot) to keep her
company.[3]   We found a different scene at Lanfin in the
new successors to ——,[4] an uncommon pleasant, happy
looking family, with such plain, frank, easy manners that
made me feel as if in the midst of old friends.[5]   Another
day we drove to Ayr and saw beautiful sea views, and also
another Tam O'Shanter and his cronies ; all admirable ;
walked about Auchencruive, another lovely but deserted
place, and a perfect wilderness of shrubs and flowers ; a
beautiful shrub, the *snow berry*, would be a great embellish-

[1] Netherplace was the property then
of Miss Campbell, an ancient cadet-
ship of the London family.   It was
subsequently bequeathed to Colonel
Ferrier Hamilton's second son,
Charles, who assumed the name of
Campbell.   (J. F.)

[2] Miss Connell's brother.   (J. F.)
[3] Miss Somervell.   (J. F.)
[4] Name undecipherable.
[5] Residence of a family of the name
of Brown.   (J. F.)

ment at your door. From all this you may guess we have
had some fine days, and I hope their genial influence has
been felt at Nithside, and that you have all been making
hay while the sun shone at Dalscairth. . . . My head is
very confused with the racketings I have had, and I
dare say I have forgot much that I meant to say. Tell
your father there has been very bad sport on the Ayrshire
muirs this season ; Hamilton says the like was never
known. Compliments to Frisk.[1]

S. E. F. TO MRS. KINLOCH

Cathlaw : September 16.

My dear Helen,—·I came here about ten days ago
under Hamilton's escort, purposing to remain *two* or *three*
days at most ; but such are the kindness and hospitality
of our friends, and the attractions of the place, that were I
to yield to their solicitations and my own inclinations
here I should remain for a month to come. But it is time
I was preparing a retreat for myself before the winter sets
in, and as I intend to be very busy when I go to Edinburgh,
I commence my lucubrations here.[2] I can give you no
idea of what I think and *feel* to be the charms of this
place, so different from all that I had fancied or remembered
of it ; it is like a bird's nest amongst hills of every variety
of form, some wooded to the top, others covered with sweet
old mossy turf and wild flowers and patches of whins and
heather, and the air so 'nimble and sweet' ; and above all,
such views ! far surpassing, in my opinion, those from
Stirling Castle.[3] Figure, *if you can*, a range all the way
from the Bass to the Argyllshire mountains, including the
Grampians and Ochills, Edinburgh and Stirling, and the

---

[1] A dog. (J. F.)

[2] She was then engaged in writing
Destiny. (J. F.)

[3] Colonel F. Hamilton succeeded to
Cathlaw on the death of his uncle,
Mr. Ferrier Hamilton, in 1814, and
also to the Westport estate, when he
assumed the name of Hamilton. This
uncle had been in the Navy, and was
at the capture of Quebec, and signalised
himself by assisting the sailors to drag
the cannon up the heights of Abraham.
He married, 1784, a Miss Johnstone,
of Straiton, co. Linlithgow. (J. F.)

Forth like a magnificent lake studded with shipping, and all the rich and varied detail of its shores without anything of map-like minuteness, for even my eyes can easily explore all this and much more.   Many parts of this view are seen from the grounds near the house, and ascent to the hilltops is so easy that I can walk to them much easier than I could to the quay ;[1] but indeed I have gained so much in strength since I came that I can scarcely believe I am myself.   Altogether it is one of the most singular and, to my taste, most enchanting.[2]

JOHN FERRIER TO S. E. F.

York Place : Friday evening.

My dear Susan,—I called for Mr. Cadell before dinner, and found him in his shop ; he seemed quite ready for the work, asked how many volumes, answered three ; what name — this I could not tell him. On learning that the copyrights of the others had been disposed of, thinks it would be for the author's advantage to dispose likeways [*sic*] of the meditated work in the same manner ; as to this I cannot pretend to judge.   He is to make a proposal for the book, which I will communicate.   As to the time of publishing, he is of opinion that, as the season is so far advanced, it should not be brought out until the end of October or November.

Ever yours affectionately,

J. FERRIER.

S. E. F. TO MR. BLACKWOOD

7 Nelson Street : April 20.

Sir,—I regret that engagements have prevented me from acknowledging the favour of your letter sooner.   The last time I had any conversation with you regarding my works I clearly understood from you that 'The Inheritance' at least had proved unsuccessful, or, as it seems I had

---

[1] Near Conheath.   (J. F.)

[2] Here this interesting and graphic description comes unfortunately and abruptly to an end, the remainder of the letter being lost.   (J. F.)

erroneously termed it, *unfortunate*, and I certainly never should have thought of *offering* a future work to you after being told the second edition of my former one was 'dead stock' upon your hands. When such was the case I naturally concluded you could not be desirous of entering into a similar speculation, and I was not disposed to press the matter.

Had I been mistaken in my supposition, however, an opportunity was afterwards afforded you by my brother of coming forward if you had any proposal to make; it appeared you had not, and there the matter ends, I hope without offence on either side. I have now only to repeat that I am ready to relieve you of the copyrights of 'Marriage' and 'The Inheritance' at a fair valuation.

I remain, sir, your obedient servant,

S. E. FERRIER.

MISS MACKENZIE[1] TO S. E. F.

Saturday, May 8, 1830.

My dear Miss Ferrier,—I was very happy to see your handwriting yesterday, and would not have lost even one post in thanking you if I had not felt it prudent not to stop yesterday. We have heard of your safe arrival in London two days before, but of course heard none of the particulars of your voyage which led you to your pedestrian resolutions. Were I to speak for my experience of the sea I should join you in them. We are all as you left us; my father looking very well, but he has not recovered his flesh since his attack of cold, so we are going to try him with animal food again. My mother and Hope walked to and from church both last Sunday and Thursday without suffering. I went on Thursday afternoon to the College Kirk to hear Mr. Tait, of Kirkliston, preach, and sat behind your friend, Mary Campbell, who won my heart quite by her manner to me, so much so that if I had been quite well

---

[1] Daughter of the 'Man of Feeling.' (J. F.)

yesterday, or my mother so to-day, I should have yielded to the impulse of not deferring a day to call on her. Our sermon was good, but confined to one point, and that point not presented in those various lights which every subject is exhibited by in the Holy Scriptures themselves. It was from Galatians, and you may imagine it from this. My mother and I have been reading your MS.[1] Never since my youthful days when I devoured 'Clarissa' have I been so completely absorbed as by the return of Ronald to his deserted home. How could you bear to write anything so heartrending? My mother felt nearly the same. After I closed the book I had to go to see a friend, and she asked me if I was ill. It is quite original, too, as far as we remember. With regard to Mr. McDow, will you forgive me for quoting poor Lady Seaforth's expression as read from her pothooks by Lady H. Hall.[2] We have a dose, and more than a dose, of him. My mother says she never saw a hieland minister like him, and I dare say she never did, for although the Strathspey ministers were some few of them no better than he, yet the extreme gentleness of her brother's manners threw a sort of quietness over the outward company demeanour of everybody at Castle Grant. But I could furnish you with some things that were under this manner as coarse as any of his sallies. Your children are better than Miss Edgeworths, but I have one or two remarks on them and other parts, which I shall submit to you when I meet. I grieve to think of your time in London being spent with oculists, but we all think his report is comfortable. You have one eye so good that if you take care of it you will, I would fain hope, see as well with it as any person who has no disease of the eyes. But perhaps I speak ignorantly. Dear Hope would say something from the overflowings of her pious soul, but I feel I have no power to do so. You will have discovered that I write in the greatest haste. I write beside my father and mother.

[1] Of *Destiny*. (J. F.)

[2] Daughter of the Earl of Selkirk, and mother of Capt. Basil Hall. (J. F.)

. . . so I hardly know what I send, but I would not delay.

Yours ever affectionate,
M. MK.

It is very lady's maid-like to bid you ' burn this,' but I am rather self-condemned for what I said of poor dear Lady Seaforth's writing.[1]

The following letter shows that Miss Ferrier, though no realist, was scrupulous in avoiding detailed errors.

BASIL HALL TO ROBERT CADELL.

London : October 6, 1830.

My dear Sir,—In reply to your questions, put by the desire of the author of ' Destiny,' I beg you will say that, by the regulations of the Service, a midshipman must serve six years before he can pass for a lieutenant, and there is no possible way of getting over this necessity. I am not aware there is any instance of such a thing having been done, and indeed it is so entirely repugnant to the feelings of the navy in this matter that no author, I should think, could venture to give any incident that turn without risk of ridicule. It is a great affair in writing about professional matters to keep strictly within the pale of usage ; for, do what we may, an unprofessional person will always make awkward slips. I wish the author of ' Destiny ' much joy in her new publication. If it equals the other it will be amongst the most amusing books in the world. I am enchanted to be in such goodly company as your prospectus sets forth, although I fear I am like the wild elephant between two tame ones !

I am ever, dear sir, most sincerely yours,
BASIL HALL.

---

[1] Miss Ferrier used to say jokingly to the Misses Mackenzie that she ought to share some of the profits from her novels with them, as they had furnished her with so many good stories. (J. F.)

S. E. F. TO MRS. CONNELL

Nelson Street [1] : September, 1830.

Now that the cows have done their part I must do mine, as I trust you are now at leisure to take some interest in your more human friends.[2]   I made out the journey very well.   Except having a worse headache than usual, did not suffer ;   I liked my male companion much ; he was very sensible, unaffected, and gentlemanly.   The well-dressed *woman* was weakness and vulgarity combined in no common degree. . . .   The weather by all accounts has been as bad here as anywhere, everybody open-mouthed against it ; there have been many deluges since I came, and very rainy symptoms still continue.   The town looks a desert, but I find it quite gay enough for me.   I had no less than five invitations for yesterday and two to-day. The Fletchers remain till the fifth, when they embark for Jersey.   He is certainly better.   Mary Camp [3] is going about the same time to Harrogate, which will make two sad gaps in my small circle.   Miss Walker paid a visit to Stirling this week and brought back such an account of the revellings at the Castle that I have given up all thoughts of going there at present. . . . This is a great stretch for my eyes, and I have had to make many a pause to rest them. . . .

S. E. F. TO MRS. CONNELL

December 10, 1830.

Our good friends the Edmonstones are all well, except that D——'s eyes are even worse than mine.[4]   They are quite happy with their new house and seem as if just begin-

---

[1] After her father's death she took a small house in Nelson Street, No. 7, and then No. 10.   (J. F.)

[2] Mrs. Connell was very fond of an outdoor country life with her live stock and dairy ; Mr. C. farmed his own property, Conheath.   (J. F.)

[3] Campbell.   (J. F.)

[4] For years she had suffered from a painful and apparently incurable affection of the eyes, and most of her more recent letters allude to this sad state of suffering.   (J. F.)

ning life again. For my part, although I have no distaste to life, as the gift of God and the means of preparing us for a better state of being, yet I cannot but be glad at every year that passes over my head. I heard Mr. Begg preach when he was here and have got a seat in his church, but it is very out of the way and close, so I fear I shall not be a regular attender. I have also a most comfortable seat in St. Stephen's with Mrs. Cunningham, so I pray I may make good use of my opportunities. By-the-bye, when you have read Dr. Arnold's sermons will you send them to me? One a day I think will carry you soon through them. The weather is dreadful, and I have seen none but my kindred and *near* friends for some time past. . . . I heard from Stirling yesterday. Jane is laid by the leg again, but in this weather legs are of little use. . . . Mary Camp is staying with Sir James and Lady Graham, who had been dining at Court, and the Queen apologised for the want of ornaments in the drawing-room, saying she had left them all at Brighton as the King did not like packages in the carriage ! Be thankful you are not the King's wife. My kind regards to Mr. C. and the girls. I hope Anne will excuse me not answering her letter, as writing is really grievous to me now.

Believe me yours ever affectionately,

S. E. F.

S. E. F. TO MRS. CONNELL

Stirling Castle : January 1831. Friday.

My dear Janet,—I can well imagine the shock you would sustain by the sad tidings of our poor brother's[1]

---

[1] The following particulars about General Graham are communicated by Mr. John Ferrier : 'Samuel Graham was born in 1756. He entered the army as ensign in the 31st Foot in 1777. In the December of that year he obtained a lieutenant's commission in the 76th. Two years later he obtained his captaincy. In 1780 his regiment was ordered to America, and he was among those who surrendered at Yorktown in 1781. He subsequently served in the Low Countries under the Duke of York. In May 1796 he was appointed to the colonelcy of the 2nd West India Regiment. In an engagement in Jamaica against some brigands and caribs, he was seriously wounded, and was sent home invalided. In 1797

sudden death, and the great anxiety you must feel to hear
how our dear sister is bearing this afflicting dispensation.
Thanks be to God she has hitherto been wonderfully
supported, and we may hope His Goodness will continue,
and as she seeks her consolation at the only true source
so she will not fail to find it there. Her medical attendant
thought it was as much as her life was worth to communicate the dreadful intelligence to her, and yet her health
has not suffered in the least. She has had two good
nights, and the disorder is so much abated we may flatter
ourselves it is now very nearly subdued, but she has had a
severe and lingering illness. I was not aware how ill she
had been till I came here. She is much reduced, but not
so much weakened as might have been expected. She
gets up about the middle of the day and comes into
the dining-room, where she remains sitting or walking
about till past nine, and she now takes a little solid food,
which she had not been able to do for weeks. James and
Helen, you may believe, are all that dutiful and affectionate
children can be to a bereft parent ; the former, indeed,
seemed as if sent by God Himself in the very hour of need,
and it was in his arms that his poor father breathed his last.
He was with him from the moment he was taken ill, which
was about two in the morning, when he went to James's
room and told him he felt very unwell, but would not allow
a surgeon to be sent for for some time. When one came
he tried to bleed him, but it would not do, and he expired
in about two hours without pain or struggle. From the
symptoms the surgeons are of opinion it must have been
ossification of the heart, a disease far beyond human skill,
and when one considers all that his poor frame has under-

he obtained the command of the 27th Foot, and in an engagement in the Helder lost an eye. He served in Egypt, and in 1804 received the rank of Brigadier-General. In 1814 he became a Lieutenant-General, and after the war was appointed Lieu-tenant-Governor of Stirling Castle, in which post he died. James Ferrier would not allow the marriage with his daughter to take place till her future husband had attained the rank of General. This he obtained through the kind intervention of Lady C. Campbell with Lord Moira, then Com-mander of the Forces in Scotland.'

gone, the surprise is not that he should have been taken so suddenly away, but that he should so long have been spared. Many will lament him, for he was a kind and affectionate husband and father, a warm and steady friend, and a hospitable and generous man.   The funeral is fixed for Wednesday, and Jane, who is all consideration for others, begs me to say, with her most affectionate and grateful regards, that she hopes Mr. Connell will not put himself to the inconvenience by taking so long a journey at this season, but do exactly what he feels himself able for.   She is very sensible of your kindness also, and will have great comfort in a visit from you, but I have arranged to remain till about the 8th, and I think it would be better for you to come when I leave her, but someone will write again before that time.   I dare say this is very incoherent, for I can only write a line or two at a time and this has been a day's labour, but I thought you would wish to hear from me.   Adieu, my dear sister.   God bless you all, and may we all lay this lesson to heart !

MISS MACDONALD BUCHANAN[1] TO S. E. F.

Ross : April 7, 1831.

My dear Miss Ferrier,—My mother is in an ecstasy of gratitude and desires me to say all manner of pretty things to you for your kindness in sending her *the book*.   She is at this moment enjoying it most throughly on a sofa by the fireside.   I am sure you think us no great judges, so it is perhaps useless and vain to tell you how much pleasure we have derived from ' Destiny.'   There will be many whose opinions are of more value to tell you how successful you have been, but none of your friends can rejoice more sincerely than we do in your success—or more earnestly hope you may long continue to pursue your brilliant, enviable, and useful career, for I will not give up my old argument anent the usefulness of good novels.   My sweet

---

[1] Sir W. Scott's favourite ' Missie.'   (J. F.)

sisters are highly indignant at the cold harsh manner in which you treat worthy Mr. McDow's excellent refreshments, and they are surprised you could introduce such an unnatural character as Miss Lucy Malcolm, a senseless affected creature pretending to prefer *potatoes* and *milk* to ducks and onions. This is the only criticism I have heard, but I believe poor Flora is rather sore on the subject, as Jemima calls her nothing but Mr. McDow. I hope Flora will have the pleasure of seeing you. She is to be in Edinburgh about the week after next, on her way to Roxburghshire to visit the Miss Melvilles and Anne Scott; the latter is better, but has really been seriously ill this season. I am happy to hear her father is much recruited and by no means looking so ill as the newspapers would lead one to suppose. The rest of this family intend meeting Flora in Edinburgh the beginning of May, when we shall, I trust, see some of our old friends. I hope the Grahams will be with you then. I have no time for any news, this being merely intended for a letter of thanks; so good-bye, my dear Miss F. We all unite in kindest love, and believe me,

Ever your affectionate friend,

MISSY.

P.S.—We have had our Highland cousins, Sir John and Lady Campbell, of Airds, here. They left us yesterday for Ardencaple. I wish they had gone there first, that I might have given you some account of Lady John the 3rd.

FROM MRS. FLETCHER TO S. E. F.

Tadcaster : April 16, 1831.

My dear Miss Ferrier,—I should not have been so long in thanking you for your kind present had I not waited to subject 'Destiny' to a severer test than that chosen by the French dramatist. *His* old woman probably partook of the vivacity of her nation, but my old aunt, as Mary will tell you, is sick and often very sorrowful, and yet 'Destiny' has made her laugh heartily and cheated her of many wearisome hours of lamentation.

My grandson, Archibald Taylor, too, forsook football and cricket for your fascinating book, and told me 'he would sit up all night to see what had become of Ronald'; Mr. Ribley and 'Kitty my dear' hit his comic fancy particularly.

My two most bookish neighbours, one an Oxford Divine and the other a Cambridge student, declare that 'Glenroy and Mr. McDow are exquisite originals.' My own favourite, Molly Macaulay, preserves her good humour to the last, though I thought you rather unmerciful for shutting her up so long in Johnny's nursery. The fashionable artlessness of Lady Elizabeth and her daughter is coloured to the life, and the refreshment of returning to nature, truth, affection, and happiness at Inch Oran is admirably managed.

Mary tells me you have returned from Fyfe with fresh materials for future volumes. Go on, dear Miss Ferrier; you are accountable for the talents entrusted to you; go on to detect selfishness in all its various forms and foldings, to put pride and vanity to shame, to prove that vulgarity belongs more to character than condition, and that all who make this world their standard are essentially vulgar and low minded, however polished their exterior or refined their manners may be, and that true dignity and elevation belong only to those to whom Milton's lines may be applied—

> Thy care is fixed and zealously attends
> To fill thy odorous lamp with deeds of light
> And hope that reaps not shame.

. . . I have another subject of gratitude to you, and I have the sincerest pleasure in acknowledging it, because I am sure, though she feels it deeply, she will not have courage to tell you so herself—your kindness to my dear Mary. She has been very much gratified by your admitting her on a footing of friendly intercourse. This has been her chief delight this winter. Neither Mary or her mother, you will observe, are expert at making fine speeches. But I hope you will find your *kindness* has not been thrown away upon them. I often wish your lot were cast for one six months upon an English country town; such a one as I now inhabit would furnish some graphic subjects for your pen. The only circulating library in the place has ordered 'Destiny,' and I hope to be edified by the remarks I shall hear upon it. Believe me, dear Miss Ferrier,

Very gratefully and truly yours,

ELIZA FLETCHER.

MRS. KINLOCH TO S. E. F.

Saturday, April 30.

. . . I had your welcome dispatch; it found me preparing for a great ball given by a Mrs. Dunlop in Russell Square, and was in truth Miss Loo's[1] *début*, as she had never been at anything so gay before. There was everything to make it a scene of delight to her youthful fancy, but oh! I was tired, tired, in spite of fine music, fine painting, and many pleasant people, and thankful to reach my own *hard* bed at three o'clock in the morning. I met the Bells[2] there, who inquired most tenderly for you, and our talk was 'Destiny,' which they have heard much discussed and much admired. The Lord Advocate[3] had borrowed their copy and they could not get it out of his hands. Mrs. Bell said a gentleman of peculiar *fine taste* preferred it to any of your works. . . . I had a note from Lady Charlotte Bury last week praying me to send her a person (I had once inquired about for her) to copy for the press, as she wished 200 pages copied in two or three days. I sent her a dirty body Duncan Campbell employs, but perfectly *honest*, though not fit, as I wrote her, for a 'Lady's Chamber.' I suppose it's another 'Journal of the Heart.'

---

[1] Her daughter. (J. F.)

[2] Mr., afterwards Sir Charles, Bell, the distinguished surgeon, and his wife. (J. F.)   [3] Andrew Rutherfurd. (J. F.)

JOHN FERRIER TO S.'E. F.

Edinburgh : July 21, 1831.

My dear Susan,—I had the pleasure to receive your letter some days ago, and as Lady Charlotte has sent me one of her papers with a few lines asking me to do what I can for her, I think it will be best for me to answer it as soon as I can send her two or three subscriptions, for I despair of being able to do more, as it is only in very peculiar circumstances that such can be asked or expected.

I see the prospectus figuring away here on the mantelpieces of the club houses, but no subscriptions as yet.

Mr. Cadell, whom I met this morning, is just returned from the south. Unfavourable as the times have been, he has disposed of 2,400 copies of 'Destiny,' and is now, he says, on safe ground. He says the work is well liked and the above is the proof of it. In regard to the copies of the other works, he tells me they are selling fair enough considering, which is all we could expect. He says that the sales are so dull that the publishers in London are resting on their oars, as he himself is doing in regard to Sir Walter's new novel.

Ever yours affectionately,

J. FERRIER.

LOUIS H. FERRIER,[1] ESQ. OF BELSYDE, TO S. E. F.

Marchmont : June 13, 1831.

My dear Cousin,—Will you have the goodness to express to the author of 'Destiny' the high gratification we have all experienced from the perusal of that work, which justly adds another laurel to the literary wreath long ago conferred by the public on the only remaining great unknown of the present day. For the considerate kindness in sending us a copy our most grateful thanks are

---

[1] He was her cousin and held a very lucrative appointment as collector of H.M. Customs at Quebec; died there in January, 1833. (J. F.)

offered. We have now passed a twelvemonth here and have every reason to be pleased with the country and its inhabitants. A large part of the society being military is subject to perpetual change. The French Canadians mix very little with the British, who here, as everywhere else, are too exclusive. The present Governor and his lady, a most agreeable couple, are trying as much as possible to check this ante-social feeling. Our climate, though fickle as our own one, is on the whole a fine one. Yesterday the thermometer stood at 90° in the shade. A magnificent thunder-storm commenced in the evening, accompanied with a profusion of most brilliant sheet lightning. This morning the temperature was only 50°. A Canadian winter has nothing appalling in it beyond the length, the ground being covered with snow from the end of November till the beginning of April. As to cold I have experienced more at a dinner-party in Edinburgh than over here. Our present residence is a truly beautiful one, adjoining the celebrated plains of Abraham and overhanging the St. Lawrence at the place where Wolfe landed. I sincerely hope this will find your sister, Mrs. Graham, and daughter somewhat recovered from the shock occasioned by the loss they have sustained in our excellent friend the General. Pray offer our united kindest condolence, and with best wishes to yourself,

Believe me, my dear cousin, yours very sincerely,

L. H. FERRIER.

Pray say to Mrs. Forbes that we get on most comfortably with her elève. Best remembrances to your friends the Misses Walker.

With the publication of 'Destiny' comes the somewhat strangely abrupt end of Miss Ferrier's career as a writer. We read of solicitations from publishers, and there are faint rumours, as we shall see, of further projects. One fragment remains, showing that the old power of merciless observation and dramatic interpretation was not a whit abated.[1] But Miss Ferrier was not one of those whose impulse to write was fed by any uncontrollable spring of inner feeling. The conditions which supplied her with material, and even more the temper which enabled her to deal with that material, were things of the past. There was no longer the joyous readiness to watch and criticise the comedy of life. Even in her last novel we see growing up between her and her old tastes and powers the barrier of religious opinions and moral principles, all the more encumbering because imperfectly assimilated.

To two of the sisterhood to which Miss Ferrier belongs was granted a fate at once enviable and tragic. Jane Austen and Charlotte Brontë passed away in the fulness of unimpaired power, with loss to the world hardly to be thought of tranquilly. With 'Destiny' before one it is impossible to say that Miss Ferrier's powers knew no abatement. If her career had ended with 'The Inheritance' I can hardly think that there would have been for any of us the sense of loss which we feel after reading 'Persuasion' or 'Shirley.' Yet at least she escaped the fate which had overtaken more than one career which began with auspices as good. No wayward perversion of judgment led her to produce anything as much below 'The Inheritance' as parts of 'Daniel Deronda' are below George Eliot's best work. There is nothing like the collapse and paralysis which overtook Miss Burney in 'The Wanderer' and in parts of 'Camilla.'

And if fate dealt kindly with Miss Ferrier's powers, so it did with her reputation. Living in a society steeped in sound literary tradition, she never had to make headway against that dismal and now unintelligible stupidity which went near to blight Miss Austen's career at its very outset. On the other hand, while meeting with fully adequate recognition and encouragement, she never became the idol of a literary *coterie*. For that she had to thank her own sound judgment and sense of humour rather than 'the discretion of her friends. From critics she met with recognition, yet not of such a character as to beget protest or reaction.

We have already seen how her work was received by those immediately about her. It is not without interest

<hr>

[1] The letter from Miss Betty Landon, 'a single lady of small fortune, few personal charms, and a most jaundiced imagination.' It is published by Mr. John Ferrier in the Introduction to *Marriage*, p. 32.

to see how her reputation fared among contemporary critics
who were free from the bias of kinship or intimacy.   Scott,
as we have seen, was lavish in praise, giving, as was his
wont, 'as rich men give, that value not their gifts.'

The following letters may serve as specimens of current
opinion.[1]

MISS JOANNA BAILLIE TO S. E. F.

Hampstead : May 1831.

My dear madam,—I received your very kind present
of your last work about three weeks ago, and am very
grateful for the pleasure I have had in reading it, and for
being thus remembered by you.   I thank you also for the
pleasure and amusement which my sisters and some other
friends have drawn from it.   The first volume struck me
as extremely clever, the description of the different
characters, their dialogues, and the writer's own remarks,
excellent.   There is a spur both with the writer and the
reader on the opening of a work which naturally gives the
beginning of a story many advantages ; but I must confess
that your characters never forget their outset, but are well
supported to the very end.   Your Molly Macaulay[2] is a
delightful creature, and the footing she is on with Glenroy
very naturally represented, to say nothing of the rising of
her character at the end, when the weight of the contempt
is removed from her, which is very good and true to nature.
Your minister, McDow, hateful as he is, is very amusing,
and a true representative of a few of the Scottish clergy,
and, with different language and manners, of a great many
of the English clergy—worldly, mean men, who boldly
make their way into every great and wealthy family for
the sake of preferment and good cheer.   Your Lady
Elizabeth, too, with all her selfishness and excess of

---

[1] They have been already published
by Mr. John Ferrier in the Introduction to Bentley's edition of *Marriage.*

[2] 'Molly Macaulay is charming ;
her niece, Miss Cumming, is an old
acquaintance of mine, and told me
the character was drawn to the life.

The old lady is still alive, in her
ninety-first year, at Inveraray, and
Miss C., who is a very clever,
pleasing person, seems delighted with
the truth and spirit of the whole
character of her aunty.' (Mrs. Kinloch to S. E. F.)

absurdity, is true to herself throughout, and makes a very
characteristic ending of it in her third marriage. But why
should I tease you by going through the different characters?
Suffice it to say that I thank you very heartily, and congratulate you on again having added a work of so much
merit to our stock of national novels. Perhaps before this
you have received a very short publication of mine on a
very serious subject. I desired my bookseller to send a
copy to you, enclosed along with one to your friend, Miss
Mackenzie. How far you will agree with my opinions
regarding it I cannot say, but of one thing I am sure—that
you will judge with candour and charity. I should have
sent one to Mr. Alison had I not thought it presumptuous
in me to send such a work to any clergyman, and, with
only one exception (a Presbyterian clergyman), I have
abstained from doing so. I was very much obliged to Mrs.
Mackenzie, Lord M.'s lady, for the letter she was so good
as to write me in her sister-in-law's stead. If you should
meet her soon, may I beg that you will have the goodness
to thank her in my name? I was very sorry indeed to
learn from her that Miss Mackenzie had been so ill, and
was then so weak, and that the favourable account I had
received of your eyes had been too favourable. With all
good wishes to you, in which my sister begs to join me,

I remain, my dear madam,

Gratefully and sincerely yours,

J. BAILLIE.

SIR JAMES MACKINTOSH TO MISS FERRIER

London: June 10, 1831.

Dear Miss Ferrier,—Let me tell you a fact, which I
hope you will excuse me from mentioning as some
subsidiary proof of your power. On the day of the dis-
solution of Parliament, and in the critical hours between
twelve and three, I was employed in reading part of the
second volume of 'Destiny.' My mind was so completely

occupied on your colony in Argyllshire that I did not throw away a thought on kings or parliaments, and was not moved by the general curiosity to stir abroad till I had finished your volume. It would have been nothing if you had so agitated a youth of genius and susceptibility, prone to literary enthusiasm, but such a victory over an old hack is perhaps worthy of your notice.

> I am, my dear Miss Ferrier,
>> Your friend and admirer,
>>> J. MACKINTOSH.

GRANVILLE PENN TO MISS ERSKINE [1]

> Devonshire Cottage : May 1, 1831.

My dear madam,—I return your book, but I am unable to return you adequate thanks for being the cause of my reading it.   I have done this (and all with me) with delight, from the interest and admiration at the whole composition, the novelty and excitement of its plan, the exquisite and thrilling manner of its disclosure, the absence of all flat and heavy intervals, the conception and support of the characters, the sound and salutary moral that pervades it all—these make me love and honour its valuable authoress, and lament that I am not in the number of her acquaintance. We all *doat* upon Miss Macaulay, and grieve that she is not living at Richmond or Petersham ; and Mr. McDow has supplied me with a new name for our little young dog, whom I have called, in memorial of his little nephew (or niece), Little McFee.   With all the thanks, however, that I can offer, &c.

> GRANVILLE PENN.

The following letter shows what perhaps one might have been tempted to doubt—that the writer herself was not the only person who took Miss Ferrier's claim as a moralist seriously.

---

[1] The recipient, Miss Erskine, of Cardross, forwarded this note to Miss Ferrier.

LADY LILFORD[1] *(DAUGHTER OF LORD HOLLAND)*
TO A FRIEND

I cannot tell you how delighted I am that my most humble but heartfelt tribute should have reached Miss Ferrier! For years, from my earliest youth, I have longed that she should know she was the first human instrument permitted to make a joyous, thoughtless young girl *pause* and reflect. I had been blessed with many advantages and opportunities—alas! but they were unheeded; 'The Inheritance,' by God's blessing alone, began to show me the worthlessness of what this world most prizes. Often in girlish enthusiasm I longed to write anonymously to Miss Ferrier, and lay my whole heart open to her! I am keeping your servant waiting unconscionably. Pray excuse, but I never can leave off on some subjects, and Miss Ferrier's novels is one!

Meanwhile, the critical reviews were somewhat strangely and inexplicably silent. In 1844, when Jeffrey's 'Edinburgh Essays' were republished in collected form, the oracle was dumb, not altogether to Miss Ferrier's satisfaction. In private he expressed admiration for the character of Miss Molly Macaulay, which most readers of Miss Ferrier will probably think exaggerated and disproportionate. When at last, in 1847, the 'Edinburgh' broke silence, it was with an article by Mr. George Moir,[2] kindly in tone and graceful in expression, but certainly not marked by any special insight or originality.

The 'Quarterly' incidentally, and by way of illustration, congratulated the author of 'that excellent novel,' 'Marriage,' on the rather obvious wit shown in the name Mrs. Downe Wright, but did not think any further praise necessary. The brilliant, fantastic, and vagrant imagination of Christopher North was unlikely to form a just estimate of work so definite and limited where observation so wholly excludes fancy. He is moved by the stagey and mechanical

---

[1] For this communication I am indebted to Miss Campbell, Albyn Place, Edinburgh. (J. F.)

[2] Advocate and Sheriff of Stirling. (J. F.)

pathos of Ronald's secret visit to his home, and he so far
reads himself into his author as to see in the novels as a
whole the tragedy of Highland chieftainship in its decadence.
His praise of Miss Ferrier does not suggest to one that he
saw in her a comedian of upper and middle class life, an
unsparing satirist alike of pretentious folly and homely
dulness.

Such criticisms go some way towards explaining how
it came about that Miss Ferrier attached, as it is plain she
did, more importance to the serious than to the comic side
of her novels. But they do not give us the whole, nor
perhaps the main, solution. Partly, no doubt, it was due
to the fact that a creative artist is apt to measure the value
of the work by the amount of effort which it costs him.
Thus arise strange delusions, such as that which made
Hogarth stake his reputation on 'Sigismunda,' and Liston
fancy himself a wasted tragedian. Miss Ferrier was easily
and spontaneously humorous; she was laboriously and
artificially sentimental and moral. And yet another factor
was at work. It is clear that Miss Ferrier's deliberate
judgment—a judgment, too, which steadily grew in her
with her years—rated amusement low and edification high.
The moralist stood apart from the comedian, deliberately
weighed her work, and found it wanting.

If comparisons in criticism be used to gauge the
supposed merits of a writer on what one may call a quasi-
competitive system, there cannot be a more deceptive or
worthless method. It brings the critic down to the level
of the small boy in Leech's picture, who liked his partner
at the child's ball better than oranges, but not as well
as tipsy-cake.[1] There can be no surer way of fastening
the attention on those features of a writer which are
common, and therefore obvious and unimportant, and
missing those which are distinctive and therefore essential.
Probably for that reason it commends itself to minds of a
certain class. But the juxtaposition of two writers, when
all question of comparative merits is set aside, may often
help one to an understanding of each. The novelist with
whom Miss Ferrier has probably been most often compared is Miss Austen. In all likelihood that is simply
because Miss Austen lived nearer to our own day, and is

---

[1] I may be wrong as to detail. It
is a kindness to my readers to give
them a pretext for verifying or cor-
recting me.

better known than Miss Burney. Between the writer of
'Marriage' and the writer of 'Persuasion' there is scarcely
anything in common beyond the fact that both wore
petticoats, and that both took their characters and scenes
from the same period, and to some extent from the same
walk of life. No two novelists could really be more remote
from one another than Miss Austen—always equable and
well balanced, and guided at every turn by an unfailing
sense of proportion and a spirit of restrained irony—and
Miss Ferrier, with her alternations of vigorous and original
comedy and conventional sentiment.

Between Miss Ferrier and Miss Burney, on the other
hand, there is so strong and distinct a likeness, as at once
to challenge comparison and to make it easy. Both are
chroniclers of humours, delighting in, and largely depending
on, daringly grotesque situations and incidents. Bella
Black is of the house and lineage of Miss Larolles. It is
not unlikely that Mr. Augustus Larkins had modelled his
manners and conversation on some younger member of
the Brangton family. It is easy enough to point out in
how many ways the later writer has the advantage. There
is no foolery in Miss Burney as good as the conversation
at Mrs. Bluemit's with Aunt Grizzy's contributions to, and
comments upon, it ; no incident as irresistibly laughable
or as well worked out in detail as Miss Pratt's emergence
from the hearse. Miss Ferrier's sentiment is almost always
conventional, and her serious incident often melodramatic.
Yet in the one work by which we may fairly judge of her
matured powers at their very best, 'The Inheritance,' she
shows that the effective construction of a story is nowise
beyond her powers. There are blemishes in detail, but
the plot holds well together, and the characters of the
story, comic and serious alike, fit into it appropriately. In
Miss Burney's novels we too often feel that the characters
and the dialogue, excellent in themselves, might be drawn
out of a bag and allotted to any portion of any of the
books. Two things, however, must not be forgotten. Miss
Ferrier grew up in a mental atmosphere far more stimulat-
ing and bracing than that granted to Miss Burney, and
she had a far larger and more appropriate stock of originals
to draw upon. Character-hunting, largely fool-hunting,
had been her pursuit from childhood, and the country
about her was well stocked with curious varieties. A critic
such as Miss Clavering, sympathetic and outspoken, and

the sense of responsibility engendered by a cultured and critical society such as that of Edinburgh, might have done a good deal for Miss Burney. Not that one can believe that mere differences of training and circumstances exhaust the question. It is one of the paradoxes of literature that a writer with a sense of humour often so bright and so acute could have been led away into the grotesque absurdities which disfigure much of Miss Burney's work. With that as an example before one it is rash to be confident. Yet one cannot imagine that Miss Ferrier could ever have marred good work with the melodramatic extravagances which disfigure 'Cecilia,' or marched her heroine off the stage in a Tilburina-like blaze of fireworks.

Another and perhaps a better plea may be urged on behalf of the earlier writer. She was the earlier. She succeeded to the traditions of the English comic novel bequeathed by Smollett, traditions which required it to be rich in grotesque and highly-coloured incident. She made it decorous; one can hardly wonder if she failed at the same time to make it artistic and well proportioned. It needed more than a single writer, or even a single generation, to do for the English novel what Goldsmith, almost unaided, did for English comedy.

A comparison almost as obvious as that with Miss Burney is with Miss Edgeworth. There is, however, one essential difference. Miss Edgeworth is didactic, not merely of set purpose, but instinctively and spontaneously. Miss Ferrier can be didactic enough, but it is only just to say that her didacticism always has an air of obligation and restraint. The likeness is strongest on those rare and happy occasions when Miss Edgeworth forgets the physic, and is content to administer the sugar without any ulterior design. Such a story as 'L'Amie Inconnue' might have been the work of Miss Ferrier. On the other hand, the very best feature of Miss Edgeworth's writings, her delicate perception and artistic rendering of the lights and shades of Irish character, above all of Irish peasant character, has no counterpart in Miss Ferrier.

As was said before, the comedy of Miss Ferrier and the comedy of Miss Austen are so wholly distinct in spirit and method that there is no room for profitable comparison. When they get beyond the domain of comedy they become more comparable in character, and probably most persons will think more widely separated in merit. Every loyal admirer of Miss Austen must be drawn nearer to her by her one happy venture upon the sea of romance. The hand that created Mr. Collins and Mrs. Bennet forgot nothing of its cunning, it bated not a jot of its innate art, when, inspired by remembered happiness and living sorrow, it pictured the grief and the constancy of Anne Eliot, the joyous courage and chivalrous gentleness of her sailor lover. With the heroine of 'Inheritance' before one it would be unjust to say that Miss Ferrier could not create a romantic character. But the presence of a wayward, lovable, and, for a time, unfortunate young lady does not by itself make a romance, and even a heroine drawn by Shakespeare or Scott would have been heavily weighed down by two such lovers as the conventionally wicked Delmour and the equally conventional and much more offensively virtuous Lyndsay. Not that Miss Ferrier has maltreated Gertrude as one of her younger sisters has maltreated a worthier heroine. The proximity of Delmour does not degrade a decent young woman as that of Stephen Guest does. But the best that can be said of him and his rival is, that their love-making is very tolerable and not to be endured by a girl with one-half of Gertrude's wit and spirit.

On the other hand, it might be urged that there is one phase of literature which Miss Ferrier has dealt with sparingly indeed, but effectively, and which Miss Austen has left untouched. We do find in Miss Ferrier traces, in one instance I think very distinct traces, of the capacity to deal effectively with a tragic situation, not indeed with the tragedy of incident, but with that subtler, though not less real, tragedy which arises out of the contrast between character and circumstances. Lady MacLaughlin is something more than a mere character of pure comedy ; Uncle Adam a great deal more. There is at least a suggestion of tragic pathos in the picture of the clever, handsome, warm-hearted woman, sunk apparently into a bundle of whims and absurdities, yet with affection and good judgment really unimpaired and ready to come to the surface when needed. And in Uncle Adam, affectionate and generous by nature, grudging, petty, and suspicious by training, never forgetting his early love, yet ashamed of anything like the least show of emotion, neither side of his character ever allowed to have free play for a moment without reproach or interference from the other, and thus in a state of chronic self-torment and restlessness, we have

a figure of blended humour and pathos not unworthy of
Scott.   Uncle Adam is a true cadet of the house of Caleb
Balderstone and Dominie Sampson.

We see somewhat the same kind of power less pleas-
ingly, but hardly less effectively, employed in that scene in
' Inheritance,' worthy of Crabbe in its grim mixture of
humour and repulsiveness, where the sick cottager's wife
is so absorbed with the care for her husband's ' dead claes,'
that she cannot pay the slightest attention to his sufferings,
or be even in the least moved by any kindly attempts to
relieve them.

Thus if any admirer of Miss Ferrier persists in the
very method of criticism which I have already deprecated,
and chooses to pit her against Miss Austen, he may, I
think, at least claim that she has for once steered into waters
where her rival's graceful and perfectly equipped bark never
ventured.

CHAPTER IV

SIR WALTER SCOTT

WE have already seen something of Miss Ferrier's inherited friendship with Sir Walter. Insomuch as it forms a distinct chapter in her life, and the letters from and concerning Scott have an independent interest of their own, it has seemed best, at some sacrifice of chronological exactitude, to place them in a chapter by themselves. Of her own intercourse with Scott, Miss Ferrier has left a record which has met with severe condemnation from one of her critics.[1] No one would deny that there was much in Scott that lay outside Miss Ferrier's comprehension. Yet no lover of Scott can fail to find interest in the clear, simply drawn picture of the home life at Abbotsford as seen by a shrewd observer, without any distorting influence of egotism ; one too, who, with old-fashioned views as to the sacredness of hospitality, felt an invincible repugnance to playing the reporter and taking down people's words under their own roof.

WALTER SCOTT TO JAMES FERRIER [2]

Ashestiel : September 18, 1811.

My dear Sir,—I am favoured with your letter acquainting me with your kind exertions on my part to supply my Lord Advocate with his materials. If I were to begin acknowledging my feeling of the friendship which you have shown me in this (to me a very important matter), it would fill a much longer letter than at present I propose to write. But as you have thought me worthy of so much kindness,

---

[1] It is published in the preface to the 1881 edition of the novels. Mr. Brimley Johnson, in his introductory memoir to Dent's edition, speaks of Miss Ferrier's ' extremely dull recollections of her two visits to Scott.' As a matter of fact, the recollections take in three visits, as we shall see.

[2] Principal Clerk of Sessions. (J. F.)

you must also give me credit for feeling it as I should do,
and that is all that can be said among friends. By an
engagement of Dr. Hume's proposing, he takes my duty
this summer, and I relieve him of his winter fortnights,
which would interfere with his class. I told him the
bargain was hugely unfair as the advantage was all on my
side, but he concluded that, as he proposed to be in town
on the 25th, it would suit him well. I would, however,
have come to town till his arrival (for I don't like bowel
complaints, and still less fighting with them), but I expect
a host of lawyers here immediately about the Roxburgh
County Election, and Col. McKenzie and his wife on
Monday next. But I think you should recall Hector,[1] as
really this hot weather is not favourable to any affection of
the bowels. And now, my dear sir, Mrs. Scott and I make
a joint petition, that if the weather be favourable in the
beginning of October (for I wish our vile teind court to be
over), Miss Ferrier and you would look in upon us for a quiet
day or two. We will take great care to give Miss Ferrier
a comfortable and well air'd room, and as we are near
Melrose and some other shewplaces, I would fain hope we
might make the time glide pleasantly away. I would be
glad to shew you this wild highland place before I leave it,
which I do with some regret, though I go to no great
distance, and hope my own place will be in time as pretty.
Meantime it is, as Shakespeare's clown says of his mistress,
'A poor thing, but mine own.' Think of this, my dear sir.
The journey is a trifle, as you can be with us to dinner any
day you have a mind, and you have no idea how you will
oblige

Yours very truly,
W. SCOTT.

Ashestiel : September 18, 1811.

Pray, as you are a ruling elder, solve me a case of
conscience. They are clearing out the modern additions

---

[1] Hector McDonald Buchanan, one of the Brethren of the Clerk's Table.
(J. F.)

from Melrose Abbey.   Will it be absolute sacrilege to build my cottage with the stones their operations afford, providing I can get them for next to nothing ?

Of the visit to Ashestiel which followed upon this invitation Miss Ferrier tells us but little.   The weather was stormy ; Miss Ferrier and her father occasionally drove with Mrs. Scott, while ' the bard,' with his son, Terry and a young kinsman of the Ferriers, took long rides on the hill through wind and rain.   In the evening Terry read plays aloud, or Scott ' recited old and awesome ballads from memory, the very names of which I have forgot.'

WALTER SCOTT TO JAMES FERRIER

Ashestiel : September 22, 1811.

My dear Sir,—There is no end of the plague I give you.   The Advocate writes to me, dated Largs 20th current, that he has not received the acts, and expresses himself anxious to give the matter dispatch.   You will be able to judge from the course of post whether this can be owing to a miscarriage, which I should think very likely.   Yet if your packet went on Wednesday 18th, it seems he should have had it before the 20th.   If you should be of opinion there is any chance of a miscarriage will you be kind enough to direct Johnstone to forward duplicates?   His address is Largs, Renfrewshire, famous for the defeat of the Danes.   I hope it will not be renowned for my discomfiture also.   The Advocate writes anxiously and in pure good humour and zeal, and it would be a pity to lose the opportunity of sunshine.   I have had a very polite note from the Premier intimating the result.   I expect brother Colin [1] here to-day, when you will be in our flowing cups freshly remembered.

Ever your truly obliged,

WALTER SCOTT.

What say you to my plan for your trip hitherwards ?

[1] Colin Mackenzie, Esq., of Portmore, one of the Brethren of the Clerk's Table.

WALTER SCOTT TO S. E. F. (1814)

My dear Miss Ferrier,—I had just written to say that Mrs. Scott's indisposition would have detained us here this week independent of the late calamity.[1] At any rate I would rather never have gone out of Edinburgh in my life than consulted my own amusement at the expense of your kind and worthy father's feelings in such a moment. Accept our deep and sincere sympathy, and believe me most faithfully and respectfully your obedient servant,

W. Scott.

We hear nothing of intercourse between Scott and Miss Ferrier during the days of her chief literary activity. Mention has already been made of the reference on which Blackwood relied as an appeal in the following letter.

Princes Street : June 1819. Thursday.

Madam,—I have the pleasure of enclosing you the concluding sentences of the new 'Tales of My Landlord,' which are to be published to-morrow.

After this call surely you will be no longer silent. If the Great Magician does not *conjure* you I shall give up all hopes.

I am, madam,

Your very respectful and most obedient servant,[2]

W. Blackwood.

In the autumn of 1829 Miss Ferrier again visited Scott, this time at Abbotsford. There is a curious and rather characteristic reticence in her language. 'The invitation had been often repeated, but my dear father's infirmities had made him averse to leave home, and when, in compliance with Sir Walter's urgent request, I visited Abbotsford in the autumn of 1829 I went alone.' One would not infer that her father had died at the beginning of the year.

---

[1] The death of Mr. Ferrier's son, Archibald Ferrier, W.S., which occurred in 1814. (J. F.)

[2] How far the personality of each 'shadow' was known or suspected by the other there is nothing to show.

It is a little unfortunate that Miss Ferrier's visit coincided with one of the gaps in Scott's Journal. As on her visit to Ashesticl, the party was a small one. Both sons were away Lockhart was detained in London by the sickness of Hugh Littlejohn, Mrs. Lockhart was ill in bed, and the party was made up by Anne Scott and Miss Buchanan—the 'Missie' of more than one affectionate reference. The critic to whom I have before referred considers that Miss Ferrier was 'little in touch with her host's real character.' And the remark 'I often wished his noble faculties had been exercised on loftier themes than those which seemed to stir his very soul,' calls forth the charge of 'pedantry and priggishness.' Can it be fairly said that one who dwelt on 'the unbroken serenity of his temper and the unflagging cheerfulness of his spirits, and the unfailing courtesy of his manners,' and who always found in him ' the same kind, unostentatious, amusing, and *amusable* companion,' had wholly failed to understand Scott ? Here, as elsewhere, Miss Ferrier frankly recognised her own limitations and did not make conventional professions of an admiration which she did not really feel. And if she did think that the antiquities of Abbotsford 'seemed crowded together in a small space, and that there was a " felt want " of breadth and repose for the eye,' was her criticism wholly beside the mark ?

In describing one scene, too, she shows a not unkindly perception of a weak side of Scott's character. There is a dinner-party where Wilkie and the Fergussons are present. Mrs. Lockhart, ill as she is, makes an effort and is carried down stairs, and is found in the drawing-room harp in hand ready to sing. Scott in his exhilaration makes the party stand in a circle with hands joined, singing

> Weel may we a' be,
> Ill may we never see.

' The glee,' such is Miss Ferrier's comment, 'seemed forced and unnatural. It touched no sympathetic chord ; it only jarred the feelings ; it was the last attempt at gaiety I witnessed within the walls of Abbotsford.' Is there any reader of the letters or the 'Journal' whose feelings have not been just once and again 'jarred' by 'forced and unnatural glee' in reading passages where a somewhat boisterous and, as it were, hectic semblance of mirth was the mark of real depression ?

Nor need any admirer of Scott, however loyal, hold Miss Ferrier much to blame for what her own generation would have called a lack of sensibility, if she somewhat failed to do justice to the merely mediæval and romantic side of Scott's genius. For if there is any discernment in our love, the Scott who holds the inmost place in our hearts is not the Scott of ' Ivanhoe ' and ' Marmion,' but the Scott of ' Waverley ' and ' Red-gauntlet.' The interpreter of Froissart, the chronicler of pageantry, the painter of tilt and battle, the storyteller of the greenwood, is ever delightful because ever human and ever manly. But it is only when joy in what is bright and love for what is gallant are blended with hereditary traditions and dominated by life-long associations that we have the Scott for whose immortality none may doubt or fear.

The following letter supplements Miss Ferrier's later and more formal reminiscences of her visit.

S. E. F. TO MRS. KINLOCH

7 Nelson Street : November 5.

My dear Helen,—I found your letter lying for me on my return from Abbotsford. . . . All your other interests I rejoice to think are well and prosperous. You will naturally expect a *narrative* of my visit to Abbotsford, but indeed I saw and heard a great deal too much to be able to detail anything ; it was all very delightful, only too exciting for one unaccustomed to soar beyond the sober realities of every day life. Nothing could exceed the kindness of Sir Walter and Miss Scott, and I was the more gratified by his attention because I felt it was not all on my own account, but for the respect and esteem I know he entertained for our dear father, and a tribute to his memory is more prized by me than any mere personal regard can ever be. Miss Scott I found very amiable and agreeable in domestic life, and she showed much kindness in presenting me with various little remembrances, which, though trifles in themselves, were gratifying as tokens of regard.[1]

---

[1] I have in my possession one of these tokens in the shape of a flat thin book, bound in red leather, and inscribed in Miss Scott's writing,

Mrs. Lockhart I also liked much ; she is very amusing, and seems most warm hearted where she takes a liking. She has been confined to bed for two months with what was *called* rheumatism in her knee, though I believe the medical people dreaded something worse ; however, she was better, and expected to be able to rejoin her husband and little boy in London very soon. The two children she had with her are delightful creatures. She hopes to spend next summer at her own cottage [1] (a little bijou within the domain), and I have *half* promised to pay her a visit there, also to return to Abbotsford and to spend some time with my *bosom friend* Miss Margaret Fergusson ! [2] I dined and spent a night at Huntley Burn,[3] but could not spend more as my time was limited to nine days (the period of all wonders), as I had to return to the preaching. Miss M. Buchanan [4] was the only other resident guest, but there were various occasional visitors, amongst others Wilkie the Painter, who by some strange, I could almost say *shameful*, oversight was allowed to depart without showing his sketches ; he is very unlike his own works, being a tall, sickly, grave, stiffish person. I talked of Fred [5] to Sir Walter, and he says he would not attempt to keep him back, but would allow him to go to Oxford as soon as he is ready ; he is for giving great scope to Nature in education.

It was on this visit that Miss Ferrier took Scott into her confidence about her novels, and received from him the advice which resulted in the severance with Blackwood.

' Miss Ferrier, from her affectionate friend,　　ANNE SCOTT. Abbotsford : Monday, Oct. 26, 1829.'

My aunt has written below : ' Remains of Sir Walter Scott's Album. 1797-9.' (J. F.)

[1] Chiefswood. (J. F.)

[2] The Miss Margaret Fergusson mentioned was a sister of Sir Adam's ; she was quite a ' character.' When her sister Isabella died Miss Ferrier went to pay a visit of condolence, and when in the middle of a speech becoming to the solemn occasion she was cut short by Miss Fergusson : ' Ye need na say ony mair, Miss Ferrier ; for Bell was aye a *most* tiresome compainion.' (J. F.)

[3] Where the Misses Fergusson lived. (J. F.)

[4] Sir Walter's favourite ' Missie,' as he called her. Her father was one of the brothers of the Clerk's Table. (J. F.)

[5] Her nephew, Frederick Kinloch. (J. F.)

The intimacy was kept up during the winter of 1829, and in the following July we read in the Journal[1] of Miss Ferrier being invited to meet an American 'who admired her prodigiously.'

The 'intimacy' with Scott referred to in the following letter[2] in all likelihood belongs to this period :

S. E. F. TO (PROBABLY) LADY CHARLOTTE BURY

Dear,—Next to seeing the summer's sun and smelling the summer's rose, nothing could have been more refreshing to my sick spirit than the sight of your vivifying characters. I confess I often lament, but indeed I never dare to *repine* at, your silence, but, on the contrary, wonder and admire your goodness in ever thinking of me at all. This has been a very cruel winter to me, but I flatter myself the worst is now over and that I may live to fight the same battle over again, for life with me will always be a warfare, *bodily* as well as *spiritual* perhaps, the more of the one the less of the other ; at least it is a comfortable doctrine to believe that the sickness of the body often conduces to the health of the soul, and I confess myself to be such an old-fashioned Christian as to have faith in such things. I am now better-hearted ; —— comes and amuses me very often, and crams me with news and with novels, and tells me what is doing in this round world, which otherwise might be standing stock-still for me. And now, having said so much upon so insignificant a subject as self, let me turn to a far more interesting theme. Your description of your travels do indeed set my feet moving and my heart longing to see all you have seen ; and this desire has been increased by reading the ' Corsair ' lately. . . . You were so kind as to

---

[1] *Journal*, vol. vii. p. 343.

[2] This letter I copied from *Diary Illustrative of the Times of George IV.*, a book attributed to Lady C. B., published 1838 and much abused at the time. It again made its appearance 1896 as if quite a *new* work. (J. F.)

Readers of Thackeray will not have forgotten Mr. Yellowplush's *Skimmings from ' The Dairy of George IV.* I must confess myself rather puzzled by this letter. In the *Diary* it is placed as belonging to the year 1817. Yet it is evident from the letter itself that it was written after Miss Ferrier had taken Scott into her confidence about her novels

say you would introduce me to Mrs. Apreece[1] and, independent of everything else, I should have had great pleasure in meeting with a person you liked. But in the first place I feel 'tis only your extreme goodness that could have made you propose it ; in the second it could only be for your sake that Mrs. Aprecce would submit to the penance of visiting me ; so I think I had better remain in my native obscurity, and not attempt to have the advantage of knowing this lady, of whom report speaks so highly. I am a wonderfully stupid person, having very little desire to see the most celebrated individuals. Ill-health, I suppose, contributes to the apathy of my feelings, and altogether I very much resemble a *dormouse* in my habits and temperament ; so if you please, dear, unless you wish to introduce me to Mrs. A. in the character of Mrs. McLarty, I think I had better forego the honour. With regard to my own performances, I must confess I have heard so much of the ways of booksellers and publishers lately that I find a *nameless* author has no chance of making anything of the business, and am quite dispirited from continuing my story and very much doubt if it will see the light of day. What a loss to the world will be the suppression of this child of genius ! Besides the cold water thrown on my *estro* by these cruel personages, the forefinger of my right hand (that most precious bit of an authoress's body) fell sick, and you may judge of my alarm when the surgeon pronounced it to have been poisoned—he, in the ignorance of his mind, supposed by some venomous particle it had imbibed when working in the garden. But for my part I have no doubt but it was a plot devised by all the great novelists of the age, who, having heard what great things it was about, had in the envy of their hearts laid their plan for its destruction. However, their malice has been defeated, as after being lanced and flayed alive, it is now put into a black silk bag and treated with all the tenderness due to its misfortunes. But, joking apart, should my book

---

[1] Married, afterwards, Sir Humphry Davy. (J. F.)

be ever published, how shall I get a copy sent to you ? And,
dear, will you *never, never* say to anybody that it is
mine, and commit this epistle to the flames and not leave
it lying about ? I am become a person of such consequence
in my own eyes now, that I imagine the whole world is
thinking about me and my books. I turn red like a
lobster every time a novel is spoken of, and whenever the
word authoress is mentioned I am obliged to have recourse
to my smelling-bottle. I mean to send a narrative of my
sufferings to D'Israeli for the next edition of ' Calamities of
Authors.'

My chief happiness is enjoying the privilege of seeing
a good deal of the Great Unknown, Sir Walter Scott. He
is so kind and condescending that he deigns to let me and
my *trash* take shelter under the protection of his mighty
branches, and I have the gratification of being often in
that great and good man's society. A few evenings ago
he gave me some couplets he wrote for our friend Lady
—— which I have transcribed for your perusal, feeling
certain that the slightest production of his muse must give
every sensible and feeling mind infinite pleasure. The
great simplicity of character and unaffected affability of
this astonishing man's manners add infinite charms to his
disposition, and he is as delightful as a private individual in society as he is supremely so in his works. The
society here nevertheless is a good deal broken up ; many
of your old acquaintances have forsaken our city for the
great Southern Babylon, and some are dead and others
grown poor or old ; in short, such changes have occurred as
generally fall to the lot of humanity. And now, dear ——
I will not longer tax your patience by adding more to this
voluminous letter, except the assurance that I shall never
cease to be your faithfully and obliged

                                        S. F.

MRS. LOCKHART TO S. E. F.

24 Sussex Place, Regent's Park :
Wednesday, 5.   Postmark : May 5, 1830.

My dear Miss Ferrier,[1]—Lockhart and myself were very sorry indeed to miss you yesterday, but it is quite out of the question to hope to find any one at home this fine weather.   Will you then dine with us in a very *quiet* way either Tuesday the 11th or Thursday the 13th ?   Our hour is half after six.   I trust one of these days will find you disengaged.   Lockhart is most anxious to make your acquaintance.   With best wishes from us both, believe me to remain most sincerely yours,

C. SOPHIA LOCKHART.

MRS. LOCKHART TO S. E. F.

24 Sussex Place, Regent's Park : Tuesday.

My dear Miss Ferrier,—I send you two autographs, one of Southey and one of Thomas Moore's, both of which I think you told me you had not.   I cannot lay my hand at this moment on one of Rogers's, but you shall have one soon, as I hear he is making most tender enquiries after me, which I dare say will come to a little *billet*, upon the eloquence of which he piques himself, and I promise it you. I made out my journey well, but am still as helpless as ever, and fear it will be long before I gain my legs.   However, I had the happiness of finding my little boy well for him ; and delighted he was, poor fellow, to see me.[2]   I remain, dear Miss Ferrier, with best respects, in which permit Lockhart to join,

Yours most faithfully,

C. SOPHIA LOCKHART.

WALTER SCOTT TO S. E. F.

Abbotsford : Tuesday evening.

My dear Miss Ferrier,—Anne returned to-day, and part of her Edinburgh news informs me that you meditated

---

[1] Addressed to Miss Ferrier, 19 Brunswick Square.

[2] 'Hugh Littlejohn,' who died December 15, 1831.

honouring your present literary offspring with my name.
So I do not let the sun set without saying how much I
shall feel myself obliged and honoured by such a compliment. I will not stand bandying compliments on my want
of merit, but can swallow so great a compliment as if I
really deserved it ; and indeed, as whatever I do not owe
entirely to your goodness I may safely set down to your
friendship, I shall scarce be more flattered one way or the
other. I hope you will make good some hopes which
make Anne very proud, of visiting Abbotsford about April
next. Nothing can give the proprietor more pleasure, for
the birds, which are a prodigious chorus, are making of
their nests and singing in blithe chorus : ' Pray come, and
do not make this a flattering dream.' I know a little the
value of my future godchild, since I had a peep at some of
the sheets when I was in town during the great snowstorm,
which, out of compassion for an author closed up within
her gates, may prove an apology for his breach of confidence. So far I must say that what I have seen has had
the greatest effect in making me curious for the rest.

Believe me, dear Miss Ferrier, with the greatest respect,
your most sincere, humble servant,

WALTER SCOTT.

WALTER SCOTT TO S. E. F.

Abbotsford [1] : Wednesday evening.

Dear Miss Ferrier,—If I had a spark of gratitude in me
I ought to have written you well-nigh a month ago to
thank you in no common fashion for 'Destiny,' which by
the few and at the same time the probability of its
incidents your writings are those of the first person of
genius who has disarmed the little pedantry of the Court
of Cupid, and of gods and men, and allowed youths and
maidens to propose other alliances than those an early
choice had pointed out to them. I have not time to tell

---

[1] Both these letters appeared in *Temple Bar*, November 1878.

you all the consequences of my revolutionary doctrine.
All these we will talk over when you come here, which I
am rejoiced to hear is likely to be on Saturday next, when
Mr. Cadell will be happy to be your *beau* in the Blucher
[stage-coach], and we will take care are met with at the toll.
Pray do not make this a flattering dream.　You are of the
initiated, so will not be *de trop* with Cadell.　I am always,
with the greatest respect and regard, your faithful and
affectionate servant,

WALTER SCOTT.

ANNE SCOTT TO S. E. F.

Sunday morning : Abbotsford.

My dear Miss Ferrier,—I am so very, very sorry I have
been so long in answering your kind enquiries ; but indeed
I did write immediately after your second kind note, but
my letter slumbered in papa's desk about a fortnight, and
it looked *so old, even in appearance*, that I did not like to
send it, and more days passed on as I have been hurried
about people coming and not coming.　In short, I would
have a thousand of good reasons were I to tell them to
you all, but I shall spare you the nine hundred and ninety-
eight.　Papa is indeed quite well ; I never saw him better
in spite of reform and east wind ; and he really does take
great care in regard to diet and exercise.　His spirits are
as good as possible, and, without having many people
staying here, we have had one or two of his old friends,
which, I think, does him much good to see.　I am now
getting quite well myself, and, except on a cold day, have
no return of sore throat ; but I mean to take great care, and
not put myself under a country doctor's hands again with
their horrid pills and potions, as I am sure Dr. Clarkson
had nearly killed me with camomile.　Papa was *so delighted
with* 'Destiny,'—*really and truly so.*　I need not say what
I thought of it !　My dear Miss Ferrier, I wish so much
papa would review it in the 'Quarterly,' or Lockhart.

Do tell me if you would *like* it to be done, for, though I am
an author's daughter, I don't know much about *these things.*
I expect Sophia and the children very soon, which will be
a great delight to me. Lockhart will leave them here and
return to London, so it will not be till July they will go to
the cottage. I have heard nothing from the Macdonalds ;
but it is my fault—I have never written to them. I don't
know what has made me feel so lazy this some months
past. I must now, my dear Miss Ferrier, conclude, as
we are just going to walk *with the cows* abroad in the
meadows—very pretty and pastoral. The Fergussons are
well ; at least, the gentlemen of the family are so. Poor
Margaret will never, I fear, be better, but at times she is in
good spirits. I hope, my dear Miss Ferrier, you do not
suffer so much from your eyes. I *do hope* you will come
here—I am *so sure* the country would do you good ; and
indeed we would have so *little* light at night, and you
would, I hope, feel as much at home here as you could do
anywhere else. But I will not trouble you with more about
the matter, as I am sure you will come to us whenever you
can. . . . Ever believe me, dear Miss Ferrier,

Yours very affectionately,

A. Scott.

ANNE SCOTT TO S. E. F.

Abbotsford : Thursday. Postmark : April 29, 1831.

My dear Miss Ferrier,—Had I not well known how
kind you are I would have written before this, but I am so
sure of your pardon I shall make no apology. I have had
much anxiety and very much to write, both for papa and
also answering letters of enquiry, &c. Papa is recovering
slowly, but mere acquaintance would think him quite well.
In mind he has always been the same. In this last attack
he has never lost it, but I think his speech is not quite
right yet. Indeed, till it comes round the disease is still, I
fear, hanging about him. He is very irritable, and will not
believe but it has been my insisting on him being bled

that has made him ill.   However, he has been much the
better of seeing Dr. Abercrombie, though all danger had
passed before he came ; but his influence in regard to diet
has been of very great use, and on that, I am well assured,
his life depends.   I am vexed none of my own family have
yet come down.   They treat his last attack too lightly, but
had they seen papa the two first days they would have
thought differently.   It is indeed a frightful disease, and
comes when most unlooked for.   I do, however, trust
Lockhart will come with Sophia and the children next
Tuesday.   I have written to beg him to do this, were it
only for a day or two.   Walter, I trust, also will get leave
and come down.   I think papa is anxious to see them both.
I am pretty well myself, though suffering from over-fatigue
both in body and mind.   Jane Erskine [1] was here during
his illness for four days, but was obliged to leave me on
account of the illness of a relation.   She was very kind and
very active, though she had not too much of the latter
quality to be disagreeable.   I hope, my dear Miss Ferrier,
your visit is only postponed, and that you will come to us
soon and, I trust, find all well.   I have behaved so ill to the
Macdonalds, never having written, but mean to do so to-
day ; but indeed I find I have not spirits enough *now* to
waste upon paper.   I look forward to the arrival of the
children with much pleasure, and Sophia will do, I am sure,
much good in amusing papa.   I was much shocked at
seeing the death of the Duchess of Wellington in the
papers to-night.   I answered a letter of hers yesterday, and
had no idea she was so ill.   My dear Miss Ferrier, I do not
like to ask you to write, because I fear you might do so out
of kindness when it must be painful to you on account of
your eyes ; but if it is really not, a few lines would be
a great pleasure to me.   I have *so* many letters from
acquaintances who do not care a bit for me, that one from
a friend will indeed be most gratifying, and you have been

[1] Daughter of Lord Kinnedder, an old friend of Scott's, and a Lord of
Session, Edinburgh.   (J. F.)

so kind as to allow me to be so. I shall conclude with
every kind wish from myself and papa.

Your very affectionate

A. SCOTT.

ANNE SCOTT TO S. E. F.

Postmark : May 10, 1831.

My dear Miss Ferrier,—I thank you for your kind
letter. I am glad to say the doctor now thinks papa has
quite got over this last attack ; his pulse is now good, and
all the bad symptoms have disappeared. We do most
sincerely hope you will now pay us the long-promised
visit, which has been so unhappily retarded. Any day
this week we shall be delighted to see you. Papa dines
always alone, but breakfasts with us and drinks tea. Sophia
and the children have arrived, and poor little Johnny, who
is very delicate just now, but that is always the case in
spring.   The others are quite well *with new nursery maids,
which* is a *great comfort.* . . . Flora—or, as we call her,
Mrs. McDow—is blooming on the banks of the Tweed,
and dispersing her smiles like her fair namesake. I was so
delighted with her objections to ' Destiny,' which was the
contempt with which Mr. McDow's luncheon was held. I
have promised her ducks and leek soup to dinner some
day soon. Will you write a few lines, my dear Miss
Ferrier, and say what day you will come to us ? I delayed
writing till to-day, because I believe that this last week
you were engaged with church. Sophia and papa desire to
unite with me in kindest regards. . . .

S. E. F. TO MRS. LOCKHART

My dear Mrs. Lockhart,—You little know what you are
doing when you invite me to join your party by steam, for
I am sure you could scarcely find in all London a less
agreeable (to say the least of myself) companion ; and
much as I like you, and long to see you and Mr.
Lockhart, I trust we may never meet at sea ! I expected

to have been on the high road to Edinburgh with my
brother before now, but he has been detained by some
cross purposes in business, and I am waiting from day to
day in hopes every one is to be the last. My sight has
become so much worse since I came here that I am now
very anxious to be home.   I made a mad-like attempt to
see you a few days ago, and shall make a wise-like one
some morning if I do not set off to-morrow or next day.

Dear Mrs. Lockhart, I am,

Truly and affectionately yours,

S. E. FERRIER.

The visit thus proposed took place in May.[1] Among
the qualities which make Lockhart the envy and the
despair of biographers is his power of bringing out by a
few effective touches the subordinate personages of his
drama, unobtrusively and without any check or hindrance
to his main purpose. His description of Miss Ferrier's
kindly thoughtfulness would be marred by any para-
phrase :

'To assist them in amusing him in the hours which he
spent out of his study, and especially that he might be
tempted to make those hours more frequent, his daughters
had invited his friend the authoress of " Marriage " to come
out to Abbotsford ; and her coming was serviceable. For
she knew and loved him well, and she had seen enough of
affliction akin to his to be well skilled in dealing with it.
She could not be an hour in his company without observing
what filled his children with more sorrow than all the rest
of the case. He would begin a story as gaily as ever,
and go on, in spite of the hesitation in his speech, to tell it
with highly picturesque effect ; but before he could reach
the point, it would seem as if some internal spring had
given way—he paused and gazed round him with the
blank anxiety of look that a blind man has when he has
dropped his staff. Unthinking friends sometimes pained
him sadly by giving him the catch-word abruptly. I
noticed the delicacy of Miss Ferrier on such occasions.
Her sight was bad, and she took care not to use her

[1] Any one who reads only Miss Ferrier's account of this visit would suppose that it was paid in 1830. But Lockhart and the *Journal* leave no room for doubt.

glasses when he was speaking; and she affected to be also troubled with deafness, and would say, " Well, I am getting as dull as a post ; I have not heard a word since you said so-and-so," being sure to mention a circumstance behind that at which he had really halted.   He then took up the thread with his habitual smile of courtesy—as if forgetting his case entirely in the consideration of the lady's infirmity.'[1]

How fully her good gifts were understood and valued by Scott himself is shown by his description of her in the 'Journal': 'Miss Ferrier comes out to us.   This gifted personage, besides having great talents, has conversation the least *exigeante* of any author, female at least, whom I have ever seen among the long list I have encountered with ; simple, full of humour, and exceedingly ready at repartee ; and all this without the least affectation of the bluestocking.'[2]   And with a repetition not very common with him Scott returns to the subject three days later : 'I wrote and rode as usual, and had the pleasure of Miss Ferrier's company in my family hours, which was a great satisfaction ; she has certainly less affectation than any female I have ever known that has stood so high—Joanna Baillie hardly excepted.'[3]

Cheerful and companionable Miss Ferrier may have been, but it was from no insensibility to the tragedy before her eyes.   No record of those latter days is sadder than her picture of Scott, spent and broken, sitting by his dying grandson : 'the child of so much pride and promise ! now, alas ! how changed.' 'Disease and death were stamped upon the grandsire and the boy as they sat side by side, with averted eyes, each as if in the bitterness of his own heart refusing to comfort or be comforted.'

The following letter, written immediately after Miss Ferrier's visit, shows with how much happy kindliness she could identify herself with the home life of her friends :

ANNE SCOTT TO S. E. F.

May 1831.

My dear Miss Ferrier,—I make use of Flora as a private opportunity to thank you for your kind present to the children.   Walter desires me to give you his love, and

---

[1] *Life of Scott* (ed. 1839), vol. x. p. 68.

[2] *Lockhart* (ed. 1839), vol. x. p. 70.

[3] Scott's *Journal*, vol. xi. p. 407.

he is *very* much obliged to you.   Baby's doll, as she calls it, gives her great pleasure and appears most beautiful in her eyes.   It has a strong resemblance to an old school companion of mine, so I also feel a sort of sentiment for it. Lockhart desires me to say he has been practising the precepts of your sermons, having only taken one tumbler and a bottle of small beer every day.   Flora has been spending some days here.   Last night, after a plentiful dinner of haggis, I took her to see Melrose Abbey.   In short, I have been doing all in my power to give her a little sentiment, but I cannot say with much effect, and Princes Street and the Dragoons will finish her.   I am sure, my dear Miss Ferrier, you will be glad to hear that papa is *now* much better, both in regard to his speech and in every other respect.   He attended both elections and was not the worse of it, but I am quite glad they are over.[1] I expect my brother Walter to-morrow for a few days. He has been obliged to come down for the Fife election. The children are making such a noise I don't know what I write, and Lockhart is shaking the table so it is like writing during a earthquake, so I had better conclude my scrawl, but not without thanking you very much for the trouble you took about the little books, which were quite what I wished.   Lockhart and Sophia desire to unite with me in kindest love to you, and ever believe me to remain,

Yours affectionately,
ANNE SCOTT.

Abbotsford : Friday morning.

Will you remember me to Mrs. and Miss Graham ? We are all determined to believe you will come to us

---

[1] Those Jedburgh and Selkirk elections described by Lockhart (vol. x. p. 74), when Sir Walter was hooted, stoned, and spat upon, and left the borough in the midst of abuse and the gentle hint of ' Burk Sir Walter,' while ' a disciplined rabble of Hawick weavers ' lined the streets, grossly insulting everyone who did not wear the reforming colours, and when the Tory candidate for Selkirk ' was grievously maltreated, but escaped murder, though narrowly.'

during the summer. I sent the book to Margaret Fergusson.
She is just the same, one day well and another ill.

S. E. F. TO MRS. KINLOCH

July 3, 1831.

My dear Helen,—I have so little to write about I
think I must soon cease to write at all; my days pass
away in darkness and silence, like shadows that leave not
a trace behind. I lament my uselessness, and fear it must
be my own fault that I am such a mere cumberer of the
ground, since none were ever designed to be such. Alas!
'the night cometh when no man can work,' as is the case
with that mighty genius which seems now completely
quenched; well might he be styled 'a bright and benignant
luminary,' for, while all will deplore the loss of that bright
intellect which has so long charmed a world, many will
still more deeply lament the warm and steady friend whose
kind, generous influence was ever freely diffused on all
whom it could benefit.

ANNE SCOTT TO S. E. F.[1]

November 28, 1832 : Sussex Place, Regent's Park.

My dear Miss Ferrier,—Thank you very much for your
kind letter and the book you were so kind as to send me.
I need not say how much *I value it.* I would have written
to you *long ago,* as I promised, had I been able; but indeed
I was not, and though I do feel most grateful to God that
poor papa is at rest, still the recollections of *past days and*
home are hard to bear. But I will not dwell on the past—
it can *do no good.* Sophia and the children are quite well.
I wish I could say the same of Lockhart; but he has had
an attack the same he had after the death of his poor boy,
which is that his pulse gets *so very low* as to make the
medical people think at least that there was disease of the
heart. This, thank God, is not the case; but he has been

---

[1] When this letter was written, Miss Scott had lost her father. (J. F.)

writing *so much* and, I fear, *also smoking*—in short, he has
far too much to do for his strength of constitution, but I
do trust that now he has consented to do as Dr. Holland
wishes we shall soon see him quite well. And now, my
dear Miss Ferrier, how are you, and are your eyes stronger?
I should like very much indeed to hear from you sometimes. Amongst the many I do regret in Scotland they
are few whose friendship I value so much as yours; and
though we, I fear, may not meet soon, if we ever do, I shall
always feel most interested about everything regarding
you. I suppose dear Missy is in town.

Jemima [1] married! It appears to me so many changes
have happened since I left England. I have never written
to Jemima, but do tell her I mean to do so soon. I would
not have thought it good luck to write a melancholy letter
to a bride. I am so glad she is so happy, but why does
not Missy marry? The generous public have been so
good as to give *me two husbands*, which is *contrary to law*
—Captain Pigot and Mr. Baillie. Now I would sooner
marry all the ship's company than the said captain; and as
for Mr. Baillie, he happens to be the brother of an intimate
friend of mine, Mrs. Ashley, who was, I dare say you know,
the fashionable London beauty for two seasons; and
because he lived for six months in the same palazzo at
Naples, I do not see *why* I should marry her brother. I
wish I could tell you any news, but there is none here . . .
Yet there is no change in anybody's living, and the expected
revolution is like the comet: it never has appeared, though
Lockhart and Sophia foretell it every day. I saw Mrs.
Leigh, Lord Byron's sister, yesterday; I never saw a more
broken-hearted-looking person. She seems, poor thing,
as if no end was ever to come to her distresses. One of
her daughters, a very beautiful girl, has eloped with her
brother-in-law, and the poor wife is left with a large family
dependent on her mother; it is one of the most horrid
things that ever I heard of. By-the-bye, I am to see

[1] She married Sir Alexander Leith, Bart. (J. F.)

Madame Guiccioli to-day, Lord Byron's last love ; I heard so much of her in Italy I am anxious to see her ; the meeting is to take place at my *élevée* cousin's, Lady Davy's.[1] And now, my dear Miss Ferrier, I have written you a long letter, or rather a long scrawl, for it does not deserve the name of a letter ; and with kindest regards from Lockhart and Sophia, ever believe me,

Your most affectionate

A. SCOTT.

[1] See p. 244. Lady Holland writes in an unpublished letter : 'Professor Davy is about to be re-compensed with the fair and healthy hand of the blue stocking widow Apreece.'

CHAPTER V

MISS FERRIER'S LATER YEARS

IF Miss Ferrier did show in some respects an inadequate comprehension of Scott, in one point at least she succeeded to a full share of his spirit. The claims and pretensions of literature did not sit more lightly upon him than they did on the author of ' Marriage.' No one reading the later letters, with their record of commonplace events, their quiet, unstudied, unepigrammatic criticisms, would imagine that he was in the presence of one who, before she had completed her fiftieth year, had produced work which gives her an abiding place among English classics. Yet withal they are, without the least touch of morbid self-consciousness, thoroughly self-revealing: and there lies their claim upon us, that they furnish the self-drawn portrait —clear, wholesome, and unaffected in treatment—of one to whom literature owes much.

S. E. F. TO MRS. CONNELL

Nelson Street : September 6, 1832.

My dear Janet,—I am happy to say I have at last found a *meet partner* in Mr. David Welsh, and my place is taken in the Saturday's ' Mail.' I should have preferred another night, but as he had no choice I had none. I expected to have been with you long ere now, but I fear I shall be soon enough, as I doubt if I shall be able to endure even your autumnal brightness. Mrs. John has had a better night, but has made no progress towards recovery. Walter left all well at Sloebiggin [1] yesterday.

Affectionately yours,

S. E. F.

I shall be just in time to open the Circuit.

[1] On the Broxmouth estate near Dunbar. It was lent by the Dowager Duchess of Roxburgh to Walter Ferrier for the summer. (J. F.)

S. E. F. TO MRS. KINLOCH

Conheath : October 5.   Postmark : October 12, 1832.

My dear Helen,—I ought to have written to you before now to have assured you of our safety in the midst of the pestilence that has been raging around us ; but truly my spirit sank within me every time I attempted to bear record to the dismal scenes that have been passing in this neighbourhood, though, thank God, we know them only by report. The papers will give you some idea of the work of destruction that has been going on in Dumfries, but you cannot conceive the consternation that prevailed when cholera reported [*sic*] to have broken out at Kirkton, and as ascertained to be actually at the Quay! Even I, though far from being an alarmist, felt as if we could scarcely expect to escape its visitation ; but the mercy of God has preserved us, while others (we may hope, also in mercy) have been taken away from evil to come. A poor man at the Quay had but just recovered from the pestilence himself when one of his children died of it, and as no human being would assist him he had to convey the body himself all the long solitary way to Caerlaverock church-yard, not a soul accompanying him ; on his return home he found another had died in his absence! Nothing can exceed the desolation that reigns all around. I have just had a very distressing letter from John, informing me that the medical people have little hope of his wife's ultimate recovery, as her strength is fast sinking.[1] That is what I have always feared would come to pass. You may imagine his anguish! . . . I would fain hope a day or two may effect a change here, and I shall set off instantly for Edinburgh. Would that I could be a help to any! But, alas! I feel as if I were rather a burden.

---

[1] She died January 1833, at 12 York Place, Edinburgh, aged 49. (J. F.)

S. E. F. TO MRS. CONNELL

1832.

My dear Janet,—Although I have almost ceased from letter-writing, I cannot allow Mr. C. to depart without a single word from me, knowing that he is not a man of many words—or, at least, not of words enough to satisfy your *enquiring* mind. After this preamble you will expect a vast deal of miscellaneous information to be poured forth, and will be much disappointed. I must have lost the art of either hearing or communicating intelligence, for I really never have anything to tell. My sphere of observation, to be sure, is very circumscribed, as I am confined to a dark room all day, and only creep out in the evening to visit some one or other of my many sick friends; for the whole town has been ill, and this is one of the very few houses that has hitherto escaped the influenza. Mrs. Walter has had it very severely, but is on the way to recovery; and Walter does not seem to have gained much by his London trip, but I hope the good effects are yet to come. I am happy to think you have a jaunt in prospect, as I am sure you will enjoy it, and travelling agrees with you. If I go anywhere it will certainly be to you by-and-bye; but I suffer so much from the common light of day I really cannot associate with anybody, and nobody can associate with me. My eyes are worse than they were last summer, so you may judge how unfit I am for society; but I have great cause of thankfulness to God for the support and consolation He affords me under this trial, and, knowing that it is of His appointment and may be for my ultimate good, I am well content to take whatever He sees best to bestow. We are too ignorant to know what is really and essentially good, and too impatient to be happy our own way to be satisfied with receiving our portion of 'daily bread' even from the hand of God. You'll think this is too serious a strain for a letter; but such thoughts are a great solace to me, and so I cannot help expressing them to others now and then.   I have heard from Jane since her arrival at *the Hall*,[1] and I hope she will enjoy it, but I have no intention of going there.   She was in great health and beauty when she left this ; so, whatever odium attaches to this house, it has not injured her, and so I hope to see her back again, if we are both alive, next winter.

S. E. F. TO MRS. CONNELL

February 1833.

My dear Janet,—I know not how long it is since I wrote to you, but it seems a long time since I heard either of or from you ; so immediately on receipt of this I beg you or one of the girls will write me a few lines.   As the winter will soon be over, I trust so your aches and pains will take their departure too ; but at present the weather is so stormy that, in spite of the old saying, I don't think it can blow good to anybody.   There is scarcely a house where there is not an invalid.   Jane[2] has had a very bad cold and been confined for a week, but to-day (though not recovered) she is gone to dine with the Edmonstones, who give a *fête* previous to Mrs. H. and D.[3] setting out on a tour of visits through Renfrewshire, and to visit some old friends who they think must be dropping off soon !   Not a word of their own dropping off—indeed, they seem rather provoked at people for being ill, and I dare say they would give you a good scold for allowing such a *crochet* to enter your head as that you could be indisposed with your charming constitution !   They are in great delight at having it announced that Sir Archibald's lady is to add a twig to the family tree, and is to come here for the purpose, that it may be a Scotch plant.   Mrs. Walter has been very unwell again, but is now better, though not much to be depended upon.   Walter and the children are well, and John and his family are all in good health and

---

[1] Stuart Hall, near Stirling. Mrs. Graham, after her husband's death, took up her abode in Edinburgh with her sister. (J. F.)

[2] Mrs. Graham, who now lived with her. (J. F.)

[3] Mrs. Halliday and Miss Dalmeny Edmonstone.

better in spirits than could have been expected. I have
not seen the Riddells very lately, but I believe they are
all well, poor things! I don't know what plan will be
adopted for them, but I fear they will be all dispersed
amongst relations, which is a very sad termination. I
don't know what Jane's plans will be, and, indeed, I believe
she is much at a loss what to decide upon herself. I have
offered to let this house and take a larger one if she will
agree to reside in Edinburgh during the winter months—
leaving her at liberty to do as she likes during the
summer ; but she has not yet come to any determination,
and there are so many different schemes afloat in her
family that it is difficult for her to decide so as to please
all—*prudence* out of the question. She has been reading
to me the 'Life of Sir David Baird,' which is extremely
interesting ; both Mr. C. and you would, I am sure,
enjoy it much, so I hope it is in the Dumfries Library. I
have also read the 'Young Christian,' and think it excellent
for old as well as young. Mrs. Crichton [1] sent a letter of
introduction by a Miss Maxwell [2] to me some weeks ago,
but I was confined to bed with a cold when she called, and
as she lives in George Square I have not had it in my
power either to see or serve her ; will you mention this to
Mrs. Crichton when you happen to see her? We had a
little *tea match* lately, and Miss Bushnan was of the party,
also Mrs. John Hay, who is a very agreeable, intelligent
person ; [3] this has been our only attempt at gaiety. My
eyes are so weak I can scarcely endure now the shaded
light of a single candle, yet I don't think the cataract is
forming, which makes the case worse. I am happy to hear
Mary and her babe are thriving [4] so well, by-and-bye he will
be a great acquisition at Conheath. The stormy weather
has made fish scarce, or I should have sent you some before

[1] Daughter of Sir Robert Grierson, of Lag. (J. F.)

[2] Niece of Mrs. Crichton. (J. F.)

[3] Wife of Dr. Hay, in Edinburgh ; she was an Irish lady, a Miss Patrick, and a cousin of Lord Stratford de Redcliffe. (J. F.)

[4] Her niece, Mrs. Bushnan, *née* Connell.

now, but I hope in the course of the week the *hadies* will be showing their heads above water—it has certainly been a good wind for them.

S. E. F. TO MRS. CONNELL

Toravon [1] : June 30.

My dear Janet,—I am sorry my billet to James should have caused such a panic in the family. I am so little of an alarmist myself I am apt to forget how sensitive some of my friends are in that respect, and certainly whatever effect the *outside* of my letters may produce, their contents are seldom calculated to produce much sensation, being commonly of a sedative description. I wish Mr. C. and you had remained longer at Moffat, since you both found yourselves so much benefited by it ; but I trust you will repeat your visit and extend your limits *at least* as far as Edinburgh, and then it is hoped you will take an hour's trip to Toravon. I came with Walter on Friday evening, and found all in great beauty and order ; he returned on Monday morning, leaving me with the youngsters, with whom I have been living most comfortably and happily, and find them all kindness and attention in a quiet way. Agnes is really a most amiable and estimable creature, as well as a pleasant, cheerful companion ; she is looking forward to her visit to Conheath with much pleasure, and I think she will be the better of a change, for she has had much to do one way and another for some time past, and she is so free from all selfish considerations. She is always occupied about others, and (as she is not very strong) sometimes too regardless of herself; that is certainly a blessed disposition, as seen in our good old friend Miss Edmonstone, whose heart is still so overflowing with benevolence and practical kindness ; she seems quite happy and never finds time hang heavily on her hands, what few can say, who have far ampler materials of enjoyment than she possesses.

<hr>

[1] Mr. Walter Ferrier's country house in Linlithgowshire. (J. F.)

1st *July*.—I can say little for the weather till yesterday, which was fine, and to-day is pleasant, and the hearts of the farmers must be rejoicing in the luxuriance of the crops. Walter is expected to-day accompanied by Eleanor. As James went to town this morning for a day or two, there is accommodation for *two* guests at a time, which could not otherwise be ; but I take my departure on Monday, when Walter returns. However, the transit from Nelson Street is so easy I shall probably return very soon ; it is such an inducement for an owl like me to be able to ' fly by night.'

Saturday.—We had the agreeable addition of Colonel Hamilton yesterday at dinner ; he had left all well at Cairnhill in the morning and met Walter in Linlithgow, came here with him, and left for Cathlaw (his place near Linlithgow) in the evening, and was to return to Ayrshire to-day ; so much for Margaret's information.[1] I am glad to hear she is so well ; she seems to thrive best in England, like many others. I missed seeing Mrs. Lester [her cousin, General Ferrier's daughter], but shall probably meet her on her return from Aberdeenshire ; she is a most meritorious creature, by all accounts, and must have done her part well to hold the respectable position she does. Lest I should forget when the time comes, I may as well mention that Mrs. Cuming of Logie begged me to bespeak her winter butter from you.

S. E. F. TO MRS. TENNENT

. . . Your mention of Miss Gillies [2] made me *blush at the bone* for not having long since executed your commission of getting my mother's picture copied.[3] I think I told you Miss Arnot (who was to have done it) had died, and I could not hear of anybody else to do it at a reasonable

---

[1] Colonel Hamilton's sister, Miss Wallace Ferrier. (J. F.)

[2] The miniature painter. (J. F.)

[3] This portrait of my great-grandmother is now in my possession ; it was painted 1765, by Sir George Chalmers, Bart., a pupil of Allan Rumsay's, and when she was Mis Coutts. (J. F.)

rate ; but as Sir Adam F.[1] says I am '*a complete screw,*
perhaps I am too limited in my terms, so please let me
know what are yours, or whether you will get it copied
yourself . . . .

Of the following correspondent Mr. John Ferrier writes
thus :

' Thorburn, the eminent minature painter, was from his
boyhood known to Miss Ferrier, whose minature he painted,
and when he went to London he never forgot his early
friend and patron, to whom he wrote now and then of his
prosperous career.   Miss Ferrier never liked the portrait of
her painted by Thorburn, and wrote, " This picture must
upon no account be shown to Mr. Thorburn, as it would
certainly displease him to see how it has been marred as a
painting since it came from his hands.   In consequence of
its having twice sustained injury, first from damp, then
from an accident, it was each time committed to professional artists here, who did their best to repair the
damage ; but, not satisfied with their repairs, a bungling
amateur next undertook the task, who made bad worse."
The likeness is supposed to have been taken thirty years
ago—S. E. F. '[2] [Written in 1842.]

Craig-y-Don, Anglesea : October 20, 1838.

Dean madam,—I thought it would be better to delay
writing to you until the close of the season in London,
when I would be enabled to acquaint you more fully of my
success.   I have now quitted the metropolis to recruit my
health in the country, and, having a little leisure, hasten to
write to you.   This spring I sent eight miniatures to be

---

[1] Fergusson. (J. F.)

[2] The miniature in question forms
the frontispiece to Dent's edition of
her novels.   This miniature is now
in my possession, and the great fault
in it, to my mind, is the gigantic
fabric in the shape of a bonnet that
she has on.   She generally, I have
been told, wore a bonnet in the
house, perhaps as a screen to her
eyes. (J. F.)

exhibited at the Royal Academy, one of them a portrait of
Sir George Anson.[1]   They were received favourably and
hung in good places.   I was gratified to learn from some
of my friends who visited the exhibition shortly after it
opened that I had improved.   And I very soon had substantial proof of this in the shape of as many sitters as I
could possibly paint, and at my new terms, namely twenty
guineas for a half-length.   My income has been more than
sufficient for my expenses.   The surplus I have laid aside
for further study, and my luck has been better than my
merit deserved ; but the less I say about this the better,
as you will be apt to imagine I am dishonest.   My health
has been good all the season in town ; for this I am much
indebted to the excellent advice I received at Slowbiggin
from Mrs. Ferrier.   I have been living a short time at
Craig-y-Don, the beautiful residence of Mr. Williams, M.P.,
situated on the banks of Menai Strait, close to the bridge.
Being in such an interesting county my sketchbook and I
have had a close acquaintance.   I shall in a very few days
leave for my native country, returning to London by
Edinburgh, when I shall have much gratification in waiting
upon you.

S. E. F. TO HER NEPHEW JAMES FERRIER[2]

Edinburgh : August 1.

My dear James,—I could not get a letter to Lord
Corehouse's German sister (Countess Purgstall), as it seems
she is in bad health and not fit to entertain vagabonds, but
I enclose a very kind one from my friend Mrs. Erskine to
the Ambassadress at Munich, and if you don't go there
you may send it by post, as it will be welcome at any time
on its own account.

Yours affectionately,

S. E. F.

---

[1] Sir G. Anson's daughter married, 1836, Miss Ferrier's nephew, Mr. Kinloch. (J. F.)

[2] When my father went to Germany, in 1834, his aunt wrote to him (the only scrap of her writing to him that I know of). (J. F.)

S. E. F. TO HER SISTER MRS. KINLOCH[1]

March, 1836.

Dearest Helen,—I should indeed have been shocked had I heard from any hand but your own of what you had undergone, for well can I enter into the sufferings of mind and body on such an occasion ; but your kind note testified that all had gone well with you, and deeply do I share, my dear sister, in your gratitude to God for having supported and preserved you under this trial. Oh that the Great Physician of souls may bless this and every such dispensation by making them the means of bringing us to Him, who alone can heal our infirmities, in whose hand are the issues of life and death. I feel much more than I express on this subject. I experience so much happiness myself, even in the small measure I have yet attained of the knowledge of God as revealed to us in Jesus Christ that I would fain impart it to others. But yet I am aware nothing injures a cause more than injudicious zeal, and they who can 'search the Scriptures' and pray to be taught by them lack little of human exhortation. May this be so with you and yours, dear sister. And this reminds me to recommend a work to Mr. K., which to one of his penetrating and searching mind I am sure will interest and entertain him beyond any books of travels he ever read. I mean ' Keith on the Evidence of Prophecy ' ; it is in one volume, and I sent it by Henry (when he was last here) that you might all read it, but especially Mr. K., as I am certain he will like it even as a *curious* book. With my kind regards ask him to read it first for my sake. . . .

I dare say you heard how Agnes Callander had eloped with a young man who had nothing but his lieutenancy and the liver ; so they dread going to India, and some of his friends think of New South Wales and are desirous of getting every information about it; so if you can send me any of Fred's letters, or some extracts from them, they would

[1] Mrs. Kinloch had just recovered from a serious illness. (J. F.)

be very acceptable. The Walters returned from Dumfries, both looking ill. Mrs. G.[1] had settled her *bit*, house, and what she had on Agnes[2] soon after she was born (I believe), but she will be a very small heiress, poor thing! I hope Loo's[3] riches won't make her set her heart on them, for they become a great snare. 'To whom much is given, of them much is required.' 'Blessed is he that considereth the poor,' and blessed may they account themselves to whom God gives the power and the will to administer to the wants of others. John is also in bed with a bad cold, and all my intimates are ill, so I'm seldom out of a sick room . . . . Jane writes me that she expects to make this headquarters, which is a pleasant prospect for me. The weather was summer, and is now winter—Thursday and Friday.

MISS HOPE MACKENZIE TO S. E. F. (1837)

Tuesday.

My dear friend,—The snow seems little likely to relent and let you come here, so I think I must tell you my matter this way, that you may think over it before we meet. Louisa[4] applied to me to persuade you to listen favourably to a request she was authorised to make to you (through her connection Mr. Sutherland Mackenzie) that you would accept 1000*l.* for a *volume anything from you* (these are Louisa's words), which a friend of Mr. S. M.'s, a gentleman *in the line* from London, is most anxious to get from you. Now, dear friend, how much pleasure may you give, and how much good would you do with your thousand pounds! But I will wait for your ears and not tax your eyes with more. I am keeping better, and had a pleasant long journal from Montpellier, from Holt,[5] to help to cheer the storm yesterday. Alas! but poor accounts of

---

[1] Mrs. Gordon, mother of Mrs. W. Ferrier; she was a Kirkpatrick, and cousin of the grandfather of the Empress of the French. (J. F.)

[2] Her niece, Agnes Ferrier. (J. F.)

[3] Another niece, Louisa Kinloch. (J. F.)

[4] Mrs. Forbes, of Medwyn (*née* Gordon Cummins); she was a great friend of Miss Ferrier, and a relative of the Mackenzies. (J. F.)

[5] Her brother. (J. F.)

our dear little boy at Ripon, much pain and much anxiety,
though still hope, which supports his dear mother, who
yet, I am sure, desires to say the Lord's will be done.
How are you and yours?

Ever your loving
H. M.

On the back of this note Miss Ferrier wrote, 'I made
two attempts to write *something*, but could not please
myself, and would not publish '*anything.*'

S. E. F. TO MRS. KINLOCH[1]

Friday, April 2.

My dearest sister,—You will understand why I have
been so long of writing to you. Had I felt less I could
have said more, but every time I attempted to write was
a renewal of anguish, which in the wretched state of my
eyes quite unfitted me for the sad task. But I will not
excite either your feelings or my own by writing at all on
the subject; you well know you have my tenderest
sympathy, but your strength and consolation, my dear
sister, must come from a higher source. You have many
ties to bind you to this life, and that makes it the more
difficult, but not the less necessary, to look beyond it for
that happiness which is *never* under any circumstances to
be found on earth. Since my dear father's death I have
felt this world is indeed no resting place for the affections ;
the most promising life is uncertain, and the longest is but
short ; but we have the blessed hope set before us that
through the merits of our Saviour we shall in His everlasting kingdom again be united to those we so fondly loved
in this imperfect state. Oh what balm there is in that
belief ! I received Dr. Arnold's sermons two days ago,
but have not been able to read any of them. I am prepared
to like them from all I hear of the author. I forget if I

---

[1] On the occasion of Mr. Kinloch's death, which occurred about 1840.
(J. F.)

mentioned that I had asked the Fergussons to mention Frederick [1] to their friends the Moultries, and they told me they had done so. . . .

S. E. F. TO MISS FLETCHER

My dear friend,—I wish I could *answer* your letter, but I can do little more than acknowledge it, for my eyes are much weaker and more averse to work; however, I comfort myself with the thought of having such a nice, long winter talk with you if my breath holds out till then, but it is getting very short. You would hear how poor Mary [2] had been hurried off to Netherby; she seemed very sorry to go and not very able for the journey; an amiable old maid has really a weary life of it! Apropos, as Mrs. Fletcher and you have always an emporium of virtuous and reduced gentlewomen, can you recommend one to act as companion to a lady whose mind is a little— not much out of order? She is English and episcopal, and therefore I think would prefer a friend so born and bred. I hope my sister G. will be able for the journey very soon. My nephew is progressing very slowly. I had a visit from Mrs. C. in *such* rapture at finding herself in town after all the cold, dirt, and dreariness of the country; but more of her anon.[3] Where am I to get 'King Rene's Daughter,' for she has never been heard of ' *in the trade* ' here? I see the Mackenzies often, but they are much in the new carpet and rug line at present. I heard from Charlotte this morning from Ayr; she had not been well, but was better. The town is to be very full, so you had best bespeak lodgings in time.

With best regards to Mrs Fletcher,

I am affectionately yours,

S. E. F.

Awfu' weather !

[1] Her nephew, F. Kinloch. (J. F.)
[2] Campbell. (J. F.)
[3] Mrs. Cuninghame, wife of Lord C., a Session Lord in Edinburgh. She was Miss Trotter, of Mortonhall. (J. F.)

S. E. F. TO MRS. TENNENT

My dear Helen,—Your note was welcome and required no apology. I was glad to hear Mr. T.[1] has got the Colonel for a *patient*, though I would rather it had been of free will than necessity that he was a sitter ; however, I hope he will be able to take his foot in his hand before the picture is finished. He should be careful of walking too much at first, and I would therefore recommend his taking a drive this way to our fine, bracing air, which never was to be had in such perfection than at present. I wonder with you at the Kinloch predilection for going beyond seas. I think this island quite small enough for any rational sized person. Great and important changes have taken place since you were here. We have got a fine grocer's shop opposite, where your mother and I may feast our eyes from morning till night on fat hams, smoked tongues, barley sugar, besoms [brooms], and what not ; and when the grocer sends in my small bills with &c., &c., &c. after my name I quite wonder at my own greatness. Your mother will say that is very *grossière*, but in spite of these honours,

I remain your affectionate

S. E. F.

MR. ROBERT THORBURN TO S. E. F.

77 Upper Berkeley Street, Portman Square, London :

September 26, 1839.

Dear Miss Ferrier,—I offer many apologies for keeping your brother's miniature so long from you. My intention was to have sent it weeks ago, indeed, to accompany your nephew to Scotland, but he left before the exhibition closed, and I also was obliged to go abroad before that event. I have returned, and Mr. Fletcher's departure for Scotland on Saturday is my first opportunity. I hope the picture and its frame will meet your approval ; it occurred to me that perhaps

---

[1] Mr. Thorburn, the miniature painter. (J. F.)

you might think I had chosen too fine a one, but I tried a plainer, and the head looked too large in it. The price is three guineas. I suppose your nephew has informed you of my success this season, and what it has enabled me to do. I do not find my extra duties troublesome, owing to a sister I have got to share them, I suppose.

My failing health at the end of this season hinted to me that I had confined myself too closely. I soon regained it by making a little excursion abroad. I do not think that I ever before felt greater pleasure than I did the first morning I awoke in the country with such a prospect before me. I intended to have gone to Venice, but on my arrival at Paris a picture there prevented me going further south, Raphael's 'La Belle Jardiniere,' which I immediately set about copying. My route to that city via Brighton, Dieppe, Rouen, and up the Seine was very pleasant and picturesque, staying sufficiently long at each place to allow me to see it. I need not tell you that I am quite ready for another fight. Permit me to remain.

Yours very gratefully,
ROBERT THORBURN.

FROM COUNTESS PEPOLI[1] TO S. E. F.

Felsina Cottage, 6 Gloucester Road : June 3, 1840.

My dear Miss Ferrier,—As you kindly express a wish to hear of my health, I take it as an excuse to send you another letter. First let me say how grateful I felt for yours, and that I so far deserved it, for it never came into my mind that you were either 'ungracious' or 'negligent.' I only remembered the too good apology you have for silence, and I thought it most kind in you to write so much. I had the pleasure of paying a visit to a friend of yours the other day, who I hope is likely to do well for himself, and to be a credit to his country—I mean Mr. Thorburn ; his success appeared to me great, as far as I could judge. I have just been regretting I had not his

<hr>

[1] Née Fergus, of Strathore, co. Fife. (J. F.)

address to give to a lady who wished a drawing done, when a friend of mine said to me 'I am sitting for my miniature,' and delighted was I when she said, ' to a young Scotch artist, Mr Thorburn.' He was much pleased to speak of you, and he is established in a good situation and very nice house. I keep quite well, but as thin as it is possible to be ; I live so quietly that I should improve a little. We receive much kindness—Count Pepoli is so much beloved by all who know him. None have shown more constant and disinterested kindness than Lady Morgan. I did not admire her writings excepting one, and never expected to like herself. She was again speaking of you the other day, and she made me promise to tell you that she has been a fellow sufferer with you as to your eyes ; for four years she expected total blindness, and sat with a single shaded candle, and even that gave her pain. She had consulted every medical man but one, Mr. Alexander, and at last she went to him and was cured ; but she still applies constantly the remedy he gave her ; all the other persons she had consulted either gave her no hope, or only tormented her with vain attempts. He is the person I long since wished my dear Miss Ferrier had consulted. Now I will not write much more, for I have little more to say.   I had at tea the other evening Monsieur Andregane, who was with Silvio Pellico for twelve or thirteen years in the fortress of Spielberg ; he has now recovered all his sufferings, looks well, and says that in his present happiness God has compensated him for all past sufferings ; he is a very religious man—it was pleasant to see one happy who had passed through so much. Farewell, dear Miss Ferrier, do not forget me. . . . We have staying with us just now an old man of ninety-one ; he was a painter, and not being in very comfortable circumstances my husband thought a little change of air would do him good, and so brought him here. He is an Italian ; his face is quite beautiful, especially his eyes, though it has little expression ; perhaps

T

it never had much, but he is now gliding very quietly down the last stage of life, and all his feelings seem placid.

Ever, my dear Miss Ferrier, very truly,

ELIZ. PEPOLI.

S. E. F. TO MRS. CONNELL (1840)

My dear Janet,—I take much shame to myself for my long silence, so I hope you will excuse it without further apology. I intended to have apprised you of Jane's somewhat sudden flight to the South, but have delayed so long that I dare say she has got the start of me herself, and written you a whole history by this time. She is a wonderful creature, but ought not to play such pranks again ; she may truly say she breakfasted here on Monday and dined at Stanmore [1] on Tuesday—very hurried doings, thinks I, and I am sure you will agree with me. I have been allowed little time to feel her loss ; my friends having plied me with attentions almost from the time of her departure. The Hamiltons came from Cathlaw to breakfast with me that morning, which was a great pleasure to me, as there are few people I value more highly ; I was happy to see her [2] so well, notwithstanding the severe trials she has had in parting with her sons ; [3] but she is an admirable person, and I am sure the children of such a mother must carry a blessing along with them, go where they may. Their house is quite an orphan [4] asylum. Cath. and Lotty Ferrier [5] are here on their way to spend the summer there, and Georgy and Jane Riddell [6] also *en route* to pass a week or two before bidding a final adieu.[7] The Ferriers seem disposed to pay you a visit on their return to the South, and I dare say Mr. C. and

[1] Where her daughter, Mrs. Tennent, lived. (J. F.)

[2] The honourable Georgina Vereker, daughter of the first Viscount Gort ; married, 1817, Lieutenant-Colonel John Ferrier Hamilton (see p. 164). (J. F.)

[3] They went to Australia to settle. (J. F.)

[4] They were very kind in giving house-room to some young relatives who had lost their parents. (J. F.)

[5] Daughters of Louis Ferrier, of Belsyde (p. 224). (J. F.)

[6] Daughters of her cousin, Mrs. Riddell. (J. F.)

[7] They went to India and married there. (J. F.)

you will make them welcome both for their father's sake and their own, for they are uncommonly pleasing, companionable creatures. I am very hospitable by proxy, you will say, which is too much the case, as not even Mr. C.'s 'splendid' joint of veal could tempt me to encounter a dinner-party, so I made free to divide it with the Walters, and I am sure he will not think it was thrown away, as both they and I relished, and are still relishing, it very much. I have got the offer of a villa from Mrs. Fletcher[1] while she and her daughter remain in England, but as she wished to let it I shall only consent to occupy it till a tenant is forthcoming, which, however, is not likely to be the case now; it is a pretty little spot near Corstorphine, and *my* friend and *their* friend Mary Camp will accompany me next week, and remain probably till about July 20, when she goes with her brother's family to Moffat; so if you will make out your visit now I can promise you pleasanter quarters than I could have done last year, for really, with all my predilection for a town life, I must own it is not 'passing sweet' at this season. Margaret and Eleanor[2] have taken a joint stock company cottage near Colinton with the Misses Gillespie, and are to occupy alternately. I fear there is little chance of Mrs. K. coming amongst us this summer. Frederick[3] is going on well at Sweethope[4] and I trust will regain health sufficient to follow out his vocation; he is much changed since his boyish days —the fire of youth is quenched; but he is sensible and amiable, mild and gentle, and really an interesting creature.

Thursday 18th.—This has been scribbled bit by bit since Saturday, but it is high time it was now brought to a conclusion. I was in Carlton Street[5] yesterday, and saw all well, the baby getting almost as fat as Grace Grierson, who seems quite domesticated there, but talks

---

[1] Old Mrs. Fletcher, the friend of Brougham and Jeffrey. The villa was near Corstorphine, Edinburgh. (J. F.)

[2] Her nieces. (J. F.)
[3] Kinloch. (J. F.)
[4] A farm. (J. F.)
[5] Where Professor Ferrier lived. (J. F.)

of leaving on Saturday; she is a fine, good-natured creature. I send you a collection of letters, in which I think you will find much that is excellent; they are by Mrs. G. [General G.'s[1] stepmother], and I have not heard anything for a great while that has interested and edified me so much. Poor Mr. Lennox! would that he had left less of this world's pelf!

S. E. F. TO MRS. CONNELL

Wednesday, 1841.

I have waited long for an opportunity of sending you an old friend with a new face, but as none seems likely to occur I must pack it off by coach, else I fear the new face will be an old one before it reaches you . . . this is a week of such extraordinary festivity among the kindred that even I have been drawn into the vortex. Lady McNeill gives a fancy ball to-morrow and a masquerade on Friday. Eleanor and Agnes[2] have offered to come and show themselves to me, and some of my friends have invited themselves to meet them, and I could not be so churlish as to refuse, especially as my poor lame friend, Mary C.[3] is to be of the party. She is now able to *creep* from one room to another with a support, after sixteen months' confinement. Charlotte[4] Ferrier's marriage takes place to-morrow at Craiglockart,[5] when forty of kindred and connections are to assemble. Changed days with the Dr.! The Hamiltons have come to town for th occasion, both (I am happy to say) quite well.

S. E. F. TO MRS. CONNELL

Friday.

My fancy fair was so brilliant and so much out of the ordinary course of my proceedings that I was quite useless all yesterday. The company assembled about eight, and

[1] General Graham. (J. F.)
[2] Daughters of her brothers, John and Walter. (J. F.)
[3] Campbell. (J. F.)
[4] Daughter of Louis H. Ferrier of Belsyde; married, 1841, Sir John Campbell, Bart., of Auchenbreck.
[5] The seat of the bride's uncle, Professor Monro. (J. F.)

we sat in the dark till ten, when the performers came *upon the stage*, which was immediately lighted up, and I withdrew for a few minutes that they might be seen. After the spectators were satisfied I then beheld them by the light of a solitary candle, and indeed it was all I could do to look upon them even in that 'palpable obscure.' Eleanor was arrayed in a robe of ruby velvet, with petticoat and stomacher of rich gold tissue, head-dress *à la* Anne Boleyn, and, as the newspapers say, 'a profusion of jewels,' lent by Lady McNeill. Agnes wore a white satin slip petticoat and tunic of thin muslin trimmed with ivy leaves, and a chaplet of the same on her head. Miss Aber.[1] personified a Roman flower-girl in long jacket of green velvet, petticoat of dark red, and all the rest of the costume most correct. Miss Gillespie[2] was in white and silver, long veil, and a chaplet of white roses. George F.[3] and Johnnie[4] in uniform completed the group; and now I have done my part in the millinery line, and hope you are satisfied, if not edified. Lady McN. has a masquerade to-night, and E.[5] enacts first a *fish-wife* and then a queen; but oh! what folly all this seems, and is! Not gaiety, real gaiety—only excitement, its vile counterfeit. In the midst of all this senseless revelry came the accounts of Miss MacD. Buchanan's death,[6] once the gayest of the gay, but prepared by long suffering and much tribulation for the happy change that has taken place. I expect Mrs. Kinloch on the 15th, and it is settled she is to bring her maid and leave her here when she goes to visit. She will be of use to me, as I am losing Emily; Peggy and she cannot live under the same roof, though both suit me perfectly. I never shop, so I see nothing, but a Moravian came to me with some work one day, and I took the

---

[1] Abercromby, daughter of Lord Abercromby; married, 1858, Colonel Brown. (J. F.)

[2] Daughter of Dr. Gillespie; married Lauderdale Maitland, Esq., of Eulisco, Dumfries. (J. F.)

[3] George Ferrier, a cousin. (J. F.)

[4] Her nephew, John W. Ferrier, died 1845. (J. F.)

[5] Eleanor. (J. F.)

[6] Sir Walter's 'Missie,' see p. 220. (J. F.)

accompanying cap, which I hope you will like. I have sent the book and the *cappy* in a parcel by the mail.

In 1840, or a little earlier, the copyright of Miss Ferrier's three novels passed into the possession of Mr. Bentley. There is nothing to show the exact details of the transaction, but it is not unlikely that Miss Ferrier carried out the proposal made in her letter to Mr. Blackwood, and relieved him of the copyright. Be that as it may be, a new edition appeared in 1841.

The letters which follow show the details of the publication.

R. BENTLEY TO S. E. F.

New Burlington Street : April 1, 1841.

Madam,—I regret much that, not being aware of your address, I have not been able to avail myself of the advantage of your correction of the proof for the new edition of 'Marriage,' owing to the great delay in receiving the corrected copy. Moreover, from some precise form pursued I did not receive your corrected copy till a great portion of the edition was set up or composed, the result of which has been that I have been put to serious expense in making the corrections to 'Marriage.'

Your request in regard to the other two works shall be punctually attended to.

I am, madam, your obedient servant,

Miss Ferrier.   RICHARD BENTLEY.

R. BENTLEY TO S. E. F.

New Burlington Street : April 5, 1841.

Madam,—I have your letter of the 2nd inst. The edition of 'Marriage' printed in my Standard Novels you will find, I trust, properly corrected[1] from the copy forwarded by you.

It is indeed much to be regretted that I did not get your introduction in time. I could not know, however,

---

[1] Miss Ferrier's own note to this is 'Quite the reverse—full of blunders (S. E. F.).'

that it was your intention to give any. This purpose may yet be in a manner accomplished by a longer introduction to 'The Inheritance.' Proofs shall be forwarded to you of this book, to enable you to see that your corrections are all attended to.

I have with this sent you the stipulated number of copies of ' Marriage ' and

Remain, madam, your obedient servant,

RICHARD BENTLEY.

The Preface to ' Inheritance ' referred to in the above letters is worth reprinting as illustrating, more strikingly perhaps than anything else could, the change which had passed over Miss Ferrier's habits of thought.

PREFACE TO 'INHERITANCE'

An introduction has been requested for the first of these three works—' Marriage '—but while the author was considering what could be said for an already thrice-told tale it had passed through the press with such rapidity as to outstrip all consideration.

Indeed, what can be said for any of them amounts to so little, it is scarcely worth saying at all.

The first was begun at the urgent solicitation and with the promised assistance of a friend, which, however, failed long before the end of the first volume ; the work was then thrown aside, but resumed some years afterwards. It afforded occupation and amusement for idle and solitary hours, and was published in the belief that the author's name never would be guessed at or the work heard of beyond a very limited sphere. *Il n'y a que le premier pas qui coûte* in novel writing as in carrying one's head in their hand. ' Inheritance ' and ' Destiny ' followed as matters of course.

It has been so often and confidently asserted that almost all the characters are individual portraits, that the author has little hope of being believed when she asserts the contrary. That *some* of them were sketched from life is not denied, but the circumstances in which they are placed, their birth, habits, language, and a thousand minute particulars, differ so widely from the originals as ought to refute the charge of personality.

With regard to the introduction of religious sentiments into works of fiction, there exists a difference of opinion which, in the absence of any authoritative command, leaves each free to act according to their own feelings and opinions.

Viewing this life merely as the prelude to another state of existence, it does seem strange that the future should ever be wholly excluded from any representation of it even in its motley occurrences—scarcely less motley perhaps than the human mind itself.

The author can only wish it had been her province to have raised plants of nobler growth in the wide field of Christian literature—but as such has not been her high calling, she must only hope her ' small herbs of grace ' may (without offence) be allowed to put forth their blossoms amongst the briars, weeds, and wild flowers of life's common path.

Edinburgh : April 1840.

When we turn from this to the correspondence with Miss Clavering we certainly understand how honesty and fear-lessness of mind may exist along with something very like a double personality.

THE HONOURABLE MRS. ERSKINE TO S. E. F.

(Addressed to ' Miss Ferrier, Cathlaw,' where her cousin, Colonel Ferrier Hamilton, lived.)

September 11, 1841.

My dear Tyrant,—Were you anything but a tyrant or a very kind and indulgent friend I should think it necessary to apologise for not writing to you before now. But in the first of these characters you had nothing better to expect, for all *slaves* are idle and negligent when they dare, and in the later [*sic*] I knew you would make large allowances for me and *therefore* neglected my duty! And this, alas! is human nature. If you wish to correct it in me you must speedily return and resume your tyranny, to which I will *gladly* submit. I think poor Whitmore was gone before you left this, but I am not sure, for my memory is growing sadly deficient. It has been a painful trial to me, but I have every reason to hope she is now happier than this world could ever have made her, and I ought not to lament that she is released from her sufferings, which have long been very great. Mrs. Callander[1] is still here, but goes on Tuesday with her family to Dunesk[2] for some time, and Mrs. Smith comes to town, not to me but into lodgings close by Dr. Handyside, that he may see her daily and watch the progress of her complaint and think if anything can be done to relieve, all having failed that has hitherto been attempted.

I do not approve this move. It will satisfy her mind and the blessing of God will I fervently hope attend it. Mrs. Callander sits by me while I write and desires her kind remembrance, and with affectionate love believe me,

Most sincerely yours,

E. ERSKINE.[3]

[1] The first Mrs. Callander, of Craigforth, a most beautiful woman, and daughter of Lord Erskine. (J. F.)

[2] A place near Edinburgh, where Mrs. Smith lived. She was a sister of the seventh Earl of Buchan, and stepdaughter of Mrs. Erskine. (J. F.)

[3] Mrs. Erskine was the second wife of the celebrated wit, the Hon. Harry Erskine, and sister to Sir Thomas Munro, Governor of Madras. She was of a frugal turn of mind, and when Miss Ferrier dined with her one day, and the butler removed the dish cover, she asked him where he got such a fine duck from, to which he replied, ' I just stepped ben to Mistress Cumin and borrowed it frae the cook (it was roasting before the fire for that lady's own dinner), for I kent Miss Ferrier was coming.' Miss Ferrier pretended to be angry, and gave her a lecture on the wickedness of stealing. Mrs. Cumin was the widow of the Hon. General Leslie, a son of the Earl of Leven ; on his marriage he took her name. She lived in Queen Street, next door to Mrs. Erskine. (J. F.)

One is reminded of Caleb Balderstone's raid in *The Bride of Lammermoor*. But that novel was written before the incident occurred.

S. E. F. TO HER NIECE[1] *MRS. TENNENT (née GRAHAM)*

Stanmore, Middlesex [1841 ?].

. . . . Indeed I am becoming very jealous of the superfluities of life from hearing so much of its wants and privations as are perpetually pressing upon one's notice in this great poor city, and more particularly in this most severe season when all human enjoyment seems concentrated in coals and blankets. I can tell you little or nothing of what is going on amongst the gay ones here, as I never stray beyond my own fireside, and its annals are short and simple, as nothing can be more quiet and uniform than the 'even tenor of our days,' diversified only by plentiful visits from friends and kindred in the morning and reading and knitting in the evening. We have been supping on the horrors of a novel by a Mrs. Crowe, called 'Susan Hopley,'[2] a very respectable woman (the only one in the book), who wears a brown gown and knits like me—but otherwise it is all full of bad doings and bloody murders, so that I could not endure it to the end. I am told Professor Wilson's 'Essay on Burns' is fine, but we have not seen it yet. . . . My eyes suffer so much I can only open them at long intervals, and now I must close them with kind regards to the Colonel.

FROM LADY McNEILL TO S. E. F.[3]

Park Hotel, Norwood : June 19, 1841.

My dear Miss Ferrier,—I felt most grateful for the beautiful little remembrance you sent us the night before

---

[1] The daughter of General Graham. Sir W. Scott happened to call on her mother one day in George Street, Edinburgh (when on a visit to Mrs. Hay, her sister-in-law), and on leaving, Mrs. Graham desired her daughter to go down stairs and open the door to him, the man-servant being very slow in his movements. When she had done so he patted her on the shoulder and said, ' That's a good girl ! I'll tell you something : Every man's man had a man, and that was how the Castle of Threave was ta'en.'

[2] Published in 1841.

[3] Many pleasant visits I have paid to Grantor House, Edinburgh, where Sir John and Lady McNeill lived. My great aunt was a most delightful person, and so kind, and her strong personality is still vivid in the memories of many now alive. Of Sir John some people stood a little in awe on account of his grand am-

we left home. It suits Ferooza[1] exactly, and is most becoming to her. This place, which I am sorry to say we leave on Monday, has done her much good. She has often wished for little Jane when going to ride her donkey or to make hay—her two favourite amusements. . . . Sir John is ordered to start for Persia on the 1st, and I think we shall go with him to Boulogne instead of going to Malvern, as originally intended. This will give us a few more days of his society, and save us some of the first bother of foreign lands ; and we have heard a favourable account of the climate, and if we don't like it after he. leaves us, we can fly to more retired regions. We have enjoyed our residence here very much. We have had enough of society without getting involved in the vortex which would have been our fate had we been in town, and one season of which is enough to last for life—at least, such a season as we had the year we were knighted.[2]

We have taken lodgings at No. 2 St. James's Place, St James's, and there will remain till our parting instruc-

---

bassadorial and somewhat pompous manner, but to myself he was always most kind and courteous. He was one of the handsomest and most dignified looking men I ever saw, and his countenance was quite beautiful. Professor Wilson used to say as a joke, when they arrived in Scotland to live from Persia, that he was known in Edinburgh then as Lady McNeill's brother ! I dare say there was some truth in it, as a title goes a long way in ' Auld Reekie,' and a good many other places besides.

The following extract is from a letter from my Aunt, Margaret Ferrier, to my father, afterwards Professor Ferrier, and shows the dangers travellers were exposed to in such long journeys as from Persia to this country. It is dated Dec. 7, 1828 :

' When you arrive, you will find Aunt Elizabeth in this part of the world, as she is at present at Elleray [in Windermere, where Professor Wilson lived], and is expected here in a few days. . . .

' Uncle James [Wilson] and his wife have been living at Elleray for a considerable time, and it is by them she has been interrupted, otherwise she would have been in Edinburgh by this time. Upon the whole, she has made out her journey very well, though she encountered some great hardships upon the borders of Russia ; when on one occasion, in spite of her certificates of health, she was thrown into a horrid prison to perform quarantine, and kept immured, I believe, for eleven days, exposed to damp, cold, and every kind of discomfort. After being liberated, she was taken violently ill, and was for some time unable to proceed, and at the same time the gentleman who had travelled in company with her was obliged by his affairs to leave her, so she had to pursue her journey alone—that is to say, with no companions except her maid and child.'

[1] Her daughter, named from the Persian word for a turquoise.

(J. F.)

[2] Sir John McNeill was knighted by William IV. in 1836. (J. F.)

tions are given ; in the meantime I must devote my 'great mind' almost exclusively to the packing of boxes and making out of inventories, having four to arrange for Pau and fourteen for Persia. The most interesting thing we have seen here is the pauper school, where a thousand children are educated. They are illegitimate children, children deserted by their parents, or the children of insane persons or criminals. They are received as early as two years old, but the majority of those we saw had been received at six or seven, the school having but recently been instituted. They may remain till sixteen. By a steady system, and by kindness and instruction without rewards or harsh punishment of any kind, they soon become cleanly and moral in their habits, orderly and decent in their conduct, and cheerful and contented. They are taught in such a manner as to make their lessons an enjoyment. They are well, though coarsely, fed, clothed and lodged, and they are instructed in habits of industry, which are considered a primary object of their instruction. We saw the boys making clothes and shoes, others working as carpenters, tinsmiths and blacksmiths, and a large body of little fellows, dressed as sailors, climbing rigging, drilled as soldiers, and practised at great guns. The girls wash, iron, mangle, cook, learn to make clothes and to knit But what delighted us most of all was the extent of their information in religion, in geography, in the theory of useful arts, and on many other subjects, such as few children acquire at the same age in any rank of life. The whole cost is four and sixpence a week for each child. I have not seen as many happy faces for many a day as we saw among those poor children. What a stave I have written you, quite forgetting that a few lines of thanks was all I had a right to impose on you. . . .

Sir John begs me to offer you his best regards, and with sincere affection, believe me

Ever yours,
E. McNeill.

The following letters refer to a tradition which connects Miss Ferrier with the authorship of the 'Laird o' Cockpen.' That Lady Nairn wrote the chief part of the song is undoubted. But it has been more than once stated in print that her version ended with the discomfiture of the Laird, and that the two verses describing Mistress Jean's repentance and the subsequent marriage were due to Miss Ferrier. No definite evidence on the point is forthcoming.

JAMES WILSON TO S. E. F.

Woodville, Edinburgh : November 7, 1842.

. . . When I wrote from Westmoreland I forgot to mention that I had, before leaving Edinburgh, sent a line to Wilson the singer in reference to the authorship of the ' Laird of Cockpen,' which he says you composed, and which you say you did not. I don't know which of you is right, but since you desire it, I will give you the benefit of the doubt. I find Wilson's rejoinder still sticking among some unburnt notes and enclose it herewith . . .

The following is the note enclosed.

Perth : August 11, 1842.

Dear Sir,—I am obliged by your writing me anent the song of the ' Laird o' Cockpen,' which I have seen in some collection [perhaps Robert Chambers's]—I am not certain attributed to Miss Ferrier. I never mentioned her name, but said merely that it was by the authoress of ' Marriage,' and I am extremely sorry if that should cause her the least annoyance. Your kindness in letting me know that she is not the writer of the song will of course prevent me from again mentioning it ; but I am almost sorry that she is *not* the writer of the song—as it is so good in its way as to be a feather in the cap of any one who could say *it's mine* . . .

MR. GEORGE THOMSON[1] TO S. E. F.

Trustees' Office : July 29.

Mr. Thomson with most respectful compliments to Miss Ferrier returns the poems which she had the goodness to send him.   He has read them with much pleasure, but not without regretting that Miss Ferrier has so successfully studied brevity in her own composition, though he deems it very prudent to follow her example

Lest any fool admire,
And clever folk should tire.

Gibbon, when in Parliament, never spoke a sentence. The bad speakers terrified him, the great ones put him in despair.   Should not nine-tenths of our rhymers be appalled in the same way when they think of a Milton, a Dryden, a Pope ?

Mr. T. has the pleasure of inclosing Mr. Curran's ' Deserter.'

S. E. F. TO MISS FLETCHER[2]

October 23.

So you have spoken at last !   High time methinks after eight months of inflexible silence, during which I have sat patiently nursing my wrath till it might have filled an Atlantic steam boiler, but now that you have opened a safety valve it has already begun to evaporate, and in the course of a page or two I expect to be tolerably cool and quite empty.   Meanwhile I shall begin to answer your letter categorically, only in the crab fashion, beginning at the last query and so retrograding to the first.

What am I doing ?

Nothing particular.

How are my eyes ?

---

[1] He wrote a *Life of Burns*, and was a friend of the poet.   His daughter, Mrs. Hogarth, was mother of Mrs. Charles Dickens.   This letter was probably written about 1809, and was inserted in its present place by an oversight.

[2] Sister of Miles Fletcher, the first husband of Miss Clavering.   She married, in August 1847, Mr., afterwards Sir John, Richardson, the Arctic traveller.

Very weak.

Is the 'wretch' to the fore?

I know nothing to the contrary, but she is living at Ravelstone, so we have little or no intercourse.

The Mackenzies came to town in rude health, and though Hope has caught cold she is so obstreperous she pays no regard to it. Mrs. Erskine is one day better and another worse, but she is able to take an airing occasionally, and she told me lately if ever she was to recover it would be by travelling. Nevertheless her intellect is clear as ever, as evidenced in a preface she lately indited for an album a young niece of mine has launched; if I can get it copied I will send it (if you behave well), but I find copiers more scarce than composers. Poor Miss Moneypenny will always be a mourner for the loss of her kind brother, but her health upon the whole is better. Sir William Hamilton is going on well, and my nephew Professor F. [Ferrier] is to conduct his lectures this winter. The meeting between Lady Bell and Mrs. Arnold must have been deeply affecting to both; that they were able to bear it all says much for the sweet resigned tone of their feelings. I read Dr. Arnold's life with the greatest interest and delight; it set my heart in a glow, which few things do now. The wife of such a man I can imagine almost reconciled to her own loss by seeing what a gain it must prove to the world. How I wished for you to read it to me. Pray tell me all about his family and whether there is to be no more of the charming 'Journal'; and the German hymns, are they ever to be forthcoming in my day? The 'Quarterly' has done itself infinite credit by its beautiful review; you have all a touch of Dr. Arnold's character in you, but Mrs. Fletcher's resemblance is most striking, only I think she is more tolerant of evil and evil-doers. I never believed she was coming here this winter; would she were and all of you, dear, Mrs. Davy included; there is much need of you here. What are Angus and Mr. Dickens laying their heads together about in Genoa?

Charlotte[1] and her chrysolite are well. Mrs. Graham is in Dumfriesshire on her way here. Oh how I wish you would all come to your senses and return to your proper sphere! It is a week since I began this, for I can write but a wee bit at a time, so I am very sick of the sight of my penmanship, and were I to con it over I am sure it would land on the fire ; so take it as it is, and with best regards to Mrs. Fletcher and Mrs. Davy, believe me, your *still* affectionate

S. E. FERRIER.

S. E. F. TO MISS FLETCHER

1844.

I'm not going to detain you, I know you're in a great hurry just setting off, and really have no time to read letters ; so I'm only going to say good-bye, which I do with a sort of feeble fluttering wish that I were going with you as your invisible familiar, merely to sit at the back of your eye or in the drum of your ear, and see all the strange sights and hear all the fine things you will see and hear ! Perhaps we might cast out now and then, or you might be for casting me out, but upon the whole I think we should put up pretty well together. I should like to hear an authentic account of the Plymouth Brethren, as I have read some of their tracts and think them good. I am reading Lord Jeffrey's[2] essays with great delight, notwithstanding the profound contempt with which (in the batch of novels of the day) my bantlings are passed by. Not even a foot-note to mark their existence poor things ! The pleasantest thing I have heard for many a day is the talk of your coming to Edinburgh next winter ; 'tis a long look, to be sure, and I may not be here, or a thousand things may happen ; but, in spite of possibilities, I enjoy the prospect and *will* trust to having it realised. My sister sends her best regards to Mrs. Fletcher and you—perhaps you may be thrown together in the whirlpool of London,

---

[1] Mrs. Christison. (J. F.)   [2] Published in 1844.

as she is preparing for her usual migration.[1]   Charlotte is
gone to Inveraray.   Mrs. Cuninghame is in Fife, the
Walkers going to and fro as usual.   I like the Browns and
wish they were stationary—but what do you care for all
such outlandish folk?   I beg your pardon, pray excuse me
for having trespassed so long on your time.   I am going
away as fast as I can now ; I'm gone.

S. E. F. TO MISS FLETCHER

My dear Miss Fletcher,—I was quite uplifted by your
commendation of me as an intelligent correspondent, and
(tho' I scarcely like to own it even to myself) I suspect
only the fear of losing that character has kept me so long
from thanking you for your most acceptable letter.   You
see I am cautious of bestowing any epithet upon it, lest (as
in my own case) it should prove a snare.   Privately I have
long been of opinion it is a dangerous thing to have a
character ; but I must not allow myself to scribble nonsense,
else my eyes will be worn out before I come to matters of
fact, the only matters I now profess to treat of.   I have
not seen our dear Mrs. Erskine for some time, as she had
been confined to bed and ordered to keep quiet on account
of her increasing weakness and debility—yet the Dr. says
there is no dangerous symptom and that her pulse continues
good.   Mrs. Drum: is living next door to her, so does not
annoy her.   Mary C.[2] set off this morning for the south.   I
felt as if bidding her a very long farewell and could only
pray it might not prove an everlasting one.   Miss Moneypenny has been very dangerously ill, but is recovering.
The Mackenzies, I am thankful to say, continue in good
health and spirits.   Nothing is talked of but Martineau
and mesmerism.   I *almost* believe there is such an influence,
but am in great doubt as to whether it is a 'lyeing wonder,'
or increase of knowledge ; pray let me hear your opinion on
the matter. . . .

[1] Mrs. Graham went annually to
visit her daughter, Mrs. Tennent, at
Stanmore, near London.   (J. F.)
[2] Campbell.   (J. F.)

S. E. F. TO MRS. TENNENT (1846)

Thursday, 25.

Anticipating the arrival of the parcel I begin betimes to thank you for its contents, which, in all their varieties, will, I assure you, be most welcome. Meantime I have to acknowledge the receipt of two very pleasant letters, for which I can make but a poor return, having heard and seen little save wind and rain for nearly a week past. To be sure one ought to be thankful who only see and hear and do not feel, for I fear the disasters at sea must be dreadful ! . . . I have been casting about for an opportunity of sending one of Lady McNeill's seal boxes—not one of the best, she says, for they went ' like snaw off a dyke ' at the sale, and produced upwards of five pounds. Professor James has put forth a pamphlet ' Observations on Church and State,' in reply to the D. of A.'s [Argyll's] ' Essay.' I have a mind to send it to the Colonel if I thought he would read it, but it is quite on the Presbyterian question. I saw Mrs. Chris. lately, and though the D. and Dss. had lunched with her, she said nought anent Lady E.'s marriage,[1] so the Cat is quite ahead of her with the news. This is the third day since my beginning, so it is time I had brought it to a conclusion and let you know when the ' parcel comes to hand,' in the shop phrase. . . . One o'clock.—The box has this instant arrived and all the gifts are most acceptable ! Mrs. Fry will be a treasure to me for many a day and evening to come, and I shall drink your health with great *goût* in a cup of Souchong. The Purse is something quite unknown to me and to the public in general hereabouts, I guess. . . . There is a calm at last, and I am going to venture forth, so Adieu. . . .

S. E. F. TO MRS. TENNENT (1846)

. . . . For some time indeed I was unable to write, but seemed as if utterly extinguished by the excessive cold ; as

---

[1] Lady Emma Campbell ; married, 1870, as his third wife, Sir J. McNeill. As she did not marry before, it is clear that the ' Cat's ' information was unfounded. (J. F.)

that abated I began to revive and am now restored to my usual state of 'dim consciousness' and to the comfort of *the* gown, which I assure you is great. Lady S.[1] and Mrs. Chris. met here accidentally, and having sat upon it (in judgment), the one said she greatly admired it, the other that she quite coveted it, and all agree that it is a great improvement on my previous habits. I wish I had anything to send you, but I am little in the way of seeing or hearing of small novelties or 'bonny dies' of any description. . . .

Wednesday.—Yesterday was so charming Lady Stuart took me to Granton, where we passed the greater part of it with Lady McN., whom we found busy with your seals, covering charity-boxes, which really look very *imposing.* You ask me to recommend books for your society, but I only do so from the report of others. Austin's 'Russia,' said to be very Romish but interesting ; 'Journey from Cornhill to Cairo,' amusing ; 'Life of Fowell Buxton,' excellent. I don't add the D. of Argyll's 'Essay,' for though clever, it is rather arrogant and petulant, and full of misrepresentations of the Free Church, though I think it is all '*tint*' that falls upon the Scottish Episcopacy and Tractarianism. . . . My delight is in Dr. Chalmers's Sabbath readings. But I must make an end of further scribbling, as the day is so fine I must take my '*Dove's Neck*' into the sun for half-an-hour.

S. E. F. TO MRS. TENNENT (1846)

My dear Helen,—I forgot to say you did subscribe to Lady Nairn's Songs, which will be forthcoming in a few days, and yr. copy I suppose will be sent to Stanmore.[2] I am much exhausted by a visit from the author of the 'Protestant Pastor!' Poor Miss Catmer[3] is drawing very near her end, and has caused her friends here to be

---

[1] Lady Stuart, daughter of Professor Monro ; married 1835 Sir James Stuart, Bart. of Allan-bank. The title is now extinct. (J. F.)

[2] *Lays from Strathearn*, by Caroline Baroness Nairn. Arranged with symphonies and accompaniments. Finlay Dun, 1846.

[3] She lived as companion to old Miss Edmonstone. (J. F.)

informed of her situation. I hope you will give me due
warning of your arrival here, that I may arrange my little
movements accordingly, as I *do* think seriously of going
to Toravon for a few days!—a gt. enterprise for me, I
assure you.

S. E. F. TO MISS FLETCHER

May 29 [1846 ?]

My dear Friend,—I am not going to write you a letter
I am only going to tell you what pleasure I had in receiving yours, and how gladly I will welcome another ; indeed,
your letters are a very great treat, so whenever you wish
to do a kind, charitable, amiable action you will write *to me* !
My sister continues pretty much the same as when you
were here, certainly not better, tho' not perceptibly worse.
I was interrupted by a visit from Hope Mackenzie and
her little deaf boy. They are to go to the country next
week. She told me what will distress many, yourselves
amongst others, that Dr. Alison was seized with apoplexy
yesterday when in the infirmary, and was carried home
speechless, but is rather better to-day.[1]   I saw Mary
C. yesterday, who has been in sorrow for the loss of
her friend Mrs. Bruce (of Kennet), but otherwise seems
tolerably well.   Charlotte has returned *quite* mesmeric, or
rather clairvoyant, under the authority of the Bishop of
Oxford, who is *said to say* that, if any one will show him
a single passage in Scripture where good was done under
evil influence, he will give up mesmerism.   I long to hear
the result of the mesmeric conference with the archbishop.
I send you a specimen of a most promising new penny
periodical.   Your dud of a shawl came after you were
gone, and it is not fit to be sent after you or given to any
one else (having been done in a violent hurry expressly for
you).   Query, What's to be done with it ?   I would fain
have written a word to dear Mrs. Davy to thank her for

---

[1] William Pulteney Alison, M.D., elder brother of the historian.   He
died in 1859.

her kind and charming billet, but I feel I have done enough ; so with my love tell her how much I prize it, and tho' I have little hope of ever meeting her or any of you here, I pray we may all meet hereafter. With affectionate regards to Mrs. Fletcher,

I am ever yours,

S. E. FERRIER.

MISS HOPE MACKENZIE TO S. E. F.

East Dalmeny : September 21, 1846.

My dear Friend,—I am sure you have all my affectionate sympathy in everything that concerns you ; so I fear it is only a selfish indulgence my yielding to the desire to say a word of loving kindness to you in this new affliction. May He who has sent it be felt to be present with you and yours in all the richness of His own divine consolations—that comfort in Christ which keeps the believer's heart amid all the trials of this world of parting and sorrow from overwhelming trouble, and points to the many mansions of the Father's house, where His word assures His redeemed that death-divided friends shall meet to part no more—far more than that, shall ' be together for ever with the Lord.' While I mourn with you, my dear friend, under such a bereavement, I desire with you to bless the name of the Lord, through whom your dear sister's [1] end was peace, thus mingling peace, *the* effectual comfort, in your cup of sorrow. I am thankful you have not suffered in health, and that Mrs. Kinloch and your niece are still with you at this time. I hope you may make out going to your brother's, but perhaps I may get a sight of you first, for if the weather be good there is a likelihood that I may be in Doune Terrace [2] on Thursday, and if so, it will be a great gratification to me to see you. But my going is not certain. If I do not appear, you know that you have my kindest thoughts and wishes with you.

[1] The death of Mrs. Graham, 1846, aged 79. (J. F.)

[2] Where Mr. Jas. Mackenzie lived. (J. F.)

We have been keeping well, and have rather better accounts of Alfred (his hearing, I mean) since he went to school. Holt is still with us; the Belmonts [1] all away on Northern visits and circuit, which they are greatly enjoying. I have very good accounts, too, of Lord Medwyn from Moy, where he has got much better and stronger among the kind Cummings.

Good-bye, dear friend, all that is truly good be with you. May the Lord bless you and comfort you.

Your ever affectionate

H. M.

ROBERT THORBURN TO S. E. F.

Brussels : September 8, 1846.

My dear Miss Ferrier,—Will you have the kindness to forward the enclosed drawing to your niece, Miss Helen ? It is for her album and the fulfilment of a promise I made her last year. The design represents the two Leonoras expecting the approach of Tasso. I hope it will please her. I have painted the subject, and an engraving of it will be published next year. Writing this at Brussels will surprise you, but it is only at such places that I have time for friendship ; for the future I am not going to work so hard as I have hitherto done. I am over here painting some portraits of the Royal Family, and my efforts to please the King will prove satisfactory to my name and purse. I will return to England about the 20th, when I shall be very busy indeed in making preparations for an event the most interesting in my life. When Mr. Harvey was in town I commissioned him to tell you all about it. I am sure I have your sympathy. My choice is after your own heart ; you would have selected her for me yourself. She is a dear girl. The consummation of my happiness will take place about the 10th of next month. My betrothed is Scotch, and we both agree we could not do better than to spend the first days of our nuptials in Scotland. If I bring her

---

[1] Her brother, Lord Mackenzie, lived at Belmont, near Edinburgh. (J. F.)

to you, will you let her be a candidate for your friendship?
With kind remembrances to my friends in Albany Street, I
am, my dear Miss Ferrier,

Yours sincerely,
ROBERT THORBURN.

ROBERT THORBURN TO S. E. F.

77 Upper Berkeley Street : January 15.

... My tour in the north has restored to me my
former energy, and increased, if it were possible, my love
for my art. This I am bestowing upon that class of my
unfinished pictures which have had no favour in my eyes ;
otherwise they might have been sent forth without adding
to my reputation ; but they have not entirely occupied all
my attention. I have occasionally given myself leisure for
the conception of future works. An illustration of the
seasons is the latest, some trifling sketches of which I
enclose, and beg that you will criticise them as fairly as the
Holy Family. When I sketched the latter design to you
I suspected not the severe ordeal it had to undergo. I
am sorry that I did not bestow more care upon it, as
Mr. Harvey perhaps would have comprehended no more.
Concerning the same picture, I still have my doubts about
the wings, but I dare say that I will reason myself into the
propriety of submitting to your better judgment. The
sketches I enclose are Spring, Summer, Autumn, and Winter.
Spring is depicted by four chubby little fellows gambolling
round a *natural* fountain. Summer appears in two girls
full of the bloom of life, and adorning each other with
flowers. Autumn shows herself in an aged couple wending
their steps to a little mountain church, their thoughts
being turned to a change in this life. Winter—dreary
winter—I have represented as the companion of death, the
witherer of all our hopes. I am coming to Scotland again
soon, but I am anxious in the meantime to have your
criticism.

ROBERT THORBURN TO S. E. F.

77 Upper Berkeley Street : September 9, 1847.

My dear Miss Ferrier,—Since my return to England
Mrs. Thorburn has presented me with a daughter and a
candidate for your friendship.   Mamma is very well, and
the baby makes full use of its lungs.   I have not yet quite
recovered from the novelty of the event.   At times I am
all happiness as the parent of the little creature, and then
all gravity with the anxious thought of its future education.

I saw my friend Tom the other day on his way to the
Continent ; he appeared very well and full of the idea of
being a traveller.   With Mrs. Thorburn's kindest regards,

I am, my dear Miss Ferrier,

Yours sincerely,

ROBERT THORBURN.

S. E. F. TO MRS. TENNENT

Nelson Street : November 8, 1847.

As my disinclination, or rather my disability, for writing
daily increases, you must not think it strange if my billets
are few and short and far between.   Moreover, my days
glide away in a quiet, even tenor, which, though pleasant to
experience, affords little to impart.   Health, to be sure, is
a never failing subject, but the less one says on that (except
to their doctor) the better ; so I shall only say, though
never *well*, I thank God I am able to go out and walk on
level ground and enjoy this sweet, mild weather.   This,
with visits from friends, and reading (or rather *listening*)
and knitting, fills up the measure of my time. . . . The
only notable incident I have to record is that of having
received a present of a most exquisitely wrought and
mounted cushion from Lady Edmonstone [1] much the
handsomest I have ever seen, only *too* handsome for me

---

[1] Wife of Sir Archibald Edmonstone, Bart.   (J. F.)

and mine, much as I deprecate paltry presents and abjure the whole bag, purse, and pocket-book tribe. She (Lady E.) is a charming creature, and, I am happy to say, now enjoys good health. Have you read her neighbour Mrs. Murray Gartshore's tale 'Cleveland ?' I think it a work of great genius and merit, and one that exhibits in a most powerful manner the evils of Romanism, though some are so dim-sighted they can't or won't see it in that light. The Islay *crisis* is come, and I fear poor Lady Charlotte must suffer with many others . . .[1]

S. E. F. TO MRS. TENNENT

I am very sorry you should have been disappointed in the result of the application, especially as I cannot devise what more can be done. 'S. G.'s' name is not only *noted*, but *especially* so, and when the time comes he 'will be cared for,' so writes Lady Graham—of course, by Sir J.'s sanction,[2] and they are neither of them people to give mere fair words and hold out false promises. For several years past I have experienced the most steady and *unremitting* kindness in various ways from Lady G., so that I should prove myself most unworthy of her regard were I to testify the slightest distrust of her on this, or any other, occasion. If Sir J. is, therefore, in office when S. G. is ready, prepared to claim the fulfilment of this promise, I have not the least doubt it will be performed . . .

S. E. F. TO MRS. TENNENT

October 13.

I have taken fright lest you should send me a brown silk gown, as I never 'walk in silk attire' at this season, but in a douce woolly garment, not of many colours, but

---

[1] The bankruptcy and ruin of Mr. Campbell, of Islay, through extravagant living. (J. F.)

[2] Sir James Graham, of Netherby ; it was fully expected that he would be First Lord of the Admiralty at this time, but the arrangements for his appointment fell through.

such as befits my extreme old age and increasing infirmities, not quite so superficial as the enclosed mits,
which are said to be the *ne plus ultra* of Shetland knitting.
I had a long visit from Lady Augusta Bruce yesterday,
when I stated Sam's[1] case to her; said she would help
me if she possibly could, but the only channel she has
to the D. of N.[2] is rather more circuitous than that of
the Jardines. . . . She is going to Paris soon for the
winter. She is a charming creature—quite unspoiled by
Courts.

S. E. F. TO MRS. TENNENT

September 22.

Many a time I have wished to write to you of late, but
during the cold weather my cough was so severe I was fit
for nothing; it is now somewhat abated with the rigour of
the atmosphere, so I must make haste while the sun shines
(which it does very benignly) to answer your letter On
reading it, my first consideration was whether I could do
anything to aid in your kind endeavours in behalf of poor
Sam. It is an easy matter to make suit when one can go
direct to the fountain head, but where there are many
interposing channels in the way one must first find out
whether these are *fordable*, especially in the case of the
D. of A.[3] who, as is well known, is not easy of approach!
The only medium I could think of was the Jardine
family, and I drove to Newington to *speir* at them; but
my intimates, Lady Mackenzie and Miss J., are both
in England, and I could not propound my queries on
paper—such as whether his Grace was likely to grant
the request, and whether, being the nephew and heir
apparent to the D. of N., they were on good terms.
When I had ascertained these facts, I should then
have asked you to send me a brief and clear statement
of what was required, and upon what grounds, and,

[1] A grand-nephew, Samuel Graham, (J. F.)

[2] Probably the Duke of Northum-berland. (J. F.)

[3] Probably the Duke of Athol. (J. F.)

indeed, I should like to have it in case of any *possibility* ensuing, though not probable in my recluse life. Now to descend to your humpy *protégé*. I find he is well known to Lady Matilda,[1] so I gave his letter to H. Walker to send to Garscube, where it may be of use . . . .

S. E. F. TO LADY RICHARDSON

December 29, 1848.

Gladly do I respond to your greeting, my dear friend, for I should be sorry if all intercourse between us were to cease here, even though I hope it may be renewed hereafter. I can well imagine how great your conjugal anxiety must be when the cause is one to excite so strong a national interest and sympathy ; but you have the comfort of possessing and knowing that your husband has the same trustful confidence in Him who is *everywhere* 'a very present help in trouble.' Still, the constant exercise of that faith is a trial, and a very great one ; but it is a noble exercise called forth on a noble occasion, and I doubt not you will be enabled to hold fast the beginning of your confidence even unto the end. I was glad to hear of Dr. Davy's return, as an event which must cause much joy in the *one* circle of both dwellings. I beg my love and felicitations to dear Mrs. Davy, as having the first claim to all congratulations, and next to Mrs. Fletcher, who can scarcely be called second in any good or pleasurable feelings. . . . Poor Miss Walker continues much in the same state—able to articulate two or three words in her own tongue, but the rest quite unintelligible. Her sister's entire devotedness to her is beyond all praise ! I saw Charlotte and her daughter Lotty on Christmas Day, both well and happy in each other. I hear Mary C. is now at Ravelstone, but we have not yet met. I am at present tolerably well *for me.* . . .

[1] Maxwell. (J. F.)

S. E. F. TO LADY RICHARDSON[1]

Edinburgh : August 1, 1849.

It was truly kind in you, my dear friend, to think of me at a time when your heart must have been full of joy, and I feel very sensibly this proof of your continued friendship. Few out of your own family, I am sure, could enter more deeply into your feelings than I do, for few can have a warmer admiration for the character of your heroic husband—having read the narrative of his *first* expedition. I have always looked upon his voluntary encounter of the sufferings and dangers of the *second* as one of the noblest undertakings in the history of man. How interesting beyond all romance must be his simple record of facts, and what a happiness is before you in the prospect of his safe and speedy return, which may God grant with his blessing on your reunion! In humble imitation of your generous example I wrote immediately to communicate the glad tidings to Mary C. and Helen Mackenzie, the former being at Killermont and the latter at summer quarters in Linlithgowshire, and my virtue has been rewarded by grateful acknowledgments from both. You may guess how few and far between are my familiar friends at present; when Charlotte C. leaves town I shall not have one left. Yet here I shall remain, as my health is now so infirm, and the weather so uninviting. I think I am better at home than I should be anywhere else. I rejoice to hear how Mrs. Fletcher continues to enjoy her green and beautiful old age, and that dear Mrs. Davy is also well and happy. How much I should like to meet you all again—but alas! I feel that will never be in this world. God grant it may be in another.

S. E. F. TO MRS. TENNENT (1849?)

Monday.

Many thanks, my dear Helen, for your kind offer of supplying my wants or gratifying my wishes; but, as I

---

[1] Sir John Richardson had gone out on an Arctic Search Expedition for Sir J. Franklin, and his return was expected when this letter was written. (J. F.)

cannot say what I particularly need or covet, I shall not tax your liberality at present. I may take shame to myself for not having long since sent the seal box I mentioned to you, but I have kept it in hopes something else would *cast up* as an accompaniment, it being scarcely fit to perform the journey alone. But, alas! nothing has presented itself, and I am not in the way of going in quest of vanities, having scarcely been in a shop these six months (indeed, I might almost say two years), having neither strength to shop nor money to spend. So all I can do is to wrap it in a bit of knitted patchwork, which (like many other things) can be of no particular use. But being of a 'frugal mind,' like Mrs. Gilpin, I bethought me how I could use to some or any purpose whatever divers odds and ends of woolgatherings (I had), and that was the result ; the remainder I am now working in the same way for Lady Edmonstone, who says it is very Turkish—set it up! The pamphlet I should have sent long ago, if I had not feared it might be rather a bore to the Colonel to receive such things, *let a be* read them. He must have much satisfaction in his munificent donation to the Church,[1] as he has reason to hope it may tend to the glory of God and the good of man. . . . I am still with Mrs. Fry, *which* I enjoy much. . . . I hear much of Macaulay's 'History,' but it must be many a day before that comes *my length.*

S. E. F. TO MRS. TENNENT (1850)

. . . . While I was writing, I was surprised by the entrance of that charming person, Lady M. Maxwell,[2] who staid with me as long as I was able to *bear her*! She has promised to come and see me very often for a month to come, which will be a great solace to me in my deep solitude and hermit cell. . . . I am much disappointed in

[1] Colonel Tennent gave the ground on which the present church at Great Stanmore stands. It is opposite 'The Pynnacles,' where he lived and died. (J. F.)

[2] Daughter of the seventh Earl of Elgin ; married, 1839, Sir John Maxwell, Bart., of Pollock. (J. F.)

'The Wide World.'[1]   It is for young people, and objectionable for them on account of the American vulgarity which pervades it; yet there are beautiful passages, and much sweet genuine piety throughout, by which we may all be edified. . . .

S. E. F. TO MRS. TENNENT (1850)

The 'Fishwife' is by the lady of your old acquaintance. Another work by a quondam associate of yours is the 'Account of Sierra Leone,' by one of the Miss Randall Callanders, afterwards Mrs. Melville.[2]   I am reading it on a loan from Mary Campbell, who, alas! is now so deaf it is almost death for me to speak to her, my voice is so much gone.   Mrs. Christison is laid up with lumbago, and I am unable to mount her stair, so we have not met for a long while. . . .

S. E. F. TO MRS. TENNENT (1850?)

. . . . The weather has been and still is bitter, even '*by ordiner*,' as the bodies say; but, whenever it has been possible for me to venture out, Lady Stuart[3] has kindly placed her carriage at my disposal, so with glasses *up* and blinds *down* I have had some gay drives!   My friends are few and far between at present, as Mrs. Christison is with her old aunt, Mrs. Clavering, near London, and Mary Camp with Mrs. Sheridan[4] at Hampton Court. . . .   I ought long since to have thanked you for the 'Harvest' you sent me, which I liked very much, but must hear it again, as I am often so drumlie and dowie I cannot do justice to what is read to me.   Miss Mary Lester[5] has put forth an allegory,

---

[1] Published in 1850.

[2] Edited by Mrs. Norton (who was a kinswoman of the writer) in 1850.

[3] Widow of Sir James Stuart, Bart., of Allanbank.   She was daughter of Professor Monro, of Craiglockart; he was the third of a remarkable trio of anatomists in the University of Edinburgh.   (J. F.)

[4] Mother of the three well-known Sheridan sisters, Mrs. Norton, the Duchess of Somerset, and Lady Dufferin.   Miss C. was her cousin. (J. F.)

[5] A cousin.   (J. F.)

'Guardian Angels,' very prettily written, and neatly done
up, and quite harmless. . . . I have heard some bits of a
book which I think the Colonel would like, 'The Lives of
the Lindsays'; it seems very entertaining, and well written
by the noble author and descendant, the present Lord, who
does credit even to that most remarkable race. . . .

S. E. F. TO MRS. TENNENT (1850)

May 5–7 [1850?]

I must now try to clear scores with you in the epistolary way, being somewhat better than when I last wrote,
though I have not much to boast of, nor can expect any
amendment while this vicious east wind blows. The lithographs will be most welcome, come when they may. I
wished much to have gone to the Exhibition for a few
minutes, merely to see Harvey's[1] pictures; there is always
so much in them suggestive of good thoughts, and that
raises one's mind above the ordinary level of this work-a-
day world. I was unable, however, to go, neither could I
go to his house to see the one he has sent to London. I
am not acquainted with Mr. H., and feel unfit to encounter
strangers, as my voice is at times so husky I can't bear to
hear it, and at others is almost inaudible. I forget whether
I mentioned that Thorburn[2] took me by surprise not long
since by entering most unexpectedly. He had taken a
run down, he said, merely by way of relaxation from his
incessant labours. If I mistake not, he said he had upwards
of forty pictures in hand, besides a long list of names
booked; he is going to raise his terms to 200*l.* for full
lengths, and do little or nothing by halves. . . . Professor
James and his whole family have been staying with

---

[1] Harvey was a native of Stirling,
and it was Mrs. Graham who discovered the great talent in him when
quite a youth. He was well known
later as Sir George Harvey, President
of the Royal Scottish Academy.
(J. F.)

[2] The eminent miniature painter,
who has been already mentioned on
p. 265. (J. F.)

Professor Wilson, to cheer him for the loss of his daughter Jane,[1] who, with her husband, is now in London. . . .

MISS HOPE MACKENZIE TO S. E. F.

9 Doune Terrace : January 27, 1850.

Mowbray can read this to you if you please.

My dear Friend,—What a sad break on our intercourse this has been, with so much sickness and suffering on both sides, yet in one way (the most precious) I am sure we have met at a throne of grace in mutual intercession. I have often wished to write to you, but I thought it might only hurt you, especially if (as too often) you exerted to write an answer ; and also one of my ails has been tendency to oppressive headache, which any exertion, particularly writing, always brought on or increased, so I was ordered to keep quiet and useless. I am now much better, and I cannot resist sending you the Apostle's greeting to his 'beloved' friend (John iii.), and also telling you *how much* we have been thinking of you, and of what you would feel when we heard of the grievous affecting death of your young cousin, Mrs. Gillon,[2] in herself, I understand, so much to be loved and lamented, and the daughter of one whom you so much valued. Oh, that all such clouded dealings of our Heavenly Father's hand may work out the 'intent' of His love, the Spirit taking these dark things and so applying them to the soul as to sanctify and make meet for the inheritance of light above all clouds and darkness. I have been much pleased with the little books that

---

[1] Married, 1849, Wm. Edmonstone Aytoun, Professor of Belles Lettres in Edinburgh University.

There is a pleasing legend about this marriage. It is said that Aytoun, imbued, as every young Scotchman of letters was (at least if a Tory), with profound reverence for Christopher North, shrank from asking him for his daughter's hand. The young lady herself undertook the service of danger. She left the room and quickly reappeared. Turning her back to her lover, she disclosed a placard, ' With the author's compliments.' (J. F.)

[2] Mrs. Gillon, of Wallhouse, daughter of Colonel F. Hamilton, died in childbed, 1850. (J. F.)

dear Mrs. Stenhouse gave us lately—they were new to us, but I see their circulation in England has been very great, especially the call to 'Come to Jesus'—the plan of which (a very small portion of man's words), introducing a large one of the word of God, is, I think, an admirable one. The other, 'The Voice of Jesus in the Storm,' is very applicable to a time of sorrow or trial. I will not plague you with the *gift* of them, but I am tempted to send the *loan* in case you like to let Mowbray read a bit at any leisure time. . . . Helen [1] keeps pretty well, and we are very thankful that my brother, Lord M., has been none the worse of resuming his labours. He and Mrs. Mackenzie are deeply grieved for Lord Jeffrey. The rapidity of his mortal illness has been most striking, and how much one does feel for kind, amiable Mrs. Jeffrey, and for his daughter, who arrived only this morning to find it was too late! Mercifully, a niece of his, who was almost like a daughter to him and Mrs. Jeffrey, has been with them.

Lord Medwyn, thank God, continues gradually, though slowly, recovering his strength. Now you must not write a word in answer to this too long note. I do hope now (weather favouring) to get to see you ere long. Meantime and ever best of blessings be with you.

Your very affectionate and faithful friend,

H. M.

S. E. F. TO MRS. TENNENT (1850-1 ?)

Saturday.

. . . This town is now such a desert, there is scarcely a person in it with whom I am on speaking terms ; not one of my intimates remain. . . . so I shall really be, what the French lady called herself in like circumstances, 'a most abandoned creature.'

Monday.—As if to say 'that's not true,' Lady McN. entered just as I had laid down my pen and closed my

---

[1] Her sister-in-law, Mrs. Mackenzie. (J. F.)

eyes for the day. She is as kindly affectionate as ever, testified by the many many tokens I am constantly receiving from Granton; but the house is always full of company at this season, so she acts the invisible fairy to her remote friends. . . . The Professor[1] has now lost the power of speech. Alas! what a subject for moralizing, and I would fain say a great deal more, but I cannot at this time.

LADY AUGUSTA BRUCE[2] TO S. E. F.

Polloc : Saturday, November 10.

Dear Miss Ferrier,—The accompanying sermons are those of which I spoke, and if it does not fatigue you to look into them, I think you will find much that is most beautiful, strengthening, and comforting. The first bears more particularly on the subject to which you alluded on Sunday. I only wish I were in Edinburgh, and could have the great pleasure of reading them to you. I shall endeavour during the course of next week, when I pass through, to call and inquire, hoping to find that my unreasonably long visit has not produced any bad consequences. I have copied the few lines which I now enclose, as it seems to me that my correspondent explains very clearly and happily how one may with perfect consistency wear a lock of Prince Charlie's hair in a bit of John Knox's pulpit !

I remain, dear Miss Ferrier, with much respect and regard,

Very truly yours,

AUGUSTA E. F. BRUCE.

Of course you have seen Aytoun's ' Lays of the Scottish Cavaliers.'[3] Are they not beautiful? It is curious to observe in the history of your dear countrymen the

---

[1] John Wilson. (J. F.)

[2] Married Arthur Penrhyn Stanley, Dean of Westminster.

[3] Aytoun's *Lays* were published in 1849.

different ways in which their loyalty has shown itself—the devoted adherence to the Stuarts on the one hand, and the stedfast maintenance of that truth that Christ alone is Head of His Church, or, as they phrase it, 'King in Zion.' The two, though they seem opposed at first, are the same principle of truth contended for civilly and *ecclesiastically* to Cæsar and to God, and there are traits in the stories of the Covenanters that might well rank side by side with the stories of the Cavaliers. Oh! how one longs sometimes for the disentangling of truth from all that has encumbered it, and for the *harmony* of the truth to be manifest.

S. E. F. TO MRS. TENNENT

Tuesday.

I fled the country ten days ago, so your letter followed me there and here, and has only just reached me. Your visit may well seem to you like a dream ; it does so to me, and like a troubled one, for I cannot but reproach myself with not having made greater efforts to show you more kindness, even though it should have been in an uncomfortable way! You may believe there were no omissions of that kind when you left me, and I enjoyed a few warm days in my own out of the world way, though I can't say I was sensible of any improvement in my health, and now the weather is cold I am glad to be in my own den and by the fire-side . . .

Wednesday.—Lady McNeill has been here laden with fruits and flowers. I showed her *Yad,*[1] and she said she would recommend Blackwood to get it. I wouldn't tell her who was the author till I had permission. I know no mankind in town, even my doctor is absent, and I should suppose there is very little reading at this season. The 'Lays' are only too beautiful ; the Colonel must read the critique upon them in the 'North British Review' for April.

---

[1] Neither of the editors can throw any light on this mysterious word.

'Facts are Chields that winna ding,' as Burns says, and there are some stated there that completely *ding* certain of the professor's averments.[1]   Many thanks for your kind offer of supplying my wants, but at present I have none— at least none in your way.   At any time if you happen to meet with a small fan of a dark colour I would be glad of such, not to cool me, but to cause a little circulation of air when I am in church.   I had one of rosewood, which is now worn out and is not to be replaced in all Edinburgh ! Mowbray says she has been in every shop, but could see nothing but *fine* ivory or painted paper ones . . .

S. E. F. TO MRS. TENNENT

Thursday evening.

On returning from my airing I found your note await-ing me, which was an unexpected pleasure and more than I deserved.   Many thanks for your kind offers, but, as Mowbray[2] says, my wants are many—my wishes are few, and I am little in the way of temptation, as I know not when I was last in a shop !   Perhaps if you are in that way, and should chance to meet with a very quiet, dark browny or purply stuff of a *cheap* kind, I might be induced to change my garment, since the wind has changed its position ; but pray let it be cheap.   I should like to hear of the Exhibition ; if there is an account of the pictures in any paper perhaps you will send it.   Poor Harvey, another mortification for him in the hanging of his picture.   Did you see Hope Stewart's 'Landing of the Queen at Dum-barton '?   I am interested for him ; he is such a good creature, and supports an aged mother and delicate sister by his labours. . . .

---

[1] A review of Aytoun's *Lays* ap-peared in the *North British* for February 1850, dealing mainly with his refutation of Macaulay's attack on Claverhouse.   The review is written in a thoroughly partisan spirit, and is unlikely to convince any one who is not convinced beforehand.

[2] Miss Ferrier's maid, often men-tioned.

The box arrived about two hours ago, and I have been busy till this moment inspecting and arranging its various contents. The foot-warmer is an excellent as well as ornamental invention, and nothing could be more suitable to one who suffers so much from extreme cold as I do. The tray is of a material unknown to me, but I admire its queer antique appearance. The tea is most acceptable, and I hope to regale my messmates, Mrs. Chris., Mary C., &c., &c., by-and-bye with a cup of ' Twining's best,' but at present my familiars are all absent. Since the meeting of the beasts [1] is over, few bipeds are to be seen, at least in this unfrequented region, though I believe travellers swarm in all other directions. . . .

THE HON. LORD CUNINGHAM TO S. E. F.

Moray Place : October 18, 1850.

My dear Miss Ferrier,—You may be well aware that it is with great regret, that I am obliged to send the enclosed unsuccessful result of our application to Lord Campbell. I hope it is in good faith ; and it might happen that he had got other favours recently from the Chancellor which precluded a new application.

I wish I could suggest another channel more likely to be successful. As Lord John Russell represents the City of London, if any of Mr. Kinloch's friends could apply to his Lordship, I have a notion it might be effectual ; or if Mr. Kinloch, from his connection with Kincardineshire, could get access to Mr. Fox Maule, by any means, he would have a good chance of carrying his point. Unfortunately, I have not for many years been on any habits

---

[1] The Meeting of the Beasts alludes to a thing Miss Ferrier wrote, but it was never published ; her friend, Mrs. Erskine, altered it, and, as she thought, *improved* it, but it was dull and prosy, I have heard. (J. F.)

with Maule, and am quite unacquainted with Lord J. I wish on the present occasion it were otherwise, and remain ever, my dear Miss Ferrier,

Yours with sincere esteem,

J. CUNINGHAM.

FROM LORD CAMPBELL (LORD CHANCELLOR)
TO LORD CUNINGHAM (EDINBURGH)

Stratheden House : February 16, 1850.

My dear Cuningham,—I should have been delighted if I could have been of any service to a kinsman of Miss Ferrier, to whom I consider myself under deep obligations for the pleasure I have derived from her charming writings, but I assure you that it is not in my power to interfere in any way with the exercise of the Lord Chancellor's patronage.

Yours very sincerely,

CAMPBELL.

I am running off to attend a meeting about the monument to poor Jeffrey.

The following correspondence with Bentley reminds us of what we are tempted to forget, that we are dealing not merely with a shrewd and observant critic watching life from within a small private circle, but with a writer who had been for forty years a classic. At last, in the edition of 1852, the worn-out mask was thrown off, and Miss Ferrier appeared before the world in her own name.[1] We need not interpret this as showing any late born craving for publicity. Rather it marks how fully the old life and associations had passed away. There was no longer the dread of alienating the victims of her sarcasm ; Edinburgh literary society with its curious traditions and superstitions of secrecy was a thing of the past.

---

[1] The following correspondence clearly shows that this was at Bentley's request. One is rather tempted to think that it was a bargain, and that in consideration of the author's name appearing, Bentley withdrew the vignettes, to which Miss Ferrier had a strong (and creditable) aversion.

It is somewhat startling, too, to find Bentley making suggestions for a new novel. Such a reappearance would scarcely have had a parallel save in the production of 'Gryll Grange,' separated by an interval of thirty years from 'Crotchet Castle.' Even a hearty admirer of Miss Ferrier may doubt whether her powers would have stood the test as Peacock's did. In 'Gryll Grange' we see occasional traces of the old spirit of reckless sarcasm which tilted alike at Byron and Coleridge, at Tory Squires and Edinburgh Reviewers. But it is everywhere softened and mellowed as in the light of sunset. And when it is lacking its place is abundantly supplied by maxims of wisdom, half cynical, half kindly, by scholarly graces of thought and speech, by unexpected touches of romance. Miss Ferrier had no such store of acquired wisdom and developed sentiment to draw upon. Her special excellences, grotesque inventiveness of incident, comic and even farcical dialogue, unhesitating descriptions of situation or character, needed to be fed from springs alike without and within, which had now run dry. The old reckless mirth, largely dependent on animal spirits and joyous surroundings, was no longer dominant. Reflection and a clear sense of the seriousness of life had not fused themselves with humour ; rather they had warred against it and repressed it. With her best gifts impaired, Miss Ferrier could no longer have won forgiveness for her short-comings. No one within the pale of salvation has ever troubled himself seriously because there is present in Miss Ferrier's works a certain crudity of expression, and a certain lack of harmony between the purely comic and the romantic, or would-be romantic, parts of her novels. Carried away in a full flood of enjoyable humour we are in no mood to be critical about niceties of construction or expression. But even in the case of 'Destiny' we see how, when once that humour had abated its easy and natural flow, the writer's shortcomings and limitations are forced upon us. It was no over fastidious dread of failure, no parsimonious husbanding of hardly won fame, but a sound and judicious estimate of her resources which kept Miss Ferrier silent.

R. BENTLEY TO S. E. F.

New Burlington Street : April 4, 1850.

Madam,—I had the pleasure of a visit from your nephew this morning on the subject of 'Marriage,' &c. I regret very much (as, indeed, I have reason to do) that these works did not receive your final corrections. The works are now stereotyped, but even now I should be happy to make any verbal corrections in them, if you would consent to give your name.

I took the opportunity of inquiring whether you had by you any materials for another work of a similar kind, and was very sorry to hear you were so much an invalid. Possibly much labour might be spared to you in preparing a work for publication. Literary aid is frequently obtained by writers of eminence to lighten their labours in the more mechanical part.

I need scarcely say how gratified I should feel if I could induce you to give the public another work of fiction. Although the honorarium which I should be happy to offer you might not be of importance to you personally, it might be gratifying to you, inasmuch as it might enable you to exercise to a still greater extent your benevolent feelings towards others. But I would venture to urge a still stronger motive to induce you to listen to my suggestion—the great value to society of such moral teaching as yours ; for the influence of a writer so justly admired will not be doubted by anyone.

It would, I frankly confess, be to me a matter of honourable pride to be connected with you in such a work.

Hoping to hear from you, I have the honour to be, madam, with sincere respect your faithful servant,

RICHARD BENTLEY.

If you should be induced again to write, I would say that it would not be necessary that the work should exceed the length of 'Marriage.'

S. E. F. TO R. BENTLEY

Edinburgh : 1851.[1]

I authorize the publication of my three novels, 'Marriage,' 'Inheritance,' and 'Destiny,' with my name prefixed to each, upon the following conditions :

1. The corrections and alterations made by me in the stereotyped edition shall be adopted.

2. The illustrations and vignettes shall be expelled.

3. That I shall have a certain number of copies for myself and friends, the boards to be lined with *plain* paper instead of the list of ' Standard Novels.'

When these conditions are complied with, I will then give up the penal bond I hold from Mr. Bentley.

S. E. FERRIER.

R. BENTLEY TO S. E. F.

New Burlington Street : January 29, 1852.

Madam,—Mr. Kinloch has placed in my hands the volumes of ' Marriage,' ' Inheritance,' and ' Destiny,' corrected by you, and will no doubt communicate with you on the subject forthwith.

I wish I could induce you to give to the public another work of fiction ; at no time within twenty years has there been a greater dearth of really good stories than at present. If three volumes should appear too arduous an undertaking, the public would be glad to receive two, or even one volume, although, of course, they might not be so advantageous to your publisher.

The times are now much altered from those when ' Marriage' appeared ; but if it were possible to meet your views, in the event of your health permitting you to contemplate a literary work, I would certainly endeavour to do so ; for I should consider it a high honour to be connected with you in such an undertaking.

---

[1] I have thought it best to bring together all the letters bearing on this fresh edition of the novels, at the expense of chronological exactitude.

If you will permit me, on hearing from you to that effect, I shall have great pleasure in making you a proposition.

I have the honour to be, madam, with great respect your faithful servant,

RICHARD BENTLEY.

JAMES KINLOCH TO S. E. F.

Office of Rolls, St. James's Palace : January 30, 1852.

My dearest Aunt,—I am afraid you will think I have fallen asleep over your work (not works), but I was only able to get Mr. Bentley's answer yesterday evening, altho' I took the books to him the morning after they arrived. He told me he was obliged to get an estimate of the expense from the printer, and altho' it would cost something considerable to make the alterations, and likewise entail the loss of the copies now on hand, he had much pleasure in complying with your terms, *but* he hoped you would not *press* the expulsion of the frontispiece in each volume—as the works having been published with the plates, he was fearful the new copies would in many instances be returned upon his hands as incomplete—adding that whatever was objectionable in the plates could not affect the author of the work, who was only responsible for the text, and could not be answerable for the bad taste of the publisher.   The vignettes, I believe you know, have already disappeared.

I am sorry to say we have quite a sick house at present, poor Sophia suffering from a bad attack of sciatica, and the two youngest with measles, with the prospect of the others being affected with the last.

Believe me, my dearest Aunt,
Very affectionately yours,
JAMES KINLOCH.

Affectionate regards to Uncle Walter, and all in A.[1] Street.

[1] Albany Street.   (J. F.)

R. BENTLEY TO S. E. F.

New Burlington Street : May 18, 1852.

Madam,—I should sooner have replied to your obliging letter of the 4th inst., but have been obliged to go from home on account of ill-health. I am sincerely sorry to hear that you have been suffering, but trust that summer, which is now at last breaking upon us, will restore you to better health, and induce you not to throw aside the idea of again gratifying the public by some production of a writer so justly popular.

I beg to thank you for your kind permission to announce you as the author of ' Marriage,' ' Inheritance,' and ' Destiny,' and I shall have much pleasure in placing at your disposal a number of copies of your works ; these shall be delivered to anybody you may authorise to receive them, or I shall have much pleasure in directing my agents, Messrs. Boyd, of Edinburgh, to send them to you.

I have the honour to remain, madam, with sincere admiration,

Yours faithfully,

RICHARD BENTLEY.

R. BENTLEY TO S. E. F.

New Burlington Street : May 26, 1852.

Madam,—I beg to acknowledge the receipt of your letter of the 24th inst. Until the corrections are made in your three stories, ' Marriage,' ' Inheritance,' and ' Destiny,' I perefctly understood that your name was not to be announced. I sincerely trust that you may be able to contribute another work to those you have already given to the world, and which have become classics.

It will not be before the autumn that the new and corrected editions of your works will appear.

I have the honour to be, madam,

Your faithful servant,

RICHARD BENTLEY.

S. E. F. TO MRS. TENNENT

Saturday, January 5, 1851.

. . . I receive very frequent visits from our friend, Dr. Maclagan, whose six sons continue to prosper to be comforts to him,[1] but he is anxious about the seventh,[2] who is bent upon going to India, if possible, in the medical line—what does the Colonel say as to the practicability of procuring an appointment ?   I believe he does not interfere with Indian matters himself, else I dare say he would lend a helping hand for your and your dear mother's sake.

Tuesday.—Another kind letter and pretty little *souvenir*; I really *ought* to blush, but you may suppose I am living on the *Revalenta Arabica*, which, amongst all other diseases, professes to cure that of ' involuntary blushing.'   The butterfly is quite a novelty, but far be it for me to make it the scavenger of my pen !   I wish I had anything to send you in return, but I neither see or hear of aught beyond my own dark walls.   I hear of no books, but I see most favourable notices of ' Humboldt's Letters to a Female Friend.'   Here comes the ' Athenæum,' which, in spite of its bad tone, I like to see.

S. E. F. TO MRS. TENNENT (1851)

Tuesday.

I can tell you little of what is saying and doing here, as I scarcely ever go out, and that only for a little airing with glasses up and blinds down, because of the glaring sun and cold east wind ; and I receive *very* few visitors, as talking excites my cough and exhausts me.   Georgy C.[3] has just been here, but was too humane to sit down, especially as poor dear Mary was with her, who is now *so* deaf !

Professor Wilson has at last resigned his Academical Chair,[4] and James F. is one of the candidates as his successor, with the good wishes of all who know him.

---

[1] See p. 16.

[2] The present Archbishop of York. (J. F.)

[3] Half-sister of Mary Campbell.

[4] He retired, 1851, on a pension of 300*l.* a year.   (J. F.)

. . . I hear 'Roughing it in the Bush' is a most amusing book. Have you seen it ? I hope you have had Lady McNeill's visit and enjoyed it. She has not forgotten me in her absence, as her gardener brings me many good things from the garden. . . .

S. E. F. TO MRS. TENNENT

Wednesday, 15th.

Your boxes put me in mind of those described in fairy tales as sent by beneficent fairies to their goddaughters on great occasions with something of everything, so that it would take a long summer's day to enumerate the various articles, and I have only a little bit of a summer's evening to bestow—suffice it to say, then, that all were thankfully received and much approved of. . . . Agnes and Helen [1] were here at the opening of the box, and the house rang with applause at sight of their mother's shawl ; it was spread out on your mother's bed, and she admired it much. Mine is very elegant, but I have been so long accustomed to the profound retirement of an old black silk one, that I feel as if the *eyes of the world* would be upon me were I to emerge in such lustre, so I shall probably avail myself of your privilege after I have duly weighed the *needs* and merits of various relatives.

S. E. F. TO MRS. TENNENT

When I received a cloak at your hands it was with the design of making it cover all deficiencies which you were evidently seeking to spy out and supply. I omitted, however, to stipulate that this comprehensive covering should be of the plainest description, and free from all incumbrances and superfluities, such as cowls, hoods, and such like gear. A few days ago I should have been disposed to beg it might be lined with fur or flannel, to

---

[1] Her nieces. (J. F.)

enable me to meet 'gentle spring' in all its usual 'ethereal mildness'; but to-day I hear the glass is up to the freezing point, so I hope in the course of time to hear tell of violets and primroses. . . . I hear of very little in the fiction way, the realities of life are as much as I can accomplish now. . . .

S. E. F. TO MRS. TENNENT

The box has arrived and the cloak is perfect! It is really everything that a cloak should, would, and could be, and all that I could have desired had I had the order-ing, not the paying, of it. I wish you had been present at the unfolding of it. Mowbray was in hysterics of delight, and could only utter broken exclamations of rapture, 'What a cloak! splendid, handsome, judicious, comfort-able, elegant, richest of silks, beautifully made, so light, so warm, so ladylike, &c., &c.' Then Eliza was summoned to bear witness, who in her gruff way deponed that she 'didna see how it could weel be handsomer.' My only fault to it, is that it is too good, and that I shall find it difficult to support the dignity of such a cloak, so much will be expected of it! . . .

S. E. F. TO MRS. TENNENT

I have a remonstrance to make to you in behalf of a certain collar and cuffs which you have cruelly consigned to the dark receptacle of my wardrobe, where they are pining away a lost existence without the least hope of ever beholding the light while they remain in my possession. Seriously, they are quite thrown away upon me, and it is a pity that anything so pretty should be thrown away ; even if they could be seen upon me, which they cannot, they would very soon cease to be fit to be seen, for though elderly maiden aunts have the credit of being very upright in their *persons* at least, it is not so with me. I am such a lounger, so given to be either lying on a sofa or leaning

back in my chair, that to be rid of Emily's vain importunities I have been obliged to tell her I must have been
born with a crumpled collar. I trust you will therefore
take pity on these poor captives and send an order for
their release. . . .

S. E. F. TO MRS. TENNENT (1851)

June 1.

The ice seems to be gathering so thick over our correspondence, that unless I make an attempt to break it I fear
it will soon become a perfect iceberg, and certainly it will
not be the summer's sun that will melt it, as the weather
savours more of January than of June. . . . Lady McNeill
came to me on her return to tell me what a pleasant day
she had spent at Stanmore. She, like myself, is much
interested in the result of Professor James's canvass for
the Chair of Moral Philosophy in the University here.
His testimonials are very high, and if you care to see them
I will send you a copy. . . . The Toravon [1] folks are all
well. Georgie Camp: [2] is on a *Tower* in Stirlingshire,
and my friend Mary and I are scarcely on *speaking terms*,
by reason of her deafness and my weakness, which pre-
cludes my raising my voice beyond a whisper. . . .

S. E. F. TO MRS. TENNENT

November 7, 8, 1851.

Having very little to do, I, of course, do nothing, which
is the only reason I can assign for not having despatched
the pictures long ere now ; perhaps another cause of the
delay may be occasioned by the vague desire of adding
something by way of accompaniment to the box, though
at the same time perfectly conscious that I have not, nor
am the least likely to have, anything fit to be sent. If
thanks and blessings were tangible things I might make a

---

[1] Where her brother Walter lived in Linlithgowshire. (J. F.)
[2] See p. 316, n. 3.

handsome package of them, as many have been bestowed in return for the *part* (only) of your bounty. . . .

Good Mrs. Robertson [1] entreats you may be told how she blesses you, and poor Peggy (no longer Vesuvia) [2] begs her 'grateful duty' for the *wee* bit I gave to her for the sake of 'Auld Lang Syne.' Sundry widows and orphans have also benefited—for I have now learned from experience to be very wary in almsgiving, as I believe few things are more hurtful than lavish and indiscriminate charity. . . . I did not see Lady A. Bruce when she was here ; her time was so devoted to her cousin, Mrs. Richard Trotter, who died the morning she left this in a very sudden and striking manner, as you may probably have heard ; if not I will relate it in my next. . . . I have Cousin Kate with me for a few days, as full of health and hilarity as ever.[3] She is reading to me 'Miss Martineau and her Master,' by Dr. Bushnan, which is really a good and clever *down set* to one of the most wicked (and fortunately weak) productions that has ever issued from the Press. I hear much of the 'Life of Bickersteth,' but have not yet been able to get it. . . .

S. E. F. TO MRS. TENNENT

Monday.

My dear Helen,—A box arrived here on Saturday evening, but too late for my feeble eyes to explore and acknowledge its various contents. First came forth a rich and beautiful shawl, which caused a prodigious sensation in

---

[1] This person nursed Mrs. Graham during her last illness. (J. F.)

[2] I regret that I can throw no light on the bearer of this romantic nick-name ! (J. F.)

[3] Daughter of her cousin, L. H. Ferrier, Esq., of Belsyde ; married her cousin, R. B. Monro Binning, Esq., in 1858. This is the cousin to whom she said, in her humorous way, 'I can't think, Kate, what it is that makes so many gentlemen come to see you? *I* never see a man except the doctor, the minister, and, *occasionally a glazier.*' As Professor Saintsbury remarked (in the *Sketch* December 5, 1894), 'There is all the creatress of Miss Bell Black in these last four words.' This anecdote appears in the very unappreciative Preface to the Dent edition, and where the word sister is erroneously put instead of cousin. There are many errors besides, either arising from the printer or the carelessness of the editor. (J. F.)

the family !   At last, when Mowbray's emotions had somewhat subsided, she declared with a sort of hysteric that shawl was the greatest relief to her mind, for she had long felt what it was to put the same black velvet cloak upon me for five winters, but she knew it was needless to speak !   Alas ! the cloak is much better than its mistress, for indeed I am a poor shred and am little to be seen out of doors at any time, but when I am I shall certainly 'row me in your Plaidie.' . . . I had a visit from Lady Augusta Bruce yesterday.   She is with your old friends the Miss Erskines, of whom she reports favourably.   It is not every day I am able to admit visitors.   My cough is at times so severe, and continues so long, I am quite exhausted. . . .

S. E. F. TO MRS. TENNENT

38 Albany Street : [1] June 2, 1851.

I am now beginning in some way to regain my identity, which for the last fortnight has been almost lost in that of smiths, carpenters, chairmen, brokers, and all the innumerable tormentors one is subject to on a change of residence, especially in 'mine own romantic town' at term time, when the whole inhabitants seem to be playing at 'Change seats, the King's coming.'   The consequence is there is no getting bipeds to do a hand's turn, and they are so overwrought, poor creatures, one's anger is turned into compassion on hearing their excuses.   I cannot accuse myself of ever having been a *hoarder*, yet, do as one will, rubbish accumulates in the course of a lifetime and in the undisturbed repose of seventeen years !   Then there had been much to *de*range here, so between packings and unpackings, comings and goings, I think the erection and arranging of the Crystal Palace must have been a bagatelle compared to the toil and trouble of my flitting ! . . .

Wednesday, 4th.—And now I must begin to pluck a crow with you, my dear Helen. Why will you persist in

---

[1] This was Miss Ferrier's last home.   (J. F.)

throwing away money upon *bonnie dies* for me when
I have so long renounced the novelties and superfluities
of life, and desire nothing more than its comfortable
' decencies ? ' N.B.--I have a mind to speak to the Colonel
about you ! I forgot to tell you of the fate of your pretty
owl, which Ferooza McNeill [1] fell so violently in love with
that I could not resist offering it to her, at which her
mother was so incensed she scolded her for admiring anything so much and would not allow her to accept it.
However, I sent it to her afterwards and told her I was
sure you would think it well bestowed, so it now reigns
paramount in her boudoir. . . .

S. E. F. TO MRS. TENNENT

1851.

. . . I think James [2] is mistaken with regard to Burns's
verses.[3] I remember Blackwood was very pressing for
permission to publish them, which was refused, and I never
either saw or heard of their having appeared in print. I
shall try to procure a sight of those in Chambers's possession, but I have no direct channel of communication at
present. . . . I see by the papers great preparations are
making to enable the public to have a stare at the Royal-
ties. For my part I had to turn away all the Queens of
England from my door t'other evening. Miss S. came,
under convoy of H. W., to take tea with me, but I was so
exhausted by my cough and catarrh I was literally unable
to speak.[4] I have been suffering very much from it of late,
and the only quietus is morphia, which I am very averse
to take—even by the doctor's peremptory orders. The
weather has been very cold and tempestuous, and there has
been snow in Perthshire, so her Majesty will meet with a
cold reception. I have seen nobody for some days past ;

[1] Only child of Sir John and Lady McNeill ; married Commander Duncan Stewart, R.N. (J. F.)

[2] Her nephew, Colonel Graham. (J. F.)

[3] The verses were those addressed to Miss Ferrier (Mrs. Graham) by Burns, and are in all the editions of Burns's poetry. (J. F.)

[4] We are told in Miss Strickland's *Life*, by her sister, that she visited Miss Walker in Edinburgh in 1851.

there are none of the natives in town, if there were I could
not hold intercourse with them by reason of this same
irritation on my lungs. . . .

S. E. F. TO MRS. TENNENT

1851.

. . . I made *wonderful exertions* in the way of entertainment and sat down no fewer than five one day to
dinner, and not only that, but H. Walker burst in upon me
in the evening, with Miss Strickland waiting at the door
wishing to be permitted (not to kiss my toe) but to shake
my hand. I was so taken by surprise and so unable to
remonstrate, that she was in the room and on the sopha
before I knew where I was ; but she didn't stay ten minutes
and was as agreeable as any stranger can be to me now,
for talking is a great fatigue, and there are times when I
really cannot speak without violent fits of coughing. My
voice at best is a mere squeak, and it is not pleasant to
exhibit one's infirmities to strangers. I hear Lady C.
Bury is in town with the Lyons,[1] but we are not likely to
meet, and I don't wish it. Lady Arthur has been very
kind in writing me all about Mrs. Ker, and I had a long
and beautiful letter from herself.[2] I can't think of keeping
Mrs. Fry altogether. She and Wilberforce I consider as
loans, and as such a boon to me who can't get (or rather
keep) books from libraries. . . . I had a long visit yesterday from Lady C., as soft and caressing as ever, so that I
begin to feel the old *glamour* coming over me. She
talked all the time and told me all about her affairs, her
happiness with the Lyons, &c., &c., &c. Do you know
aught of the translation of ' Plato ' in Bohn's cheap Library ?
Two volumes. I have a reason for wishing to read it, but
can't get it, a-hem !—no hint. . . .

---

[1] Mrs. Lyon was Lady C.'s
daughter by her second marriage.
(J. F.)

[2] Lady Arthur Lennox and Mrs.
Ker were daughters of Lady Char-
lotte, by her first marriage. Mrs.
K.'s first husband was Mr. Langford-
Brooke, of Mere Hall, Cheshire.
(J. F.)

S. E. F. TO MISS MARY CAMPBELL

1851,[1]

Many thanks, dearest Mary, for your latest of unremitting attentions. Our friend has done her part well and it is wonderful how much she has made of what seemed a completely worn out subject. It must have been very gratifying to her to be able to plant a fresh sprig of laurel on her loved poet's grave. I can say nothing good of myself. My cough is very severe and will probably continue so, *at least* as long as this weather lasts; but I have many comforts for which I am thankful, amongst these I must reckon silence and darkness, which are my best companions at present. Oh! for faith to pray more fervently for the blessings promised to the believer, but you will help me, dear friend, and may God bless you!

S. E. F. TO MISS MARY CAMPBELL [2]

My dear Mary,—Although I have omitted to answer Miss Kelty's [3] query I have kept in mind the purpose of propounding it to my nephew, Professor F., when I should see him. This I have been in daily expectation of doing for the last ten days, but as he has not yet appeared I can no longer delay apologising for my seeming neglect. I still think he must be forthcoming some of these days, when I shall not fail to *speir* him. I know nothing of the matter myself nor am acquainted with the Messrs. B.[4] I send you a little merry go round sort of a thing, which you who knit in shade may find useful, at least I did in my day. I do it in fear and trembling for a *return*, which I do assure you would annoy me exceedingly, as I really don't know where to bestow my goods. All my friends

---

[1] This letter alludes to an article Lady Richardson wrote for Mrs. S. C. Hall's Magazine on Wordsworth's Home Life, 1851. Miss Campbell has been mentioned at p. 289 and elsewhere.

[2] There is nothing to show the date of this letter. I have, therefore, placed it with the only other one to the same correspondent.

[3] An authoress. She wrote several books now quite forgotten. (J. F.)

[4] Blackwood. (J. F.)

have kindly helped me away with some bit of some sma'
trash or other (the sma'est of a') I think may be of some
sma' use to you.   I am wearying to see you and hope we
may meet on Sunday, D.V.

Ever yours affectionately,
S. E. F.

S. E. F. TO MRS. ¡TENNENT

October 8, 9, 1852.

. . . I have nothing new to tell you of anything or
anybody here, and I find nothing readable after 'Uncle
Tom's Cabin.'   I never was so stirred by any book, and
I'm glad to hear the whole world is the same.   There is
to be a great emancipation bazaar at Glasgow, and I'm
going to work like a nigger for it!   Should the whole
proceeds purchase but one slave that is something—how
much of weal or woe may be in that *one*! . . . The
weather is very cold, and I have been screwing my courage
up to invest a small sum (as the MacDonald Buchanans
used to say) in the purchase of a winter gown, as *Hightem*
is truly in its sear and yellow leaf, and Mowbray's sighs
every time she fastens it are really piercing; but as you
kindly propose *traatin* me to one I willingly submit to
your choice, requesting it may be a very plain, quiet
garment of any dark colour, except brown, as I think I
shall get the name (without the character) of the *Brownie*,
and wish I had anything to send you, but, except my
precious autograph, I have nothing, and I *think shame* to
send such a pitiful thing even at your bidding. . . .

S. E. F. TO MRS. TENNENT

. . . My cough, tho' less violent, is still troublesome,
and my lungs are so weak I am often unable to speak, so
a companion in these circumstances is very tantalising.
Of course I receive very few visitors, so know very little of
what is going on in this gay city.   The D. of Argyll seems

to be gaining golden opinions from all classes and sects, and most deservedly, for he appears most sincere and zealous in his endeavours to do good ; and in spite of his phillippick [*sic*] against the Free Church,[1] he and the Duchess of Sutherland have attended Mr. Guthrie regularly during their stay and been *hand in glove* with him and several of its ministers. If you read the Edinburgh papers I am sure you must have admired his speeches at the meetings where he presided. I have not seen the Memoir of Dr. Chalmers, but I hear it is admirable. . . .

S. E. F. TO MRS. TENNENT

1853.

. . . Mrs. Ker has kindly placed her house in London at her [Lady Charlotte's] disposal, but I believe she is no more fit to manage a house in London than one of her own pugs or parrakeets![2]   The Lyons are going to Italy and the Lennoxes to Malta, he having got the command of the regiment, so I hope the change will be for the better. I am reading the 'Memoir of Mr. Allan,' a Quaker, which I find very interesting and which gives most favourable impressions of crowned heads and dignitaries, such as Emperor Alexander, Duke of Kent, &c., &c., but I am having it read rather cursorily and hurriedly, being the loan of a loan viâ my kind Mary Campbell.   I last year presented Lady A. Bruce with a copy of ' Little Things,'[3] which she took

---

[1] She joined the Free Church after the disruption. (J. F.)

[2] Both Lady Juliana in *Marriage*, and Lady Elizabeth Malcolm in *Destiny*, must have been copies of Lady C. in her love for animals *only*. She never travelled without being accompanied by her canine favourites, and there was a footman who attended to them and made up their beds in the carriage ! Lord Dunmore, it is said, once refused a visit from her because she would bring these four-footed travelling companions with her. (J. F.)

[3] By Miss Henrietta Wilson, a niece of ' Christopher North.' She always lived at Woodville with her uncle, Mr. James Wilson. She was the daughter of Andrew Wilson, who died young. Beside the two pleasant healthy books of homely morality, *Little Things* and *Things to be Thought of*, both referred to in these letters, she wrote the truly delightful *Chronicles of a Garden*. In it the teaching of Ruskin is grafted on a stock of good sense and right feeling, and bears sweet and wholesome fruit. In her love of Nature, above all in her observant sympathy with animals, Henrietta Wilson is a true kinswoman of Christopher North, a sister in heart and mind to the master of Camp, and the chronicler of Rab.

to Abergeldie this Autumn. The Princess Hohenlohe read it, and was so much pleased with it, that she asked leave to *lend* it to the Queen—who I hope would order a copy for herself on her return to London. As you were one of the early patronesses, I think you will be glad to hear it has attained such eminence ; indeed for a little *nameless* book from an *unknown* author, its success has been great. . . .

I shall try and do my best in a signature, but I have so long indulged in the lazy S. E. F. that I feel quite nervous about signing my name proper. . . .

S. E. F. TO MRS. TENNENT

Saturday, 1853.

My guests left me, to my great regret, on Thursday, but Town is not the best place at this season, especially as the east wind still prevails, to the great detriment of invalids like me. Lady Stuart kindly drives me whenever she can to be rid of its influence, and really makes a sacrifice in shutting herself up in a darkened carriage with a coughy, *squealy* companion when she might be basking in the sun and hearing the birds sing ; but she is one of those who consider others more than herself. Apropos, I hope you have got ' Things to be Thought of,' which is about as admirable as its predecessor and bids fair to be as much appreciated, five thousand copies having been sold the first week, something almost unprecedented in an anonymous and very unattractive looking work. Miss Brewster's ' Work ' is of a rather higher grade and does honour to womankind ; at the same time it makes one feel very insignificant, and so is humbling, which is one good effect. . . . The whirling of tables &c. is practised with great success in several respectable families here—one of the Judges is particularly successful it seems.

S. E. F. TO MRS. TENNENT

February 11.

It was a rash promise I made to give you an account of my life and conduct for the last two months, as I have really little or nothing to say of or for myself; great part of my time has been passed in bed and great part of it in coughing, diversified with a little reading and knitting. I never go out, and see few people at home, so am of little use to anybody; yet here I remain, doubtless for some good purpose—may it be that of 'redeeming the time' so much of which, alas! has been misused and mis-spent. . . . I congratulate you in having got an *abstaining* curate, as I do think it is high time the clergy were using every means by precept and example to counteract this most hideous vice of intemperance which has so overspread the land. There is, perhaps, not much to be done in the way of reforming drunkards, but much may be done by preventing the young from beginning the habit even in *moderation.*

17th *Friday.*—It is high time I was bringing this long-winded scrawl to an end. I have been poorly and only able to write a wee bit now and then, and here is such a day as dark as night, with wind, rain, snow, and piercing cold. . . . . Thanks for your offer of handsome habiliment, but your cloak is as good as new. My shawls would be quite uplifted if they knew of the honour you put upon them—pray let me know when you will be ready to receive another. . . . I take Mr. Bushnan's 'Hope Companion' as it is not costly, only three-halfpence a week, so I don't think he will make a dash on the profits—poor creature. . .

S. E. F. TO MRS. TENNENT

Tuesday, October 1.

I was glad to receive the 'Athenæum' this morning bearing the Stanmore postmark, and nicely directed, as usual, in the Colonel's hand. . . . The weather is now very cold and broken, and I have been suffering from incessant irritation of the lungs, and seldom get out, and indeed at times am scarcely able to speak. I have not seen Lady McN. lately, as she has a houseful of relations, who, though readers, are not buyers of books—indeed I believe few people are nowadays as everybody (except myself) subscribes to clubs or libraries, and *they* are still deserted. James W.[1] is not returned, and when last heard of was at Dunrobin. . . . I dare say you have no idea of the demands upon the charitable in this ' romantic town '—romantic, alas! would there were less of that and more done for the sad realities of poverty and destitution which surround us! Amongst the many uncomplaining sufferers who come within my limited sphere, I fear poor old Mrs. Robertson and her daughter[2] are of the number, though they would be at the last extremity before they would beg or make their wants known. Mowbray kindly goes to them when I can spare her, and though it is little of gold or silver she has to bestow, she does what she can to aid them in Christian offices, no less precious in the sight of God! . . . . I am very anxious about this as I feel my life to be very frail and precarious, and if I were gone poor Mrs. R. would soon be forgotten ; there is nothing I envy in riches but the power of relieving others.

Wednesday.—I was interrupted yesterday by a visit from Lady Arthur L.,[3] but I was scarcely able to speak to her, though glad to see her looking well and happy.

S. E. F. TO MRS. TENNENT

. . . I enclose a Prospectus of a work which is forthcoming from the pen of my young friend Fanny Mackenzie ; it has been highly approved of by competent judges, so I hope it will be successful, as the profits are for a charitable purpose. She is a very uncommon creature both for intellect and accomplishments, and both devoted to the glory of God and the good of her fellow creatures. . . .

S. E. F. TO MRS. TENNENT

I am not to be trusted with money! I told you I had put aside one of the sovereigns you sent me for Mrs. R.[4]

---

[1] Wilson. (J. F.)
[2] See p. 320. (J. F.)
[3] Lennox, see p. 323. (J. F.)
[4] Robertson. (J. F.)

[Robertson] till next rent day, but every time I open my desk, and see it lying wasting its substance there, I think of the enclosed touching appeal. I am sadly tempted to do what I have no right to do—to give it, or a part, to the poor widow and her babes; yet without your sanction I cannot venture to put your name to the list of subscribers I have commenced. I fear it will be a very small one, as I am not able to see any but very intimate friends, and most of them are as poor (or as *well picked*) as myself. Lady S. [Stuart] though an Episcopalian, is always willing to impart to all churches and sects, and I doubt not you are no less liberal. You will see from the list of collectors, Walter [her brother] is one of the number, as the case is known to him and he takes a great interest in it. I have been better and worse since I wrote to you. My cough is at times *very* severe, and my voice is at times scarcely audible, so I am obliged to live quite *à la hermit.* . . .

This, and not a few other touches of a like kind, remind one how little real truth there was in Miss Ferrier's remark of humorous self-depreciation : 'The Lord loveth a cheerful giver, but I can never give cheerfully.' There is not much in common between the author of 'Marriage' and the author of 'Don Juan,' but one is reminded of:

> So for a good old gentlemanly vice
> I think I must take up with avarice.

S. E. F. TO MRS. TENNENT

Friday.

I was amused to hear of your *rencontre*, and glad to have tidings of my old friends, having not only lost sight, but sound of them for many a day. I may expect to see Annie [1] stalk in some of these mornings, as I don't suppose she will be *overpressed* to prolong her stay, either at Stapleton or Dunglass,[2] at least, not after she has displayed the treasures of her wardrobe, and exhibited her last cap to an

---

[1] Miss Walker. (J. F.)
[2] Sir J. Hall's place near Dunbar. (J. F.)

admiring circle.   The weather is now so charming, I long
to hear your mother is enjoying it out of doors, and is in
training for the long journey before her.   The aged Aunt is
now safely housed at Conheath—having made out the journey
with ease in two days ; it is wonderful that she should have
remained entire upon exposure to the fresh air, after having
been immured so long in that horrid receptacle.[1]   I have just
been paying my daily visit to John ; he suffers less from
pain than he did, but has a sensation (if it may be so called)
of *numbness* in the limb, for which he is now undergoing
galvanism ; he is very patient and wonderfully cheerful, poor
fellow ![2]   It is as much as I can do to climb the long stair,
for I am now very breathless and feckless.

S. E. F. TO MRS. TENNENT

1853.

. . . My good friend H. Walker has lately expended
five hundred pounds in erecting and establishing temperance inns for the lower orders in town and country, and
her nephew, John Hope, is (for he is much abused by all
do-nothings) accused of spending *at least* two thousand per
annum on the temperance education, anti-popery, and other
good causes. . . . I should be much obliged to you if you
could get for me a little book called 'Gentle Influence,'
which I cannot procure here.   Pray tell the Colonel to get
Sir John McNeill's pamphlet reprinted at the request of
the publisher, Murray,—' The Progress and Present Position
of Russia in the East.'

Poor Lady Leith is in fear lest her three sons should
all be sent to the wars.   Mrs. Stuart Ker [3] was in town for
a few days, and came to see me, and though the very sound
of her voice is music in my ear, I could not admit her ;
there are days when I am unable to speak without pain
and difficulty, so you cannot wonder that I should decline

---

[1] Old Miss Connell; she lived in
Charlotte Street, Edinburgh. (J. F.)
[2] Her nephew, John Wilson
Ferrier; he died 1845. (J. F.)

[3] She was a most charming and
fascinating person, like all the members of Lady Charlotte's family.
(J. F.)

all introductions, and confine myself entirely to relations and old *familiar* friends. . . .

S. E. F. TO MRS. TENNENT

Monday, 23rd and 24th.

I have been long of welcoming your return home, but I am a very languid correspondent now, and you must place all omissions to the true account— bad health and weak eyes, I might say at once *old age* ; but while I receive such frequent and well-penned little volumes from sister K. [Kinloch] (so much my senior in years) I dare not lay my claim to that apology. . . . I trust James[1] has given up all thoughts of relinquishing his situation, as, whatever may be its inconveniences, he might be long of getting anything as good.   McLeod of McLeod, a great Highland proprietor and a most excellent man, has been completely overwhelmed by the debts of generations, that he is now working hard in office for 200*l.* per annum, with a wife and family to support ; and a brother of Sir R. Menzies, a very fine young man, is clerk on 80*l.*   Sir J. McN. was very desirous of getting a relative of *his* put on the constabulary in Ireland, and with some difficulty got his *name* put to a list of (I fear to say how many), and the prospect of its coming to be his turn in the course of a few years.   I mention these *facts* that James may not act rashly in this matter, and lose the substance in grasping at the shadow. . . .

S. E. F. TO MRS. TENNENT

October 18.

. . . Writing becomes daily more painful and irksome to me.   I can still discern objects as clearly as ever, but I cannot look steadily at anything for more than a very few seconds without a great effort, so I often shrink from the touch of a pen as though it were a torpedo. . . . Many and various are the trials we are called upon to endure in

---

[1] Her nephew, Colonel Graham.   (J. F.)

our earthly pilgrimage, each and all ordained in heavenly wisdom and love, and adapted to the various states and conditions of those who are to be exercised thereby. But for that consideration, and the many blessed assurances given to us in Scripture, what a fearful mystery this world would appear to those who have lived in it as long as I have done! At present all my dearest and best friends are in tribulation of one kind or other.

I had almost forgot to ask whether you desired a Miss Helen Halkett to call upon me? I was not able to see her, and never heard you mention her. Is she a real person? . . .

The following letters came to hand too late for insertion in their proper place. They are all later than 1846.

S. E. F. TO MRS. TENNENT

September 23.

My dear Helen,—It was only two days ago I received the enclosed, and as I guessed its contents could only be a repetition of what I had communicated, I thought it needless to forward it *post haste*, so have kept it till I could acknowledge your own letter at the same time. I will send the pictures by-and-bye, and I think that of the Holy Family [1] will be in its right place in your possession, as a pleasing remembrance of those who are gone and going, for it was done by your mother and given by her to my father, and when I succeeded to it with other things I suggested to her to present it to one who I knew would value it dearly for her sake, and highly she was gratified by the token of regard.[2]

I could not have believed that you had *bought* the lithographs ; I shall either return or keep for a little the one belonging to you, but I think it would be too much

---

[1] Copied in Indian ink from Sir Joshua's picture. It is quite like an engraving and is most beautifully done, and is signed 'Jane Ferrier, 1800.' (J. F.)

[2] Miss Barbara Ferrier, a distant relation. (J. F.)

to bestow upon Lady A. B., unless by so doing it might serve James in any way; if he comes this way I shall at any rate put in some good words for him in case they might help to Lord E's.[1] better appreciation of his merits.

I am going to call on the Miss Erskines to-morrow to tell them all about the Canadians. To-day I have been to the West-end to meet Mr. Walter and Helen at the railway station—*en route* to D-shire. Walter has been with me for a day, but I don't think him very well. However, I hope the change and variety may do him good. Agnes is still at Toravon reddin' up, but leaves for St. Andrews in a day or two.

Wednesday.—'Friar's Chicken!' in these times! I hope you are not in the way of pampering any of the fraternity? My cook is much too strict a Presbyterian to have any hand in such a dish, and on referring to the Scotch cookery-books, it seems to have been expunged from their orthodox catalogue of dainties—I am just going to apply to Lady McNeill, whose principles I dare say are sufficiently lax to admit of her being able to furnish a most approved recipe, which I will send forthwith.

I called for the Misses E., but they were out. I must now say adieu (a very blurred one), not forgetting my best regards to the Colonel and thanks for the trouble he takes in sending me the 'Athenæum' so regularly.

Dear Helen, ever affectionately yours,

S. E. F.

S. E. F. TO MRS. TENNENT

January 12.

My dear Helen,—As you said in your last you should write to Agnes in a day or two, but as nearly a fortnight has elapsed, I begin to fear you are again invalided, whether at Stanmore or Torquay remains to be told.

My eyes have been better and worse according to the weather, with which I dare say the Colonel also sympathizes in a lesser degree. Mine were at ease during the thick

[1] Lord Elgin, then Governor-General of Canada. (J. F.)

fogs, but are now bewailing the hard frost—though indeed one is ashamed to mention their own trifling ailments when they think of the sufferings of thousands of their fellow creatures. At such a time one can scarcely help wishing for wealth, that they might enjoy its only true luxury—that of relieving the necessities of others—but God chooses His own channels, and so, instead of *wishing* for more, we ought to *pray* for liberal hearts and open hands to give freely of what we have.

13th.—I make little way in this cold dry weather, which brings me many visitors—amongst others Katherine F., who I am in hopes of having for an inmate, though she is so *recherchée* it is difficult to excuse her even for a week or two. I had a letter from Hamilton a few days ago, giving a more favourable account of his dear wife, so I would fain hope it may please God to preserve her precious life. Mrs. Walter still coughs and continues delicate, all else and others much as usual.

We were rejoiced to hear of James's [1] advancement— for such it must be—and for the very gratifying manner in which his past services have been acknowledged. All who know him I am sure must rejoice in every increase of his prosperity, which I trust will not stop here, but be merely a step to something still better. I have had no opportunity of returning the books you left, but will when I can. Have you ever heard of two, which I think must be interesting, though nobody here can tell me anything about them: 1st, 'The Influence of the Soul over the Body'; 2nd, 'The Influence of the Body over the Soul' I had almost omitted to thank you for your leather pocket-book, which was one of many New Year's gifts, and you will laugh at some specimens of the various *Bagatelles*—such as a sack of meal, a skep of honey, turkeys, hares, pheasants, illustrated Fairy Tales! and sundry Goode Bookies. There is no want of papers. Good kind Lady G. [2] sends the 'Standard' most regularly, and the 'Athenæum' is a great

<hr>

[1] Colonel Graham. (J. F.)   [2] Lady Graham of Netherby. (J. F.)

treat.   With best wishes and regards to the Colonel, including yourself,

I remain affectionately yours,

S. E. F.

S. E. F. TO MRS. TENNENT

February 12–13.

My dear Helen,—I must seem to you very remiss in having been so long of thanking you for your kind letter containing sundry particulars anent Penzance, for which Lady McN. begs her best thanks—as also for the Colonel's and your gratifying invitation to Stanmore—but that is all she can say at present, not having yet obtained Sir John's consent to the expedition, which to be sure is a very material point ; if she does prevail, their stay, I should suppose, would be short, as he cannot be long absent from his official duties.

It was very stupid in me not to think of saving you the trouble of applying for a letter to G. F. from his sister. But I am liable to attacks of great stupidity at times.   I forwarded your note to her as she returned to Cairnhill with Ham [1] and Mr. G., to both of whom she is a great comfort.   Poor Margaret has been quite overcome and cannot be of use to any one—before the sad event [2] she had really been very well for a length of time ; the baby is very thriving and is under its grandmother's care.

Walter and Mrs. F. return many thanks for your kind invitation to Helen, but she is still too delicate to be sent from home ; she is a very fine amiable creature with an excellent understanding, and quite unspoilt by the admiration she *used* to excite, for alas ! her beauty has been much marred by sickness ; but I trust in God she will be spared, she is such a blessing in the family.   Agnes is still at Marchmount, and Wat is doing well in America.   I suppose it is as easy to get into office as into the Navy nowadays. I heard of a most influential family who could not get a son into the service by any means.   I ought to have

<hr>

[1] Colonel Hamilton.   (J. F.)   [2] The death of Mrs. Gillon.   (J. F.)

written to dear Jane long ago, but I am very languid and
lazy. Thanks for the offer of Hoffmeister, but I got a
present of it from the McKenzies when it was published—
it is a book I think the Colonel will like. Beware of
' Railway Speculation.'

I have books of yours waiting an opportunity. Mrs.
Christison had not heard of Mrs. B. Ker [1] lately. The Lyons
have taken Castle Menzies, in Perthshire, for the summer.
I was sorry I could not see Miss Aber [2]; but there are days
when my *parts of speech* are so weak, I can scarcely articulate, and at best I can only see one or two in the course
of the day. The weather has been dreadful in all possible
ways—hurricanes of wind, torrents of rain, and storms of
snow ; to-day the sun is shining by way of —— I fear all
this is against the Colonel's rheumatism. With kind
regards to him, believe me, dear Helen,

Your Affectionate,

S. E. F.

Those who like to classify men and women in definite
groups, according to their formulated views on the great
subjects which divide the world, will find little in Miss
Ferrier's letters to gratify their curiosity. Special subjects,
such as temperance and the anti-slavery movement, appealed
strongly to her. But her judgments were too soundly rooted
in humour, in perception of and value for individual character, to accept the bondage of system either in politics or
religion. She could attach herself alike to the Campbells,
with their inherited Whig principles, and to Scott with his
mediæval sympathies and Tory convictions. One tradition, and one only, tells of something like definite party
feeling. Henry Brougham had, as a child, been one of
Susan Ferrier's schoolfellows and playmates. In 1834,
when Lord Brougham and Lord Grey were on a political
visit to Edinburgh, Miss Ferrier and her old schoolfellow
again met. The interview was described by one of Miss
Ferrier's nieces. ' By-the-bye, Susan had a meeting with
the Chancellor, who received her with the greatest cordiality
and alluded to their acquaintance in olden times ; but,
somehow or other, he failed to win her heart, for she talks

---

[1] Mrs. Ker, her cousin. (J. F.)   [2] Abercromby. (J. F.)

of him with positive dislike, though I think she certainly used to stand up for him.' A tradition is extant in the family that after this a bust of Brougham which used to stand in Miss Ferrier's house was banished. There were characteristics in 'The Learned Friend,' quite apart from his political opinions, which might well alienate one who was at once a severe satirist and an earnest moralist.

No one can read these letters and doubt that a deep sense of religion, of the overwhelming importance of man's spiritual nature, ran through Miss Ferrier's life. But it is equally clear that neither the details of ecclesiastical machinery nor the differences between religious forms and creeds greatly interested her. That may have been in part due to the conditions of her birth and training. The Ferrier family were Presbyterians. Helen Coutts, like many inhabitants of the east coast of Scotland, was an Episcopalian. The eldest daughter was brought up in the mother's church, the rest of the family in the father's. Thus Susan Ferrier grew up in an atmosphere where the possibility of honest divergence of opinion had to be fully recognised. There was much, too, of the eighteenth century in Miss Ferrier's view of life, and she would in all likelihood have subscribed readily to the doctrine, ' he can't be wrong whose life is in the right.'

Nor was it only from the tyranny of political and ecclesiastical system that Miss Ferrier was free. We find neither in the novels nor the letters any tendency to formulate theories of life, or to pronounce cut and dried judgments on classes of mankind.

In this, as in other matters, her weakness (if weakness it were) and strength went hand in hand. Untrammelled by theory, she could fasten with all the more certainty on the shades of individual character and the concrete facts of individual life. In that respect she may be said to stand almost alone among distinguised novelists, perhaps quite alone among those of her own sex. With Charlotte Brontë, with George Eliot, with Mrs. Gaskell, with Mrs. Oliphant, even in some measure with Miss Austen, one can foretell the treatment of a person from the category in life to which he belongs. Miss Ferrier is as free from external prepossessions as Fielding or Thackeray. In that respect, perhaps more than in any one other, the letter writer reflects and illustrates the temper and methods of the novelist.

On November 2, 1854, Miss Ferrier died. Her remains lie in the family burying place in St. Cuthbert's Church, Edinburgh.

One can hardly take leave of her better than in the words of one who may be said, in some sort, to have succeeded by inheritance to *the* friendship of Miss Ferrier's life :

'The wonderful vivacity she maintained in the midst of darkness and pain for so many years, the humour, wit, and honesty of her character, as well as the Christian submission with which she bore her great privation and general discomfort when not suffering acute pain, made every one who knew her desirous to alleviate the tediousness of her days ; and I used to read a great deal to her at one time, and I never left her darkened chamber without feeling that I had gained something better than the book we might be reading, from her quick perception of its faults and its beauties, and her unmerciful remarks on all that was mean or unworthy in conduct or expression.[1]'

'Unmerciful' no doubt Miss Ferrier could be, but her severity never spared herself. To her every phase of petty egotism, manifest or disguised, vanity, self-pity, self-depreciation, were wholly strangers. Sincerity and fearlessness are the keynotes of her life—in them the humourist that Miss Ferrier was and the moralist that she sought to be, find their meeting-place.

[1] Lady Richardson, quoted in the preface to the 1881 edition of *Marriage*.

INDEX

PRINTED BY
SPOTTISWOODE AND CO., NEW-STREET SQUARE
LONDON

www.ingramcontent.com/pod-product-compliance
Lightning Source LLC
Chambersburg PA
CBHW051113120726
47905CB00005B/1266